Stranded

Don & Stephanie Prichard

ISBN-10: 0986229806
ISBN-13: 978-0-9862298-0-0

Scripture taken from The Holy Bible, New International Version,
Copyright 1973, 1978, 1984 by International Bible Society
Used by permission of International Bible Society

Cover Design: Ken Raney
Editor: Natalie Hanemann
Formatting: Polgarus Studio

Printed in the United States of America

First Edition: November 2014

Dedicated to our beloved children
Gail, Andy, Sarah

Do you not know?
Have you not heard?
Has it not been told you from the beginning?
Have you not understood since the earth was founded?
He sits above the circle of the earth,
And its people are like grasshoppers.
—Isaiah 40: 21, 22

PART 1

June–July
1981

Prologue

The heavens faded from black to dusky blue, arching like an inverted bowl over the inky waters below. Sprawled across a fragment of boat, Jake Chalmers scanned the horizon. Darkness cloaked the expanse to the west, but in the east the circle of the earth etched a line of gold between ocean and sky. Pushing himself chest high, arms shaking, he studied the line for movement. Nothing. Nothing but the rising sun.

He rolled to his back and threw an arm over his eyes. Seawater dripped off his sleeve, stinging the cracks in his lips. He winced and pressed them together. A scum of brine coated the inside of his mouth, numbing his tongue and the back of his throat. Swallowing to generate saliva blazed a trail of salt down his esophagus. His stomach heaved, but there was nothing to expel, not even bile.

So thirsty. The craving ground like fine sandpaper against every cell in his body. Forty-two years old and he'd never experienced misery like this, not even in Nam. He raised his arm and flexed his fingers, blinked until the crinkled skin on the back of his hand came into focus. Were the wrinkles a symptom of dehydration? Or the result of floating five nights in the ocean?

He shifted back onto his stomach and hooked his left arm over the edge of the fragment to keep his balance. The flat-bottomed vessel, split in half lengthwise by the explosion and flipped into an upside-down V, barely accommodated the stretch of his six-foot-two frame. The submerged air compartments that had doubled as tourist passenger seats kept the damaged craft afloat, but the V tipped precariously with each swash of a wave.

He'd count, clear the haze from his mind. Count the days since he'd boarded the cruise ship. The days alone on the ocean after the explosion. The hours, the minutes, every second of the rest of his life he'd spend hunting down Captain Emilio.

He sat up, catapulted by the heat of rage. The boat fragment jerked, and he fell on his back and slid, grasping with outflung arms at the wet surface. The ocean swallowed his feet, his chest. The bucking craft smacked his head as he slipped off. Blood filled his mouth, stinging his tongue where his teeth slashed it. He caught the edge of the vessel, pulled up, and spat. Crimson dots spattered the craft's white paint.

Ginny. The ache for her pressed against his chest. Where was she? Floating like him in the ocean? Or had she slipped under the waves to a briny grave? He closed his eyes. Tired. So tired. Wanting to save her. Failing. His throat tightened.

He repositioned his grip and willed himself not to let go. Willed himself to fill his lungs and release the air in a slow exhale. Willed himself to crawl back onto the broken sea vessel. He lay on his stomach and stretched his limbs into a sprawl.

God and man may have abandoned him, but he wouldn't yield body and soul easily. The ocean would have to wait.

He dozed in snatches until the change came. Awareness of it crawled into his dreams and elbowed him awake. He opened his eyes. Rain? He raised his head, body trembling, to scan the heavens. Empty. Only the sun glaring from its own ocean of blue sky.

No, beneath him. Motion, tugging him—a surge forward, then a stop. Surge forward, stop. He shook his head, lifted himself off his stomach. At the next swell he glimpsed the horizon. A green smear creased its edge.

Land.

LAND!

His heart slammed into high gear, and he struggled to his knees. The water dipped and the land disappeared. The boat fragment slid forward. Stopped. Rose on the slow elevator of another swell. He held his breath.

An island slipped onto the horizon. High on one end, sloping to sea level at the other.

He sucked in air and hurled it out in a cry that reverberated across the waves.

As if startled, the boat fragment jumped, and he fell on his stomach. He grabbed the vessel's edge. It rotated in a half circle and lurched forward on a new path. A path headed back to sea.

An ocean current—it must have caught the longer part of the fragment submerged in the water. He studied the distance to the island. The current might veer back and sidle up to the island, or, just as likely, it might tow his broken sea vessel farther away.

Didn't matter. He didn't need the boat. Just the island.

He slipped into the water and set his strokes on autopilot.

Chapter 1

Five days earlier

Jake Chalmers leaned on his forearms against the cruise ship's railing, his back to the crowded buffet table. The light fingers of the harbor breeze carried his wife's voice, rising in unsuppressed gaiety behind him. Exactly what he'd hoped for. Planned for. To take all the pain and stuff it into his heart, free hers to soar.

He swallowed back the lump crowding his throat and focused on the deck below. Captain Emilio stood alone at the gangplank. He'd been there all morning, personally welcoming each boarding passenger. No question he made a good impression—tall, trim, young for holding the position of captain.

As a seasoned officer sizing up a younger officer, Jake had given him high marks. The captain's white uniform was crisp; his jacket, immaculate; and his hair, though a bit long, was neatly groomed under his captain's cover. The ship gleamed with fresh paint and shining metal surfaces. The crew, all Filipinos except for the first mate, were attentive and friendly. Captain Emilio's attention to detail as good as guaranteed the cruise from Guam to the Philippines would be a memory-maker to cherish.

The stream of passengers trickled to a few last-minute boarders. Now would be a good time to slip down and join the man for conversation. As small as the ship was, with only twenty-four guests to attend to, the captain might be up for several visits on the bridge during the five-day trip.

A ship's horn blared nearby, and the passengers, evidently mistaking it for the *Gateway's*, flocked like starlings to join Jake at the railing. He made room for Ginny to squeeze in front of him, her back against his chest. The Cherokee wedge sandals she'd purchased especially for the cruise raised her four inches to where she could fit just under his chin. Impulsively, he kissed the top of her head.

She tipped her face up at him and smiled. "Watch it, Marine."

He wrapped his arms around her, inhaling the fruity scent of her shampoo. "I'm watching, and you aren't getting away."

But she would get away. Months, the doctor had said. Six at the most. A tight knot constricted his chest.

The horn blared again, and the passengers, grumbling that the cruise wasn't leaving after all, drifted back to the buffet table. Ginny shifted to his right side and slipped her arm around his waist. "Shouldn't the captain be on the bridge? We leave in fifteen minutes."

"Must be waiting for someone. Here comes the first mate now." Jake nodded at a short, balding Caucasian striding toward the captain. "He'll take over so the captain can go."

"He's sure ticked about something. Look at the roster."

Behind the captain's back, he clutched the ship's roster, rapping it like a jackhammer against his spine. Jake shrugged. He'd be annoyed too if his men came up short.

At the first mate's approach, the hammering shifted to ominous whaps. The captain's nostrils flared above clenched teeth. For one beat, the hammering stopped. "I told you to wait."

The mate jerked to a stop. "Yessir." His lips pinched into a thin line. He turned and slunk away.

Jake scowled. Nineteen years in the Reserves had exposed him to every kind of officer the Marine Corps attracted. This one was a bully. He managed his men through intimidation.

"Look!" Ginny nudged him with her shoulder. "That's who he's waiting for."

He followed her line of sight to a woman stepping onto the gangplank. She wore a calf-length dress the colors of a brilliant red and orange sunset, a slit on the left opening to just above her knee as she trod up the passageway. Like the captain, she was tall and slender, a looker. A good match for him.

Ginny sighed. "So gorgeous."

The blonde or the dress? Didn't matter. He booted his disgust with the captain. What mattered was a perfect cruise. One last, happy experience before Ginny's suffering began. Unless God chose to remove it …

"Gorgeous is what I've got in my arms." He drew her into a tight hug. Stuffing the pain. Trying mighty hard to let his heart soar with hers.

* * *

Evedene Eriksson strode up the gangplank, a pool of sweat suddenly swamping her armpits and dribbling down her sides to her waist. She hesitated. She could still turn and—not run, certainly—but walk away as fast as her legs could carry her.

No.

One clue, one little bit of evidence—that was all she needed. She could do this.

At the other end of the gangplank, the captain stepped forward to face her. Elation bubbled up her chest to her throat.

The man was handsome—dashing, really, in those crisp white cottons and flashy blue jacket with its gold braid and brass buttons. His cap sat at a jaunty angle on his head, revealing dark, curly hair, which probably that very morning had been cut and styled. No doubt every female boarding the ship thrilled at the sight of him.

But what set her heart thumping was that he had the same hawklike Roman nose as Danny Romero, the same square jaw and cleft chin. Her heartbeat pounded into a drumroll. Eight frustrating years of Danny Romero dodging her every effort might finally come to an end. All she had to do was prove the two men were related, and *United States vs. Romero* was her win.

She peered at the deck above him, locating the source of chatting and laughing passengers. A couple stood at the railing, locked in an embrace. The tightness that had clamped her shoulders all morning loosened. She was making the right decision to board, in spite of her boss's reluctance. With all these people here, nothing bad could happen.

She stopped in front of the captain.

"Eva Gray?"

She blinked. The captain was holding the ship's roster, eyebrows raised. She almost corrected him, almost said, no, she was Evedene Eriksson.

"Yes, Eva Gray." She stared boldly into his eyes. She wasn't a field agent like Scott, but she could lie just as well.

Captain Emilio glanced at the roster. "You're traveling alone? The reservation says two staterooms."

The question smashed like a fist to her stomach. She'd been only a few steps behind Scott when someone pushed him onto the track with the El bearing down on him. For a moment, the switch she'd turned off in her mind flipped on, and she saw Scott fall, heard people scream, felt the swoosh of air slap her face as the train braked.

She snapped the switch off. "Just me."

"Then one of my crew will show you to your cabin. You'll find your luggage inside." The captain made a mark on the roster and bowed slightly, the gesture a wooden tilt from the waist up. "Welcome aboard, Ms. Gray."

She followed the crewman across the deck, but at the captain's shout to cast off, she found her legs suddenly stilt-like, her sandaled, toenail-polished feet like sandbags. What was she doing? Her stomach twisted. She shouldn't have let herself think of Scott and the El.

"This way, please." The crewman held open a door into the ship's bowels.

The gangplank growled into place behind her, and the deck shuddered beneath her sandals. She should run, leap onto the pier. Her feet betrayed her, yanked her forward through the hatch. The crewman brushed past, and the door clicked shut.

She inhaled sharply. Tiny hairs at the nape of her neck prickled like icicles and spiked shivers down her spine.

"Here, ma'am, your room." From the end of the corridor, the smiling crewman beckoned her.

She straightened her shoulders and marched down the passageway. This was exactly where she wanted to be. One last piece of evidence, and 1981 would mark the year she put Chicago's premiere drug lord, Danny Romero, behind bars.

Chapter 2

Their second night out, Jake entered the ship's dining room and breathed in the fragrance of ginger and anise and other Oriental spices wafting from the evening buffet table. Paper lanterns festooned the ceiling. White tablecloths and pale rattan chairs gleamed against the rich turquoise carpet and faded cocoa walls. Intricately carved pictures of rural Filipino life hung on the walls, reminding him of Nam. A boy on a water buffalo. Two workers in domed field hats, cultivating a rice paddy. A mother and baby outside a hut. The perfect setting to celebrate with Ginny tonight.

Ginny stepped in next to him, pretty in a red, sleeveless wraparound dress. The first night at sea, the cruise had honored newlyweds. Tonight it was oldyweds' turn. He wore the black polo shirt she'd given him before dinner as an anniversary gift. She had sewn a gold insignia of the Marine Corps on the pocket and embroidered Lt. Colonel Jacob A. Chalmers, USMCR, in tiny, neat letters beneath it.

"My brag shirt?"

"That's what Marines do best." The hug said there was no getting out of wearing it.

His gift to her gleamed under the soft light of the paper lanterns. Gift-giving wasn't his strong point, but this one swelled his chest. The ring was a delicate white-gold band, set with four birthstones—a ruby for her, two sapphires for the twins, a peridot for him. In the tough months ahead, he wanted the ring to be a reminder of this evening and their happiness.

"Look, there are our guests." Ginny waved to a young girl accompanied by a thin, white-haired woman standing at the other entrance to the room. "Crystal is eleven, and Betty is her great-aunt. Poor things were eating all by themselves last night." For sure, Crystal and Betty would not lack dining companions the rest of the trip.

The four of them joined the buffet line, and Jake piled his plate high with rice and every vegetable and choice of meat offered. Though the fare was simple, a festive bottle of wine sat on each table, along with goblets and a pitcher of water. As soon as they sat, a waiter brought champagne in delicate, fluted glasses.

The captain called for toasts, and the chatter in the dining room hushed. Jake was the first to stand. "Twenty years ago I proposed to this lovely lady." Applause rippled through the room as he pulled Ginny to her feet and put his arm around her. "She didn't turn me down then, and she hasn't since."

"Jake!"

He kissed her soundly and the room reverberated with hoots.

"Bragging is what Marines do best," he whispered.

"Next to best." She cast a sultry look at him and took his hand, laughing as they sat, fingers entwined.

When the toasts were done, Captain Emilio rose to make his rounds to the tables. Why so early? Was something special planned?

The captain approached their table. "Congratulations on your anniversary." His gaze rested on the Marine Corps insignia and slid up to the two scars on the right side of Jake's face. "Nam?"

"Dog. Pit bull." Jake narrowed his eyes, waited to see if the bully caught the mimicry.

The captain's lips thinned into a straight line. "Ladies, enjoy your meal." His smile slid over them like a tanker over seaweed. He walked, shoulders rigid, to the next table.

"I got bit once," Crystal said, "but it was just a puppy. It didn't hurt much."

"How long ago was that, Jake?" Betty put her hand on Crystal's arm, as if to hush her.

"About forty years ago. I was two and didn't know any better than to pick up her pup by its neck."

"Did kids at school make fun of your scars?" Crystal whispered.

"You mean with nicknames like Jagged Jake and Chewy Chalmers?"

"Oh." The corners of Crystal's lips turned down. "They call me Crybaby Crystal at my school."

"I was Shrimp," Betty interjected. "Every year the kids got taller, except me."

Ginny hunched her shoulders into a shrug. "With red hair, what else but the Freckled Freak?"

If he and Ginny had been alone, he would have slipped his fingers into that golden-red hair and pulled the woman he loved into his arms. Freckled Freak? He wanted to guffaw, belt out a good, hard laugh. The Freckled Freak had grown into a beautiful woman who still made his heart thrum. He'd never stop thanking God for her.

Without warning, sorrow slammed like a wrecking ball into his chest. Thank God? His lungs tightened in a sharp ache. When the doctors said Ginny would die of stage IV colon cancer at age forty-two?

"Jake?" Ginny's hand pressed against his arm, and he steadied his eyes on hers. They crinkled at the corners, a sheen of moisture refracting light from the paper lanterns overhead, and he knew she was smiling bravely. Smiling for him.

He sucked oxygen back into his lungs and laid his hand over hers. They'd agreed not to let grief claw away their joy of being together.

"Dance?" He led her to the small dance floor and took her into his arms, cradling her against the jostle of other couples.

He'd lost control. He wouldn't let it happen again. The cruise was only the beginning of the good things he'd planned for her.

* * *

Eve slipped out of her dress and hung it in the narrow closet. Thank goodness she'd already laid out a change of clothes on her berth. Captain Emilio had left the dining room sooner than she expected, and his wink as he passed her table had set her nerves to jangling. Up till now, switching from prosecuting attorney to field agent had proved fun. She'd worked on the crew by first ordering room service, then gaining a tour of the galley, and eventually a trip through the entire ship. The crew loved her interest in them and eagerly answered all her questions.

But what had she discovered? Nothing. She shook out the cobalt blue, V-neck blouse and white, cuffed shorts and put them on, then plucked out the pins holding her hair in a French twist. Her visit in a few minutes with Captain Emilio had to look casual, like it was no big deal. No giveaways like trembling fingers or forgetting her name was Eva Gray.

She squinted into the tiny bathroom mirror and settled on a light application of lipstick, no powder. Okay, so she hadn't discovered the hold stuffed full of drugs. But she had unearthed two puzzling events that sat like lead in her gut.

Why was the ship operating with a skeleton crew—maybe half what it needed? The men were scrambling from room service to meal preparation to the mechanics of running the ship. Then there was the fact that every member of the crew was sailing the *Gateway* for the first time. That couldn't be a coincidence. Only Chester, the first mate, was an old-timer. She blew out a breath, remembering how unfriendly and close-mouthed the officer had been.

She slid her feet into high-heeled sandals and buckled the straps. Somehow those two discoveries were important. They pointed to something, but what? Three more days until they docked in Manila. She needed to pull things together.

She found Captain Emilio alone on the bridge, leaning over a map spread on a chart board. He had removed his jacket, and the back of his short-sleeved shirt was pasted in a line of sweat bracketed by his shoulders and running down his spine to his waist. He turned to face her as the wooden deck creaked under her sandals, his eyes constricted, hard, like a hawk sighting its prey.

Her breath froze, and for a second she couldn't move, couldn't think. Then he smiled, and the icy bullet in her lungs dissolved. Had she imagined animosity? She took a deep breath. This wasn't going to be as easy as questioning the crew.

"We still on course?" She nodded at the map and forced a smile.

"We're right where I want us to be." His voice was deep, confident, a man used to getting his way. He stepped around the chart board, his eyes sliding appreciatively over her body. His hand pressed lightly against her waist as he guided her to a tray offering an assortment of drinks.

She stiffened at his touch, and his hand dropped.

"An after-dinner drink?" His eyebrows rose—over her choice of beverage, or over her reaction to his brash familiarity?

She delayed her answer, examining the offerings on the tray, regrouping to take over the reins of control. "How about a tour first?" She pointed to what looked like some kind of communication apparatus. "What's this?"

"A single side band radio." He explained it in detail and moved to the next piece of equipment and then another.

She lost interest at the third item. What she needed was some way to link him to the Romeros. The facial similarities weren't enough, of course, to make a legitimate connection. But wasn't it an interesting coincidence that Emilio, an Italian, commanded a ship that the feds knew ran drugs from Guam to the Philippines to Chicago, home turf of the Romero family?

If she could tie him to the family, or even just to Chicago, she might well have found the link that could secure a win for the Justice Department. Eight years of chasing Danny Romero would finally end with his backside in a corner he couldn't slip away from.

The captain's finger hovered over the last piece of equipment. "This is the radio locator beacon—the distress signal. It alerts other ships or aircraft that you're in trouble and need help."

Enough about equipment or she'd have to send out her own distress signal. She infused fresh curiosity into her voice. "How long have you been captain of the *Gateway*?"

Again, the man rattled on. Definitely oriented to details. Her interest perked as his autobiography moved backward through time. Vanity made one vulnerable. What question could she ask to lure him into a trap that would give the information she needed?

Captain Emilio stopped abruptly. His eyes narrowed, focusing on hers. "Where are you from, Eva?"

Exactly what she wanted to ask him. "Chicago. How about you?"

His eyebrows shot up. "Small world—my father lives there."

Her heart leaped. The trap had caught its mouse.

* * *

Captain Emilio smirked as Evedene Eriksson, alias Eva Gray, clattered down the steep ladder stairwell. How her eyes had danced after he'd shared the information she so badly wanted to hear. A rather pathetic game of cat and mouse on her part, but worth it to see her think she was the cat.

He snorted. So, she should be done with her pitiful interrogation of him and the crew now that he'd revealed he was Danny Romero's son. If only she'd been willing to offer herself in his bed to get the information out of him. He shrugged and picked up a microphone. Just as well. His mission tomorrow required all his attention.

For a moment he tried picturing his father's face when the old man received the news of his son's death. Would he crumple into tears at the loss, or scowl at what he perceived as incompetence? Who cared? His father was a goner, whether through the Romero trial or through his emphysema. And without his father's protection, so was Emilio if he didn't make his escape now. Either he faked his death, or the other three Romero sons—the "legitimate" ones—would make it a reality. Their plans didn't include him as part or parcel of the Romero empire.

"First mate to the bridge," he announced over the public address system.

Chester appeared promptly. He had been with the captain five years, and his clenched jaw said he knew his performance had better be up to snuff.

"The radio locator beacon can be moved now. Are both lighters set?" It was important to Captain Emilio's purposes to not use the lifeboats. The flat-bottomed lighters rode high in the water and were used for brief sojourns of sightseeing in the shallow waters surrounding the outer Philippine islands. They weren't necessary components for the sale of the ship.

"Yessir."

"The keys?"

"Yessir." Chester reached into his pocket and produced two sets of ignition keys. His hand shook, and the keys clanked against each other.

"Don't go getting soft on me."

Chester shoved the keys back into his pocket and blinked several times. "We're only supposed to take out the attorney."

"You want to back out, now's the time."

"No, sir." The first mate swallowed and looked the captain in the eye. "The explosives are ready, one on each lighter and an extra one for the locator beacon."

Chapter 3

Sleep snapped at Captain Emilio like a shark attack. Awake he felt sure of his strategy, but the moment he closed his eyes, the sharp teeth of anxiety bit chunks out of him. He woke and reviewed everything—what could go wrong, what had to go right, all the contingencies—until finally he allowed his eyelids to slip peacefully down. Then the sharks started on his hide again. At last he gave up and went to the bridge to relieve Chester.

The skin around the first mate's eyes and lips was tight and pale, as if his face had been wrung out and shrunk. He grunted in acknowledgement when the captain appeared, but left without speaking. Nor did Emilio have anything to say to him. Tension was a monster they had to live with until they completed the last and worst part of the plan.

He checked every instrument. The red and white lights on the equipment glittered against the backdrop of night sky outside the windows. The ship was on course. Twenty-three passengers and half a dozen crewmen, gliding thousands of feet above one of the deepest and darkest troughs in the Pacific Ocean. The Philippine Trench—a bottomless pit. A bottomless trash can. He drew a long breath and exhaled it slowly. The muscles in his chest and shoulders remained tight. He refused to pace. Instead, he tapped his fingers on the chart board.

They had been sailing over the top of the trench for two days. This evening the schedule called for their departure from the trench to the Philippines. He traced a finger over the route he'd always followed, a shallower channel that threaded its way through thousands of islands to

Manila. Ahead and to the west lay the seven thousand islands of the Philippines. Beyond that and a bit to the south were the ten thousand islands of Indonesia.

But he wouldn't be going to the Philippines. He slapped the chart board and turned to pace the floor. Today he was changing course—both the ship's and that of his own life. Nothing, nothing could go wrong.

The crew assembled at 0600. Captain Emilio entered the engine room, and the men halted their conversations midsentence. A cocoon of noise enveloped the sudden hush—the rumble of the diesel engine, the softer chuffs of the gears turning the propeller's drive shaft, the pulse of lungs pushing and pulling air through nostrils and tight throats.

He faced them, his lips firm, and stared each man in the eye before he spoke. "Today we shanghai the *Gateway*."

The men murmured, shoulders taut.

"Today you become rich. Rich beyond your dreams." Captain Emilio relaxed his mouth into a smile, and the tightness in the men's faces dissolved. They laughed, nodding at each other, united in a conspiracy of prosperity at little cost.

"One last time, we review the plan."

They had the details down pat, but he wanted them hammered nail-tight. He started with the big picture. They would use the two lighters to abandon the passengers at sea. Chester had already placed the locator beacon in one of the boats. The castaways would be rescued while the *Gateway* fled to its black market purchaser in Hong Kong. The twenty-four-passenger cruise ship had excited a bidding war. Top dollar—that's what they were getting. They'd all begin new lives, rich beyond belief.

The captain's gaze fell on the first mate. Among the crew, only Chester knew the real plan.

* * *

Prizes for everyone? Eve leaned against the railing and surveyed the passengers milling about on the lower deck. Who'd miss out on a drawing like that?

The tables and chairs from the dining room were grouped in front of the first mate, who held a microphone in his hand. An assortment of packages wrapped in blue tissue paper lay on a table next to him. A crewman—Carlos, maybe?—walked among the passengers, distributing numbered slips of paper.

She spotted a table of lone females and clambered down the steps to join them. She hated sticking out in a crowd. Scott would have taken care of that, at least for appearances' sake.

"Eva, come sit." Ginny Chalmers patted the empty chair next to her.

"I don't want to take your husband's seat."

"No, no, he's got five books he's reading. Please, sit." She introduced the other two occupants at the table, Betty and Crystal.

So, she wasn't the only lone female on the cruise. Eve eyed the two with interest. Had they booked the love boat by mistake?

The older woman looked to be in her late sixties. Nicely preserved, no surgical help. Wealthy, judging by her jewelry and clothes. The kid leaning on her, chair scooted close—her granddaughter, maybe? Ten or eleven, not yet into puberty. Pale, obviously not feeling well.

Ginny she'd met yesterday, the second day out. Friendly gal, the chatty type. Fortyish and still attractive, no middle-age spread. She'd seen Ginny's husband in the gym twice. He was one of the few who hadn't gawked when she worked out. Nice, but he should be here. The cruise was meant for couples.

Captain Emilio, hair rumpled, the armpits of his shirt damp with sweat, strode to the microphone and seized it from the first mate. Eve froze. Something was wrong.

"Ladies and gentlemen, your attention, please." The captain's voice was calm, but the stern look on his face said trouble. He waited until everyone had shushed each other. "We have a problem in the engine room."

A murmur of anxiety swept through the crowd. Several people nearest the bulkhead jumped up from their seats. They pointed at the door and yelled, "Smoke!"

A thick, gritty cloud drifted out the doorway. A Filipino crewman emerged, scowling, his face pinched. Several women shrieked, and everyone shot to their feet.

"Sit down!" Captain Emilio bellowed into the microphone. "Sit down and listen to me!" He flared his nostrils as everyone took their seats. "As a precaution for your safety, I need you to immediately vacate the ship."

Once again people leaped to their feet.

"Sit down and listen to my instructions!" he roared. *"Now!"* Like a pack of trained circus dogs, they sat.

"Do *not* go to your cabins for anything! Everyone must proceed aft—straight to the back of the ship. We will use the two lighters there. They are like lifeboats. There are life vests stored beneath the seats. Get into the boats first and then put on the life vests. It is urgent that you do *exactly* as I say. Two crewmen will be there to get you into the boats and out on the water, away from the ship." He paused, his dark eyes sweeping the crowd. "Go, *now!*"

The passengers jumped to their feet, eyes wide. The men grabbed their women and pushed them, pulled them, shoved them toward the fantail of the ship to the safety of the lighters.

Eve heard Ginny's cry in the din of stampeding passengers. Her voice bleated like a frightened sheep. "My husband! I've got to get my husband!" She held Crystal by one hand, while Betty had a firm grasp on Crystal's other. The girl's face was ashen. The three were being dragged along in the dash to the lighters.

Ginny's concern was understandable, but foolish. Her husband could take care of himself. Something far more significant bothered Eve. Her tour of the ship had included the engine room. It didn't make sense that smoke from that part of the ship would come out this particular door. Nor did it make sense that they would be sent all the way to the back of the ship to use the lighters instead of the lifeboats. Most of all, it didn't make sense that they weren't putting on life vests. First and foremost, they should be putting on the vests.

DON & STEPHANIE PRICHARD

The crew had been diligent in showing her around the ship. She wasn't sure what was happening now, but she did know the location of the life vests adjacent to the lighters.

"Ginny, over here!" Eve grabbed Betty's arm and hauled the trio to the door of a nearby locker. It proved to be a closet of sorts, filled with life vests and other safety equipment. "Put these on." No one else was looking out for these helpless females, so she would.

When they emerged from the locker, one of the two crewmen stationed at the lighters ran up to them. "No! No! These for crew! Yours on boat!"

Eve shoved him away. He ran to the locker, where other people were now helping themselves. Taking advantage of the opportunity, she pushed Betty and Crystal into the closest lighter. Already, it was almost full. She turned for Ginny, only to discover the distraught woman pleading with the second crewman.

"My husband, he's not here! He's still below!"

The crewman's mouth dropped open. "Not here?"

"He left the drawing. He's in our cabin, reading. Please, let me go get him!"

The other crewman ran toward Eve. It wasn't hard to tell he was angry about the invasion of the locker. He had managed to stop the other passengers from obtaining life vests, and it looked as if he were determined to secure hers and the other three that had escaped. She climbed into the lighter and shouted to the crewman attending Ginny. "Push us off! We're full!"

When the lighter landed in the water, Eve watched to see what would happen to Ginny. The two crewmen had their heads together while the remaining passengers crowded unassisted into the second lighter. Surely one of the crewmen would go with Ginny to fetch her husband.

Across her own lighter, a few people down, Eve spied Betty and Crystal. The kid wasn't doing well. The water was choppy, and the high riding lighter was kicking waves. When Eve saw someone pointing back at the *Gateway*, she turned to look. Surprise smacked her in the face at how far their boat had drifted away. Or had the *Gateway* moved away from them?

The other lighter plopped into the water, sloshing its passengers. Eve spotted Ginny, still wearing the life vest, clutching the edge of the small boat. Her head was tipped back, her face upturned to the cruise ship. Eve's heart skipped a beat. Ginny's husband was still on board the ship.

* * *

Captain Emilio climbed to the bridge. Almost done. His footsteps rasped on the wooden deck as he crossed to relieve Chester at the wheel.

"Time to radio the authorities that we're in trouble."

"Yessir."

Everything was on track. The crewman attending the second lighter had already activated the radio locator beacon. It would guide rescuers to the ailing cruise ship—only now, of course, the beacon was on the lighter instead of the *Gateway*. The cruise ship would be halfway to Hong Kong before any rescue ships arrived. Once the crew destroyed anything identifying the ship, they, too, would be eliminated. Couldn't have any witnesses around.

Almost done. He allowed himself a congratulatory smile. Waiting in Hong Kong, safe from the threat of his brothers, were his wife and infant son. He'd pulled it off.

The deck creaked. The voice of the crewman who'd set off the smoke bomb spoke at his back. "Captain, one passenger—he stay below deck."

Captain Emilio spun around to find himself face-to-face with Jake Chalmers.

Chapter 4

Hunched on her seat toward the back of the lighter, Betty hugged Crystal to her side. Other passengers crowded the bow. Several cried out at the growing distance between the lighter and the cruise ship. A young couple ran to the stern and searched the outboard motor for ignition keys. Eve and three others hunted for life vests. They opened the storage lockers under the seats, but the promised vests were not there. Only a small, telescoping mast, a sail and its rigging, and a pair of oars. Two men nabbed the oars and shoved them into brackets on either side of the boat. The vessel rocked under their efforts to synchronize.

Crystal's chest jerked. She gagged and spewed the contents of her stomach onto her life vest and Betty's. The foul odor swept into Betty's nostrils. She whisked Crystal around and held her while the child vomited over the edge of the lighter.

"Poor baby, you done?" She touched Crystal's forehead. It was clammy with sweat. Vomit clung to strands of Crystal's hair and smeared her chin and the back of her hands. The stench from both life vests curled Betty's toes. "Here, let's clean you off." She kneeled on the seat and stretched for a handful of water from the choppy waves.

Before Betty could stop her, Crystal shrugged out of her life vest.

"No, don't take it off."

"But it stinks!" Crystal shoved the vest at Betty.

The push threw Betty off balance. She grabbed at the life vest. For a moment the weight of Crystal's clutch on it steadied her. Then the edge of the boat slammed against her stomach, catapulting her headfirst over the side. She snatched a lungful of air just before she hit the ocean.

The cold water invaded her pores and chilled her bone-deep. She kicked to the surface, heart thudding at something far worse. Her right hand still held Crystal's life vest. She hadn't let go, and she was certain Crystal hadn't either.

"Crystal!" Her cry was a tiny mew against the vastness of ocean and sky. She caught her breath. Crystal didn't know how to swim.

The water churned next to her, and Crystal—choking, arms flailing—crashed to the surface. She spotted Betty and lunged at her. Fingers of steel grasped Betty's shoulders, plunging her head beneath the water. She kicked frantically toward the surface, but Crystal's weight bore her down. The air in her lungs pushed for release until her face felt like it was going to pop .

Suddenly Crystal let go. Betty opened her eyes and looked up. Crystal's arms and legs were lashing the water, propelling her toward the surface. Of course—once Crystal's own head dipped beneath the water, she gave up on using Betty as a life raft.

The empty life vest was still in Betty's hand. She slipped her hand through an armhole and jerked it to her shoulder. No matter what, she couldn't lose the vest. Without it, Crystal would drown.

The pressure in Betty's lungs leaked air bubbles out her nose. She thrashed to the surface, gasping for air. She got in one lungful before Crystal's fingers grabbed her left arm. Hating herself for it, Betty shoved the child away.

She gulped in another lungful of air. "Put this on." She thrust Crystal's life vest at the girl. "Put it on."

Crystal ignored the vest and clawed at the water. Her eyes were wide, the whites around her irises showing.

Betty rammed the vest into Crystal's chest. "Hold onto it!"

This time Crystal obeyed, bobbing, coughing out water.

The lighter. Somebody needed to haul them in before Crystal let go. Betty rotated toward the boat. "Help!"

The lighter was moving away from them, oars flipping up sprays of foam. Her insides crowded into her throat. Where was everybody? Had no one seen them fall? She screamed louder.

A face appeared at the stern, hands gripping the side of the boat. Eva Gray peered across the water at her, a stunned expression on her face.

"Help!" Betty yelled.

Eva disappeared. Her voice rose in a piercing shriek. "Stop! Man overboard! Turn the boat!"

Betty spun back to Crystal. Her niece's pale face barely hovered above the water. "They're coming to get us. You see that?" Did Crystal's head nod in assent, or was it simply the bob of a wave? "Feel around and find an armhole in your life vest, sweetie. We need to get you into it."

Crystal didn't move.

"Put your arms through both armholes. I'll come fasten you in back. It won't matter that you have the vest on backward." She waited. She wasn't going to get close enough for Crystal to grab her again.

"Crystal, put the vest on!"

The corners of Crystal's mouth turned down and her lower lip trembled. A groan tumbled out of her mouth and quavered into a hiccupping sob. Her shoulders stirred, and the yellow material of the life vest peeked above the surface of the ocean, disappeared, and bobbed up again tight against her.

"Good girl. You got it on? Both arms through?"

Crystal clearly nodded her head this time.

"Okay, I'm going to your back now. The vest will hold you up. Just relax and breathe. I'll fasten it and then we can hold hands. Would you like that?"

Betty dog-paddled just out of reach to Crystal's back. "Don't turn around now, or I can't help you." She pulled the edges of the vest together and overlapped the Velcro straps so the vest fit as tight as possible. She groped for Crystal's arm and slid her fingers down to the child's. Crystal's skin felt like cold rawhide.

"I've got your hand. See?" She raised Crystal's fist out of the water. Goose bumps prickled the white flesh of the child's forearm. Betty rubbed it with her other hand. "Move your arms and legs, sweetie. Don't let them get cold."

Her own energy was down to a trickle. She was sixty-nine years old. What was she doing out here in the middle of the ocean, grappling for her grandniece's life? Shouldn't someone be saving them instead?

She twisted around to look at the lighter. The oarsmen were making an awkward half-circle in the water. The boat was even farther away than before.

"Here, over here!" she hollered.

The tall, slender figure of a woman wearing a life vest climbed onto the seating. For a moment she stood, one hand shading her eyes, facing Betty. Then she bent her knees, swung her arms back, then forward into a dive that hurtled her over the side of the boat and into the water.

Betty choked back a sob. Someone was coming for them. The gaping mouth of the ocean wouldn't swallow them after all.

* * *

The deck of the bridge squeaked under the penny loafers that Jake had shoved onto his bare feet. He halted, planting himself in front of the captain. The man reeked of sweat. "Your crewman said you wanted to see me."

Captain Emilio's eyebrows flicked up. He looked surprised for someone who'd sent for him.

"We have a problem, Mr. Chalmers. I need your help." The captain grabbed a pistol out of a drawer, beckoned Jake with it to follow him, and sped out of the room.

Sparks crackled across Jake's nerves. He ran after the captain. What kind of trouble required a pistol? His heart beat faster. Ginny. Where was she? He scanned the decks. Where were the passengers? Weren't they supposed to be at a drawing on the lower deck?

They arrived at the fantail of the ship. Captain Emilio stopped and pointed to two white lighters bobbing on the ocean. The closer one was a hundred yards off.

"We had a problem we needed to deal with. See the boats out there?" Captain Emilio stepped back, as if to give Jake an unobstructed view of the ocean. "All the passengers, including your wife, are on those lighters."

Jake gripped the railing. Ginny was out there? He whirled around to face the captain. "What problem?"

Captain Emilio aimed the pistol straight at Jake. A corner of his mouth crooked into a smile. "I want you to join them, Chalmers." He nodded at the railing. "Jump."

Jake scowled and turned back to the railing. He raised his left knee as if to climb over, but instead wheeled around and with his right fist struck the captain's hand, followed by a slam with his left fist to the captain's head.

Emilio staggered backward but held onto the pistol. He straightened and pointed it at Jake. "Marines. Always thinking they can outsmart a Navy man." Without delay, he fired the pistol.

The turbulence of the bullet licked Jake's cheek with a hot tongue as it skittered past. His left ear rang.

"The next one's coming between your eyes, Chalmers. Jump."

This time, Jake ceded. He climbed over the railing and pushed off in a wide dive. His backbone prickled, expecting a second bullet.

He hit the ocean and sliced in. No pain, no sting of salt on an open wound. Was the captain waiting to shoot until he surfaced? He arched his back and kicked up.

He surfaced next to the *Gateway*, out of reach of the ship's churning propellers. Emilio stood at the railing, his gaze fixed on Jake. Instead of holding the pistol, the captain pointed at the lighters. He locked onto Jake's eyes and raised his other hand until it was high over his head. Then, in one swift movement, he swung his arm straight down.

A blast, then almost simultaneously another, roared from the direction of the two lighters. Jake whipped around in time to see water, wreckage, and human bodies thrown high into the air. For a moment he couldn't move, couldn't shove what he'd seen and heard into his brain. Couldn't grasp the sense of it.

He rotated back to Captain Emilio. The captain leaned against the handrail, eyebrows lifted, eyes probing Jake's as the ship pulled away.

Then it hit him. The explosions were deliberate.

"Ginny!" He took off for the lighters.

Chapter 5

Eve reached Betty and Crystal just as a loud explosion cracked the air behind her. She spun around. Hot pain stabbed her ears and she screamed. Screamed louder as passengers and pieces of the lighter hurtled into the air. A foggy mist enveloped the boat and raced to engulf her, Betty, and Crystal. Debris smacked their bodies and plopped into the water. They shrieked and grabbed each other. A huge wave inundated them. They resurfaced, still clutching one another, coughing out water, gasping in air. Eve gripped Betty and Crystal as hard as she could, afraid she would lose them in the aftershock ripples.

The mist cleared, and she cried out. The bodies of passengers and fragments of the lighter lay scattered across the rocking sea. Hovering over the wreckage like an anxious hen over her chicks was the lighter itself, still intact except for the stern. An eerie silence prevailed where only minutes ago a frightened group of passengers had chattered. Neither the cruise ship nor the second lighter was anywhere in sight.

* * *

Jake stopped to get his bearings. His chest heaved from swimming so fast. He treaded water, fighting to wheeze in air and spit out ocean. The vapor caused by the blast had settled. He scanned the dark water for white boat fragments.

Suddenly the lighter itself rose like a pale ghost on the crest of a swell. He inhaled sharply. What was this? The lighter had survived the explosion?

Then he saw the bodies. They floated aimlessly in the debris surrounding the boat. None moved; none attempted to swim; none struggled to keep their heads above water. He shouted Ginny's name and took off. Over and over, with each stroke forward, he pleaded the same three words: *Please, God, please!*

He reached the bodies and searched for Ginny. Some of the bodies were submerged below the surface. Some were more body parts than bodies. Retrieving and inspecting them churned his stomach. *Please, not Ginny!*

She's not here. She's on the other lighter—he'd only imagined a second explosion. The hope lifted him, and he paused to look for the second lighter. In the distance, the cruise ship marked a fading speck on the horizon. He spun around to scour the opposite direction. Nothing. He clenched his teeth and continued his hunt for Ginny.

Several torn life vests floated on the water. Jake grabbed one and strapped it on. Why weren't the passengers wearing them? His mouth tightened at the only rational conclusion—they'd never had the chance.

A yellow life vest supporting a body caught his attention. He swam toward it. Strawberry-blonde hair, darkened to a deeper red by the water, swirled around the head. Dread snatched the air from his lungs. Trembling, already knowing, he rotated the body toward him.

* * *

"What happened?" The child's bewildered voice pierced Eve's stupor.

She answered, overwhelmed even as she spoke, by the simple explanation. "There was an explosion. Everyone's gone."

"Two explosions," Betty said. "The other lighter blew up too."

For a moment, no one said anything. Then Betty asked, "Can we get to our lighter?"

The practicality of the question grabbed Eve. The wave had deposited them even farther from the broken vessel. If it floated out of their reach, their chances of survival disappeared with it. The distance was most likely too far for the old lady and kid to make by themselves.

"I'm going to tow you two like I'm the engine of a train. Hold on and kick your legs to help us move." She took hold of Betty's life vest and pulled Betty, who in turn pulled Crystal in tandem. Twice, Eve had to push away bodies. She recoiled at having to touch them, even more at shoving them aside as if their lives meant nothing and their deaths were only a hindrance to getting to the lighter. She wept for them in a ragged, low moan, her body shivering at the horror that had taken twenty lives and left three behind.

They reached the boat and clung to its side, out of breath and coughing up a nasty bile of brown seawater. Crystal shattered the ocean's hush with loud sobs. Everything in Eve screamed to join her, but instead she said, "Stay here while I take a look."

She edged herself to the rear of the lighter. A gaping hole designated where the outboard motor and back panel had blown away. She peered inside. Chunks of scarlet flesh and tattered cloth dotted the boat. Her stomach heaved and she gripped the side harder.

"Can we come now?" Crystal pleaded.

"Betty, it ... it needs cleaning."

"We can't hold on any longer. Crystal can close her eyes, can't you, sweetie?"

"I just want to go hooooome."

The two appeared around the corner of the lighter, and Eve helped them board. Since there was no rear panel to climb over, she was able to push Crystal and then Betty straight onto the floor and climb in after them. The child collapsed in a heap, but Betty looked around at the carnage.

"Oh, Lord, no!"

"How about if you two close your eyes and hug each other to get warm. While you do that, I'll clean things up a little."

"I'll help you." But before Betty could get up, Crystal slipped into her arms. With a glance of apology at Eve, Betty began to hum and rock the sobbing child.

"That's okay, stay where you are." But inside, from far back in a childhood long abandoned, Eve ached for a mother's arms around her.

* * *

Time stood still while at the same instant it expanded into all of eternity. Jake hugged Ginny's lifeless body to him. Ginny was dead. His throat quivered.

No.

She couldn't be.

This trip, their second honeymoon—he'd planned all kinds of delights for her. Things she loved. He wanted to see her eyes jump to his, catch the corners of her mouth twitch up, hear her laugh and look at him like he was her hero. See her eyes soften, know he was telling her he loved her.

A tremor spread down his nerves, and his chest began to quake. Anguish ripped through his guts and tore his lungs open in great, wrenching sobs. He clasped Ginny's body to him, not wanting to let go. Not wanting to be left behind.

Ginny was gone.

She couldn't be, but she was.

He closed her eyes and kissed them, cold and salty against his lips. There had been no chance to say good-bye. He'd meant to be there for her until the end, to hold her hand, keep it warm for that split second of time when she transferred from this life to the next.

He swam toward the lighter, bringing Ginny with him. The vessel floated sideways in a trough of water, revealing both ends damaged by blasts. The distinctive odor of detonated C-4 permeated the air as he got closer. He recognized the military explosive and shuddered at the memory of bodies flung into the air. Ginny had died instantaneously—the overpressure of the blast would have collapsed her lungs. Anger blazed red-hot in him. She'd never stood a chance.

He swam to the stern and slid Ginny's body directly onto the floor and pulled himself in. The craft held, in spite of the damage fore and aft. He examined the blast areas. Whoever had placed the explosives obviously hadn't thought about the sealed air compartments under the seats. The blasts on each end of the boat had mostly expanded into the air and done little structural damage. Except, he thought grimly, for the passengers.

He sat and pulled Ginny into his arms, cradling her as if she were the one holding back tears. There were things he needed to say.

He took a deep breath to steady his voice. "Ginny, I love you. I should have told you how special you are to me. Every day I should have told you. How you made my life full, my days happy. I didn't know ..." Tears streaked down his face and the words began to come in gasps. "You've been God's precious gift to me—you know that, don't you?" He stopped, his throat too tight to go on.

How would he tell their two children? He and Ginny had left the twins at West Point Military Academy two weeks ago to begin college. Ginny had been a devoted mother. She had stayed home full time to take care of them, to immerse herself in their lives. He tried again to talk to her, to tell her how dear she was to the three of them. But all he could think of was how devastated they would be without her.

The water lapped against the boat, rocking them with the gentle hand of a mother tending her newborn. He looked up at the deep dome of the sky. He had assumed he and Ginny would finish out the year together. The oncologist had promised the chemo would give them up to six months. But God in His sovereignty had let it be otherwise. Ginny was in Heaven; he was left behind on earth.

He hugged Ginny's empty body to his chest and wept.

Chapter 6

Eve picked up a shred of cloth from the lighter's deck and washed out the blood. The fabric came from a shirt, pink, with some kind of pattern at the edge. She tried not to think about which passenger had worn it, but her mind wouldn't let it go. The girl barely in her twenties who had searched for the motor's ignition keys? Or the petite Asian woman who politely asked if she could look under Eve's seat cushion while everyone else screamed and shoved? Their faces pushed against her soul.

She rubbed at her tears with the back of her hand. Only a short while ago, eleven living, breathing people had occupied the lighter. Now eight of them floated in the ocean, chunks of their bodies left behind in the boat. She used the cloth to wipe away the gore, to soak up the bright red blood and rinse it into the ocean. Twice she vomited. She muffled her sobs so she wouldn't wake Betty and Crystal.

Where was the *Gateway*, anyway? It had vanished from sight. She kept looking up, waiting for it to return. What was going on? Why had it disappeared?

She sat back and gazed dully at the cloth dripping seawater from her hand. Why clean the boat if she expected the cruise ship to come back? The question puffed at the haze covering her mind.

Because the ship wouldn't be back. She blinked, and the mist evaporated.

Because the *Gateway* had abandoned them.

She stood, legs shaking. *No.* The cloth dropped from her hand and plopped onto the deck. This was no accident.

Piece by piece, the puzzle came together. Both lighters had exploded—she remembered the two boats flaring in a mirror image of each other. Their simultaneous explosions precluded coincidence. And the blasts had been more than mere motors blowing up—the detonations had been powerful enough to kill everyone aboard. Her ears still stung from the impact of the shock wave. No, there was only one reason why the cruise ship wasn't returning. Horror gripped her by the throat.

The explosions had been planned.

She clutched the edge of the lighter. The crew—no wonder there had been so few. A skeleton staff could get by if the passengers were disposed of a few days out. The men had been ignorant of Captain Emilio's background and character—she didn't believe they had lied to her about that. Had they known about the captain's macabre plan? Or would they, too, end up floating in the ocean?

But worst of all, worst of all, was the part she had played. Oh, how she had gloated when Captain Emilio just happened to divulge the very information she sought. Fool! Her death was the motive for the explosions. She was the target.

But why not kill just her? She sank to the deck and covered her face with her hands.

Twenty people dead, and all because of her.

* * *

Jake held Ginny to his chest, rocking her, smoothing her hair, kissing her forehead. She couldn't be dead. Any second now she'd open her eyes, cough up seawater. She'd smile that frail little lopsided grin of hers she used when she was sick and didn't want him to worry. They still had half a year together. He was going to be there for her just like he'd planned.

He straightened and inhaled deeply. No, their life together was over. He clenched his fists. But their journey wasn't done. It would end when Captain Emilio sat in the electric chair.

He rose and laid Ginny on the deck floor, positioning her head as far away as possible from the water flowing down the middle. Though no one could possibly have survived the blasts, he should still check on the other lighter. He shielded his eyes from the late afternoon sun to search out the other boat. The rise and fall of the ocean revealed nothing. Perhaps the other boat's damages had sent it to the bottom of the ocean.

Dorsal fins sliced the water off the bow. He grimaced at what the sharks were feeding on. At least he had a boat. The injured craft wasn't much better than a crutch in a marathon race, but it beat fighting off sharks.

On one side of the lighter, yellow shreds of life vests plastered the back of a shattered storage compartment. The vests must have been locked inside. He examined a second blasted compartment on the other side. The boat's sailing equipment and two oars lay secured to the floor. He removed the mast and sail. Both had been damaged by the blast. The mast wouldn't telescope to its full extent, and the tattered sail wasn't in any better shape. But they would have to do.

He inserted the base of the mast into the floor bracket in the middle of the boat and slid in the pin to secure it. Shaking out the sail, he attached the rigging to the crippled mast and fastened the bottom two corners to metal eyes on each side of the boat. That done, he lashed an oar to each side of the lighter so the blades protruded into the water to function as dual rudders. They would keep the craft moving in a straight line.

A breeze slapped the nylon cloth, and the lighter leaped forward. Water spurted through the hole at the front of the boat and rushed down the deck and out the larger break at the stern. The damage slowed the progress of the boat, but it was moving. He adjusted the oars so the boat sailed west, toward the Philippines.

Two days, maybe four at the most, and he'd have the law on Captain Emilio's tail.

* * *

Eve crouched against the shadier side of the lighter, her arms wrapped around her knees. Thirty-three years old, a successful federal prosecutor, and here she was whimpering for her mother's arms around her. She bit back a sob. She never cried. Never. But twenty people … twenty people dead because of her ambition. She never should have boarded the *Gateway*.

She mentally slapped herself. *Stop.* No more thinking about it. Not forgetting, just not going over and over it until she dissolved in stomach acid. The past was only good as a springboard for the future. She snuffed in a lungful of air. And Captain Emilio's face was dead center in that future's bull's-eye.

She raised her face to the steady wind skimming over her head and shoulders and filling the nylon sail above her. She knew how to run a motorboat, but not the intricacies of rigging a sail. Her hands had shaken so hard anyway, she'd been worthless trying to help Betty do it. All Eve could think about was what if the *Gateway* returned? What if they were looking for her?

Afterwards, Betty had cuddled back up to Crystal. Eve watched as Crystal stirred. Opening her eyes to half-mast, she spotted Eve and stared at her. "You saved us, didn't you?"

Eve's stomach tightened. "I think you saved *me*. When you fell overboard, I swam out to you and missed the explosion."

"What's your name?"

"Eve—Eva Gray," she corrected herself. "But most people call me Eve. And you're Crystal, right?"

Crystal's blue eyes didn't waver as she nodded. "You saved us. You came after us, and you brought us back to the boat."

Eve looked away. Crystal considered her a heroine, but truth was she was the villain. If she hadn't boarded the *Gateway*, none of this would have happened.

She turned back to Crystal. "It's hot." The child's face lacked color. "How are you feeling? You okay?"

"My stomach hurts. I swallowed a bunch of water and my mouth tastes yucky."

Betty patted Crystal's arm. "When it rains, we'll catch the water and get a drink."

"Are we going home, Aunty?" Crystal's chest rose and fell in a choked sob. She clutched Betty's hand. "I want to go home."

"We're going to the Philippine Islands, sweetie, then home. They're a bit south and mostly west of us. If this wind keeps up, we could make it to the closest island in two days."

Crystal's chin quivered. "What'll we eat? I'm hungry."

Eve looked with keen interest at Betty. They both knew there was no food aboard.

"Nothing, honey. We'll just do a bit of fasting until we get there."

* * *

Jake straddled the stream of water coursing down the deck and searched the ocean for signs of the other lighter. Bodies, debris ... there ought to be something out there. He found himself looking out at the ocean, then back at Ginny. The ocean, then Ginny, until finally he gave up and sank to his knees beside her. Her body slipped further into the middle of the boat, and he lifted her back to the edge of the lighter.

His heart stopped when he saw her feet. Half of her left foot was missing. The blast had ripped off her toes. The bone of her heel lay exposed.

Rage suffused him, booting the numbness shrouding his mind. Ginny wasn't just dead—she had been murdered! The memory of Captain Emilio's arm swinging down, giving the signal to blow up the lighters, blazed afresh in Jake's memory. That man, that lowlife, was responsible! He had made sure Jake realized that. Not only had Captain Emilio murdered every passenger in the two lighters, but he had wanted Jake to suffer through the discovery of Ginny's death and then drown with her.

His mind reeled. He had been so consumed with finding Ginny and grieving over her that the big picture had slipped past. The atrocity of the event staggered him. Not just Ginny, but twenty-two other people had been slaughtered.

Why? Clearly Captain Emilio had premeditated the mass murder. He had herded the ship's passengers into the lighters and blown them up, counting on the sea to dispose of their remains. The *Gateway* had made a hasty departure, but surely not to its original destination. The disappearance of the passengers would require an explanation. In fact, neither Captain Emilio nor the ship's crew could ever show their faces again without being questioned. That meant either defection or new identities. But neither of those required a mass murder.

Then it struck him. The disappearance of the ship meant its owner would collect insurance money. No survivors would be left to testify to the contrary. But Captain Emilio had made a serious mistake.

He hadn't waited to make sure Jake had drowned.

* * *

Eve's confidence in Betty's claim to be an experienced sailor wobbled like the fragile lighter on the ocean's swells. They had been sailing for hours, huddled in a small patch of the sail's shade. Endless miles of ocean undulated beneath them, behind them, all around them. The sea was an immense monster, and they were caught in its belly. How did Betty know they were going anywhere? How did she know they weren't going in circles, prisoners of the sea's vast bowels?

She waited until Crystal's eyes closed and a soft snore whispered from her lips. "Betty, have you done much sailing on the ocean?"

"No, only lakes. But the principles are the same: catch the wind and set your rudder."

Eve frowned. "We could sail past dozens of islands and never know it."

"As long as we're headed west, we'll run into them. And if there's no wind, a ship may spot us."

"And if there's no ship?" Eve's grumpiness seeped into her voice, but she didn't care. She was hot, hungry, and most of all, thirsty.

Betty shrugged. "Then I guess you hope in God."

"God?" Eve spat out the name. "What hope was God for all those passengers on the *Gateway*?"

Betty stared dumbly at her.

"And what about us—and this poor child? No food, no water, our skins burned to a crisp. The blast that ended the lives of those people will be a mercy compared to the torment we face."

"We don't know that will happen, Eve."

"We know about a world out there full of misery. Where is this God of hope? Tell me, Betty, how long has happiness ever lasted in your life? How long in Crystal's? I bet it's come in pretty short installments, hasn't it?"

Betty looked down, her shoulders sagging.

When Betty gave no answer, Eve turned her face away and squeezed her eyes shut. She was well acquainted with misery. What was the courtroom, anyway, but a Dumpster filled with damaged and soiled lives that she—like an over-dressed bag lady—sorted through for scraps of justice? And she knew happiness too—it was the court's constant victim, always stabbed in the back.

She had hoped to move on from prosecutor to judge. Perhaps even a Supreme Court Justice. Reagan's pledge to appoint a woman to the Court had paved the way. But now Eve's dream was dashed. Happiness stabbed in the back. If there were a God, she would shake her fist at Him.

"Aunt Betty, look!"

Eve opened her eyes. Crystal's raised arm, pink from a long day in the sun, poked a finger at the sky. Eve peered over her shoulder, past the billowing sail. A black curtain of rain pounded the waters ahead, and the whitecaps were churning.

The front of the lighter jerked up, then plunged down. Eve clutched the side of the boat as water at the gaping stern splashed deeper into the lighter.

Betty's promised drink would soon arrive, but at what cost?

Chapter 7

Rain awoke Jake. It drummed on the hollow air compartments and splattered onto his face. How could he have fallen asleep? He bolted upright and checked for Ginny's body. It lay a short distance from him, her hair plastered across her face. He reached out to smooth it away, but stayed his hand. Rigor mortis had set in. A leaded heaviness settled over him, sinking through skin and bone until it stopped and wound itself around his heart.

He shifted to fence in Ginny's body by placing himself between her and the hole at the stern. If the wind started pitching the boat, he'd remove his life vest to take off his shirt and use it to fasten her down. But at this point, all it would accomplish would be an unnecessary chill for his upper body.

He remembered how Ginny liked to tease him that she could fry eggs on him, as hot as his skin got under the covers at night. Her toes were always cold, and she liked warming them under the soles of his feet as she lay curled against his back.

The memory lifted the weight from his heart. He should get up and take the sail down in case the downpour turned into a storm, but remembering bore a sweetness he didn't want to chance losing.

Remembering ... how every morning he made a pot of coffee and brought Ginny a cup. Placed it on the sink, where the aroma soaked into the steam of her shower and she'd call out, "Thank you, Jakey!" The only person to ever call him that ridiculous name. And when he came home in the evening, they'd sit on the back porch after supper and talk about their day and what was happening with the kids. At night he locked the front and back doors, checked on Brett and Dana, and crawled into bed with Ginny. They snuggled a few minutes, never long enough for him. She always slipped out of his embrace into a spread-eagle slumber that took up two-thirds of the bed. She'd sleep through the alarm the next morning, and he'd get up and make a pot of coffee …

The rain lightened to a brisk shower, and Jake roused himself lest he miss out on quenching his thirst. He took off his shirt, soaked it in the rain, and wrung it out several times to remove the salt. Then he saturated the shirt and squeezed the rainwater into his mouth, again and again, until his stomach protested.

Ginny. To think of her now meant to think of her gone from his life forever. Everything that had meant anything to him—their travel plans, a getaway cabin in Montana, his purchase of H&F Design and Construction from his boss—all of these were tied to Ginny, were given life by her presence. Now they were meaningless. Their future together had turned from a yellow brick road to a gaping crater.

* * *

The day dawned hot. By noon it was blazing. The wind that had blown all night and all morning stilled. Betty took down the sail and spread it over the boat to provide shade, but it was stifling underneath.

"Please, Aunt Betty, let me cool off in the water."

"The salt will only make it worse once you get back out. You're nice and clean now."

"I don't care, I'm hot."

Crystal jumped in, and Betty made sure the child had a good hold on the back of the boat. Crystal's legs trailed behind her in a comfortable float, two thin, white sticks winking back at the sun.

Eve slipped in beside Crystal. "Sorry," she mumbled to Betty. "The way things are going, I'm living for the moment."

Betty didn't protest. The rain had energized her, but the new day had beaten back everything she'd gained the evening before. How wonderful to be in charge yesterday, to be the one who knew what to do. She'd added a day to their lives. Maybe two. Maybe enough to get them to an island.

She listened to Eve and Crystal's chatter. Should she join them? It was warmer than she'd expected under the sail.

"I think Aunty's sad because Uncle Frank died in January."

"I didn't know that."

"My mom died when I was born. I'm an orphan."

"When did your dad die?"

"I don't know. Grandma says Mom didn't know who he was."

"So you live with your Aunt Betty?"

"No. With my grandma and grandpa. Aunt Betty and Grandma are sisters. Do you have a sister?"

"No, a brother …"

Had she slept? She felt the jostle of the boat as Eve and Crystal climbed back in, heard them gasp when they lifted the sail. The fresh air made her realize she was soaked in sweat.

"Quick! I need water." Eve's voice snapped just short of panic. "We need to cool her down."

Was she that bad off? Crystal stripped off her dripping shirt and shoved it into Eve's hand before dropping to her knees beside Betty. "Please, Aunty, don't die! Please, please don't leave me!"

"It was an oven in there, Betty. Why didn't you come out?"

The coolness of the water against Betty's skin made her gasp. "Musta been cookin', didn't know it." The words tangled on her tongue. Her fingers found Crystal's hand and latched onto it. "'M okay, sweetie. No need t' cry."

She swallowed and turned her head to Eve. "Look for land t'day. Maybe t'morrow. Go west, always west." She licked her lips and tried to swallow again. Her tongue felt fuzzy and two sizes too big for her mouth. She pushed herself to finish her instructions. "No food—can survive weeks." That was the good news. "No water—maybe three days." That was the bad news. "Worse with sunburn."

She sighed and closed her eyes. There now, she could rest. She'd passed on the baton.

* * *

Jake awoke and found Ginny gone.

The air in his lungs punched tight gasps out his throat. His heart thumped erratically in his chest. He turned the boat back on its path to find her. Lurching on quaking knees, he sped from bow to stern and back again, zig-zagging from one side of the boat to the other to search the water. She was still in the life vest and would be floating. The thought of her body, forsaken in the sea, tore at him.

Maddeningly, the wind worked against him. He stripped down the sail and dismantled the oars, but the lighter proved unwieldy for one man to row. Locked into position, the pair of oars barely touched his fingertips when he stretched out his arms between them.

No, no, no, it couldn't be! Disbelief knotted his gut and yanked hard. He had lost her all over again. He glared at the rolling sea until its restless energy mesmerized him. Sapped him. Sucked out his insides until there was nothing. Only a hole, dark and empty.

A gust of wind slapped his face, and the image of Captain Emilio shooting his pistol, its bullet roughing Jake's cheek, rose in his mind. He drew in a slow breath. That man alone was reason enough to keep going. Numbly, he reassembled the mast and rudder and aimed the boat west again.

At noon the wind died and the boat floated aimlessly. He tore off his life vest and in a fit, slammed it to the deck. All morning, his urgency to reach land had been matched by the steady pressure of wind against sail—as if he and God were teammates, yoked together to bring about swift justice. Now there wasn't even that. He dove into the water to cool off.

When the wind started up again, he climbed aboard and picked up the vest. His heart stopped at the sight of a crack running down the middle of the floor from bow to stern. He dared not remove the vest again. If the boat split apart and sank, the life vest was his only chance to reach land.

He reoriented the boat westward and positioned himself on the side of the crack holding the mast. The wind was stronger than before, but it failed to cheer him. The pressure against the sail stressed the crack, and he had no idea how long—hours or days—it would be before it split open.

Ginny's death pounded on his soul like a fist on a hollow-core door. Over and over he asked himself what he could have done differently to prevent it. Over and over he came to the same conclusion: nothing. Everything that had happened had been beyond his control. It was Captain Emilio who had made all the choices, Captain Emilio who had molded the clay of their lives into the shape of hapless victims.

But over and over, another question shoved him against the wall: *We are Your beloved. Where were You?*

* * *

Eve opened her eyes. Stars overhead, millions of them, sparkled in densely layered eons of light-years. She sat up and sought out the constellation Betty had shown her. It confirmed the wind was still blowing them westward. Gratitude welled within her that the storm had proved nothing more than a rough cloudburst, and that if Betty was right, the Philippines lay within a day's reach. They were going to make it.

She got to her feet and peered over the billowing sail. If land was out there, it was impossible to tell. The only distinction between black water and black sky was the twinkling stars.

She checked on Betty and Crystal. The child was curled against Betty, probably more for emotional comfort than warmth. Surprising herself, Eve stooped and kissed Crystal on the forehead. At least she had her aunt to love her. And grandparents. More than Eve ever had.

Betty's pulse clipped at a rapid pace, but was short of racing. After the cloudburst, the sun had steamed all three of them into wilted seaweed. They needed another dose of rain—or better yet, land bursting with streams. She stepped over the sleeping forms and walked to the rear of the boat. The wind whipped her long hair away from her face, and she had to brace herself. Pulling down her shorts and panties, she crouched over the broken stern.

There was a microsecond of realizing she was off-balance, and then the abrupt shock of hitting water. Its coolness surged through her like icy electricity. She clutched her shorts, struggled to tug them over her knees into place and at the same time kick upward to the surface. She churned, bewildered by the darkness. Which way was up?

Blackness pressed in on her. Terror gripped her chest. She could never be alone in the dark, never. The air in her lungs squeezed for release. She had to let it go. Bubble by bubble it bullied its way up her throat and through her lips. Her body went limp. Her consciousness swirled like tub water spiraling down the drain. In one last effort, she clawed at the ocean, willing herself not to breathe in.

Her head broke the surface, and she gasped at the air. Oxygen burned the lining of her throat and lungs like iodine on a raw sore. She choked and wheezed and coughed up seawater until finally she could breathe.

The boat. Where was it? She twisted one way, then the other, until she saw it—a smudge against the stars as it sped away from her.

"Help, Crystal, help! Wake up! Wake up!" She swam after it, stopping only to yell.

She swam until she could swim no more.

Then she shouted until she could shout no more.

* * *

The shriek woke Jake. Every hair on his body prickled in icy horror. Ginny! She was out there—alive—screaming for him! He jumped to his feet.

The shriek came again, piercing his ears. Not Ginny, he realized, but the boat. The vessel shuddered as the crack down its middle split open like a zipper. In one final howl of agony, the injured craft burst apart and dumped Jake into the ocean.

Chapter 8

Crystal's eyes darted frantically beneath her eyelids, her scream stuck to her throat. A gigantic sea monster hovered above her. She writhed helplessly as its raspy tongue slicked over her legs and tugged her into its huge, horrid mouth. Finally, a tiny squeal escaped her lips, and she opened her eyes. She was hanging halfway out the stern of the lighter, her legs flailing against something soft—the monster's tongue! Its saliva sloshed at her waist, soaking her, disintegrating her.

She squealed again and scrabbled onto the boat and grabbed her aunt. "A monster!" she screeched. "A monster's swallowing us!"

Betty sat up and peered sleepy-eyed at Crystal. "What in the world are you talking about?" She brushed her hand over Crystal's legs. "Where'd you get this sand, child?" When she glanced over Crystal's shoulder and her eyes widened, Crystal yelped and spun around.

There was no monster. Instead, the rising sun revealed an expanse of bright turquoise water laced in rows of white froth. The water splashed giddily toward them and landed again and again in a heap of salty bubbles at the stern of the boat.

Crystal and Betty rose, holding each other steady, and gaped at the beach. "Land!" they cried in unison. They turned to tell Eve.

* * *

Jake dozed in snatches until the change came. Awareness of it crawled into his dreams and elbowed him awake. He opened his eyes. Rain? Raising his head, body trembling, he scanned the heavens. Empty. Only the sun glaring from its own ocean of blue sky.

No, beneath him. Motion, tugging him—a surge forward, then a stop. Surge forward, stop. He shook his head, lifted himself off his stomach. At the next swell he glimpsed the horizon. A green smear creased its edge.

Land.

LAND!

His heart slammed into high gear, and he struggled to his knees. The water dipped and the land disappeared. The boat fragment slid forward. Stopped. Rose on the slow elevator of another swell. He held his breath.

An island slipped onto the horizon. High on one end, sloping to sea level at the other.

He sucked in air and hurled it out in a loud *Ooo-rah* that reverberated across the waves.

As if startled, the boat fragment jumped, and he fell on his stomach. He grabbed the vessel's edge. It rotated in a half circle and lurched forward on a new path. A path headed back to sea.

An ocean current—it must have caught the longer part of the fragment submerged in the water. He studied the distance to the island. The current might veer back and sidle up to the island, or, just as likely, it might tow his broken sea vessel farther away.

Didn't matter. He didn't need the boat. Just the island.

He slipped into the water and set his strokes on autopilot.

At first he swam, but after several minutes, he flipped onto his back. No way could he swim the entire distance to the island. No food for two days, no water for a day and a half. He'd best conserve his energy for the final stretch. The damaged life vest provided minimal buoyancy, but by paddling his arms and legs he kept his nose and mouth far enough above the surface to breathe.

The broken lighter crept away from him, dawdling on the crests of swells, inching forward in the valleys where the current gripped it. He forced himself not to keep checking and rechecking his progress. Was it because he was so tired that the island never seemed closer, or was it the chill seeping through the pores of his skin and crawling toward his heart that made him miscalculate? Maybe he should have stayed on the boat fragment. He could have clung to it, no matter where it took him.

His legs drifted downward as if weighted with lead sinkers. His head sank deeper into the water. He groped for the surface and came up sputtering. Hypothermia. Alarms clanged like cymbals between his ears. He was a dead man if he reached the point of chattering teeth and a shaking body. The water at the equator was warm, but not as warm as his body temperature. Given enough time, the ocean would suck every drop of heat from him, and he'd be lunch meat for sharks.

He grabbed a lungful of air, turned face down into a dead man's float, and rubbed and squeezed and massaged his right leg and foot. Another breath, and he attacked his left leg and foot. Then his arms, then his legs and feet again, until his skin tingled and he could feel the blood coursing through his arteries. Forget floating, he'd swim for it.

He nourished his strokes with prayer, and his prayer with steadfast glances at the island. At the northern end of the landmass, a volcano towered. Its southern rim had crumbled and the lava flow had run south, forming the rest of the island. Patches of white indicated beaches here and there skirting the coast. Most important, everything on the island was green—somewhere there was fresh water.

Water! He rolled onto his back and swam, spitting out brine, picturing himself at a stream. Yes, he'd immerse his whole face and suck in a cheek-busting mouthful. Slosh it around, spit out all the residual salt crystals, cough out the slime on his tongue and throat. Then finally, finally, he'd swallow that first mouthful of water. Sweet, untainted, salt-free water.

He emerged from his reverie, nerves sparking alarm at the roar reverberating across his eardrums. He flipped onto his stomach and caught his breath. Steep rock walls loomed above him. Waves blackened by the cliff's shadow smashed against the rock base and plummeted back in white, foaming shreds. Beneath him, an undertow whisked swirling patches of froth to the surface, tugging at his arms and legs, grasping cold fingers at his clothing.

Stomach acid surged to his throat. He forced himself to breathe evenly and swim in measured strokes away from the tumult. The roar of the hungry cliffs urged him to slash through the water, to burn up his energy. He quaked with the desire and fought against it.

Swimming first on his back, then on his stomach, he watched the cliffs alongside him gradually stoop lower to the ground, heard their snarls lapse into grumbles. At last, his breath shaking out of his chest in short gasps, he allowed himself to float. At the tip of the island, where sea and land met, he'd swim in. For now, it was all he could handle to paddle on his back and let the bobbing current carry him parallel to the island.

A wave smashed against him and rolled him over. He surfaced, choking and gagging, unable to pull air into his lungs. He thrashed helplessly as another wave clenched him in its salty jaws and dragged him off like a lioness with her prey. He gasped in air and fought the wave. It dropped him, but another pounced on him and lugged him determinedly toward its destination. Wheezing for air, dreading what awaited him, he twisted around.

Instead of rocks, a swatch of sand lay a short distance away. He mouthed a grateful *Ooo-rah* heavenward.

In control now, he sprawled on his stomach and rode the wave in. Then another, and another, until his feet struck bottom. He stumbled toward the beach, relishing the weight of his body on the soles of his feet. Beneath water that shimmered an indigo blue, he stepped over shells half-buried in the sand. Little fish darted away at his clumsy approach.

Toes numb, he fell several times and staggered in the shallow water lapping the shore. When he stepped onto the beach, his feet glared in the sun like the pale bellies of dead fish. Somewhere in the Pacific Ocean he had lost his shoes.

No one came running to meet him. Either the island was deserted, or its inhabitants were hiding. He scanned the sand for signs of disturbance—footprints, depressions from boats shoved to or from the water. Nothing.

He squinted at the wall of palm trees and jungle growth behind the beach. Again, nothing. A sea gull, and then a second and a third, coasted overhead, adding their squawks to the slap of ocean waves.

He spotted a coconut under a palm tree and tucked away his unease. The sand burned his hands and knees when he fell twice, but his anesthetized feet were as good as encased in jungle boots. He tromped over to the jungle's edge, where several nuts lay on the ground. A brown object launched out of the palm tree and swooped past his head. He ducked and pivoted to face it, laughed when it plopped onto the sand and dashed under a bush. A flying lizard.

He scooped up the largest coconut and pounded it on a sharp outcrop of rock until the hairy husk fell away and the inner shell cracked open. The first mouthful of milky fluid he spat out. The salt crystals caking his tongue loosened, and he spat out the next mouthful. The third time, he swallowed the sweet juice and dug into the coconut meat. Only then did he allow himself to collapse and sleep.

When he awoke, he consumed another coconut. The sun hung directly overhead, baking the beach, steaming the flora into an aroma of pungent leaves and bark. A globe of tiny insects hovered around his head like a helmet. The only sounds were the murmur of waves and the flutter of palm fronds.

He stood, grunting as a hundred needles pierced his feet from ankles to toes. Good, at least his feet were recovering. He hobbled in the palm trees' shade until the pain subsided, and once again scanned his surroundings. No signs of human life on the beach or the nearby jungle. Most likely he had landed on one of the remote, uninhabited islands of the Philippines. He grimaced at the thought of island-hopping his way to civilization.

Holding his life vest over his head as a shield against the sun, he returned to the shallow water of the beach. South, toward the lower elevation of the island, was his best bet for finding a stream.

The beach stretched farther than he'd figured. The vista was like walking onto a movie set—palm trees waving in the breeze, sun and gulls overhead, ocean waves lapping at his feet—except the film crew had gone home. Only he and God on the island. He clenched his teeth against the tightness rising from his stomach to his throat.

Ginny. She should be here with him.

His footsteps slowed. No one knew he was alive. No one knew where he was. Who would tell Brett and Dana about their parents' deaths? Dana would crumple to the floor; Brett would stand stalwart but shred inside. Jake quickened his pace. He needed to get to civilization, get a phone call through to his kids, get the authorities after Captain Emilio.

He stopped, his breath rushing out of him at the sight of a man-made object down the beach. A boat. It sat on the sand, barely out of reach of the waves. In spite of sore muscles, he jogged over to it, breathing raggedly, his heart pounding. It couldn't be, but it was—the other lighter from the cruise ship.

He stood at the bow and peered down the length of the boat. Sure enough, it had sustained severe damage from the explosion, but only at the stern, where the motor had been. Why two explosions on his lighter but only one on this boat? Had the explosives on the bow not detonated? He climbed over the side and squatted to examine the bow's interior. No evidence of C-4 or other explosives. He huffed in frustration. What distinguished his lighter from the other, that Captain Emilio had placed two explosives on it?

Close by on the deck lay the detached sail, neatly folded next to the mast, and a set of oars. Unlike the equipment on his lighter, no damage marred them. The wind would have swept the boat far ahead of his to the island, easily skimming the lighter over the current onto the beach. But who had sailed it? Could someone have survived the blast and overpressure? Impossible.

He inspected the rest of the boat. A crack zigzagged down the length of the deck, promising a dunk in the ocean. No matter, he'd risk it. One thing was for sure—this vessel was his ticket home. A supply of coconuts was all he needed, and he'd be on his way.

At the lighter's stern, he stepped back onto the beach. The sand at his feet was heavily disturbed, as if there had been a struggle. From there, footprints headed toward the jungle.

As badly as he wanted to confiscate the boat, he couldn't leave without checking out the owners of those footprints.

Chapter 9

If there was trouble, Jake wanted both hands free. He picked up his life vest and slipped into it, wincing as the hot rubberized fabric sizzled like a steam iron on his sunburned shoulders. The trail leading away from the beach was pocked with disturbed sand, and the jumbled footprints made it hard to tell how many people he was following. Two, maybe three? He trotted alongside the tracks, gasping with each step as his bare feet smoldered like coals on the hot sand. At the jungle's edge, the trail curved toward a tall palm flapping green fronds in the wind.

A scream pierced the air. A child's scream! Jake took off in an all-out sprint. Why hadn't he thought to bring an oar for a weapon?

Approaching the palm tree, he spied—of all people—the young girl who had joined them for dinner with her aunt. Crystal, was it? She was crouched halfway on her feet, breath rasping in and out of her throat in squeaks of terror. Near her lay Betty, eyes closed, mouth slack. His mouth dropped open. How had they escaped the explosions?

Crystal lunged and jabbed a stick at something near Betty's legs.

Snake!

Adrenaline landed a grenade in every muscle and nerve. A coconut lay a step away. He snatched it up and hurled it at the snake. The reptile turned on him, its slender body puffing to twice its size along its vertebrae, revealing blue spots between olive-green scales. Jake grabbed another coconut and stepped closer, aiming for the head. His nerves prickled dagger points from his spine to his fingertips. He hated snakes. *Hated them!*

He slammed the coconut down. The blow struck its mark, but the snake bounced under the impact, and apparently none the worse, darted into the underbrush. Jake bashed the vegetation with two more coconuts, until Crystal's wail penetrated the red haze in his mind.

"It bit her, the snake bit her!"

Jake dropped a fourth coconut and took a deep breath to clear his head. "Where?" He stooped at Betty's side.

"Right there." Crystal pointed at her aunt's right thigh.

Jake pushed up the cuff of Betty's shorts, exposing pale skin above sunburned knees. Two tiny, red dots identified where the snakebite had punctured her skin.

Crystal resumed her ear-shattering wails.

"Here now, be brave," he growled.

"My aunty's going to die!" The corners of Crystal's mouth plunged downward until her bottom lip protruded in a lump of rosebud flesh. She snuffed hiccupping sobs through her nose.

Jake mentally smacked himself. *She's just a kid, Marine.* "It's only a tree snake." He gave her shoulder a squeeze. "It's not poisonous." In Nam, they were all over the place.

Or did she mean Betty was dying before the snakebite? He checked the older woman's pulse. It was racing. "She didn't open her eyes when you screamed. Did she seem all right before she got bit?"

"I don't think so." Crystal sucked in the rosebud. "She kept falling when we walked up here."

That explained the pockmarks in the sand. "How long has she been asleep?"

"Since we got here. It's been a long time, and she won't wake up." Crystal's chin quivered, but she didn't cry.

Dehydration? Jake pinched the skin on the back of Betty's hand. The wrinkles didn't smooth out. He took Crystal's hand and did the same thing with the same results. No tear tracks on her face, either, for all the bawling she'd done.

"I'm going to get you something to drink. Keep an eye on your aunt, okay?" He looked around for coconuts and gathered several. Under Crystal's close observation, he beat one against an outcrop of rock until the husk broke away.

"I tried, but I couldn't open any."

"Good for you for trying." The corners of Crystal's mouth tweaked up, and a spasm of warmth touched the ache in Jake's chest. He pierced the inner shell of the coconut and handed it to her. "Drink this while I open one for your aunt, then you can help me with mine."

This time Crystal's smile stretched across her sunburned face. Hairline cracks split her lips. They had to be painful, but her blue eyes shone at him like he was Santa Claus.

He opened a second nut and inspected Betty's wound before he tried to rouse her. Crystal stopped drinking. Her face scrunched into the precursor of another wail.

"Wound looks good, doesn't it?" Jake spread his cracked lips into a stinging twitch of a smile. "No swelling and no change of color. Probably no worse than that puppy-dog bite you told us about on the ship."

Crystal pressed her lips together and narrowed her eyes. "It didn't break my skin, and dog bites aren't poisonous." She hoisted the coconut back to her mouth.

So much for sharing the pedestal with Santa.

He turned his attention to Betty, patting her hand, calling her name. Her eyelids fluttered but didn't open. He lifted her head and put a splash of coconut milk on her tongue and closed her mouth.

"Betty, I've got a drink for you. Do you taste it? Sweet, isn't it?" He massaged her throat and was rewarded with a convulsive gulp. Her eyelids fluttered each time he fed her, but her eyes stayed closed.

"That's enough for now." Jake took off his life vest and slipped it under Betty's head. Crystal's gaze reminded him of his promise. "You ready to open my coconut?"

Crystal selected one and pounded it against the rock. She stopped twice and swept mournful eyes at Jake, but he simply nodded at her. "You're getting there." When her shoulders sagged, he stooped and put his hands over hers. "Good job. Just a few more jabs and you've got it."

She stuck with him. Her body jerked with each brutal stab at the rock, but when the husk fell away, she beamed in triumph. Yes, sir, he was back up there with Santa.

He fed Betty a second round of sips, and her eyes fluttered open. By the third round, she sat up and held the coconut.

"Jake Chalmers," she murmured. At his nod, she asked, "Are there others?"

"No." He swallowed back a tsunami of pain.

Betty blinked. "Your wife?"

He looked down, shook his head.

"I'm sorry. So sorry."

The tsunami filled his eyes. He wiped the moisture onto his cheeks. "How did you survive the blast?"

Betty took in a shuddering breath and clutched the coconut to her chest. "Crystal and I fell off the lighter, and Eve swam over to help us. We were far enough away, we escaped the explosion." Betty took a sip from the coconut before continuing. "Eve helped us back to the lighter and we set sail. Landed here this morning." She looked at Jake. "Eve was with us until last night. She must have fallen off."

Eve. Ginny had pointed her out to him, and he had recognized her as the last-minute arrival on the cruise ship. He glanced at the two life vests lying under the palm tree. "Was she wearing a life vest like you and Crystal?"

Betty nodded, and Jake scrambled to his feet. "If she's close enough to the island, we might be able to save her."

If the current hadn't already swept her past.

He grabbed all three life jackets and strode toward the lighter, but stopped part way. How was he going to wield the boat? Manning the oars required two people, and neither Betty nor Crystal was in shape. Certainly not to row against the current. And what if the boat split? He swallowed at the thought of the ocean current bearing away another victim.

To the south, a rock the size of a house jutted onto the beach. Several young palms topped it. Their fronds waved in the wind as if beckoning him. Perfect. He changed course.

Nervous energy prickled up and down his spine like a spastic neon sign. Cuffing his hand over his eyes, he peered at the sun's position overhead. How many hours—two?—since he'd swum to the island? Could she be that far behind him?

He ran along the jungle's edge where towering palm trees shielded the sand from the sun's rays. The tingling in his feet was as good as gone. When he got to the rock, he slowed to climb it, wary of cutting the bottoms of his feet.

At the top, the ocean greeted him with a panorama that was more than he could hope to scan. His heart sank. Eve would be a dot as tiny as the puncture wound on Betty's leg. But he needed to save the only other survivor. He needed it—*please, God*—because ... he sucked in the tsunami of his pain ...

Because he had failed to save Ginny.

He slumped against a palm tree and focused on the water to the north. Gradually the ocean became a matrix of lolling waves and blues and indigoes that untangled what did and didn't belong. Eve didn't belong. *Please, God, let me spot her.*

He studied the water, organizing it into a grid. His tongue became cottony. His muscles ached for another nap. He blinked to keep from getting hypnotized.

A pinpoint of yellow twinkled on the waves. A reflection of the sun or Eve's hair? A splotch of brighter yellow bobbed beneath the dot for a fraction of a second. He held his breath, his heart thudding. He didn't dare look away until he was completely convinced.

Yes! It was Eve!

He tore back to Betty and Crystal. "I found her. Out on the ocean."

Their mouths rounded into perfect O's, but before they could say anything, he swooped Betty to her feet. "Help me," he commanded Crystal. "We need to run."

He put Betty between them, her arms clasping their shoulders, and lifted her off her feet. "Keep in step with me," he directed Crystal. "Right, left, right, left. Faster." He matched his stride to hers. "Faster. Atta girl." In a rush of adrenaline, he bore the brunt of Betty's weight and pushed Crystal to run as fast as she could.

When they arrived at the foot of the rock, Betty's sunburned face was pasty. She sank next to her wheezing niece.

"I'm sorry, but to save Eve, you need to climb the rock." Jake lifted Betty to her feet and Crystal stumbled to hers. "I'll go first and hold your hand. Crystal, you reach up and steady her."

He climbed part way and was pleased to see Betty watching where he placed his feet. When he reached down for her hand, she clasped his without hesitation. Plucky old dame. They just might pull this off.

Blood seeped from several scrapes on Betty's legs by the time they reached the top. He plunked her under a palm tree and searched for Eve. His breath left him when he saw how much closer she was. Any minute the current would catch her and drag her past the island.

"She's not moving." Betty's hand jerked to her mouth. "What if—"

—she was dead? Jake grimaced. "I'm going after her." He lowered himself over the edge of the rock. "I won't be able to see her when I start out, so you need to keep adjusting my direction with hand signals until we intersect."

While making his way back down the rock, he slipped in his haste and crashed to the base. He shook out his arms and legs. No bones broken. He got to his feet and put on his life vest. Plucking up the other two, he limped across the beach and splashed into the ocean.

Chapter 10

Jake staggered against the crashing waves as if he were a drunk flailing a bouncer. The breakers shoved him backwards, slugged his face, and snatched at the two life vests tied to his own. He fought past the fracas to the swells of deeper water and swam on his back, his gaze nailed to Betty. Her arms remained at her side. His gut churned. What was she waiting for? Had she lost sight of Eve?

Finally she waved her right arm over her head and pointed south. His stomach looped into knots. Surely Eve hadn't slipped past him? Three times, Betty signaled him with a big circle followed by churning arms to flip onto his stomach and swim hard. He chopped the water, heart hammering, until his lungs clamored for oxygen. Each time he raised his head, Betty gestured him with another big circle to flip onto his back again.

At last she stood and pointed. Next to her, Crystal jumped up and down. Eve—she must be nearby.

He treaded water until he spotted her several arms' lengths away. Nothing moved but her long, ropy hair swirling around her head. *Please God, not again.* He swam to her and grabbed her arm. It was cold. Icy cold.

He slipped his other hand to her neck. Above his fingers, her face was red and swollen with tiny, cellophane blisters. Her lips and eyelids and ears bulged like crimson party balloons about to burst. The pain had to be severe, but beneath his fingertips her pulse beat.

61

Jake shot a clenched fist high over his head. On shore, Betty raised hers, and Crystal clapped. He smiled, knowing they were cheering with him. Him and the heavenly host.

"Eve." He shook her shoulders. Her head lolled without her eyelids giving a twitch. He didn't dare slap her face or pull her hair to wake her up. Not with that angry red skin already torturing her. He pinched her arm, hard. She didn't respond.

All those hours chilling in the ocean—she might never regain consciousness. His stomach clenched. What she needed was warmth. Get her to the beach, and they could take care of that.

The knots securing the two extra life vests resisted his efforts to release them. He huffed, frustration sawing at his nerves. If Eve's face slid under water, her lungs would not survive. She needed the aid of the extra vests to keep her head up while he pulled her to shore. He worked the knots with both hands, herding Eve with his shoulder so she didn't drift away.

When the knots finally loosened, he tied a vest around each of Eve's thighs. Her torso rose in the water, giving her buoyancy that made her easier to tow. Floating on her back, she was now, in effect, a human lighter.

The last thing her injured face needed was his hand clutching her chin. Instead, he gripped the shoulder of her life vest and swam toward the beach. A glance back showed her head slipping lower in the vest. Another stroke forward and her chin sank into the ocean. Jake jerked her up. Reluctantly, he shifted to hold her head to keep it from going under.

In spite of Eve's buoyancy, his feet kept kicking her butt, and if not that, her dangling legs. Towing her was like lugging a tanker. His arm tired of plowing a path for them, and his legs seemed to kick against liquid lead. With each ocean swell that lifted him, the rock on which Betty and Crystal sat slipped farther behind him. He adjusted his angle to the beach, but the ocean persisted in mastering his direction.

When the end of the beach came into view, a glimpse north showed Betty and Crystal inching their way down the face of the rock. Would they wait for him in its shadow or follow him to see if the number of survivors became two instead of four?

The sun crawled westward until it hung over the tip of the island. Jake's heart spiraled downward. Nothing lay beyond the farthest point of land except water. He didn't dare rest. Didn't dare stop kicking.

Eve's hair floated into his face, and he pushed the strands away. His right arm tingled with exhaustion from pulling them forward, over and over, without the relief of switching arms. If he quit, even for a second, fatigue would drop his legs like bait to the current. This time it would swallow them. The lead in his legs wasn't going to let him kick-start once he stopped moving.

He shoved aside Eve's hair as it swished again into his eyes. Was there a way he could tuck the dratted mass into her life vest? He released her chin and slid his left hand alongside her head to corral her hair. It was surprisingly long. Long enough to wind in a loop around his palm. Suddenly he had a cord handle he could grip. He didn't need to haul Eve by her chin, he could pull her by her hair. Better yet, he could do it with either hand.

The reprieve gave him an edge over the current. Switching back and forth between arms, he gained momentum. He was only, what, a football field away now from the island? He could make it. Locking his mind into the tick of a metronome, he chopped at the water. Left arm, ten strokes; right arm, ten strokes.

His arms grew heavier. The number slipped to seven strokes, then five. He traversed the current, but the wind had dropped and the breakers were too mild to carry their bodies to shore.

Three strokes each. He slugged mechanically toward shore. The white sand of another beach wavered before his eyes. Tiny beach. Better not miss it. He fixed his eyes on the white blur.

His left arm—numb. Couldn't risk switching arms, opening his hand, fumbling for the cord handle …

Water gushed into his mouth and bit the inside of his nose. He jerked his face up, gagging at the brine. One foot struck bottom, then the other. He stumbled forward two steps before he could stand.

The breakers slapped his back and swept around him as if congratulating a teammate for bringing home the victory. Jubilation erupted in his chest, warming his insides. He raised his arms over his head, fists clenched in triumph. Then horror pierced his gut.

His hands were empty.

Where was Eve?

* * *

Jojo swatted the partially open door so that it whacked against the wall, emitting a sharp crack like a pistol shot. Every face in the BahalaNa Bar jerked toward him. A hot lava of glee rose in his chest as the expressions changed from surprise to fear. Inhaling the pungent incense of beer and liquor sweetened by the sweat of sudden dread, he stepped into his kingdom.

The bartender reached under the bar and produced a bottle of Jim Beam, pounding the bottle onto the counter along with a smile on his gaunt face. Above him, a small black and white television blared into the room's abrupt silence. Jojo halted his steps to listen to the news bulletin. Was it about the sailor who had vanished at sea?

No, the bulletin was about a cruise ship, the *Gateway*. Ship, crew, and passengers had disappeared over the Philippine Trench. All were presumed dead. The Filipino announcer's face registered sadness, but after a few terse sentences, he recovered and moved on to the next item.

Jojo grabbed the bottle and a stack of plastic glasses. So, rich *turistas* had died. The rich lived good lives, however long or short. The only real tragedy in life was to get in Jojo's way—like the sailor who had accused Jojo of cheating at cards.

He strode to the poker game in the far corner of the room. The players' lips tightened and their Adam's apples bobbed in choreographed swallows. They knew Jojo's rules. Everybody played until Jojo was done with them. Until that exact moment, no one dared bow out.

He scooted a chair to the table and dropped onto it. Even sitting, he towered over every man in the room. The light skin and round eyes passed on to him by his American father had been a magnet to back-alley bullies. Puberty toppled the tables, and by age sixteen, the six-foot-four giant with broken teeth and a maze of facial scars had avenged every evil word and deed ever directed at him.

He slammed the Jim Beam and glasses onto the table, and five bottles of cheap beer rattled on the wood. "American whiskey for my friends." Each man, eyes lowered, took a glass and filled it halfway with Jim Beam.

Jojo selected his target. Hadn't Paco made himself scarce the whole month before Jojo left on the transport ship? And yet, here sat the twerp now, sporting a new watch on his right wrist and a chain of shiny gold around his neck, obviously comfortable in thinking Jojo wouldn't dock for another week.

"Paco." Jojo waited until Paco raised his eyes. "For you—your welcome-back gift after being gone so long." He shoved the bottle at the quivering man.

The shoulders of the four other men relaxed. The player with a greasy eye patch shuffled the cards. The man to his left with a hairy mole cut the deck, and One-eye took back the cards and dealt. No one looked at Paco. Only Jojo, grinning, a second bottle of American whiskey next to his shot glass.

He played with his back to the wall, facing the room. The number of stragglers grew to a small crowd. Men slouched onto the six rickety bar stools and scraped chairs across the scarred wooden floor to fill tables. The television pasted background noise onto the men's murmurs and grunts. Cajoling, ridiculing, bullying, Jojo performed for his audience.

When the room was at its noisiest, Jojo kicked back his chair and bellowed like a crazed carabao. Mouths snapped shut. Eyes stared. Paco groaned and slumped against the table, shoulders quaking, hands covering his face. His wrist was empty, his fine, gold necklace gone.

"Drinks for everyone!" Jojo roared. "Tonight Paco makes our hearts dance."

Chapter 11

Jake's euphoria snapped like a broken wishbone. He'd lost Eve. He stared dumbly at his empty hands. *Go back and get her.* He could do it. That was all that mattered, wasn't it? To do what he couldn't do before—to save a life instead of letting it slip away as if it were inconsequential pocket change? He lowered himself into the jostling breakers to turn around, but his legs sprawled helplessly and he barely caught his breath before his head plunged beneath the surface.

"Jake!"

The shout brought him up sputtering. *Ginny?* He could do it—he could save her.

Heaving against gravity, he lurched to his feet to return to the ocean. A wavering blob on his left came into focus. Crystal—yelling at him, tugging a caravan of life vests.

Eve? He blinked in confusion.

The youngster stopped in the shallow water, leaned over Eve's head, and grasped her under the arms. Crystal's blue shirt and shorts plastered her thin frame. She must have waded in after Eve. Gratitude choked Jake's throat. But why was the child's face scrunched like that?

Crystal's wail slapped him like an open hand to the cheek. Blood rushed to his head, stinging his face. Noooo! Eve. She was dead …

He cried out and smashed through the waves to them. The life vests had wedged Eve's body into the wet sand at the edge of the beach. Her head was tilted back, her eyes open and vacant.

"Her face," Crystal blubbered. Her fingers lost hold of Eve's arms, and she plopped onto her backside.

Her face? Crystal was crying about Eve's face? Jake dropped to his knees beside them. He raised Eve's head and pressed his fingertips against her neck. His breath untangled from the knot in his chest. "She's alive."

Crystal clambered to her feet. "But, but what happened to her face?"

Her voice shook with horror. Did she think fish had been nibbling on Eve, eating her alive? He could see why. "It's sunburned, that's all. There's nothing to cry about."

Crystal stepped back as if he'd smacked her. Great, she'd taken his words as a rebuke instead of as a comfort. Seizing her hand, he drew her back to him. "Hey, I meant she's going to be okay. You're her friend, aren't you? How about if you call her and see if she replies?"

Crystal drew in a shaky breath while he shifted Eve into a sitting position. Averting her eyes from both Jake and Eve, Crystal dropped to her knees beside them. A wave trickled across the wet sand and batted her legs. She dangled her fingers in the foam, the corners of her mouth twitching into a frail smile.

How long since she'd last played like a normal kid? A twinge of guilt pinched Jake. His wasn't the only world that had turned upside down.

"Eve?" Crystal's voice quavered. She peeked to see if Eve responded, then glanced at Jake. She called again, louder, her voice shrill against the backdrop of tumbling breakers. After her third attempt, Jake closed Eve's eyes against the burning sun.

"She's out cold. We've got to warm her up, fast."

Crystal hunched her shoulders and rubbed her arms. "We could bury her in the sand. It's nice and hot."

"Scorching hot, don't you think? That's what my bare feet say. How about if we make a human toaster instead?"

The high pitch of Crystal's voice cascaded into a giggle. "What's that?"

"Did Betty come with you? I need both of you for the toaster."

Crystal pointed at the jungle encroaching the back of the beach. A bundle under the shade of a stumpy tree raised a slender arm and waved. "Aunt Betty said you'd make it, and you did."

Jake's chin quivered. An old lady with a snakebite and a scared kid known as Crybaby had tromped through sand and vegetation to be with him. He wasn't with the one person in the world he wanted to be with, but how good of God that he wasn't all alone either.

He blinked away the pricking in his eyes and stood, half lifting Eve. His legs wobbled and he sank into a crouch. No way he was going to carry Eve to Betty.

He shaded his eyes and squinted at Crystal. "I need your help again. You game?"

Crystal's prompt grin, spreading white teeth across a face burned almost as badly as Eve's, squeezed his heart. The kid had the wail of a foghorn, but the brightness of a sunbeam.

"We're going to slide Eve across the hot sand on these life vests. I'll pull her by her legs while you hold up her head, okay?"

Crystal's mouth and eyes rounded into circles. Was it the idea of touching Eve's head?

"Her face is a stomach-turner, isn't it?" Might as well face the facts as run from them. He stood and tugged Eve onto the beach. "She'll never recover if we don't get her out of this sun. You ready?"

Was *he*? The long swim towing Eve had drained him, and here he was going to do it again, only over a sea of blazing sand. But to rest would be to penalize Eve. He'd make it. The journey's end was as good as within spitting distance.

He clasped Eve's legs under his armpits so that he faced Betty, and leaned into a mule-harnessed pull. He didn't look back, but a jerk on Eve's body followed by a piggy half-squeal, half-grunt told him Crystal was on board.

Halfway to Betty, the sand sizzled the soles of his feet. No leaping his way over the coals this time. It was all he could do to put one foot in front of the other. If he ever ended up in the ocean again, he'd stow his shoes in his pockets.

The heat crackled up from his bare toes to his tongue. How long since he'd drunk that coconut juice? Stomach acid pitched flames into his mouth and scorched the back of his throat. Every breath he took was a chore. Exhaustion pressed against his face from the inside like a balloon ready to burst.

And then, there was Betty, reaching out to him, guiding him with her tiny hands on his arm into the shade.

"You're a hero, Jake. You saved her!" Betty's eyebrows rippled into a funny crook as she peered up at him.

A hero? He'd done it? He crashed onto the sand, dumping Eve's legs.

Betty and Crystal rushed to his side. Why were they undulating like that, mouths moving, no sound?

"Hug her," he blurted, gesturing at Eve. His mind jumbled the words on his tongue. "You two, toaster ... Eve, bread between." His words jerked with the effort of keeping them straight.

His eyelids quivered shut. Had he made sense?

* * *

Crystal shrieked as Jake's eyes rolled to the back of his sockets and his eyelids slid shut. Aunt Betty glared at her, lips squeezed in that cut-the-nonsense look Crystal hated. She clenched her bottom lip between her teeth to keep from crying. But she'd never seen eyeballs swivel like that—it was awful, like they weren't attached any more.

A shiny green fly with bulging red eyes and translucent wings landed on Jake's mouth and scuttled across the tire tread of his lips. Noooo! Hadn't she learned in science class that flies spit saliva on the spot they want to eat?

"Scat!" Aunt Betty flapped her hands above Jake's face. The fly buzzed away, circled several times, and finally disappeared. Aunt Betty placed four fingers to the side of Jake's Adam's apple. "He's okay. Poor guy only swam half the ocean to get Eve here."

Aunt Betty removed her hand, and Crystal slipped her fingertips onto the four white splotches fading from Jake's sunburnt neck. His pulse thumped against her third fingertip, and she giggled. It was as if that fly had snuck under his skin and was trying to shove her finger away.

"His skin's burning." Betty reached over and grasped Eve's ankle. "And she's cold as ice. Let's get her out of those vests and slide her and Jake together to help each other out."

Crystal was good at untying knots. She had the two vests off Eve's thighs before Aunt Betty finished untying her one knot. Together they rolled Eve onto one shoulder and then onto the other to free her of the vest on her chest.

"No sense trying to move Jake. Let's bring Eve to him." Aunt Betty stooped to Eve's head and seized her shoulders. Crystal joined her, and they shoved, tugged, and pulled on Eve.

"Good grief, I didn't know she was that heavy." Aunt Betty released Eve and sat down. "Unless we roll her like a log, we're not going to budge her."

"Let's just do a toaster, like Jake said." Crystal stepped to Eve's back and crouched next to her aunt. Aunt Betty's face was bright red, like all her sunburn had rushed up and pooled there. And now her eyes were wobbling, like Jake's had.

Her aunt's eyelids fluttered. Her shoulders sagged forward, pulling her head and fluff of white hair into her clothes like a turtle into its shell. Crystal stifled a sob. Not again! This was what Aunt Betty had done when they got off the lighter—passed out, leaving Crystal all by herself.

She wasn't alone, though. Jake and Eve were with them now. She helped her aunt stretch out on the sand to hug Eve's back, one arm flung across Eve's stomach. Her aunt's eyes drifted shut, and the familiar puffs of her snores rose like invisible smoke signals over Eve's right shoulder.

Wait, she didn't want to be the front part of the toaster! Crystal's lower lip trembled as she stared at the nasty cellophane blisters on Eve's face. Please, no, the blisters weren't moving, were they? Crawling like hungry maggots around Eve's nose and lips, bumping into each other across her cheeks and forehead?

She gagged and turned her head away.

Across from her, Jake hadn't stirred. Was his chest moving, or were those heat waves shimmering like when they'd carried Eve? He was a hero, Aunty had said. He'd swum half the ocean to save Eve. And Aunt Betty, she was a hero too. How many times walking down here had she fallen, but got up? She kept pointing to Jake, a tiny dot on the ocean, and saying, "We've got to be brave, sweetie, like him."

Crystal whimpered and lay down. She rolled herself against Eve, shuddering as the front of Eve's damp shirt pasted itself against the back of Crystal's. Her head bumped into Eve's chin. An icy chill crawled down Crystal's backbone. Ick, had she squished Eve's blisters? She whimpered again and wriggled lower against Eve's body, away from the horrid head.

Her legs touched Eve's, skin against skin, and Crystal gasped. Eve was cold—really, really cold. Eve wasn't just bread—she was frozen bread.

Taking hold of Eve's arm, she clamped herself against the frigid body. The coolness invaded her, sucking on her body heat like she was a popsicle. Now *she* was a hero, wasn't she? Both she and Aunt Betty—a human toaster defrosting Eve, bringing her back to life. Eve had saved their lives, now they would save hers.

She lifted her T-shirt and pressed Eve's arm against the warmth of her stomach. Eve's hand and fingers were crinkled like Grandma's when she'd had her hands in dishwater too long. Crystal laid her arm alongside Eve's to create another toaster, and used both hands to enclose Eve's wrinkled fingers with their long, polished red nails.

What had happened that Ginny and all those passengers had died? Crystal sniffled. When she and Aunt Betty were sitting on the rock, she'd asked if her mom was like Ginny. Mom would've been, if she'd lived, Crystal was sure of it. But Aunt Betty said no and had mushed her lips together in that way that meant she didn't want to talk about it. Crystal closed her eyes against the pain and clutched Eve's arm in a tight embrace.

She woke with sand in her mouth. She'd rolled onto her stomach and broken the toaster. She grabbed Eve's arm. The flesh was warm.

"Hey!" She sat up and sputtered sand, wiping it away with both hands. "Hey, everyone!" She shook Eve, then Aunt Betty. Neither moved. She crawled to Jake and shook him. "Jake!"

Were they dead? All three lay in the exact same positions she'd last seen them in. Her insides froze, and for a moment she couldn't move.

Forcing herself, holding her breath each time, she checked the pulse in their necks. Jake's and Eve's were strong, but Aunt Betty's was faint. Crystal pushed up the leg of her aunt's shorts and inspected the snakebite. It didn't look any different. She pinched the skin on the back of Aunt Betty's hand. It stayed wrinkled. Her own too.

As if tapped on its shoulder, her thirst blazed. That's what they all needed—coconut juice.

"Jake." She jiggled his arms. His shoulders. His head. "Please, Jake, wake up!" When he didn't respond, she poked him hard in the ribs. Nothing. She wanted to slap his face, but he was an adult. She couldn't bring herself to do it.

She got to her feet. The only palm trees she could see were in the direction she and Aunt Betty had come. How many trees had she trudged by with her aunt hanging onto her shoulder? One or two coconuts had to be close. Nothing bad would happen if she walked far enough to grab one but stayed close enough to keep everyone in sight.

None of the bodies stirred as she stepped farther and father away. The gulls had abandoned the sky and were plopping along on sturdy, webbed feet at the ocean's edge. Were they eating, or had the sun dropped low enough to signal bedtime? The granules of sand that had steamed her sandals earlier were cool now under the shadows stretching across the beach from the jungle.

Where were all the coconuts she'd seen? Fear prickled the back of her neck. Wait, there up ahead was a nut, a dark smudge on the white sand. She'd have to step out of sight of Jake, Eve, and Aunt Betty, but only for a minute.

She raced toward the coconut, its sweetness already on her tongue and halfway to her stomach. She'd open it and take just a sip, then first dibs went to Aunt Betty because her pulse was faint. Or should it be Eve, barely hanging onto life? Or Jake, so tired from saving Eve he couldn't be roused?

The buzzing registered just before the sight and smell of the rotting animal made her veer. Her feet slipped and she fell smack on her face, her fingers only inches away from the putrid flesh. A blanket of shiny green flies hurled upward from the lump, hovered like a magic carpet, and zoomed down on her. Squealing through her nose, her eyes and mouth scrunched tight, she rolled over and over in the sand until she could scramble to her feet and run.

The gulls screeched and took to the sky as she dashed past. They scolded her with raspy caws, flapping away over the ocean and circling back.

Jake, Betty, and Eve had not moved. They were dying, and the flies would move in on them next. Crystal didn't bother to check anyone's pulse. She dropped to her knees beside Jake's head.

Raising her hand, she brought it down hard and slapped him full across the face.

Chapter 12

White lightning slashed Jake into consciousness. He opened his eyes to blinding brightness. Silence stuffed his ears. He blinked, and beach and sky appeared. The noise of gulls, ocean breakers, and flapping palm fronds clicked on at full blast. What had happened? His left cheek stung as if touched by an electric wire. He rubbed it gingerly and sat up.

Crystal huddled nearby, eyes wide, body motionless, as if watching Lazarus rise from the dead.

He must have passed out. The last thing he remembered was telling Crystal about the human toaster. Had it worked? A few feet away, Betty and Eve lay stretched out against each other, sound asleep.

He got to his feet and stumbled to the women. Betty was snoring, but Eve's chest wasn't moving. He touched her neck and found her skin warm, her pulse strong. Evidently a shallow breather. Her fingers and hands were blanched and wrinkled from the water. Her feet too. No shoes. No calluses on her toes and heels. He shook his head. Those pampered feet were going to have a tough go of it.

The sun was sinking behind the island. How long had he been out, anyway?

He glanced back at Crystal. She hadn't stirred. Mighty unusual for her. "What happened? I must have fallen asleep."

"I slapped you."

"You—" He stopped. "That's what woke me up?"

Crystal's nod was barely perceptible. Her body hunched into a tighter wad.

Crybaby Crystal had slapped him? Jake rubbed his cheek, hiding his smile. The kid had really whopped him one. That explained why she was sitting there knotted up like that.

"Which was harder, smacking me or the snake?"

Crystal's lips twitched. "You." She grinned and her shoulders relaxed. "You wouldn't wake up."

"Looks like you did a good job with the human toaster while I slept."

"They won't wake up either." Crystal pinched the skin on the back of her hand and held it up for Jake to observe. "We need coconut juice. I looked but I couldn't find any—only a dead animal covered with flies." The corners of her mouth crinkled downward.

"Tell you what. Eve has immersion foot. How about if you massage her hands and feet while I get some coconuts for us?"

"Immersion foot? Ewww!" Crystal slipped her hands behind her back. "What's that?"

"She was in the cold water so long the blood stopped circulating in her hands and feet. If we don't get it going again, she won't be able to use them. Ever." Disfigured face, useless hands and feet. Would she wish he'd left her in the ocean? Tightness squeezed his chest.

He sat and lifted Eve's right foot. "Start gently, using the palms of your hands to squeeze, like you were flattening Silly Putty."

Crystal crept next to him and sat, crisscrossing her legs. She grasped Eve's left foot.

"Then, before your hands get tired, press harder and use your fingertips."

"My hands are already tired."

"Count to ten, then shake your fingers out." Jake shifted to Eve's right hand. "Let's do the same thing with her hands. Squeeze each finger ten times like they're in hot-dog buns, then rest and go back to her feet."

"Okay, but I'm thirsty."

"Right." Not a marathon runner here. He rose on stiffened legs. "One coconut shake coming up."

Before he'd taken ten steps up the beach, he turned around to find that Crystal had fallen asleep. He hesitated. The shadows had deepened, and a murmur of animal life seeped from the dense tree line. He should shake Betty awake to keep watch. Or he could hurry and pray nothing bad would happen.

* * *

Eve opened her eyes. Her vision flitted like a bird caught in a storm, seeking a place to land. It tumbled onto a moving blur and focused. A man. Sunburned face, scraggly whiskers, two jagged scars on his right cheek. Alarm spat electricity across her nerves.

Quick, get away! Run! She tried to move, but her head spun so that she teetered at the edge of a dark chasm.

"Hey, you okay?"

The voice brought her back to the man. He sat cross-legged next to where she lay. Way too close. Course dark hair lay on sand-crusted legs barely inches from her face. She jerked her head away. The movement tingled life down her spine and into her limbs.

Wait—he was holding her hand? She whipped it away. "What are you doing?"

"You've got immersion foot. I'm massaging your hand to get the circulation back."

"Don't touch me!" She tried to wriggle away from him, but her body parts lay in a disconnected heap. Her mind swirled, dragging her into the depths of a black whirlpool. *No!* She fought back. Not with this man here.

She willed herself to grasp the jagged edge of consciousness, to pull herself over its razor-sharp lip. *Breathe. Think.* Where was she?

She gulped a lungful of air and risked a glance away from the man. Sand. She was lying flat on her back on a stretch of sand. The rhythmic crash of ocean breakers broke into her consciousness. A beach? She wrenched her attention back to the man. What was going on? She struggled to sit up.

The man sat immobile. When she collapsed, he spoke, his voice soft against the ocean's rumble. "Betty and Crystal are here. Look to my left and you can see them."

Betty and Crystal? The memory dropped like a bomb. She'd fallen off the lighter—had swum after them, screaming, yelling, pleading for them to hear. Horror at her abandonment gripped her anew. She gasped to breathe.

"They're right over there, see?"

She turned her head. Betty and Crystal lay nestled nearby, eyes closed, heads pillowed side by side on a yellow life vest.

The grip on her throat loosened, and air seeped back into her lungs. Safe. They were all safe. She peered up at the man. "Jake Chalmers. Your wife—" Hadn't she worn a life vest too?

"She didn't make it." The words scraped in a whisper from his throat.

The words cut into her soul. Ginny—dead, trapped in an explosion meant to kill Evedene Eriksson. Sobs crammed her chest.

"I have some coconut juice here. How about if you take a swallow." Without waiting for an answer, Jake scooted closer and raised her head. With his free hand he picked up a coconut pierced at one end and held it over her mouth. "Can you stick out your tongue?"

She winced as her tongue touched her lips. "My mouth—"

"Your lips are swollen from sun poisoning. We'll try not to touch them. Just a bit of juice now." He tilted the coconut until it dribbled a dab onto her tongue. "Atta girl."

The drop of liquid crystallized into salt. Her tongue was coated with it. She swallowed the bitter saliva and panted to keep from vomiting it up.

"More? Gets better as the salt dissolves."

She nodded reluctantly and stuck out her tongue. In between swallows she breathed deeply, willing her stomach to settle, closing her eyes until the black whirlpool threatened, and she popped them open again.

"Good enough. Let's give it a rest." Jake lowered her head and took her hand. He kneaded her fingers. "Can you feel that?"

"Yes." She squirmed. "Pins and needles in my fingertips."

"Good. Betty and Crystal and I are taking turns massaging your hands and feet. By tomorrow you should be okay."

Tomorrow? She turned her head for another glimpse of the beach, absorbing the fact that the sun had set and a gray gauze of twilight clung to the sky. Behind her a bird chattered. She pivoted her head toward it. Was that the howl of monkey in the distance? A breeze fluttered the shadowy fronds of a line of palm trees, and she caught the faint scent of flowers.

"Where are we?"

"An island, probably on the edge of the Philippines. Appears to be uninhabited. We'll check it out tomorrow."

The Romero trial. It jumped out at her like a jack-in-the-box. "I need to get off."

Jake squinted his right eye and raised his left eyebrow. "We aren't staying any longer than we have to."

"I mean there's a—" She halted. Should she talk about the Romero trial? What if she slipped and mentioned Captain Emilio in connection with it? Jake would figure out she was the target of the explosions. All those passengers, Ginny, dead. But the target escaped. The target lived.

She coughed. "I'm sorry. I'm confused. I—how did I get here?"

Jake switched to massaging her other hand, and she stifled a yelp at the pinpricks.

"Betty and Crystal landed here this morning, then I swam in from a piece of wreckage. We spotted you in the current and fished you out."

"You weren't in one of the lighters with the rest of us. How—?"

"Captain Emilio forced me overboard at gunpoint. I swam out to save Ginny, but ..." Jake's lower lip jerked. He paused. "But I was too late."

The sobs beat hard fists against her lungs again. Jake turned fierce eyes on her, and the fists froze.

"There's a man out there who murdered nineteen people." Jake's eyes, weighted with pain, blazed into hers. "He made sure I saw it. Made sure I saw him raise his hand and give the signal to detonate those explosions. Made sure I knew my wife was on board one of those lighters." He stopped, and the air hurled out of his lungs like a category five hurricane. He flared his nostrils and gasped in a fresh storm, his chest shaking.

"Nineteen people. They never had a chance." His jaw tightened, accentuating the two pale scars on his sunburnt cheek. "Captain Emilio thinks he killed twenty-three, but four of us escaped." His eyes bored into Eve's. "And that, Eva Gray, will be his downfall."

Eva Gray. She shuddered. That name was key to why nineteen people had lost their lives. Until they got off this island, she must make sure Jake never found out.

Chapter 13

Jake's heels sank deeper into the sand with each sweep of the waves until both feet lay buried. The water crept past his legs and soaked the backside of his shorts where he sat. On the horizon, translucent hues of orange and red smeared the sky, painting the undersides of clouds mounded over the circle of the earth.

Another morning. Using his left hand, he drew hash marks in the sand: two and a half days on the cruise ship, two and a half on the broken lighter, and now a new day on the island. Six days since he and Ginny had boarded the *Gateway*. He ran his palm over his face and flinched at the sting of sunburnt skin. Its nip contrasted the icy numbness in his chest.

Instead of feeling sorry for himself, he ought to be grateful he hadn't been shark meat. He inhaled the tang of brine off the sea and focused on the horizon, where the rising sun flung its radiance like a king donning his robes. He wasn't alone—Nam had taught him that. *Lo, I am with you always.* God's promise. And he'd made it home to Indy, hadn't he?

But there was no home now. Only a wide, gaping hole where Ginny had been.

"Jake!" Crystal raced across the beach and plopped down next to him. "What are you doing?"

For a second, the muscles in his neck and shoulders knotted. He ducked his head to hide the resentment dead-bolting his jaws at her intrusion. She was just a kid. She wouldn't understand the enormity of his loss, what it meant to be hollowed out and left behind.

He eased his shoulders into a comfortable slump and faced Crystal with a smile that felt like cardboard. "Reading."

Crystal's eyes widened as he raised his right hand to show her a notecard-sized book. "You found a book? What is it?"

He handed it to her and she rubbed her fingers over the stiff, plastic brown case sealing off the pages. "*The New Testament with Psalms and Proverbs.* You found a Bible?"

"Got it from a Navy chaplain in Viet Nam. I carry it with me everywhere I go." He patted his back pocket and grinned. "Waterproofed for shipwrecked Marines and long swims in the ocean."

"Why do you want it?" She ruffled the pages and handed the book back to him.

"I read some of it every day." He paused. "You ever get a love letter from your dad?"

The corners of Crystal's mouth drooped. "No."

A pang yanked Jake's heart. A father not expressing love to his child? What wouldn't he give to wrap Brett and Dana in his arms right now? Warmth seeped into his chest and nestled against the chilly place of Ginny's absence. He took a quick breath. He still had his kids. Still had his life as a father and their love for him.

He pressed his lips together until he could speak without choking up. He tapped the book. "This is a love letter from God, our heavenly Father. Every day He tells me in a new way that He loves me. I wouldn't want to miss out on that, now, would I?"

"No." The color drained from Crystal's face and she stared motionless at her hands. "Can I read it?" she whispered. "I don't have a daddy."

Air slammed into Jake's lungs and rushed back out in a tight rasp. He wanted to sweep the kid into his arms, to squash the ache pinching that tiny whisper of despair. "Tell you what," he whispered back, his voice hoarse, "every morning, you find me and we'll read it together."

A flush sprang to Crystal's face, and she raised her head, eyes blinking back moisture to look at him. Her chin and lower lip twitched in a tug-of-war between crying and smiling.

He encouraged the smile with a warm one of his own. A real one this time. "How about if we get some coconuts going? See how Eve and your aunt are doing?" He stood as a smile won the battle on Crystal's lips.

Who knew how many mornings they'd have together? He knew where they'd start their reading, though. *Lo, I am with you always.*

* * *

It took every bit of self-control Eve could muster to not kick Betty in the face.

"Stop! Please." Beach, palm trees, and bright morning light flashed on and off around her like a blinking neon sign.

Betty dropped Eve's foot that she'd been massaging. "Am I hurting you?"

"Yes!" Eve's head spun. She jerked onto her elbows and turned her head just in time to retch onto the sand instead of on her shirt.

"I'm sorry. What should I do?" Betty tottered to her feet, her voice shrill against Eve's wobbling eardrums.

Eve's breath jolted into her lungs and back out. *Go. Just leave me alone.* She collapsed onto her back and waited for the world to stop twirling.

Betty squatted next to her, careful to avoid Eve's vomit. "Would you like to sit up?"

Eve gritted her teeth. Mother Teresa was not going to leave her alone. She grunted her assent.

Betty gripped Eve's bare shoulders, and white-hot vises clamped onto raw, tissue-thin skin. Eve shrieked.

"Don't worry, I've gotcha." Betty tugged Eve upright and steadied her. "There you go."

Eve gasped and thrust stiffened arms to her sides. She peered at her sunburned shoulders sizzling with ten white ovals where Betty had grasped her.

Was there any part of her that didn't hurt? Top to bottom, inside and out, every cell in her body crackled with pain. There was no marrow in her bones. Only smoldering coals, glowing, pulsating, feeding off the tinder of her body.

Crossing her legs in front of her, she tilted forward enough to free her hands and poke her big toe. She drew in a hissing breath. She might as well have used an ice pick.

"How about some coconut juice?" Mother Teresa snatched away a hulled coconut from some ants in a fire brigade line and brushed them onto the sand. "Jake's got a supply stacked here, but this one's open."

Eve held out a trembling hand. She'd crunch an army of ants if that's what it took to get moisture inside her.

She lifted the nut to her mouth and took a sip. Her lips throbbed, but not like they had last night. The pinpricks in her fingertips were subdued too, almost gone. But the coconut juice pinched her stomach, and she gagged the last swallow back into her mouth. She spat it out and let the nut fall to the ground.

Sleep. That was all she wanted, to curl up in the fetal position and let time nurse away her aches and pains.

"Eve, you're awake!" Crystal sped across the beach, arms outstretched, her path a direct collision course with Eve.

Eve whimpered.

Betty stepped between them and caught Crystal. "Careful, child. You don't want to hurt her."

"Oh." Crystal peeked around her aunt, the eagerness on her face shifting to uncertainty.

Eve shammed a smile. "How about a rain check on that hug?"

"Okay." Crystal dropped onto the sand and sat cross-legged like Eve. "What happened to you? We woke up on the lighter and you were gone."

"I fell off. It's as simple as that."

"Jake rescued you. You saved us, and then Jake saved you. He swam out and got you."

Eve glanced at Jake trudging barefoot toward them from the beach. He hadn't told her that last night. Guilt punched another red-hot poker into her body. He'd saved her, but not his wife. She swallowed the ash in her throat. He must never, ever find out about her part in Ginny's death.

"Guess what? A snake bit Aunt Betty. See?" Crystal pulled up the hem of her aunt's shorts to expose two red, puckered dots.

Betty touched them with the tip of her finger. "It hurts, but at least the snake wasn't poisonous."

Eve's skin pricked into goose bumps. "I hate snakes." She couldn't even look at them in zoos. She did a three-hundred-sixty-degree scan. "Do they slither onto beaches?"

"They're more afraid of you than you are of them." Jake grinned at her from where he stooped over a pile of four coconuts.

Bile rose to the back of Eve's throat. Her father used to say that, the same smirk on his face. "Which is precisely why it bit Betty," she snapped.

"No, I … I whacked it." Crystal scrunched her head into her shoulders and looked down at her hands squeezed together in her lap. "It was slithering right toward her. I thought I'd scare it away, but it bit her instead."

"I'd say that was pretty brave of you, Crystal." Jake straightened, juggling three large, hairy coconuts in his arms. He glanced at Eve, his facial muscles stiff, then past her to Crystal. "How about grabbing that fourth nut and we'll crack these open."

Crystal jumped up, spattering sand on Eve. Eve whipped her face aside in time to protect her eyes. The sand pelted her hair, and what didn't stick fell onto her neckline and slipped underneath her shirt, grinding against her skin. Crystal and Betty didn't even notice. Their eyes and smiles were focused on Jake.

Molten lead pulsated against Eve's temples. She groaned and folded into a tight curl on the sand. She wasn't going to move another muscle until they got off this horrid island.

* * *

A bead of sweat slipped from Jake's forehead to the end of his nose as he hammered the coconut hull against a rock. Three days with nothing to eat, and then only coconut for the last twenty-four hours, made the task grueling. Crystal's help, simple as it was in using a sharp rock to punch holes into the hulled nuts, was a welcome relief.

When all four were opened, he and Crystal sat on warm sand not yet crisped by the sun and took hefty gulps from two of the nuts. He savored the sweetness, rolling the moisture on his tongue before swallowing. The breeze off the ocean bore the coolness of morning. Overhead, the gulls' raucous cries carried a note of glee, as if pleased at the prospects the day held for them.

From where he sat, he could see the tip of the volcano above the tree line. He rose, eager now like the gulls. The four of them should get going before the heat of day sapped their energy.

They gathered the other two nuts and brought them to Eve and Betty. Eve lay curled on the sand, her eyes closed as if sleeping, but the furrows on her forehead belied a relaxed condition. So had her words. Jake grimaced. She should be in a hospital bed, receiving treatment for sun poisoning, dehydration, and exhaustion. Instead, she was going to be asked to get up and suffer some more.

He gave Betty a coconut while Crystal offered the fourth one to Eve. Out of the corner of his eye, he watched Eve push herself into a sitting position without help. Her hands shook, but she manipulated the nut to her mouth with ease. Good, her hands had recovered. That meant her legs and feet should be fine too. She should be strong enough to walk.

"We need to find water," he said.

The three women looked at him, squinting their eyes at the sun forming a backdrop to where he stood.

He nodded toward the west side of the island. "I did a little exploring this morning and found a swamp. The source of its water is probably the volcano at the other end of the island." He pointed north, but the women didn't turn their heads to look. "If we don't find any people, we'll want to set up a signal for help at the island's highest point."

"And leave this place?" Betty clutched her coconut to her chest.

Jake scowled. "No one knows we're here, Betty. No one is out looking to rescue us."

Her face and shoulders sagged, and he immediately regretted his sharpness. He wasn't commanding troops here, he was dealing with scared, sun-sick women. They needed to know his plan so they could get on board.

He consciously relaxed the muscles in his brow and jaw and softened his voice. "Our first priority is to stay alive, which means securing water, food, and shelter. There may be someone here already and we just need to find them." He smiled to encourage them. "If not, we need to get to the best site for a signal beacon."

"No!" Eve sat up taller, her backbone rigid, her shoulders taut. "Maybe tomorrow, maybe the next day, but not today." Her eyes narrowed at Jake. "There's not one part of my body that doesn't hurt. I can barely sit up, much less walk." She waved her hand at her feet. "And I don't have any sandals—I'd have to walk barefoot."

Jake kept his voice even. "None of us feels good, Miss Gray, but we—"

"Tell me, Mr. Chalmers, who put you in charge?"

Jake stiffened. "This isn't a matter of elections. The issue here is survival. I've been trained as a Marine to—"

"My question stands." Eve folded her arms across her chest and glared at him.

"Your question is inappropriate to the situation."

"No, it's your presumption of taking charge of my life that is inappropriate."

Jake stopped. He clenched his jaw, and for a moment no one spoke. "Very well," he said at last. "If you ladies would rather stay here, I'll explore the island by myself."

Crystal's face crumpled. "I want us to be with you, Jake. Please don't leave us!"

"I'm not talking about abandoning anyone." The words came out harsher than he intended. He took a deep breath. "I'll be back by nightfall." He'd travel faster by himself anyway.

"Wait!" Betty stood. "Jake's right. We need water." She put her hands on her hips and faced Eve. "We should start out right now. And we're not going to leave you behind." She extended a hand to Eve.

Eve frowned, but she took Betty's hand and struggled to her feet. She took a step and fell onto her hands and knees. "I told you! My feet are numb; I can't walk."

Jake reached for her arm. A few steps, and she'd be okay.

Eve jerked away. "I don't need you to—"

"Hush!" he growled. "Betty, take her other arm, please." The two of them boosted Eve to her feet.

He held onto her as she swayed between them. "We'll need to help her. What do you think, Betty? Are you feeling strong enough?"

"I can do it." Betty slipped under Eve's left arm and clasped Eve's hand.

Jake did the same with Eve's right arm across his shoulder, and together he and Betty steadied Eve's waist with their free hands.

Eve gasped. Her body quaked, her head rolled forward, and her knees buckled. "Sick!"

Jake and Betty froze.

"Should we lay her back down?" Betty gazed wide-eyed at Jake.

He paused. He didn't like leaving them alone for the whole day. Too many things could happen. Snakes, animals, men … Whether Eve liked it or not, he was responsible for the three of them now.

"Let's wait a minute and see if she recovers. If not, I won't go far. Not all the way to the volcano."

Chapter 14

Eve hung between Jake and Betty, gasping shallow breaths until her stomach settled and the dizziness faded. She raised her head and straightened, bearing her weight on both feet. Jake's clasp of her right arm over his shoulders raised her almost to her toes, but Betty's shoulders were a foot lower than Jake's. To stay upright, Eve had to brace her arm on Betty, all but grinding the frail woman into the sand.

"I'm hurting you." Eve withdrew her arm.

"I'm okay, don't worry." Betty lifted Eve's arm back into place.

"Here." Jake's hand tightened on Eve's waist and shifted her weight off Betty's shoulders. "I've got you. Just use Betty to stabilize yourself."

At the sour scent of Jake's armpit, Eve turned her head and gagged. How far could she walk holding her breath?

Jake took a step forward. Eve raised her right foot and set it down with a clumsy plop on the sand. Needle pricks, hot and razor sharp, shot up her calves, crested in her thighs, and plunged back to her feet.

"Hurts!" Her stomach lurched, and she panted to keep from vomiting.

Jake and Betty stopped and held Eve steady until her breathing normalized. Sweat drenched her face. She needed to lie down.

"Ready?" Jake asked. As if reading her mind, he added, "Walking's the only cure."

"Then go without me."

"Ten steps. Ten steps and then you can rest."

Crystal, her thin arms clasping life vests and coconuts to her chest, stepped in front of Eve. "You helped us swim to the lighter. Now we can help you." She beamed as if she'd handed Eve a box of chocolates.

Did the child think life was a series of carefully balanced paybacks? Eve saved them, Jake saved Eve? Eve dragged them to the lighter, they dragged her to the volcano? She clamped her teeth against the acid words crouched on her tongue. Life had no sense to it—only consequence. There was no Judge in the sky handing out rewards, seeing to it that the scales of justice tipped in favor of good. The only justice that got meted out came from the courthouse, and even that was too often shackled.

The Romero trial. Her breath stopped. The trial was coming up in a little over two months. She had to get off the island!

She filled her lungs and released the air in a spurt. "I don't need to rest. Go."

The pain chewed at her strength and fogged her mind until she no longer clung to Jake or braced herself on Betty. Vaguely, she felt their grips on her arms tighten, felt the pinch of their fingers on her sunburn, felt Jake's clasp on her waist squeeze deeper into her flesh. She didn't care. Hell was an eternal path of smoldering coals, and she was going to walk her way right out of there.

* * *

Jake fixed his eyes on the beached lighter, a dull white speck against the sand sparkling in the morning light. Some other day he'd have appreciated the beauty of their pathway—palm trees to their left, branches bowing and skittering in puffs of wind, and to their right a palette of blue ocean and crystalline sky. But not today. Today the beach was a tunnel of sand blistering underfoot and sun blazing overhead.

"Lighter," Betty murmured.

From the way she spoke, her tongue was as dry and leathery as his. No stopping to drink from the coconuts Crystal carried, though. Eve's fatigue was growing with each step. Barely walking, head hanging, legs bearing less and less of her weight. Betty was staggering too.

"We'll rest in its shade," he promised.

He dragged Eve the last few steps when her legs stopped working. He should've picked her up and carried her to spare Betty, but he couldn't. He needed Betty to be his crutch, to keep Eve upright, or they'd all three collapse on the hot sand.

His knees gave way at the boat, and the three of them fell. Eve tucked into a tight curl, mouth slack, eyes shut. He took a coconut from Crystal and dabbed juice into Eve's mouth. She moaned and swallowed. He dabbed more, again and again, until she stopped swallowing and her mouth went slack again.

He put up the sail to provide shade while Betty and Crystal drank from their coconuts and fell asleep leaning against each other, their backs against the boat. He split his coconut open and ate the meat, debating whether to eat the other three coconuts too. That would mean replacing them. Hulling them. Delaying the trip. He closed his eyes. He wasn't that hungry.

He woke with a start to find Crystal shaking him. The sun hovered directly overhead, leaving only a sliver of the shade they'd fallen asleep in.

"I'm hungry." Crystal held up her coconut. "I sucked it dry."

"Wake up Eve and Betty and we'll all eat."

Crystal shook the two women until they opened their eyes.

"Chow's on." Jake forced his lips into a grin.

Eve uncurled and sat up straight. Betty stretched and squinted at Jake. Both of them looked expectantly at him.

"Coconut meat on the shell." He pried Betty's open and handed the two halves to her, then did the same for Eve and Crystal. Crystal scooped the fruit into her mouth, but Betty and Eve couldn't hide their disappointment. What did they expect, lobster?

He swallowed his irritation. "Maybe we'll find something more on our hike up the coast."

Betty glanced at the two halves he'd emptied and tossed aside before his nap. "I can't eat all mine. Here, you take one of these. If anyone needs the nourishment, you do."

"Mine too." Eve handed one of her halves to him. "You only lugged me all the way here."

Warmth pinched his cheeks at their kind words. He was such a grouch, way too hasty in his judgments.

"I only want half too." Crystal added her piece to the lineup of shells.

He took their offerings only because he knew he wasn't snatching food out of their mouths. And he was hungry. Famished.

Crystal finished her meal first. "Why's there white on your noses?"

They looked at each other's noses.

Eve and Betty shrugged, so Jake answered. "When people get a sunburn, they either get out of the sun or get some kind of medication. We haven't been able to do that, so the pores on our noses secreted this white fluid. It hardens into a crust so no more damage can be done."

Eve rubbed the top of her head. "What I can't figure out is why my scalp is so sore. It's more than just sunburn."

Jake flinched as she looked his way.

"What?" She glared at him.

"Nothing."

"No, tell me."

"All right. It's probably because I pulled you ashore by your hair."

Eve's voice rose. "You're telling me you never learned that towing by the chin is the proper procedure?"

Jake stiffened. Push him, and he'd push back. "I'm telling you that pulling you by your hair made the difference between life and death."

Betty reached across him and touched Eve's hand. "I watched him, Eve. Two different times you both went under. I thought he'd lost you for sure, but he never let go."

"The important thing," he growled, "is that by God's grace we made it to shore. Your head will heal."

Eve set her empty coconut shell down, slow and deliberate. "So it will. But if there was any grace involved, it was from you, and not from any God who let all those other passengers die."

Everything inside Jake went quiet. Ginny's face slipped into the silent space of his mind. His gut tightened, stiffening his belly, his lungs, his jaws. He should argue with Eve, but his storehouse of Bible answers was empty. Answers wiped out by an explosion that didn't need to have happened. Shouldn't have happened.

He stood and dismantled the sail, pushing, stuffing, cramming his pain into the hollow places his heart wouldn't find. "Let's head out. The sooner we get to that volcano, the sooner we get off this island."

Chapter 15

Eve avoided looking at Jake when he extended his hand and hauled her to her feet. She grabbed the edge of the beached lighter with her other hand but jerked it away when the heat of the wood stung her fingers. She toppled against Jake.

"Uh, sorry." She glanced at his face and saw his eyes clearly averted from hers. She knew it—she'd as good as slapped him, reminding him of his wife's death like that.

"It's okay." The words were flat, his mouth tight. He steadied her and slid her arm across his shoulders, not once looking at her. "You ready, Betty?"

Betty's expression said she'd seen Jake's pain too. Betty peered up at Eve as she braced her arm across Betty's shoulders. Betty's eyes asked, "Why?" but her mouth said, "Ready."

They took their first step. The stink of Jake's armpit, freshened by his nap in the hot sun, rushed into Eve's nostrils. She flinched but didn't whip her face away this time. The odor was a nuisance, nothing more. Nothing like the deep well of pain bored into Jake's soul.

"Still got the pinpricks?" Betty asked. The beach was lava hot now, so they walked in the wet sand along the shore to protect Jake's and Eve's bare feet.

"No, but my legs—it's like they have no bones."

"I can tell you're wobbly." Betty pointed up the beach to a daub of gray. "That's the rock Crystal and I sat on while Jake swam out for you. There's shade there, if you can make it."

"All right." Eve swallowed, her mouth dry at the reminder of what Jake had done for her. As much as she hated apologies, she owed him one. "Jake. Thank you for risking your life to save mine. I'm … It doesn't matter how you did it."

The long draw of air into his lungs told her the apology, lame as it was, mattered. His knotted shoulder muscles softened beneath her arm as he breathed out.

"It was the only way I could hang onto you."

Acid scoured the back of her throat. Did he have to keep defending himself? Why couldn't her apology be good enough? Just like her father, Jake had to be right or he wasn't happy.

She prickled at having to be helped by him, at having his sweaty hands clasp her hand and waist, at having to comply with his marching orders in the first place. That would end as soon as she could stand on her own. She targeted the rock Betty had designated and aimed every fiber of her will at it. Behind the rock, the volcano towered far away in the distance. It would take more than a day, more than two, to get there. Was it worth it?

With every step, the sun baked the sunburn on her head and shoulders. Her skin steamed in the unrelenting heat until she wanted to sob when Jake at last lowered her into the shade of the rock. Thirst shriveled her tongue, making it difficult to swallow. Water. They needed to do whatever was necessary to find water.

She opened her mouth to tell Jake to go. *Don't come back until you bring us water.* The command to the presumptuous, mighty Marine hunkered like a sweet after-dinner mint on her tongue. But before she could speak, the words melted in the hot, sweet salve of sleep. She woke to find Crystal nudging her. The child thrust half a coconut into her hands. Beside her, Betty stirred.

Crystal handed her aunt what looked like the other half of Eve's coconut. "Almost all the nuts were green or rotten. A half's all we get."

"We need to find water." Jake stood outside the shade, mouthing the words around a jaw full of coconut meat.

Eve twitched in irritation that he'd beaten her to the words. "We've got shade. We'll stay here until you find a stream."

"No." Jake swallowed his mouthful. "We've got to get to higher ground for that. The end of the beach is just ahead. Let's assess the situation there."

Eve refrained from throwing her coconut at him. At least he'd included the rest of them in deciding what to do when the beach ended.

She felt stronger on the next leg of the journey. She still needed Jake and Betty's support, but she bore most of her weight and walked like a human instead of plopping down one foot after another like a life-sized puppet. Though their pace was still agonizingly slow, they arrived at the end of the beach without once stopping.

Jagged black rocks replaced the white sand. A short distance away, a tangle of undergrowth swallowed the rocks and spread inland toward a backdrop of towering trees.

"Now what?" Betty glanced pointedly at Jake's feet. "You and Eve have no shoes."

"We need to get to the volcano. You can wait here for me if you want."

"In the hot sun instead of the shade?" Eve snorted. "Nice choice."

"Feet in the ocean, head in the breeze." Jake shrugged. "Not a problem."

"Unless you have a second-degree burn." Eve pressed her fingers against the top of each shoulder. When she removed her hands, five white spots faded from each reddened shoulder. "Like it or not, Commander, the troops are advancing with you."

The muscles in Jake's jaw tightened, highlighting his own pale spots from the scars on his right cheek. "Better to wait until you can walk in that tangle by yourself. Three abreast will be—"

"Get me a sturdy branch for a staff and I'll manage just fine." Eve lifted her right foot and wiggled her toes, then did the same with her left foot. "The pain is gone."

"Good, you can trail us, then. We'll flatten the path for you and maybe make better time."

Before Eve could answer, Jake turned and batted through the underbrush. Apparently his feet were tough enough to take on the rough vegetation. She'd barely sat down before he returned with branches for each of them.

"Ready?"

As if she could say no. But she did. "After I take a dip." She used her branch to get to her feet and with all the dignity she could muster limped into the shallows of the ocean. Betty and Crystal followed her, but Jake splashed by them and dove into a wave.

Jerk.

Out of the water, he lined up Crystal to follow him, then Betty behind her. By default, without a word or gesture from Jake, Eve's position was last. She hobbled into the lineup and he headed inland.

"We'll stick as close to the ocean as we can," he said over his shoulder, "but the farther we go, the more we're going to find rock cliffs between us and the ocean."

Eve glanced at her pampered, painted piggies. *No squeals out of you, girlies, not a one of you.* She clenched her teeth and followed Betty into the vegetation. It was an obstacle course that stood between her and the Romero trial, that was all. She'd get to that courtroom if she had to crawl on her knees.

They followed an animal trail that snaked between outcrops of volcanic rocks and patches of twisted undergrowth. The pungent odor of heated vegetation assailed their nostrils, vying with tiny, flying insects determined to investigate every orifice on the travelers' heads. The number of beaches diminished, while the rugged terrain looming over them became more and more difficult to climb.

"This is probably our last beach." Jake helped each of them clamber over a rocky incline to a scrap of sand at the ocean's edge. "We'll travel on top of the cliffs now."

Betty collapsed onto the sand. "Jake, I've got to rest." Her hair and face were drenched in sweat, and her green T-shirt and shorts clung to her like paste. She fanned her face, more to drive away the bugs hungry for her eyes, Eve guessed, than to create a breeze against the noon heat.

Eve eased down next to her and sheltered her swollen face against her knees. Her mouth was cottony with thirst. Two days of coconut juice had taken a toll on everyone's bowels. The embarrassment of the frequent side trips it occasioned was topped only by the odor clinging to their shorts when they returned.

Their fearless leader sat down next to them. "Let's bathe and take a break. You gals can take a nap while I look for water."

No protest here. Eve waded into the ocean, scrubbed what she could of her body and clothes, and crawled back to shallow water to lie submerged except for her aching face. She closed her eyes.

"I want to go with Jake," Crystal said.

"Go." Betty's assent was a puff of air out of her lungs.

She expected Betty's pillow-soft snores to follow. Instead, as soon as Jake and Crystal were out of hearing, Betty spoke, her voice sharp. "What is it with you and Jake?"

Eve sighed and opened her eyes. "I know Jake saved my life, and I'm grateful to him. But I also know the nature of men." She sat up. "You watch: he's going to expect us to be running around like his personal slaves, waiting on him hand and foot."

Betty scowled. "I don't think Jake is that kind of man."

"That's the only kind of man there is. If you don't look out for yourself, he'll expect everything to revolve around him—with his word as the law."

"Come on, Eve, you can't tell me you've never known a good man."

"Never."

Betty snorted. "Come on! Your father? Brother? Teachers, doctors—"

"All looking out for themselves."

Betty stared at her, her face sober. When she spoke, the words came out softly, tiptoeing as if Eve lay bandaged on a hospital bed. "Then I think you'll find you've met your first good man in Jake."

Eve laughed, the sound harsh, grating her ears, grating her throat. "Watch with me, Betty. You show me—show me exactly when I should believe that."

"No, Eve." Betty's smile was sweet. "I want you to tell *me*—tell me the exact moment. Because you will see it."

Chapter 16

Jake helped Crystal climb the last few steps back down to the beach. The kid was nimble as a monkey, but her determination to not spill one drop of the precious water she carried made her footsteps cautious. Between her and Eve slowing them down, they'd do well to make it to the stream by nightfall.

"How about if you give the gals their water while I clean up." He handed his half coconut shell of water to her. Betty and Eve lay asleep, submerged to their waists in the swirling, white coattails of the waves. He waded past them a short distance and sat down. The salt stung the cuts in his feet. He'd have to tear off a piece from his shirt to wrap around them so they wouldn't get infected.

"Aunty, wake up, we found water! Do you want me to pour it on your head?"

Betty opened her eyes and bolted upright. "Don't you dare waste it, child! Eve, wake up."

Beaming, Crystal handed them the two shells. "We scraped all the coconut out so we could bring the water to you."

Betty took a swallow and grimaced.

"It tastes awful and there's sand in it, but it's real water, Aunty."

"I can tell. Thank you, sweetie. It's wonderful to have it."

"We saw bananas too. Jake's going to get us some tonight."

"How far did you have to go?" Eve took a sip from her coconut and made a face. She held the water in her mouth, as if debating whether to spit it out or swallow it.

Jake growled under his breath. He had shed blood for that water. He waited for Eve to swallow it. "The stream isn't far, but a good ways at the pace we've been going. As soon as you finish your drinks we'll head out so it doesn't get dark on us."

"And spend the night in the jungle?" Eve twisted around to confront him. "Why not stay here to help Betty and me recover? We can start out in the morning."

He should have seen it coming. "We'll camp at the edge of the jungle, not in it. The stream will give us fresh water, and the bananas a good start on a tough day. No sense wasting time here."

To his surprise, Eve ended her protest. She turned to Betty and raised her eyebrows. "Well, I guess we should do what the man wants, right, Betty?"

Betty smiled and raised her coconut shell. "Beginning with drinking the water he brought us, Eve." She directed her smile to Jake. "Thank you, Jake, that was good of you. I'm glad we didn't have to wait till we got there."

"You're welcome." Inside, he squirmed. Something was going on here. Something beyond cooperation on Eve's part and gratitude on Betty's. He rose to tear the hem off his dripping T-shirt. The two women sipped their water as if it were hemlock and watched him sit and bandage his swollen cuts.

Aha! An expectation—that's what it was. They'd never tell him, but it'd be there waiting for him, a steel trap he'd step into as sure as if he were blind. He huffed. What they needed was a good dose of gratitude that they weren't stranded on the island by themselves.

Their progress proved even slower than before. Eve refused to abandon her branch and let him help her move along faster. A hand up a steep incline was the most she'd accept. And, sure enough, it was dusk by the time they got to their new campsite.

He glanced from the stream's trickle of water to Betty's and Eve's faces registering disappointment. He shouldn't have called it a stream. The bed was broad and deep, but the amount of water flowing down its middle was barely a foot wide and only inches deep. They had to practically bury an empty coconut shell in order to fill it with water.

"Not exactly the Hilton," he said stiffly, "but it's got running water, no limit on how much we drink, and enough splashes to wash off every bit of salt you've got patience to deal with."

"I'm all for that." Eve knelt next to the water and splashed it on her face. She winced every time the water spattered her reddened skin, but she didn't stop.

The tough rind of his exasperation sloughed to his feet. He'd forgotten about her pain in his determination to conquer distance. Barely able to walk, sore feet, sun beating on her sunburn—she had to be in agony. Really, she'd been a trooper. He should admire her resilience, ignore her mulishness.

"Crystal, want to help me with those bananas?"

The trees weren't far, but his feet were tender from the cuts. Even if he could handle climbing the rough bark, he had no way to cut off an entire cluster of bananas. When they arrived, he hoisted Crystal onto his shoulders. Stretching to her fingertips, she harvested an entire tier of twenty fruit.

The trip back to the campsite was difficult in the dark. The night noises of the nearby rain forest leaped at them like invisible demons. Whoops and cries, snarls and screams, and snapping sounds. He remembered a similar sound in Nam.

"I don't like it here," Crystal whimpered. "Something's out there."

"You're okay. It's mostly monkeys and birds. Nothing for you to worry about."

His stomach knotted. Just something for him to worry about.

* * *

He woke before sunrise. Three dark lumps identified his companions, lying side by side on the dry stream bed, with Crystal sandwiched between her aunt and Eve. He drank from the stream, savoring each swallow, until his belly protested. Then he soaked and rewrapped his feet. When the sky lightened, he stood and grabbed several bananas, pocketing them for later. No sense waking anyone—they'd just worry until he returned. He'd hurry.

The path back to the lighter was easy to follow, trampled almost flat by its four travelers the previous day. He ignored the stinging twitches in his feet and trotted where the path was level. Without the women to slow him down, he'd arrive at the lighter in no time at all. His task would take only a few minutes. He might even get back before they woke, tired as they were.

The silence of being alone poked at the emptiness inside him, opened him to the pain fisted in his soul. The words erupted, unbidden, clamoring.

God, why?

Why take Ginny away from me? Our time was already reduced to months— why steal that from us?

A leaded heaviness halted his steps. It rose to his lungs, locking his air passages, paralyzing his breath.

He closed his eyes and squared off with God. *I don't want to live without her. I can't bear it. I can't.*

The torrent came then. Flooding his eyes. Roaring down the canyon in his heart. Hollowing a cavern in his soul.

He fell to his knees, and a hush followed. It wrapped him in its folds like a mummy. Tight. Numbing the pain.

At last, he got to his feet. His direction was clear. He had no choice.

He had to go on. The lives of three people depended on him.

A gull cawed overhead. Morning heat wafted a faint perfume off the vegetation. A coven of tiny, flying insects welcomed him into their swarm. He brushed them aside and broke into a trot.

The beach was dazzling after the shadows of the rain forest. Sea and sky winked, brilliant gems of aqua and turquoise, the sun a golden amethyst in their midst. He stood for a moment and let the serenity stretch its arms around him. He could do this.

In the damp sand at the ocean's edge, salt water soaked through the bandages on his feet, biting his cuts as he walked. He trudged past the large outcrop of rock where Betty and Crystal had watched him rescue Eve. The beached lighter came into view, and he increased his pace.

Was it an illusion, or were the waves tugging the boat into the ocean? He'd meant to pull the lighter farther up onto the beach yesterday but had forgotten with the distraction of helping Eve. Depending on what they found at the elevated end of the island, several days could pass before he returned to repair the boat. In the meantime, he didn't want the tide to dislodge it and float it out to sea.

His mouth went dry as he neared the lighter. Something in the water had washed ashore during the night. A body. His knees wobbled.

Please, God, not Ginny.

The odor of decomposed flesh permeated the air. The corpse was bloated, swollen by the fermentation of death. Blowflies buzzed frantically about it, covering it in a shroud of shifting black dots. Jake held his breath and threw sand over the corpse to dispel the flies.

It wasn't Ginny. He released the air in his lungs, gagging as he inhaled the putrid odor with his next breath. The body was a Filipino man—a sailor, from the looks of his clothing. A red gash stretched across the man's neck, clearly identifying him as the victim of a cruel and swift murder.

Jake's hair stood on end. He stood stock-still and scanned the beach. Nothing. The body's presence could mean civilization was nearby, perhaps even on the island itself. On the other hand, the fact that the man had been murdered spelled danger for all of them. And he had left the three women alone.

He needed to hurry. He stepped toward the lighter but stopped. He couldn't leave without burying the body. Any man was owed that dignity. Fetching an oar from the boat, he dug a hole in the sand near the tree line and dragged the corpse by its clothes to the shallow grave. He planted four sticks at its corners to mark its boundaries. Hastily, before closing the grave, he searched the man for a wallet or other form of identification. Nothing, except a knife slipped into the man's waistline. Jake took it.

The stench of the corpse clung to his hands and arms. His stomach roiled at the nastiness of the task. He made a quick attempt to wash the stink off in the ocean, then pulled the lighter to the edge of the tree line.

Burying the sailor had detained him long enough that the women would be awake now. In spite of his fatigue and the sand slipping into his bandages, grinding against the tender flesh of his feet, he made himself jog.

He'd been gone far longer than he'd intended.

Chapter 17

Jake stepped into the cone of silence pyramiding the stream bed. Birds, monkeys, everything but insects had fled the premises of the human invaders. Betty, eyes closed, lay curled on the sandy bed where he'd seen her last. Next to her, Eve sat chewing a green banana, her face somber. Crystal crouched over the stream, fingers curled around a coconut shell, three more lined up next to her like children at a water pump.

The knot in his stomach dissolved. Nothing had happened to them. Not this time. He took several breaths, his heart thumping from running back to the campsite. He needed to discover what dangers lurked on the island. Get a supply of bananas, head for the volcano, and spy out the land.

None of the women detected his approach. He shook his head. They didn't need to do sentry duty, but surely they could tune in to what was happening around them. "I'm back," he announced.

Betty opened her eyes and jerked to a sitting position. Relief flitted across her face, followed by a scowl. "You were gone so long, I was afraid you'd left us."

Behind her, Eve stared daggers at him.

"I'm sorry. I thought I'd be back before you woke."

"You said you could go faster without us, and then you just disappeared." Betty pushed her hair behind her ears. Her hands shook.

Jake's conscience crunched down hard. He was supposed to protect them, not scare them. "I'm sorry." His heart felt the words this time. He stooped and took Betty's hand. "I won't go off again without telling you first."

"Where were you?" Eve demanded.

He prickled at her tone of voice. Okay, he deserved the harshness. He'd scared her too. Crystal's quivering lower lip made the rebuke unanimous.

"I went to the beach to move the lighter so the tide wouldn't get it. If we don't find anyone here, we'll need to repair the boat to keep going. I thought I'd let you sleep until I returned."

"What took you so long?" Eve jabbed the question at him as hard as she had the first one.

"I found a dead body."

The women gasped in unison, and he took perverse pleasure at being able to justify himself before the firing squad. But he was frightening them again. Not what he wanted. "It washed ashore near the boat." Their eyes widened. "No, it wasn't Ginny."

"Was it one of the passengers?" Betty gripped his hand tighter.

"No, but it was a Filipino man, probably a sailor. Before I buried him, I searched his clothes and found this." He released Betty's hand to show them the knife he had placed in his belt.

"Is that the stench I smell, the dead man?" Eve's curled lip indicated her disgust included more than the odor.

"Sorry." He took a step back. "I guess I didn't get it washed off."

"Give me your shirt, Jake." Betty held out her hand. "I'll see what I can do with it in the stream."

He took his shirt off and handed it to her. Crystal gasped. He didn't have to look at the three of them to know they were gawking at the ragged path of scars etched into the right side of his chest.

"Dog," he muttered. He turned to walk away, then stopped. "I'm leaving to get more fruit."

Crystal didn't ask to join him. Great—no doubt he'd frightened her, as gruff as he'd been. No more growling, Marine. Ginny had told him to boss the troops, court the ladies. He huffed at the practice he was in for.

He was pleased to find riper bananas. He examined the fruit for tarantulas, but the battle against other hungry insects was beyond winning. By the time he arrived back at the campsite, his chest and arms bore the reddened battle scars of their victory.

Betty handed him his sopping shirt while Eve and Crystal selected their bananas. "Smells good, feels good. Thanks, Betty."

In turn, they thanked him for the bananas. Graciousness abounded as if they were the star pupils at a Victorian finishing school.

He stuffed down all the bananas he could eat, then took his life vest and cut a slit in it.

"What are you doing?" Crystal dropped down next to him.

His heart warmed at her presence. The courting was working. "Watch." He removed the stuffing from the life vest and cut the rubberized fabric into four equal pieces. Then he placed some of the stuffing on two of them, put his feet on top of the stuffing, and secured the fabric around each foot. He stood and took a few steps.

"Good enough." He took the other two pieces and the remaining stuffing over to Eve and got down on one knee. "May I?"

Eve leaned away from him. "I'll do it." She took the materials, all but stiff-arming him. With a few deft movements, she assembled the moccasins and tried them out. "Thanks. Nice idea."

They exchanged polite smiles.

"But Jake …" Crystal frowned. "What about when we're out on the ocean? You won't have a life vest."

Eve put her arm around Crystal's shoulders. "Don't worry, kiddo. If he needs help, I'll tow him by his hair."

Silence, then a cackle from Betty. Warmth flooded his chest, and he laughed.

* * *

Jake led the way over a winding path that skirted the coastline. Every step raised them higher above the ocean until they looked down from steep walls of volcanic rock to the foam of crashing waves below. Trees the size of saplings replaced the palm trees. Beyond them lay the towering rain forest, a green sea that tossed as restlessly as the ocean booming in their ears.

"Can't we just cut through the jungle to get to the volcano?" Betty sighed. "Seems like we're getting farther away, not closer."

"We'd have no way to orient ourselves in the jungle. The layers of leaves are so thick we wouldn't be able to see the volcano. Besides, the coastline is where we'd find anyone, if they're here."

"There's no one here." Eve leaned on her staff, swaying slightly. "The beach we landed on was too gorgeous for anyone to pass up living on it."

"Unless there's something better. That gorgeous beach was just around the corner from a swamp. No telling what lives in there."

Betty inhaled sharply and Crystal whimpered.

"Thanks for goosing our imaginations," Eve snapped.

"Look, I'm not trying to scare you, just asking you to be sensible. You need to be alert to what's going on around you. This morning I walked right up to you, and until I spoke, none of you knew I was there. I could have eaten you for breakfast."

"Thanks, that should help us sleep tonight."

"Okay, you two!" Betty halted. "Let's start being reasonable by taking turns and rotating who stays awake."

With age, injury, and a wild imagination to arm them? Jake sighed. But was there any alternative? He couldn't stay up all night and expect to function the next day. The murdered sailor was a warning that their lives could be at risk. "I agree. From now on, someone always needs to be standing watch."

* * *

Jake stared in disbelief at the wall of rock blocking his way. It jutted straight up from the ground like a black granite tombstone. Where had that come from? Every time the women wanted to rest, he'd scouted ahead for the best route to take. Twice they'd been forced to retrace their steps. Now it looked like they would have to double back over everything. All the way back to their morning campsite.

Crystal, Betty, and Eve, still following the pattern of trailing him in single file, joined him one by one. Betty's steps wobbled, Eve's dragged. They sank to the ground as soon as they saw Jake wasn't moving.

No way did he want to tell them they'd climbed that last, steep incline for nothing. "Ready for a rest stop?"

Eve and Betty answered by shrugging off their life vests and using them as pillows. Before Jake could say anything, they were asleep.

He turned to Crystal. "I'm going to explore how to get around this piece of rock."

"Can I go with you?" She discarded her life vest and flapped the front of her sweat-soaked T-shirt. "I'm not tired."

He nodded at Betty and Eve. "Looks like your turn to do guard duty. Do a good job and stay alert. I won't be gone long." He winced at the disappointment on her face as he walked away.

On the ocean side, as he expected, the volcanic rock cliff plunged straight down. He turned and trailed the wall inland until the jungle opened its maw and swallowed the wall in vegetation so thick, his stick was useless against it.

The only other option was to go over the cliff. It wasn't particularly high, maybe fifteen feet, not at all impossible if he could find a way to climb it. He followed it back to their campsite, studying the rock face for footholds. Nothing. The vertical edges were as finely honed as if a straightedge had sliced down them.

"We hear you, Jake. About time," Eve called out.

She and Betty were eating bananas they had stuffed into their pockets that morning. Short naps, or had he taken longer than he thought?

"Where's Crystal?" He frowned that they'd let her out of their sight.

Betty gasped. "What do you mean? We thought she was with you."

Chapter 18

Jake drew in a sharp breath. Crystal, gone? Betty and Eve scrambled to their feet, eyes wide, complexions zombie-white. The crash of a wave against the steep rock cliff slapped into his consciousness. His heart jumped.

Please, no!

He ran to the cliffside.

Two gulls screamed overhead. He fell to his stomach and peered over the edge. The cliff dropped guillotine-sharp to turbulent ocean swells. A line of froth barreled in from the ocean and walloped the cliff, spraying the wave into a geyser of foam. It arched away from the rock and plunged into the murky turbulence.

No one could survive a fall into that.

His breath came in gasping jolts. He should have taken Crystal with him. Should have thought of the cliff. Should have never, ever left her alone.

"Jake." Eve's voice, soft, compelling, reached into the swirling tumult inside his head. "Jake, she may have gone to get water. Remember that last little stream?"

He pulled back from the cliff's edge, aware of her fingers tight on his right shoulder. He sat up and grabbed her hand. Held it. Latched onto the compassion in her eyes. "I shouldn't have left her."

"We all left her. We're all responsible." Her voice quivered. She took a deep breath. "And now we're going to look for her. Where do you want us to begin?"

He released her hand and rose to his feet. What was wrong with him? Of course there were other possibilities. The swirl in his head settled and he swallowed the tight pinch in his throat. "Not alongside the wall. She couldn't have passed me, or I'd have seen her. Same goes for the jungle. She must have gone to the stream. I'll go back and look for her."

"I'm coming with you." Color returned to Betty's face. She turned and set off at a fast clip downhill.

"No." Jake caught up and grabbed her arm. "Please, I want you and Eve to stay together." His gaze fell on the pile of coconuts shells they used for water. Four shells. Crystal hadn't gone for water. His stomach clenched. "You and Eve follow the rock wall toward the jungle after all. Maybe she decided to explore a bit. Maybe she slipped by me."

He took off running, slowing only when the path cut to the edge of the cliff. "Crystal!" Behind him, Betty's and Eve's calls echoed his. *Please, God. Help us find her.*

At the tiny stream where they'd last stopped for water, he paused long enough to drink. The stream bed showed no signs she'd returned, nor did the vegetation give evidence she'd followed the trickle of water inland.

Of course not. This was Crybaby Crystal. She wouldn't have gone off by herself. Not far. She had to be near the rock wall.

"J-a-a-ke." Eve's shout as he strode up the steep incline halted his steps. She was calling his name—not Crystal's. He broke into a run, his heart hammering.

When he came into view, she yelled, "We found her!"

Relief burst like a floodlight into darkness. He sped up the hill, wanting to laugh. He'd hug that little girl. Then he'd chew her out good.

Crystal was not standing with Betty and Eve.

Chest heaving from the run, he scanned the campsite. "Where is she?"

"Here."

He followed the voice skyward. Crystal's head and shoulders poked up from the top of the rock wall. His mouth dropped open.

"I'm sorry, Jake." The corners of Crystal's eyes and mouth scalloped downward to a quivering chin. "I didn't mean to scare everybody." She snuffled and gulped in a whimper.

"She's been up there all this time." Betty's voice was tight. Hot with anger, hot with tears held back.

He swallowed his own. "Crystal, how'd you get up there?" If he'd stood on his own shoulders, he still wouldn't have been able to touch the edge.

"Over there." She pointed to the ocean side of the cliff.

He walked over to the edge. The sheer incline of the precipice jutted upward in irregular protrusions from where he had lain on his stomach to look down at the ocean. He leaned out and peered at the cliff face. She couldn't mean here. Not where it meant hanging out over the ocean. "Where?"

"I'll show you." Crystal disappeared.

He looked above him in time to see her legs push out from the top of the rock wall. They dangled over the ocean far below her, while her bare toes searched for a foothold. His heart shot to his throat.

"Crystal, go back." It was all he could do not to yell. If he scared her and she let go …

He spied the footholds she must have used. He forced calmness into his voice. "I see the stairs you used. You don't need to show me. Go back to where I first saw you so I can talk to you."

Her legs withdrew at a snail's pace onto the top of the wall. A moment later her head and shoulders reappeared where he'd first seen her.

"I'm back." A grin replaced her former sniffles.

He wanted to shake her. "Do you know how dangerous that was?"

Her smile flattened.

"You could have fallen! Did you think about that?"

She nodded her head. "I took off my sandals so I wouldn't slip." The corners of her mouth sank downward.

"Don't ever, ever do anything like that again! You could have fallen into the ocean and we'd have never known it. We looked all over for you. You scared us, Crystal. Scared us badly."

Hiccupped sobs shuddered from her chest.

"How are we going to get her down? Not ... over there." The tears Betty had held back dripped off her chin. Eve's arm encircled the trembling woman, holding her up as much as comforting her.

"No. I'll catch her from here."

He took a breath of air and cleared his head of the fog of emotions. "Crystal, stop crying and listen to me. Lower yourself over the edge, right where you are. I'll catch you."

She quieted and peered through tear-blurred eyes over the wall's rim. "You're too far."

"Look." He stretched his arms toward her. "Not so far. I'm right here."

She didn't move, just stared down at him.

Eve stepped to his side. "I'm here too. I'll make sure he doesn't catch you by your hair."

Crystal giggled. Slowly, ever so slowly, she shifted until her legs stuck out over the wall. "But how are we going to get to that big beach on the other side?"

Jake blinked. "Whoa. What beach? On the other side of this wall?"

"Uh-huh. I was looking down on it when I heard you guys calling. There's a cove and a really big stream and—"

"People?" Jake didn't breathe. That one factor decided their next move. Either they'd find help getting off the island, or they'd have to repair the boat and island-hop.

"Nope. No people."

"You're sure?"

Crystal hesitated. "I didn't look real hard. I got to the edge just as Eve and Aunt Betty yelled, and I hurried back."

"Stay there." He turned to face Eve and Betty. "I'm going up."

"How?" Betty glanced at the cliffside. "Not ..."

"I don't know how she got around that corner to the first step, but it doesn't look too bad after that."

"Please, Jake." Tears flooded Betty's eyes. "It's not worth the risk."

"If Crystal made it, I'm sure Jake can. Maybe all of us can." Eve walked to the edge of the cliff. "It does look like a staircase."

"Noooo," Betty moaned.

Eve stepped back and Jake positioned himself at the corner, chest flat against the wall, left arm extended back across its surface. There was nothing to hold onto. He reached seaward around the corner and searched with his right hand. His fingers found a hold, a good one. He gripped it.

Below him, a wave crashed against the cliff, darting up at him like a tongue spattering saliva. His heart quaked at the distance. The wave couldn't begin to touch him, but its violence foretold his fate should he fall.

The first foothold on the precipice required a step up from where he stood. Balancing his weight on his left foot, he extended his right leg and planted his foot on the projection. His jerry-rigged moccasin held.

It was do or die. Plastering himself against the wall, he pushed off from his left foot to his right. Too late he realized he didn't have enough room for both feet. He teetered. Gripped the wall. Grubbed for a toehold.

Pressure against his left hand stabilized him. Eve peered around the corner. "Gotcha."

Shoot him if he ever complained about that woman again.

Wiggling his toes, he burrowed his left foot underneath his right until he stood with both feet crunched on the foothold. He raised his right foot to the next stair step.

"Okay, let me go." A new hold on another projection. Then a step up. Then another. And another. At last he pulled his chest onto the top of the rock wall.

Crystal sat facing him. "I knew you could do it."

"Don't you ever do it again, do you understand? The shortcut isn't worth losing you."

"But what about Aunt Betty and Eve?"

"We'll find another way around for them."

"Jake, here comes Betty," Eve yelled. "You'd better help her."

"What?" His heart skipped. He scrambled to the edge and found Betty clinging to the cliffside. Eve's arm pressed Betty's bare feet against the first foothold.

"What are you doing?" His scream sent sea gulls whirling toward the ocean.

"Shut up and reach for her."

Fury percolated to the crown of his head. "She's too far down!" He extended his arm toward her anyway.

"She's coming up. Ready, Betty?"

A grunt rasped from Betty's throat.

"Do you see where to put your foot?" Eve's voice was calm, reassuring. Exactly as it had been when she'd encouraged him to look for Crystal. "On your right there—up just a little. Put your foot on it. I've got you steady here. You won't slip."

Step by step, Betty rose toward him.

"One more, atta girl." He clutched her arms and stabilized her until she climbed high enough for him to haul her over the edge. She sat panting, swallowing in between gasps.

"You okay?" He patted her hand.

She nodded, and he turned to help Eve.

"Don't need it." Eve refused his hand and climbed unassisted onto the top of the wall. Betty's sandals protruded from her shorts' pockets. "Here you go, Betty. We should have thought to toss our coconut shells up here."

"The plan was for you and Betty to stay down there," he said evenly. "If we don't start working together—"

Eve's eyebrows shot up. "Working together? Did you share your plan with us?"

"You were on the way up here before I could say anything."

"We're not your troops, Jake. We can make our own decisions without your approval."

He stepped closer, glare to glare. "That sailor I found was murdered. If anyone is on the other side of this rock, there's no room for independent decisions."

She folded her arms across her chest. "Then we'd better go see what's there and discuss our next move, don't you think?"

Chapter 19

Crystal dropped her life vest and ran screaming into the gurgling stream. She plopped face down, rolled over, then back again onto her stomach. Mouth wide open, she gulped down the cool water. She'd drink the whole stream, she was oh so thirsty.

How long had Jake made them sit on that hot, black rock, waiting, waiting, waiting? If Aunty hadn't fainted, they'd still be there. C'mon, like Eve said, nobody was on this island. There were no boats, no huts, not even footprints in the sand. Creepy, that's what this island was.

She sat up and faced the broken rock cliff she'd scampered down ahead of everyone else. Eve and Jake were still winding their way toward the stream. Jake carried Aunty in his arms like she was a big baby. Guilt twisted rubber bands around Crystal's stomach. She glanced up and down the stream. There ought to be something she could carry water in.

Her shirt. It was stinky with sweat, but it'd be wet and cool. She whipped it off and sloshed it around in the water. By the time she got to the adults, the sun had already dried her naked chest except where her hair touched her shoulders.

She handed the sopping shirt to Jake. He set Betty down and mopped her face and arms and shoulders. "How about a couple of drops on your tongue?" He squeezed the shirt over Betty's open mouth.

Betty's eyes bulged. "Get your shirt back on!" she croaked. "You're too old to walk around like that."

Heat flamed Crystal's cheeks as Jake and Eve took a gander at her. "No I'm not." Granny had told her she'd be thirteen before she had to worry about things like that, and she was only eleven. Jake handed her the shirt, and she jerked it on.

Her aunt walked the rest of the way to the stream, with Jake and Eve supporting her on either side just like Eve had been supported when they started out yesterday. Eve had been such a grump, and now it was Aunty's turn. And Jake, he had freaked out, yelling at her about climbing the wall. Would telling him she was the best in her gymnastics class help? Probably not. She had liked him until he bawled her out. She sniffed. Had even imagined her dad was like him.

The three adults stopped short of the stream to gaze beyond it. "Look at that cove," her aunt murmured. "A perfect inlet for boats, maybe even deep enough for ships if the entrance isn't too narrow."

"Postcard perfect with that crescent of white sand around it." Eve's furrowed brow scrunched her sunburn blisters together. "I can't imagine why no one lives here."

Because of what lives in the jungle? Crystal shivered.

She hung back while the others waded into the stream. Really, things were not postcard perfect. On one side of the stream a few scraggly trees and plants grew. On the other side, nothing. Just flat rock until you reached the sand around the cove. And then, past the beach, nothing but a field of long, sun-bleached grass slanting uphill toward the distant cone of the volcano. The dry stalks rasped in the breeze as if they were whispering a secret they dared not tell.

Goose bumps popped up on her arms. The island was creepy. Something bad was going to happen if they didn't get away quick. She scurried to join the adults.

"We've got to spend the night here, Jake." Her aunt stretched out onto her back in the water. The stream pattered over her body and around her face, wagging her white hair.

Eve stretched out too—eyes closed, fingers fluttering water onto her swollen, red face.

"Fine by me." Jake sat hunched over in the middle of the stream. He'd hardly said anything since they'd looked down on the empty cove.

Was he still mad at her for climbing the wall? The rubber bands tightened again around her stomach.

He stood and ran his hands over his wet hair and face. "We've got a few hours of daylight left. I'm going to check out the source of this stream. Anyone else interested?"

Betty shook her head.

"Eve?"

"Not until I have immersion foot from head to toe."

"What about you, Crystal?"

She shrank back. "I don't like jungles."

"We'll turn back the first time you get scared. How about that?"

She was scared now. But would he get mad at her again if she said no? Reluctantly, she nodded her head, hoping he'd see she really didn't want to go and let her stay.

He pointed to a spot where three green-leaved trees grew next to the stream. "We'll make camp up there, under those trees."

Betty lifted her head high enough to glance upstream. "Please, be careful."

Crystal slogged behind Jake in the stream, past the three trees, up to where the vegetation grew thick and tall along the banks and enclosed them. She looked back. Aunt Betty and Eve were no longer in sight.

Jake stopped. "What do you think a jungle is like?"

She swallowed the landslide cramming her throat. "Scary."

"Let's see if you're right." He stepped out of the stream into the foliage. "It's okay to be scared, but it helps you be brave if you know exactly what it is you're scared of."

But, she didn't want to be brave.

"To make sure we know how to get back, we're going to mark our path." He snapped a pencil-sized branch and left it hanging. "Come on, you can help."

She followed him, reaching out and snapping something with every step. They didn't go far before he stopped again. "What do you think? Could you find your way back to the stream?"

She looked back at the waist-high trail of dangling wood and brightened. "Uh-huh."

"As you get better at it, you won't have to mark it so often. And when you're really good at it, I'll show you how to hide it so no one sees it but you."

Happiness marshmallowed in her chest. She followed Jake several steps before snapping a branch, waited a few more steps before snapping another. A map, that's what she was creating. A map with invisible roads only she could see. She and Jake. Her heart thrummed. Maybe her daddy was like Jake after all.

Then, as if she'd walked through a door, the world changed. The air seeped damp and muggy into her lungs. Shadows merged into a spooky wall of darkness as layer upon layer of leaves far above her shut out the sun. Hoots and screeches rained down from the dark clouds of leaves. "Jake!"

He halted. "When your eyes have adjusted, tell me what you see."

Her heart thumped so hard she could barely breathe. "Trees," she squeaked. She wasn't going to cry. She wasn't.

"Some of them look like big, wooden tepees, don't they? They're called triangular buttress roots." He stepped next to her and pointed at the treetops. "Up there is what's called the canopy layer."

She craned her neck to peer at the trees looming tall as skyscrapers above them.

"The crowns of the trees crowd against each other and form a big awning that pretty much keeps the weather out. Makes it like a big hothouse down here."

"You mean zoo!" She put her fingers in her ears, and Jake laughed.

"That's mainly the monkeys and birds that live up there. They've got their own little world in the canopy."

Dead leaves polka-dotted with tiny, green plants lay in a thin carpet on the forest floor. Walking between the trees was easy. "Where are all the jungle plants? It's not like this in the movies." She grabbed a huge vine hanging from the canopy and swung on it.

"Surprised, huh? They can't grow inside the rain forest. Only at the edge, where they get sunlight." He stood, hands on his hips, smiling at her. "So what do you think, not so scary after all?"

He'd done this for her? Happiness jammed her heart so hard against her lungs she could hardly breathe. Nobody but Aunt Betty did nice things for her. It was always *hush up, be still, find something to do* from everybody else. Especially Grandma and Grandpa.

She let go of the vine and dropped to her feet. "I like it." Maybe not the jungle so much, but definitely Jake.

"Let's see how you do finding your way back to the stream."

She led the way, spotting the broken branches way too easily. Next time she'd space them farther apart. Her heart skipped a beat. Next time? Hoots and howls and screeches from the canopy prickled her skin into a thousand goose bumps. "What about gorillas and … animals like that?"

"You thinking of Tarzan?"

Her cheeks burned. "Yes."

"That was in Africa. No gorillas here in the Philippines. No lions or tigers. Probably nothing bigger than a monkey on this island."

"What about the swamp? You said—"

"I was thinking of snakes and crocs. Reptiles you wouldn't want to snuggle up to."

She giggled at his silliness. A question she'd wanted to ask ever since she'd seen him with his shirt off popped into her mind. "You were in a jungle …"

"In Viet Nam. During the war."

"Is that where you got those three scars? The round ones?"

"Bullet holes, yep."

"What happened?"

"We were defending a bridge the enemy wanted to destroy. They wanted to stop us from getting supplies to our troops. Fortunately the bullets hit me on the right instead of on the left where my heart is."

"What did you do?"

"A buddy bandaged me up to stop the bleeding. The bullets went right through me, so I didn't need anyone to dig them out."

"So you just had to lie there and wait till they could get you to a hospital?"

"No lying around, kiddo. I was in charge of the men. My duty was to see that they were okay and doing what they were supposed to be doing. We needed to protect that bridge, and that's what we did."

She sucked in her bottom lip and chewed on it. He'd been brave in a scary situation. Could she be brave on a scary island? Maybe … with Jake next to her.

Sunlight seeped through and the vegetation became a tangle again. They arrived at the stream and doused their sweat and bug bites. Before they started out again, she broke off one of the dangling branches and set it afloat down the stream. Would Aunt Betty know it was from her?

The water moved faster the farther upstream they waded. When the stream entered the rain forest, even though her heart pounded in her ears, she found comfort in its familiarity. The rain forest was a hothouse with skyscraper trees and a canopy zoo. Nothing bigger than a monkey. Not like the swamp with snakes and crocs.

Was that a log halfway in the stream? She swallowed. "Jake, would there be crocs here?"

"Too shallow. They need to submerge to eat their prey."

Had her dad been in a jungle? Maybe gone to Viet Nam and been a hero like Jake? Her mom had been a hippy, Granny said. Hippies had protested the war. But maybe she'd met a soldier and admired his bravery.

The dark cloud that hid in her heart rolled out from cover. Why hadn't her mom left at least some kind of clue as to who her baby's daddy was? Just because her mom didn't like her own dad didn't mean Crystal and her father wouldn't love each other.

"What do we have here?" Jake stopped, and Crystal bumped into him.

She shoved away her black cloud and peered around him. A triangle of light lay ahead. Out of it echoed a faint, steady roar.

Chapter 20

The faster Crystal ran, the harder the current pushed against her shins. Jake was getting farther and farther ahead of her. "Wait!" she almost screamed, but then remembered, no, she was going to be brave. She shoved harder against the water. Ahead of her, Jake ran silhouetted in the triangle of light, elbows bent, arms pumping. She imitated him.

He stopped abruptly and turned toward her. Had he found people in the light? The grin on his face said whatever it was, it was good.

A stitch in her side pinched hard. She stumbled the last few steps, clutching her waistline. "What is it?"

He stepped aside, and she rasped in a breath. An oblong pool ten times the size of her best friend's swimming pool stretched out in front of her. From a ledge even higher than the soaring tree line, a waterfall tumbled into the pool, spattering noise and a fine mist that sparkled in the sunlight.

"It's beautiful." Picture postcard perfect. Other than where the waterfall churned the water, the pool was clear all the way to the bottom. Small, round pebbles glinted like thousands of pennies. The bottom rose in a gentle slope until the pebbles merged with larger rocks, and then larger, until there was no more water but only the rain forest on one side and a steep hill on the other.

They waded to the edge of the hill and climbed its slippery, grass-covered side until they reached the level of the rain forest's canopy. Soaked to the skin by the mist, they perched on the side of the hill like two giant birds and gawked at the sea of green leaves swaying around them.

Everywhere she looked were birds and monkeys, fruits and insects, and huge, spectacular flowers.

How often had she dreamed of going to the Detroit Zoo with her mom and dad? And now, here she was, right smack in the middle of the real thing.

"Keep your eyes on the monkeys," Jake whispered. "What they eat is what we can eat."

"Oh!" She jumped when, only yards away from them, a snake darted out to catch a tiny bird in its fangs. She hadn't even seen the snake, camouflaged as it was by its snappy green hues among the leaves. She made a sad face at Jake.

He shrugged his shoulders. "You just have to go with the flow, Pumpkin."

"Why'd you call me that?"

"Pumpkin? That's what I called my daughter when she was your age. Is that okay?"

Crystal's heart skyrocketed. Jake had told her yesterday on the beach that God adopted believers to be His children. God could become her heavenly Father, too, if she wanted. But, really, a heavenly Father couldn't take her for a walk in the jungle. Or show her how to make invisible trails. And, for sure, He wouldn't call her Pumpkin. No, what she needed was a real father. She smiled up at Jake. "It's okay if you call me Pumpkin. I like it."

Warmth overflowed her heart and radiated into the cold cavity that had stood empty, aching for someone to love her, all her life. No more being a scaredy-cat. No more Crybaby Crystal. From now on, she'd be brave. She'd think of something to prove it, and Jake would be real proud of her.

* * *

The sea gulls' raucous cries woke Jake to a rising sun. For the first time since the four castaways arrived on the island, they'd slept in the open instead of under trees. Eve had volunteered for the first watch, but had she wakened Betty for the next one? Both of them lay asleep near the stream, mouths slack, heads cushioned on their life vests.

So much for that plan. Did it matter, anyway? With no one else on the island, what could possibly threaten them?

The fiber filling for his moccasins was dry from last night's washing at the stream. He reassembled the footwear and tested it for comfort. If he didn't get the filling cushioned just right, the rubberized material rubbed his toes raw. Today he needed his feet to stay in good shape. It would take him most of the day to make the round trip to the top of the volcano.

Remembering his promise to not leave without telling anyone, he shook Betty awake. "I'm going to poke around the cove and then head out for the volcano," he whispered.

Crystal popped up like warm toast. "I want to go with you."

Eve raised her head. "Why aren't all of us going? Is this another unilateral decision?"

He sighed. "I figured Crystal could take you to see the jungle pool. You know, a day at the spa? The trip to the volcano will be grueling—uphill all the way." Not to mention he could go faster by himself.

Betty got to her feet and brushed off the sand clinging to her clothes and arms and legs. "How about if we explore the cove together? We can decide about the volcano after that."

Before he could protest, Crystal, Betty, and Eve were on their feet and headed for the cove, decision presumed by a majority vote.

The flat expanse of beach and grassland made it easy to see each other. They scattered. Eve sauntered along the shoreline, and Betty waded into the waist-high grass at the back of the beach. Jake opted for exploring the cove. Crystal followed him, scouting for seashells.

"I'm going to check out how deep the cove is." He slipped off his moccasins. Tiny, black mussel shells lay half-buried in the shallow water. Protein. Larger ones had to be nearby. His mouth watered as he stooped to scoop up a handful.

"Jake, there's a barbed-wire fence here," Betty yelled.

A fence? He dropped the clamshells and spun around to face her. The terrain snapped like a photograph into his mind—the cove, the sloping mount to the volcano, the cover of long grass. "Stop!" he screamed. "Don't—"

An explosion cracked pistol-sharp through the air. Betty dropped out of sight. Overhead, the sea gulls shrieked and veered toward the ocean.

He sped across the beach. "Crystal, Eve, stay where you are! Betty, don't move!" He halted at the grass. With painstaking care, he stepped exactly where Betty's footsteps had crushed the grass. If he was right, one wrong step, a slight miscalculation, and he was a dead man.

"Betty?" Sweat trickled into his eyes. The explosion had been minimal. Silly to hope, but she might have survived. The grass rustled. "Betty?"

"Here."

The air whooshed out of his lungs. "Don't move. Not even a finger."

His heart hammered with each step forward. How far had she penetrated the field? The trampled stalks cut into his bare feet. Unbelievable she'd gotten this far.

He found her. Sitting on the ground. Speckled with dirt. Grasping her left ankle.

"My foot!" she groaned. "What happened?"

"I think you walked into a minefield."

She caught her breath. Her face froze in horror.

"You'll be okay. We'll get you out of here the same way we got in."

"Where are you?" Crystal shouted. "What happened?" Dry stalks crashed against each other.

Fear jammed his heart into his throat. "Crystal, stop! This is a minefield! Stop!"

"Jake, she ran in," Eve yelled.

"I stopped." Crystal's voice, pitched high, teetered on the edge of tears.

"Don't move. Do you hear me, Crystal?"

"Yes." Then, words squeaking, "Eve's here too."

What? "Stay where you are, both of you. Don't move and you'll be okay." He held his breath. Please. This time comply.

Silence. Blessed silence. The acrid stench of his sweat swept into his nostrils. "I'm bringing Betty out. Stay still, no matter what, until I get to you."

The indistinct murmur of their voices filtered through the rustling grass. He took a deep breath to focus his mind. "Betty, give me your hands. I'll help you stand up."

"I can't." She raised her foot. Her leather sandal was gone. Blood seeped through black dirt caked on her sole and toes. He could only hope the sandal had protected her foot from metal fragments.

"Must have been the detonator that went off and not the explosive charge." No guarantee that would hold true for the other mines, though. "I need to carry you out of here. If you can stand up on your other foot, I can get ahold of you."

"I'll try." She gripped his hands and let him pull her to a shaky stand on her good foot. Her breath came in rapid, shallow jerks. She crumpled just as he grabbed her.

He folded her into his arms, cradling her like a baby. Her body was completely limp, her eyes open but unseeing. He should lay her down, but not here. Not where they could be blown to smithereens.

He retraced his steps. Forced himself to go slowly, to study the path of crushed grass. Listened at each step to the flutter of air in and out of Betty's lungs. Cupped the faint race of her pulse against his palm.

"You're almost there, Jake."

At Eve's voice, he lifted his gaze to where she and Crystal stood waist-high in the grass a few yards away.

"Just a few more steps." The tight lines around Eve's mouth belied the calm of her words. "Do you think there'd be mines this far out?"

"Not taking any chances. Stay put and I'll come get you after I put her down."

"Her foot is dripping blood. We've got to stop the bleeding." Eve spoke sharply.

"I'll deal with it after I get you and Crystal out of here. Just don't move. Promise me."

126

"I can see where we stepped."

"No! Risk your life and you risk Crystal's too."

She glared at him. He knew what she was thinking—if he could walk out, so could she.

"You'll never forgive yourself," he pleaded.

Her lips tightened. "All right. We'll wait."

The footprints of his bare feet replaced flattened grass. He stepped onto the beach and carried Betty to the pile of seashells Crystal had stacked near the cove. Betty was still out. Bright red drops dribbled off her foot onto the sand, marking their trail over the beach. He laid her on her back and made sure her eyelids were closed to the sun.

"Crystal, stop!"

Eve's shout hurled him to his feet. Across the beach, Crystal's head and shoulders bobbed through the grass toward him. Behind her ran Eve.

Chapter 21

White-hot horror flashed through Jake's body. Muscles and mind locked up. Lungs and heart slammed shut. Only his vision worked, beach and sky disappearing as he pinpointed Crystal and Eve. The head and shoulders of each rose and sank, rose and sank, as they ran. Any second, any footfall, and a land mine could wrap them in a geyser of sand, metal, and blood.

Adrenalin slammed the On switch and he jolted into an all-out sprint. Before he could reach them, Crystal broke through the grass, then Eve. She grabbed Crystal. Their legs tangled and they fell onto their faces in the sand. He stopped, chest heaving. Shaking. Relief barely holding his rage at bay.

Crystal, sand pasted to her face, squirmed out of Eve's grasp. He grabbed the child by the shoulders as she stood. It took every bit of control he had to not scream at her. "Why did you do that?" She stared at him, blue eyes wide. How could she look so clueless? "Why did you run? I told you to stay there until I came for you."

"I ... I was being brave."

"Brave?" He choked back a hot lava of fury. "Running over land mines is not brave. If you'd stepped on one, it would have exploded."

Her chin trembled. "I followed my footprints ... like I followed the trail of broken branches. I wanted to"—she jerked in a gasp of air—"make you proud of me."

He released her shoulders and took a deep breath. "Crystal, I want you to be brave. But I want you to be smart-brave."

"What's that?" She brushed her hands over eyes brimming with tears.

"Putting your life in danger is not smart, and it's not brave. It's smart-brave only when there's a good reason to do it. When you climbed the cliff over the ocean, you could have fallen and been killed. That was danger that wasn't necessary. Not smart. Not brave. Just foolish, hugely foolish, because you put your life in danger for no good reason."

Crystal frowned. "But I'm good at gymnastics."

"In gymnastics you won't fall hundreds of feet into an ocean full of rocks. On a cliff you might."

Crystal blinked.

"When you ran in the minefield, your foot might not have landed exactly on top of your footprint. Right next to it could have been a land mine. Smart-brave would be to go slowly and study where to put your foot. But running wasn't smart or brave. It put your life in danger—and Eve's."

Crystal's face crumpled. "I made you mad, but I just wanted—"

"Yes, you made me mad. And I'll keep on getting mad every time you do something stupid that puts your life in danger." Tears toppled off her lashes, and he pulled her into a hug. "But only because I care about you, Pumpkin."

Her body jerked in a loud snuffle, then yielded to his embrace. "I'll try to be smart-brave," she squeaked.

He gave her a squeeze and let her go. Tucking his finger under her chin, he stooped to meet her eyeball to eyeball. "And you'll make me proud." The brightness of her smile, the eagerness to please reaching out so desperately from her eyes, grabbed his heart.

"Jake, we need to take care of this foot." Eve beckoned him from Betty's side.

Crystal dashed ahead to her aunt. Betty was awake, clenching her jaw as Eve washed the grime off the injured foot.

Jake examined the torn flesh. "I need to probe for metal fragments. It will hurt." Already Betty was pale under the splatter of black dirt clinging to her hair on down to her toes. Her face was contorted with pain. "I'm sorry, Betty. We can't leave anything in there."

"Be quick then." She squeezed eyes, jaw, and fists shut.

He cleaned his hands in the salty water of the cove, then gently clasped her foot. At his first prod, she lashed her foot away and kicked him with surprising force with her other foot.

"Jake, I'm sorry. I didn't mean to do that."

"And here I thought you were a frail, little thing." He chuckled and patted her fisted hand. "But we're going to have to apply a bit of restraining action now. Eve, pin her legs down—lie on them if you have to. And Crystal, you hold your feisty aunt's hands and keep her from slugging me."

When everyone was repositioned, he probed the bloody flesh of her sole with his fingertips. He blocked out her writhing and shrieks. He was no doctor, but he'd learned in Nam there was no mercy in leaving metal to fester.

As soon as he stopped, she collapsed. Crystal was bawling, Eve shaking.

"She's clean," he said. "Before I carry her back to camp, I need to bandage her foot. Run up there and bring me the T-shirt bandages I used on my feet before I made the moccasins. And several coconut shells of water from the stream. Please," he added, as Eve stiffened. He wasn't commanding the troops.

As soon as the two were out of sight, he grabbed a large seashell and turned his back to Betty. He filled it and turned to kneel next to her. She opened her eyes when he picked up her injured foot. "I know this is gross, Betty, but it's the only sterile liquid on hand to disinfect your wound." He waited for her to catch on while he poured the warm, yellow fluid from the seashell onto her foot.

"What is it?" she asked. Then the odor of Jake's urine hit her nostrils. She jerked her head away. "Oh my!"

"The Marine Corps tells us to use this in medical emergencies. I'm afraid your injury fits the criterion."

Her nostrils flared and she blew out a spurt of air. "Can't argue with the Marine Corps, now, can we?"

Crystal arrived with the bandages. He scrubbed them in the cove and used one to wrap Betty's foot. Blood seeped through but stopped before soaking the entire bandage.

"How about a drink?" Eve lowered herself next to Betty and raised her head for sips from a coconut shell. Crystal used the second, unused bandage to mop dirt from her aunt's face.

They moved her to their campsite near the stream, under the three trees' spotty shade. Crystal did her best to plump up her aunt's life vest for a pillow, then lined up shells of water for her to drink. Eve took on the job of washing the dirt off Betty's arms and legs and hair.

Jake put on his moccasins. "I'll get breakfast." He itched to examine the fence Betty had found, but until she was okay, he couldn't ask Eve and Crystal to help him.

Getting to the fence meant he needed to enter the field. Enter and exit it. Not exactly what he'd planned for the day.

* * *

"Your color is back." Jake opened the pouch he'd made of his shirt, and bananas, star fruit, and dark purple mangosteens tumbled out against Betty's good leg. She was sitting up, her injured foot propped on a life vest. Eve and Crystal gathered around her and exclaimed over the two additions to their fruit choices.

Betty smiled up at him. "We've been talking about the minefield."

His mouth twitched in amusement. Men would have discussed it first thing. To the women, it was secondary to Betty's injury. They had mussed and fussed over making her comfortable and hadn't asked him a single question. He was eager to get back to the minefield, but he relaxed and peeled a banana and stuffed it into his mouth. "And?"

"We think the land mines are Japanese," Betty said, "left over from their invasion of the Philippines in World War II."

"I agree." He sliced open a mangosteen for each of them, and two for himself.

"How did you know Betty stepped on a land mine?" Eve cut open another piece of fruit. "It sounded like a gunshot."

"The fence. The first thing an invading army would do is take the high ground—in this case, the volcano. To get there from the cove, they'd have to cross the grass field. It was the perfect location for a minefield. The mine Betty stepped on must have deteriorated over the years and was no longer functional. What exploded was the detonator that sets off the mine. It's made of stainless steel and wouldn't rust away like the explosive."

They ate silently, their faces somber, until Betty asked, "Why was a fence there too?"

"As soon as we're done eating, I'd like Eve and Crystal to help me answer that—if you're okay with being left alone." He glanced at Eve. "And if they want to help."

"I'm ready now." Crystal scrambled to her feet and wiped her hands on the back of her shorts.

Eve's eyes narrowed. "Help how?"

"I'll show you when we get there."

She raised both eyebrows and looked away.

Could the woman ever cooperate without a protest? "I have to determine the angle of the fence first. Then I'll know how you and Crystal can help."

"All right." Eve popped the last of her mangosteen into her mouth and rose to her feet. "Let's go."

What? He'd barely begun his meal. He stood and jammed a banana into each pocket. "You okay being alone, Betty?"

"I'm halfway to a nap already. I'm fine, Jake." She dismissed them with a wave.

He led the way, heart pounding at what he was about to do. The risk was minimal, but still, it was a risk. The whole course of getting off the island would change if anything happened to him.

They stopped where he had emerged with Betty. "See the rocky ground surrounding each side of the field?" He pointed at two locations rising on either side of the grassy area. "That's where I want you to walk. There won't be any land mines there. But wait until I tell you to go. I need to get to the fence first."

"Whoa." Eve grabbed his arm. "You aren't going back in there?"

"To get to the fence I am."

"Not worth it." Her grip tightened.

How was it that she didn't want him to order her around, but she was certainly ready to tell him what to do? He bit back the rebuke. "If the Japanese were here, they had shelter and supplies. That fence could be our key to finding them and getting off the island."

Her hold loosened, but she shook her head. "If you step on a mine, we don't gain anything. We can search around instead."

"Look, I know what I'm doing." He removed her hand from his arm and stepped into the grass.

Chapter 22

Jake halted as his foot sank into the first flattened clump of grass. *Idiot!* He gazed at the increased space his foot took up. Why hadn't he thought about the danger of wearing his moccasins? Here he'd bawled out Crystal for risking her life with the tiniest of missteps, and now he was doing the same thing. One extra inch, and a detonator he'd missed before could be set off.

Should he go back, take off the moccasins, and start over? Trouble was, the soles of his feet were bruised. Stepping on the broken grass on his first trip in had left his feet tender. A sudden stab of pain, a bit of a stumble, and he could be thrown off the safe path he and Betty had forged.

No, his feet needed the protection. He splayed the grass around the next footprint and studied the ground for the telltale spike of metal that would end his life. Once his weight depressed the detonator, stepping off it would explode the mine.

A breeze blew off the ocean. The sunbaked stalks of grass rasped against each other like the tail end of a rattler. The noise was relentless. It crept up his spine, jangled his nerve endings. Each step forward, each lift of his foot, stopped a heartbeat. The gulls, as if holding their breaths, coasted silently overhead. At the edge of the field, Eve and Crystal said nothing.

Sand stuck to the sweat on his hands and fingers. Twice he got granules in his eyes from swatting insects that landed on his nose and cheeks and eyebrows. His back ached from stooping to minutely examine the area of his next footstep.

Then he was there. He stood at the fence, heart thundering, skin and clothes soaked in the sour odor of his sweat. "I'm here!" he yelled, for the sake of Eve and Crystal, for the jubilation of success, for gratitude to a God who was looking out for him.

The breeze rattling the grass parted the stalks into bowing waves that revealed the length and breadth of the fence. It was exactly what he expected: a giant X that stretched some thirty yards across the open area of the field. The waist-high grass was slightly taller than the fence and thick enough to conceal it. Each leg of the X consisted of barbed wire stretched in three tiers of parallel lines—a single wire at the top, more strands in the middle, and several more at the bottom. Together the three tiers formed an upside-down V over the ground.

"Eve." He twisted to face her over his right shoulder. "Can you get to that spot?" He pointed to a location on his right that lined up with the farther tip of the fence. "And, Crystal, can you go over there?" He pointed to the opposite tip on his left.

Staying on rocky ground outside the minefield, they each walked to the place he'd designated. Crystal stopped when he signaled her, but Eve ran forward and bent over the ground. She bobbed back up with widened eyes. "There's a skeleton here. Human! Next to something rusty."

He blew out a breath in relief and inhaled the next one with glee. So, he hadn't taken the risk for nothing. "Perfect! Just what I'd hoped for." Better, even. "How about you, Crystal?"

Crystal turned her gaze away from Eve and took two stiff steps. Mouth dragged down and eyes wide open, she looked as if she expected a boogeyman to jump out at her. She turned in a half circle and halted. "There's a rusty thing here too."

"Excellent! Stay right where you are and wait for me."

She plastered her arms to her side, fingers worrying the hem of her shorts. He'd better hurry before she bolted. Cautiously, but with more confidence than when he'd entered, he retraced his footsteps through the grass to the beach and on up to join Crystal.

"Let's check out the terrain before you show me what you found." They climbed the embankment separating the minefield from the stream and looked over the grassy field to Eve. "See that?" He pointed to a depression running the width of the field between Eve and Crystal. "That's a trench where the soldiers hid."

"Are they skeletons?" she whimpered.

"I'm pretty sure there aren't any more skeletons down there. Can you see the rusty thing you found?"

She pointed to a red lump below them. "Can I go back to Aunty now?"

He waited while she ran to Betty. The kid had done well. No crying, no fleeing. She had stood her ground in the face of a boogeyman attack.

He climbed down to the trench and found a rusted chunk of metal at the tip of the fence. Clearly a machine gun. An escape route had to be somewhere nearby. He pushed aside the heavy grass at the back of the trench until he found a small hole just large enough for a man to crawl through. A tunnel? If so, no doubt it would have one—maybe several—exits.

He'd save it for another day. At least in the minefield he'd been able to see what he was facing. No telling what had made its home in the tunnel.

He tromped through the grass to the other side of the trench. "Eve?"

"Over here. There's a cliff." She trotted back to him and pointed out the skeleton. "Looks like we were right about the Japanese being here."

Jake brushed aside the long grass covering most of the skeleton. The bones appeared intact, clothed in a tattered khaki uniform and faded leather boots. The figure was kneeling against the trench, arms, chest, and head atop the embankment. Nearby, a second rusty machine gun stood at the fence's tip.

"The uniform definitely looks Japanese." Jake examined the insignia on the collar. Red, faded to pink by the weather, with a yellow stripe and single star. "I'm not familiar with their ranking system."

Eve hitched her hands on her hips and squinted at the figure. "One lone soldier, left behind, looking out to sea for a ship to rescue him. Abandoned and alone, he dies."

Jake snickered at her drama. "Probably not the lone soldier, but the last. I suspect there are a dozen or two buried somewhere nearby. Being the last, there was no one left to bury him."

She shot him a look of irritation. "I think 'Lone Soldier' fits him just fine. What did Crystal find?"

He gestured at the lump of rust. "A machine gun like this one. Your Lone Soldier was manning a second machine gun position. Enemy soldiers who got through the land mines would run into the barbed-wire fence and be held up. The gunners' job was to fire along the fence and cut them down."

"Was that a trench you crossed to get here?"

"Yes. More soldiers would be positioned along it with rifles. I found what I think is an escape tunnel in case the enemy got through."

He showed her the opening. "If they were here any amount of time, they probably carved out a place to live in. This volcanic rock begs for it."

"At the other end of the trench maybe?" She jogged back to the skeleton and shoved aside grass on the back slope of the ditch.

The trench abutted a rocky bank that led to a drop-off of about forty-five feet straight down. Jake peered over the edge. The roots of a tree buried long ago in lava stuck out of the cliff's side like whiskers. He stepped back. The higher slope of the bank between him and Eve didn't look natural. The stone was not consistently lava. Some of it looked imported. "Let's look over here," he called.

Eve brushed past him and picked up a stick at the edge of the cliff. "Jake, I found something—a wire."

"Wait, don't touch it!" He rushed to stop her. "It could be rigged to a booby trap."

He caught a blur of movement in his peripheral vision. He turned to see a huge log rolling directly toward Eve.

"Look out!" He lunged forward and grabbed the back of her shirt. Before he could yank her away, the log mowed her down and bounced off the cliff.

Screaming, Eve toppled after it.

He grasped at the bare rock for a hold, then tumbled after her.

Chapter 23

The edge of the cliff scraped against Eve's belly. Booted her off.

She scrabbled at empty air. Abruptly, the full weight of her body jarred to a stop. Her breath punched out of her lungs. Punched back in.

She dangled in midair. Gazed numbly at the log cracked in two on jagged rocks below her. Way below her.

"Eve!"

She startled and looked up. Jake was suspended by one arm from a root above them, his face contorted in pain.

"Grab my belt! I can't hang on."

Hang on? She blinked. Pain under her arms. She gasped. Her shirt was cinched in a stranglehold around her chest. Jake was holding her by the back of her shirt.

"Hurry! You're slipping."

She groped behind her for his legs, used them to swivel around. Her nose banged into his knees.

"Reach up for my belt. Hurry!"

She felt a jerk as his hold slipped. She shot her hand up. Fumbled for his belt. Grabbed it with both hands. Jake let go of her shirt, grunting as her weight transferred to his torso.

The two of them swayed like a pendulum. Craning her neck, she got a clear view of his left hand clutching a root embedded at both ends in the cliff. He grunted again and joined his freed hand to it.

His belt and shorts inched down his hips. "Jake!" She glanced at the smashed log.

"Walk your feet up the cliff. Climb up me like a ladder."

Her breath came in short, raspy puffs. Sweat on her hands made his belt slippery. She gripped it tighter, walked her feet up the cliffside on either side of him, grabbed his shoulders.

"Now my neck. Clasp your hands behind my neck."

She slid a hand into place. His neck was slick with sweat. If she lost hold—

"Quick!" His voice creaked with pain.

Her heart beat wildly. He was going to lose his grip on the root. There were no others nearby for her to grab onto. A feral whine rose from her chest. She clutched his neck and slipped her other hand into position. Clasped her fingers so tight that crackling pain shot down her arms.

Her feet slipped off the side of the cliff, and the weight of her body jarred against Jake's neck. Her face skated down his chest to his belly.

Air hissed through Jake's teeth in a sharp inhale.

She clung to his neck. Gasped in shuddering breaths. Released them in spastic bursts. They were going to fall.

"Walk back up, put your feet on my belt."

Legs shaking, she shuffled one leg higher against the cliff, then the other leg. Bent her right knee. Snaked her foot onto his belt.

"Good, now the other foot!"

She slithered it over his torso and onto the belt.

"Stand up, grab the root. Hurry." His words came out pinched.

She pushed her feet against his hips and straightened her legs. "My fingers. I can't unlock them."

"Lean into me, they'll loosen up." His eyes were squeezed shut, his brow and cheeks crunched tight.

She shoved her chin onto his shoulder. Loosened her hold on his neck. Released the dead bolt on her fingers.

"Almost there." She raised her hand and slid it up the side of the cliff until her fingers found the root. Clasped it. Slid her other hand up and grabbed a second hold. She tightened her grip, willed her toes to slide off the belt.

Jake groaned as her weight shifted off his body. He opened his eyes and peered up. "Lemme get a better hold. Then climb onto my shoulders and onto the cliff."

The root jiggled as he repositioned his hands. Her heartbeat accelerated. What if one end pulled out? She peeked down at the log. It was old and weather-beaten, but still, it was solid, and it had cracked in two. If she fell, she would die a slow and painful death.

"I'm ready." Jake's feet were braced in back of him against the cliff. "Go."

"The root—"

"I know." His voice was solemn. "Hurry."

Hurry. How many times had he said that? Hurry—so that only one of them fell? Tears rushed to her eyes.

She locked her fingers onto the root and put her right knee on Jake's chest.

"Atta girl."

Then the other knee, farther up. "I can't—" She strained to lift her first knee to his shoulder, but her arms were too spent to pull herself high enough.

Jake's left shoulder lowered, and a shove pushed her knee onto it.

It took her a second to realize Jake had let go of the root with his left hand to help her. His teeth were clamped tight with the effort.

"Jake, no!"

"Hurry!"

She lifted her other knee to Jake's right shoulder and straightened. The cliff edge was within reach. She stretched up for it. She'd have to stand to pull herself over the edge.

Hurry. She rose shakily, lopsided on his shoulders, and worked her hands, then her arms, over the edge onto the top of the cliff. When her head and chest crested the edge, she stepped off Jake and onto the root.

"Almost there." She looked down at him. He was still dangling by one arm. Had she hurt his shoulder?

Hurry. She bent her knees and pushed off the root with both feet to boost her waist onto the edge.

Her foot slipped as the root gave way.

* * *

Jake smacked into the side of the cliff as one end of the root broke loose and sent his backside scraping down volcanic rock. He shot his left arm up to hold on with both hands. They slid down the root, shredding skin. His mind numbed at the horror of smashing to his death in one final splat.

His clasp found traction on the dirt that had buried the dislodged end. His fall stopped. A bare yard of root hung between him and a long plunge to the rocks.

A thread of blood snaked from under his left palm and slithered down his arm. He twisted around to face the cliff and brace his feet against it. Pinching the root between thumb and fingers to prevent further sliding, he climbed higher on the root until he was holding it where it disappeared into the rock. His body ached like he'd been stretched on a medieval torture rack.

"Jake!"

He glanced up. Eve's head poked from the cliff's edge.

"What should I do?" Her voice quivered, and she choked on the last word.

A boulder-sized lump formed in his throat. He hadn't expected to survive. He took a big breath and swallowed. Still no guarantee he'd make it. "Wait till I get closer to you, then pull me up."

The rubber of his moccasins worked well on the cliffside's rough surface. He walked his feet up it until his elbows were bent root-high. Keeping a tight hold with his right hand on the root, he bent his knees, then straightened enough to grab the edge of the cliff with his left hand.

"Gotcha." Eve seized his wrist.

"Don't—" Her tug loosened his fingers, and he dropped like an elevator with a snapped cable. Face and chest scratched rock as he descended to a shoulder-jarring stop. Once again he dangled from the root by one arm.

Stupid woman! He clenched his teeth to keep from yelling it at her. Clutching the root with both hands, he started over again.

"Don't touch me!" He glared up at her, and her abashed face withdrew from the edge of the cliff. Exhaustion slowed his second climb. He needed badly to rest, but to relax his grip for even a second was to invite a dive into the sharp teeth of the rocks below.

When he had a good grasp with both hands on the cliff's edge, he called to her, forcing what kindness he could into his voice. "Eve, three things I want you to do. First, grab my hair and pull me up while I get my arms aboard. Second, when my head is close enough, hold me by my chin and the back of my head and keep pulling. And third, when my chest is aboard, slide your arms under my armpits and pull me the rest of the way. Got it?"

"Got it."

She hauled him onto the cliff top exactly as he'd specified, not missing a step. His body shook uncontrollably from the effects of being a human bungee cord. Chest heaving, he rolled onto his back and pillowed his head on his hands. An army of gnats attacked the scrapes on his cheeks and forehead. Groaning, he rolled onto his stomach and hid his face in a stockade of arms. The bugs now landed on the scrapes on his back. Let them feast. At least they weren't mosquitoes.

"You saved my life. Thank you." Eve's voice was teary.

He turned his head to peer at her. She hadn't been this emotional when he'd saved her from the ocean. Maybe because this time she'd seen the options—die or be saved. "The log got both of us."

"Only because you held onto my shirt."

He raised his head and grinned at her. "I couldn't reach your hair."

She laughed, but only for a second. "Twice now, you haven't let death snatch me away. You held on at your own risk." Her voice caught as a sob jerked out of her lungs. "Betty's right—you are a hero."

He blinked back a sudden rush of tears. "You risked your life too. Betty told me how you swam out to rescue her and Crystal."

She looked away from him. "Jake—" She pinched her lips together so tight the skin around her mouth turned white. "There's more to that story—"

"I know. Betty told me about that too. How you tried to save Ginny. Thank you." His chest quaked. "It means a lot to me."

"Jake." Her words came out hoarsely. "I'm trying to tell you it's my fault she's dead."

He frowned. How could she blame herself? "You can't hold yourself responsible. She chose not to get into the boat with you. And even if she had—"

"No, I'm talking about Captain Emilio."

"Captain Emilio?" Anger boiled up from his gut at the name. He sat up. "You weren't his *girlfriend*, were you?"

She jerked back, her eyes wide. "No!"

He took a deep breath to calm down, but his words still came through gritted teeth. "I'm sorry, I shouldn't have yelled at you." He swatted at the gnats. "As far as I'm concerned, anyone connected to Captain Emilio should be strung up with him."

She said nothing. Just stared at him.

"I'm sorry, Eve. What did you want to say?"

She hesitated, as if she'd lost her thought at his outburst. "Captain Emilio—why did he want to kill everyone?"

"So his boss could collect insurance money is my guess. The explosions made it look like a shipwreck."

"How would the authorities know where to look for the wreck?"

He had to think about that. "When I went to the bridge, a crewman was on the radio. He hung up when I entered. He may have been sending a Mayday. He may have told them the coordinates."

"And a rescue ship would have come?"

"Ships and planes." He closed his eyes. "I should have thought of that. I should have stuck around."

She was silent until he opened his eyes. "The bugs are eating you up, Jake. You should go bathe, wash off those cuts and scrapes."

"You too." Her knees and hands were also scraped, although she had a lot more skin left than he did. They rose, and he led the way to the cove.

Was she done talking? Something didn't seem right. Eve had been a pain every one of their four days on the island. Her sudden appreciation was a welcome change, but right now he felt somehow manipulated. Why would she say Ginny's death was her fault and then bring up Captain Emilio? Her connecting the two baffled him. It wasn't like her not to make sense.

He glanced at her over his shoulder. Her chin was trembling. Had the fall shaken her up and confused her? Or was the confusion in his mind?

He huffed at the prospect of her tears. He had always given in to Ginny's.

Eve was no wuss. After they washed off, he'd push her for an explanation.

Chapter 24

Eve wanted to slap herself. What had she been thinking? Just because Jake had saved her life didn't mean she had to bare her soul to him. She owed him no allegiance. No duty to confess the truth and nothing but the truth. She shuddered at how close she'd come to disclosing her guilt for Ginny's death. *Fool!* What if Jake had caught on to the fact that there was some kind of connection between her and Captain Emilio?

At the cove, Jake waded out to the deeper water, leaving her to sit in the shallows and splash water over her wounds. She hated salt water. Hated the crust it left on her skin, the sting on her sunburn and now on her abrasions from the cliff. Hated it most of all because it, too, had almost snatched away her life. How was it she hadn't drowned? Hadn't been eaten by sharks?

Sobs crowded her chest. She couldn't stop them. So what if Jake saw her cry. She'd nearly lost her life, nearly cost Jake his. She bawled, let it all out, until the fear and guilt and unanswered questions shriveled to a size she could once again ignore.

She'd tell Jake nothing. Tell him the fall shook her up and she'd jabbered nonsense.

Jake waded ashore and she tensed, but he didn't ask any questions. Because he'd been put off by her crying? Or because he had no issues with what she'd said? Maybe she'd lucked out and she was off the hook.

At the campsite, Betty and Crystal gaped at them. "What happened?" Crystal exclaimed.

145

"I set off a booby trap." Eve sat and told them about the log pushing her and Jake over the cliff and their struggle to climb back up. She was surprised at how calmly she related the incident. No more riding the emotional roller coaster. The cry had been just what she needed to get back on top of things.

Betty frowned when Eve was done. "Mines and booby traps … so we were right about the Japanese being here. Crystal says you found a skeleton."

"Yes, a lone soldier." Eve described him. The uniform, the trench, the two rusty machine guns at the farthest tips of the fence.

Betty turned to Jake. "What happened that he got left behind?"

"I suspect we'll find a dozen more soldiers somewhere. Japan must have lost the records detailing they had personnel here. For years after the war, Japanese soldiers were found alive on Pacific islands, unaware the war had ended."

"What if some are still here?" Crystal's chin quivered. "They might come after us."

"No." Jake shook his head. "They would've buried the soldier we saw. I can assure you he was the last one."

"Why did they set a booby trap up there?" Betty asked.

"Because we were too close to something they didn't want found." Jake broke a small branch off the tree and routed the gnats harassing his face. "That last soldier was manning the most important position in their defensive scheme. His hair was gray, which probably means he'd been living on this island for years. He had to have shelter somewhere. My guess is that his unit had a cave nearby for living quarters. It was probably also where they planned to hide if their defensive position got overrun. The booby trap was set up to divert attention from their hiding place."

He downed a coconut shell of water and reached for another. "I'll check it out tomorrow. The three of you have given me enough excitement for today."

Eve blurted out a laugh. "It's true. All three of us have taken a turn."

Crystal giggled, then Betty joined in. Jake managed a weary grin.

He plopped down next to Betty. "How's your foot?" It was swollen, with more colors to it than the fruit piled near her.

"Not good, but at least it's still there. In fact, I'm grateful all of me is here! Thank you for that, Jake."

Eve smiled. Jake—all-around savior and good guy. Was it just two days ago she'd told Betty there was no such thing as a good man? Savior—okay, she'd grant Jake that. How could she not? But good? No. She still needed more evidence before she could agree to that.

"It's been over thirty-six years since the war ended," Betty murmured. "And nobody ever found that Lone Soldier."

Eve caught the implication. That lonely old man had died waiting for his country to come save him. How many days? Months? Years? Poor guy, he'd spent his last breath, still hopeful, still patient, still looking out to sea.

She jumped to her feet. "Wait, I just thought of something!"

* * *

Looking out to sea.

Eve sped back to the minefield. Why was the Lone Soldier hunched halfway out of the trench? She clambered up the rocky slope on the east side of the field. Why else, but to face the sea? To look one last time for his country's return—a ship, at first only a dot on the horizon, then growing larger and larger as it hastened toward the men it had left behind.

She stopped at the skeleton, her heart saddened for a moment by the Lone Soldier's unrequited hope. His bones had been cleaned of every bit of flesh. A few tufts of gray hair adhered ghoulishly to the top of his head. Had he worn a cap? If so, it was gone, blown away long ago. His uniform, though tattered and bleached by the sun, was still intact. It held his bones in position from his neck down to his feet, which were encased in ragged leather boots. Too bad they were too small for any of them.

She brushed aside the long reeds of grass concealing most of the skeleton. The skull lay face down, partially buried in a layer of soil. His arms were spread wide, holding him on top of the embankment. It was as if, in death, the Lone Soldier had accepted his fate and embraced the island on which he had been abandoned.

Careful not to touch the soldier, she searched first near his right hand. Then, inches from his left, she found what she was looking for. Triumphantly, she lifted up the prize.

Looking out to sea. As she'd suspected, the Lone Soldier had used binoculars.

* * *

Crystal dumped her shirt-load of dried grass into a pile near Aunt Betty. "Don't let it blow away. There's not much since Jake won't let me get some from the minefield." She wanted to kick the pile. When would everyone stop treating her like a little kid?

"Mercy, child, why would you even think of going there?"

"Because the grass is tall and thick. Two trips, just to the edge, and I'd be done."

"That wouldn't be smart-brave. One little tug on a clump near a detonator, and you'd be done, all right."

Crystal turned on her heel and stomped to a spot far away that she'd been too lazy to go to earlier. "*Smart-brave* belongs to Jake and me," she muttered. "Anyways, you're not supposed to hit me with it like a stick." Jake should have let her go into the jungle with him instead of Eve. When had Eve last stood guard, huh?

Grumping loud enough not to be heard, she ripped the parched grass out of the ground and stacked it until she had enough for another load. Eve hadn't even wanted to go with Jake, so why had he insisted? Because Crystal was just a little kid who couldn't carry anything bigger than a stinking wad of grass, that's why.

Jake and Eve sloshed down the stream as Crystal stooped to pick up the grass. Their shirts bulged with their cargo, and each carried a pile of sticks and branches heaped to their eyeballs.

Crystal perked up and grinned. Wow, this was going to be quite a fire! She made a pouch in her shirt, scooped in her grass, and ran to join them.

Fruit tumbled out of their shirts, along with dried leaves, twigs, and small branches. Larger branches, some of them the size of small logs, dropped from their arms into a jumbled mound.

So why didn't they look happy? Jake's lips were pinched against his teeth, like when he'd been mad at Crystal for climbing the cliff. And Eve had her don't-push-me face on. Ha! They'd had another fight. Well, Jake deserved it for asking Eve to go with him instead of her. Didn't he know all Eve ever did was complain and make life miserable for everyone?

"You're bleeding." Crystal pointed to Jake's scrapes from the cliff. They were seeping bright red drops on his forearms and biceps where he'd hugged the firewood. "Your fingers too."

"I'll wash off." He trudged to the stream, sank down in the middle of it, and closed his eyes. Eve waded in upstream of him and did the same thing.

They didn't get up. They just lay there and lay there and lay there.

"It's gonna get dark," she yelled.

"Crystal!" Aunty said her name like Crystal had let out gas or something. "Let them rest."

Crystal turned her face away and snarled.

Jake opened his eyes and sat up. Water streamed down his face and chest and arms. It turned pink every place he had a wound and dribbled down to join more pink places. His cheeks were bleeding into his beard. With his two facial scars and the dark hollows under his eyes, he looked like Frankenstein's brother.

"You're right, it's getting late." He squinted at the sky, then stood and ambled to where Eve had put the binoculars. His hands were pink with blood, but after Aunt Betty's reprimand, Crystal didn't dare comment on it. Besides, what could he do about it? They didn't have a towel.

"What we need is a large, sharp rock." He searched along the bank, and she helped him find one.

"Where do you think we should hit this to get the big lens out?" Jake held out the binoculars to her.

Easy peasy. She pointed to the part of the casing encircling the large lens.

"The metal is strongest around the lenses to protect them. If we hit hard enough to break it there, we break the lens too." His finger touched a place halfway down the binoculars. "How about here?"

She shrugged. He didn't really want her advice.

Bam. The casing bent open exactly where he'd pointed. He used the knife to pry out the lens. "Want to try lighting the tinder?"

Her heart leaped. "Really?"

"She shouldn't be playing with fire." Aunt Betty's voice bristled.

"Your aunt's right." Jake seized a handful of leaves and dropped them in front of Crystal. "I want you to be smart about this. Be responsible. Fire is not a toy." He wiped the blood off the lens onto his shorts and handed the thick circle to Crystal. "Here's how you hold it. Put it right between the sun and the leaves, just like this."

Crystal didn't look at Aunt Betty for permission. Heart hammering because Jake had defied her aunt, and that now she was doing it too, she held the glass exactly as he'd shown her.

"Keep it steady. I'll get some grass and twigs." Jake patted her head as he got up.

"I see smoke!" Goose bumps prickled over her arms. The wisp hung like a wriggling gray thread, then disappeared.

"You let it go out." Aunt Betty scowled and reached for the glass.

"Keep trying, Pumpkin. I'll put some grass and twigs under the leaves to give the fire something to dig into. You can do it."

Crystal glared at her aunt. "No, I can't. I'm a loser! That's what *she* thinks!" She threw the lens as hard as she could at the leaves, jumped to her feet, and sprinted toward the cove.

She was almost to the water before she heard the thud of running feet behind her. A wail burst through her throat and out her mouth. "Leave me alone!"

"Hey, what happened? Are you okay?"

At Eve's voice, Crystal plopped onto the sand and covered her face with her hands. "Go away."

"You sound like you need a friend."

"Losers don't have friends."

"Can losers be friends with losers?"

Crystal sniffled. "You aren't a loser. Only I am."

"I fall off a cliff, and I'm not a loser? Want to go see where it happened?"

Crystal dropped her hands. Wow, would she ever! "I guess so."

Eve extended her hand, and Crystal let her pull her to her feet.

"Want to see the Lone Soldier too?"

"Huh-uh. I don't like skeletons."

"He's a loser too. The three of us can start a Losers Club."

A giggle burbled out of Crystal's heart. "He's the king of the losers."

"How about the general? That way we can salute each other. It can be our secret Losers Club signal."

They crossed the beach to the rocky ground on the other side of the minefield. Eve took Crystal's hand and swung it as they walked. "Sometimes losers hold hands."

Crystal smiled up at her. "Sometimes friends do too."

* * *

Jojo woke with a hangover. He was surprised. When he was with a woman, he was careful to drink only enough to sharpen every sense to its keenest point. He lived off the memory of every minuscule detail for weeks. Only when the urge had him trembling once again, his feet at the very edge of the brink, would he set up another occasion.

The bed stank of sweat and alcohol and years of filthy bodies. He rolled over. The woman's eyes were swollen shut. Blood crusted her lips. Fresh bruises spotted her body. But there were no broken bones, no missing teeth. Nothing permanent that could give evidence in court should she be foolish enough to go to the police.

He studied her carefully, prompting his groggy memory, stocking his mind with visuals. Then he dressed and left. His hangover was in bad need of attention.

Chapter 25

Rain bombarded Jake awake to a starless sky. Eve, Betty, and Crystal sat up and cried out as if they were under attack. Beyond the cove, the ocean roared its own protest. The wind spattered them with wet bullets and set their teeth to chattering.

"Put your life vests on." He helped Betty into hers. The vests would conserve their upper body heat. Their heat—he didn't have a jacket any more. Just moccasins.

His moccasins! He felt under the rock where he stored his footwear. His fingers identified the rough squares of fabric, but the filling was gone. He had laid it out to dry.

"Eve, your moccasins."

"Got them on."

They huddled around Betty, shoulder to shoulder, heads down. Crystal's arm was cold against his.

"Shouldn't we go to the jungle?" Eve shouted.

"The rain will quit before we get there."

"You're a weatherman?" she flung back.

"Look up. The stars are back out. Tells us the wind is blowing the clouds away."

Minutes later, the rain shut off as if someone had closed a spigot. The clouds rolled westward like army tanks, attacking the volcano, barreling on from there to battle the ocean. In the east, a line of gold split the ocean from the sky, and the stars faded. Shivering, rubbing their arms, the four castaways sat and watched the sun burnish the horizon.

Sadness—every morning it threw its dark cloak around Jake's heart. Every morning marked another day without Ginny. She should be here. And what about his children—they must think their parents were dead. A week was a long time to wait for news.

"The wood is wet," Crystal whined. "We can't light a fire." Betty put an arm around her.

Whatever Eve had said or done last night with Crystal, it had resolved the flare-up between Crystal and Betty. Good, because he needed a day off. Needed to get away, to be free of the burden of their unrelenting demands. Most of all, he needed space between him and Eve. Her stubborn refusal yesterday to explain the connection between her, Ginny's death, and Captain Emilio had finished off his patience.

He stood, muscles stiff, bones creaking. Old. Weary. "I'm going to the lighter to get the sail. It will give us some cover and keep the wood dry." Before they could say anything, he added, "I'm going alone."

Crystal's eyes filled with tears. Eve's eyebrows puckered into a frown. Betty's lips tugged down at the corners.

He didn't care.

"Wait, Jake." Eve slipped off her moccasins and offered them to him. "Wear these until you can fix yours."

"Here's some fruit." Crystal grabbed his favorites from the pile near Betty and handed them to him.

"You deserve time alone, Jake." Betty's voice was tender. "We'll be just fine."

He stuffed the fruit into his pockets, sat, and put on the moccasins. The morning sun removed the chill from his skin. And maybe his heart was just a little warmer too.

"Thanks." He stood and jogged away from them. Maybe he'd come back after all.

* * *

A fire glowed in the dusk when he returned hours later. A dollar to a donut, Crystal had lit it, with Betty and Eve hovering over her like clucking hens. How had they done with the supply of fruit? It was too dark to get more. And he was bushed. His discovery today had been worth the time and effort, but all he wanted to do now was sleep.

"Jake!" Crystal's grin in the firelight confirmed his guess. "I got the fire going. We dried out the wood, and Eve got more twigs and leaves. And fruit."

With bare feet? He dropped the folded canvas and rope and lowered his tired body next to Crystal's. "Atta girl, I knew you could light it." A glance at Eve's feet revealed she was wearing his moccasins. "Did you find my filling?"

"No. I took some out of my life vest."

"Good. I could use your jacket—someone's jacket," he corrected himself, "to make torches tomorrow. I want to explore that tunnel in the trench."

"I thought you were going to the volcano top." Eve didn't try to hide her irritation.

"I changed my mind."

"Then I'll go by myself. I want to get off this island."

"Can I explain my reason tomorrow? Tonight I—"

"No."

Why had he held onto her shirt when the log bowled her over the cliff? "Okay." He refrained from making his sigh audible. "Here's why. Today makes five days we've been on the island. We've seen no passing ships, no planes overhead. The only sign of civilization has been a murdered man that washed ashore." He flinched at Crystal's gasp. Oops. "And now, with the discovery of the Lone Soldier, I realized that what we actually discovered is an island so long deserted that an enemy from four decades ago died. Forsaken … forgotten … abandoned … This island exists in a vacuum. No one—"

"Jake." Betty's protest roused him. What had he said? In his exhaustion, he'd shared his soul, not his mind.

He straightened the slump of his shoulders. "I want to explore that tunnel. Get what facts I can on what happened to the Lone Soldier and his companions—how they lived, how they survived. With that information, I'm ready for what we find from the top of the volcano."

Across the fire, Eve frowned. "I don't see the connection. There's no reason for the tunnel to have priority over the volcano."

He shrugged. "Then go."

"Please, Eve, wait for Jake." Betty grabbed Eve's hand. "What if I'd been alone when I went into the minefield?" The fire flickered shadows onto Betty's face, emphasizing deep lines around her eyes and mouth that hadn't been there on the cruise ship. She turned to Jake. "Would there be more booby traps above the minefield?"

"I wasn't going to risk it. Safest path is through the jungle."

Eve's cheek muscles twitched. "I'll wait one day, nothing more."

He shrugged again. Did he even want her along? He'd accomplished a big task today with no one to distract him. Chances were, she wasn't going to be happy with what she found from the volcano top anyway.

* * *

He couldn't sleep. He'd spent the day with Ginny, talking to her, recounting their years together, wondering with her how the kids were doing at the Point. Now that he was back with flesh-and-blood humans, the ache for her returned. If he'd been alone on the island, would he have found happiness with her ghost? Had the Lone Soldier fought loneliness with the aid of invisible loved ones?

Rolling onto his back, he stared up at the stars. He'd prayed today too. The emptiness was bearable when he took it to God. But the prayer and the remembering didn't remove the pain. The ache had become his second skin, squeezing him, crimping the hollow space inside where his heart had been. In daylight he could keep busy, keep his mind distracted. At night, memories waited at the door for body and mind to yield to them.

"Can't sleep?" Betty lay nearby. She didn't sound any sleepier than he. Behind her, Crystal bent over the low flames of the fire, the faithful handmaiden determined to keep it alive. Eve sat facing the cove, silhouetted by a sliver of moon.

"Yeah, having a hard time."

"Thinking of Ginny?"

He swallowed. "Yeah."

"It helps to talk."

"Been talking to her all day."

"I thought so. Talk to me now."

He sat up. Half-reluctant, half-eager.

"She was a lovely woman, Jake. I appreciated her kindness. She was the only one on the cruise who bothered to talk to Crystal and me the first two days."

"She loved people." That was why he'd chosen the small cruise ship. She'd have gotten to know every passenger, their hopes and dreams, their heartaches.

"Where did you and Ginny meet?"

"High school." He chuckled. "She beat me out of being valedictorian by one point."

Crystal stopped poking the fire. "Tell us about your first date. I bet it was so romantic!"

"Romantic blunder was more like it."

Betty cackled. "Sounds like a story. Tell us." She scooted closer to the fire. Eve joined them, so he got up and settled into their circle.

"It wasn't really a date—more of an accidental get-together—but I liked thinking of it as a date. It was 1955, the summer before our junior year in high school. We knew each other before then, of course, but neither of us was dating."

"Why?" Crystal asked.

"Because I was self-conscious of my scars, and because Ginny would only date a Christian."

Eve's head jerked toward him. "What kind of prejudice is that?"

"It wasn't a matter of prejudice. She didn't want her faith compromised."

"He's right," Betty interjected. "My husband wasn't a Christian, and I found my faith compromised time after time. Frank's stance was that we each were free to act as we believed."

"Seems sensible to me." Eve wrapped her arms around her legs.

"Was it?" Betty's voice fell. "I eventually gave up my faith."

"You shouldn't have—you don't have to give up who you are just to be married." Eve's words vibrated with indignation.

"It's not that simple. Differences—big ones, important ones—push you apart." Pain crumpled Betty's face. "But we want to hear your story, Jake. Please, go on."

It was hard to crank up the enthusiasm after Eve's fuss. He cleared his throat. "That summer, there was a carnival in town for the Fourth of July. I can't remember why now, but I was alone when I ran into Ginny and her friends. The two girls Ginny had started the day with had met some guys from our class and had paired up. That left Ginny as an unpaired extra, which was awkward for everyone. So when I came along, the two couples latched onto me and asked me to join them. Ginny went along with the impromptu arrangement only because she knew how uncomfortable it'd be for everyone else if she didn't agree.

"We had a wonderful time. I'd had a crush on her since the beginning of high school, so I was thrilled to get to spend time with her. She let me pay her way on the various rides, but only after she whispered she had a job and would pay me back later."

"So what was your blunder?" Betty asked.

"Ginny was so lovely, and when we did something fun, she'd look at me and we'd laugh and smile at each other. This went on all evening. When she congratulated me for winning the state wrestling title for my weight class, I felt like a hero in her eyes. I was just sure she liked me and was having a great time. Then she agreed to let me take her home, and I was even more confident. It wasn't until we got to her door that I realized she'd let me drive her home so she could pay me back the money I'd spent on her. She kept insisting I take the money, and I kept refusing, and then, well, I kissed her."

He took a deep breath, reliving the moment. "I'll never forget the expression on her face. She pushed me away like I'd violated her or something. 'What's the matter?' I said. I felt pretty stupid. I thought we'd had a good time and she'd want me to kiss her."

"That's what feminism is all about!" Eve's eyes blazed across the fire at Jake. "Men forcing themselves on women—men feeling they have the inherent right to dominate—men assuming there's an invitation where there's really an invasion."

Jake's mouth fell open. "It was just a kiss, Eve." He glared back at her. "Boy-chases-girl was the cultural norm back then. Ginny was—"

"I'm not looking for a social studies lesson, Jake. Which, by the way, you have all wrong. Men dominating women is not a cultural norm—it's a male norm, for all cultures and all times."

"Stop it! Stop it!" Betty clapped her hands over her ears. "We have enough problems on this island without you two squabbling."

For a moment, no one said anything. Then Eve rose to her feet, her back rigid. "How about a walk, Crystal?" She held out her hand. The child joined her, and they strolled toward the cove.

Jake huffed. Was she using Crystal to get at him?

"I'm sorry, Jake." Betty put her hand over his. "I'd hoped for a better ending to your hard day."

"Part of it was good. I discovered a way around that ocean cliff."

"You mean Crystal's suicidal staircase?"

He chuckled. "Yeah. The path is a long ways around, but it beats that drop to the ocean."

"Good, because I swore I'd never risk that climb again."

Truth was, the path was a luxury. The cave tunnel, though, was a keyhole, and he and Eve were the key to unlock it. The log booby trap all but screamed that something was hidden there to be discovered.

Chapter 26

Silence hung like a dark shadow over the camp when Jake returned with the morning fruit. He sat and chewed a banana and waited. His gut told him the women had discussed something. Either the outcome wasn't unanimous, or they were nervous about telling him. Didn't matter what they'd decided, he was going to explore that tunnel.

At his third banana, Eve spoke. "You can use my life vest for torches, but I'm not coming with you." She dropped the vest at his feet. "I'm going to the pool. I'll bring fruit back with me."

Acid erupted like a hand grenade in his stomach. "I'd rather you back me up in the tunnel than go to the volcano with me. No telling what's inside—"

"I want to get off this island, Jake, not explore its nooks and crannies."

"I'm telling you, the volcano top isn't the ticket off."

"And the nooks and crannies are? If I'm going to waste my time, I'd rather do it at the pool." She plucked a banana from the pile and sauntered to the stream. The steady splash of her feet marked her progress toward the jungle.

"That's a low blow." To his surprise, neither Betty nor Crystal responded. Did they agree with Eve? He glanced at them, but they looked away. "I'm going to need someone's help."

"I'm sorry, Jake, but I'm not crawling in there with you, and neither is Crystal."

He picked up Eve's life vest and huffed. "I don't need someone to go in with me. I need one of you to stay at the entry. If for some reason I can't find my way out, your voice will guide me back."

At their silence, he slashed the vest into four pieces and stalked off to retrieve three sticks and several handfuls of dry grass and bark.

Betty frowned as he rejoined them. "Why isn't the volcano top our ticket off?"

"Because the Lone Soldier died here. There is no ticket."

Her mouth fell open. "You're saying we're stuck here?"

"I'm saying the island has secrets. Until we know them, we don't know how to get off."

He twisted the grass, fiber, and bark into three tight wads, wrapped the vest pieces around them, and attached them to the three sticks. All the while, Betty said nothing. Was she really going to let him go alone? He stood, swallowing back his anger. "I'll need the lens to set a torch on fire." Crystal handed it to him and he pocketed it.

Betty cleared her throat. "Crystal, will you go?"

Crystal's chin quivered. "I don't like the trench."

Or the boogeyman in it? "I could use your help to make one more torch while I'm inside. Can you do that for me?"

She hesitated only a moment. "Okay."

He didn't give her time to change her mind. They gathered the necessary materials and took the shortcut over the rocky embankment straight into the trench. He tore away the dried grass covering the tunnel's opening—what he hoped was a tunnel, anyway.

The hole was smaller than he expected. His mouth went dry. Would he be crawling into a booby trap? An animal's lair? In the minefield, he'd at least known what its secret was.

"Let's see if this material will light." If not, he'd have to start over with pieces of the canvas sail. He focused the lens onto the fabric until a spot blackened and opened a hole to the combustible material inside. A nasty stink of burnt rubber pervaded the air.

He took his Bible from his pocket. "When you're done making the torch, read this real loud into the tunnel and don't stop until I return. Real loud, so I can hear you."

How long would the torch last? He tucked the two unlit ones into his belt, poked the lighted one ahead of him into the tunnel, and squeezed through on his belly. The stench of the torch filled the enclosed space, burning his nostrils and throat. Then, suddenly, the odor dissipated.

His heart beat faster. The dim light of the torch revealed what had to be a man-made tunnel high enough for him to walk at a stoop. The floor was level, and the walls midway down were smooth, as if human hands had rubbed them, feeling their way through the passageway.

He counted his steps. At twenty, he bumped head on into a wall and smashed his torch. The smoldering bundle sagged precariously atop the stick. Holding his breath, he tugged the bottom of the fabric to pull the bundle back into place. The fire dimmed, then settled into a steady burn. As a precaution, he lit the second torch against its heat.

The passageway turned sharply to the right, its ceiling now above his reach. He straightened and raised the torch. The stale odor of decayed flesh assaulted his nostrils. He gagged, then inhaled sharply at what the torch revealed.

Twenty Japanese soldiers encircled him in a chamber of niches cut into the walls. Empty eye sockets gaped above grisly grins bared in death. Their uniforms, rotted by flesh, had collapsed onto their skeletons. Battle gear and a few personal possessions lay tucked against the side of each soldier.

The first torch sputtered out, and he discarded it. Clenching his teeth against the shivers spiking down his backbone, he examined the skeletal remains. Each man had a rifle, but a quick check revealed none had ammunition.

He huffed with satisfaction when he identified the remains of the officer in command. His katana sword, standard issue for Japanese officers, lay askew at his side. Jake picked it up and pulled it out of its scabbard. The blade was still sharp. He slid it back in, slipped the scabbard into his belt, and selected a couple of entrenching tools and two bayonets from other corpses.

What was that? The back of his neck tingled. Slowly, stomach tight, he turned around. The scant light of the torch fell on a dark mass occupying a ledge he had thought empty. The mass moved, bulging upward. A narrow head rose, identified by eyes glinting in the torchlight.

The air bolted from Jake's lungs.

Snake!

Bayonets and shovels clattered to the floor. He whipped the katana sword out of its scabbard. With all his might he swung the blade straight down on the beast. Loosened by the jolt, the smoldering tip of the torch dropped onto his hand. He yelped and flung the torch to the floor. The flame winked, then went out.

Total darkness enveloped him.

He scrambled backwards until he was tight against the cave wall. Recognition of the serpent sucked the marrow from his bones: a giant python, more than capable of squeezing the life out of him. He must not, *must not* let those coils wrap around his body.

The monster's thrashing ricocheted against the cave walls. He couldn't tell which direction the noise came from. He lashed out again with the sword. The blade encountered only air. He kept slashing anyway.

The noise subsided. A faint scraping sound rose from the floor, then stopped. His own heavy breathing pulsated against his ears. He held his breath to get total silence.

Nothing.

Was the snake positioning itself outside its prey's reach, getting ready to strike? Jake anticipated his head would be the target. He lunged forward again, flaying the sword. It hit nothing but air, the floor, the wall of the cave.

He backed against the wall and listened. Nothing. Only the sound of his labored breathing and the staccato of his heartbeat.

Out of the corner of his eye, he glimpsed a speck of red on the floor. He caught his breath. A cocooned ember was glowing inside the disabled torch head. He snatched the third torch out of his belt and used the sword to scoop the ember and the unlit torch together.

Hair prickled on the back of his neck. He was taking a chance, making himself open to attack if the snake was waiting to strike. He gripped the hilt of the sword so it couldn't be knocked out of his hand. The weapon was his only chance for survival.

Sweat drenched his shirt. His heart thudded at the thought of the monster's coils wrapping around him. The snake would knock him off his feet … render him helpless … pin him down. Who was he kidding? The katana sword would be useless.

A tiny flame shot out as the third torch caught fire. Jake jerked it up and swept it in an arc. No snake. No massive pile positioned outside the reach of the sword. He moved the torch in a slower semicircle to make sure. When he was confident of his safety, he made a more thorough search of the cave.

A long section of the snake lay on the ground where it had been severed from the body. A bloody trail identified where the injured reptile had exited into a second passageway that led away from the one Jake had entered. Probably the escape tunnel he had expected to find instead of a burial chamber.

The cave dust revealed the trail of a second giant snake in addition to the one he'd injured. No wonder there had been such a huge pile. Considering their sizes, they could have taken on about anything. Why hadn't they attacked while he examined the corpses? Could the acrid smell of the torch have held them back?

His torch sputtered. No way he wanted to be in that darkness again. He stuffed the sword and tools into his belt, then grabbed the severed tail of the snake. After all, it was meat.

When he turned the corner, Crystal's voice echoed in the tunnel. He'd forgotten all about her. What if the snakes had gone this way instead of out the other exit? His throat tightened. *Thank You, God, for Your sovereignty over snakes.*

Softly, echoing in the chambers of his heart, came a response: *I am sovereign over explosions too.*

No.

Jake halted. He tightened his grips on the python's tail and the expiring torch.

Yes.

He forced himself to breathe. Yes, Lord, You are.

The torchlight died. He lowered himself to his hands and knees to avoid hitting his head when the passageway narrowed to its exit. The floor stung his kneecaps where they'd been cut on his crawl in.

I believe in Your total sovereignty, Lord. The declaration gave him peace. No matter what, he was loyal to God. He tucked the affirmation into a safe place in his heart.

Crystal blew out a breath of relief at his appearance. "You were gone a long time."

He gave her a hug, he was so glad to see her alive. "I found a burial chamber and used up all three torches looking around."

She recoiled. "More Lone Soldiers?"

"Twenty of them." He decided not to tell her about the snakes. "And look what else." He reached into the tunnel and retrieved the sword, bayonets, and shovels.

She glanced at his precious booty as if it were covered in slime. "You aren't going back in, are you?" She fingered the sad excuse for a torch she had assembled while waiting for him.

"No. But thank you for making the torch. Okay if we save it for later?"

"I know it needs fixing."

"I'll work on it some, but what counts is that you didn't quit." He grinned at her. "Neither the torch nor waiting on me."

The corners of her mouth tipped up. "Here's your Bible. Could you tell what I was reading?"

He hadn't listened to a word of it. He slipped it into his pocket and picked up the supplies from the cave. "You can read it again while I work on your torch. But first, let's get these back to camp. Then I've got one more thing to do while you tend to your aunt."

On his return to the cave, he picked up two of the large seashells Crystal had stacked at the cove. He washed the snake carcass, removed its skin, and cut up the meat. All the while, he thought of the two monsters he had faced. Shells piled high with meat, he carried them with the same jubilation he was sure David had felt dragging Goliath's head into camp.

Surely the three women would hail him as the conquering hero.

Chapter 27

Eve stepped out of the pool. Gathering fruit was filthy business. The sweat and the scratches didn't bother her so much as the bugs. There were hundreds, thousands of them. They bit and stung, crawled into her long hair, attacked the soft mucous of her eyes. Her ears, nose, and mouth—all were targets of investigation. Where were the birds and reptiles that were supposed to create a balanced ecology? No matter—she was determined to help Jake out by gathering fruit.

She harvested more aloe leaves for Betty and herself and stuffed them into her pockets. The fruit she'd collected earlier was soaking in the shallows of the pool. She gathered them into her shirt and slogged downstream to camp.

How had Jake done in the tunnel? Shame prickled over her conscience. The man saved her life, and what did she do? Punish him for what, being male? She snorted. Her boss said she let the courtroom color her opinions too much. And now, instead of helping Jake, she had deserted him. All right, she'd do better from here on. No matter how much he irritated her, she'd be nice.

From a distance, she saw the glow of their campfire. Why a fire when it was only midmorning? The aroma of roasted meat drifted into sniffing range. Her mouth watered, and she slogged faster.

When she entered camp, Jake rose, beaming. "Today, we feast!" He held up a seashell piled high with steaming lumps. "Today, we eat meat!"

"What is it?" She set down the fruit and aloe leaves and reached for a morsel.

"Protein!" His smile spread across the red stubble of his beard and crinkled the corners of his eyes.

She dropped her hand. What was this? Why the evasion?

"Careful, they're hot, all right." He set the platter down to remove several more pieces from a stick. After heaping them onto a second seashell, he did a ta-da wave over the two platters. "Eat hearty, everyone!"

Betty and Crystal shrank back.

"And why is the identity of the meat being kept a mystery?" Eve hitched her hands on her hips.

"I like to know what I'm eating," Betty grumped.

Crystal wrinkled her nose and turned her head away.

"I can't believe all this wonderful meat is for me." Widening his eyes, shaking his head, Jake bit a piece of the cooler meat in two and chewed it, rolling his eyes to the sky. "Ahhh, this has to be the *crème de la crème* of delicacies!" He popped the other half into his mouth and moaned.

His humor was pitiful, but she'd promised to be nice, right? She eyed the diminishing pile as Jake helped himself again, smacking his lips. "All right, Jake, I'll eat some just to shut you up." She took a piece and chewed it.

Oh, how excruciatingly delicious! She licked her lips and offered a piece to Betty. "You know, it is pretty good. I don't think I'll go into convulsions or pass out in ecstasy like Jake, but it is tasty."

Betty hesitated but finally took it and bit into it. "Tastes like turtle. What do you think, Crystal?"

"I don't like turtle."

"It's not turtle." Jake all but giggled.

What was with this guy? He seemed awful pleased with himself. Eve shot her hand to her mouth. "It's not monkey! Tell me you didn't kill a monkey!"

"Nope. Not monkey."

The guessing became a game. Crystal ventured a piece, then several more, and joined the bantering. Was this the first time since the explosions that anyone had laughed? Eve savored the pleasantry. Meat and laughter—they had needed both.

When the last piece was gone and they still didn't know the answer, Eve put it to Jake. "All right, confess. What was it?"

Jake hunched away from them. "Oh, please, ladies, you aren't going to gang up on me, are you?" He grabbed Crystal's hand. "Crystal, you're my only hope—stand by me in my time of need!"

"But I want to know too!" Crystal bit back a grin.

"Now, this is pressure!" Jake stroked his scraggly beard. "What do I get for telling?"

"I don't have anything." Crystal displayed her hands, palms up.

"Sure you do. How about a kiss every morning to start the day? That would brighten things considerably for me."

She giggled and immediately planted a kiss on his cheek. "What about Aunty?"

"I'd say a hug from her every day would mean a lot too."

Betty smiled. "It's a deal."

Eve folded her arms and glared at him as he sized her up.

"And you, Eve, how about if you and I take a hike up that volcano today?"

Well, she certainly wasn't going to argue with that. "Okay, then, Mr. Gourmet Chef, let's have the answer to this big mystery. What was the meat you're so giddy about?"

His chest swelled with obvious pride. "Snake."

"Snake?" Impossible. "Those were big chunks of meat. Too big for a snake."

"Not for a python."

Her breath caught in her lungs as her mind matched the snake's size to the pieces of meat.

"Was it in the trench?" Crystal's voice rose to a high pitch. "Where I was sitting?"

Jake's grin disappeared. "It's okay, Pumpkin—here, let me tell you the story." He put his arm around her. She was shaking.

Eve's mouth went dry as he told the story. The dark cave, the rotted skeletons, his torch going out … And snakes. Giant snakes. She shivered. She hadn't thought about pythons being on the island. And Jake had been left to face them alone.

"I don't ever want to go in any cave!" Crystal wailed.

Jake turned the child's tear-streaked face to him. "We might have to, Crystal. If we don't get out of here before the monsoon, we'll need shelter. But believe me, I won't give any snakes a chance to get in."

"What about other places?" Crystal shrank into a tight wad of compressed arms and legs. "I don't want to get eaten by a snake!"

Eve opened her mouth but caught herself. Surely one of them would always be there to protect her—but would they? She didn't want to make a promise she couldn't guarantee.

"You know what helps when I get worried?" Jake pulled a small book out of his pocket and opened it. "Read this, Pumpkin. Psalm Twenty-three."

Crystal's voice trembled as she started.

"The Lord is my shepherd, I shall not be in want.
He makes me lie down in green pastures,
He leads me beside quiet waters.
He restores my soul.
He guides me in paths of righteousness for His name's sake.
Even though I walk through the valley of the shadow of death,
I will fear no evil, for You are with me;
Your rod and Your staff, they comfort me.
You prepare a table before me in the presence of my enemies.
You anoint my head with oil; my cup overflows.
Surely goodness and love will follow me all the days of my life,
And I will dwell in the house of the Lord for ever."

By the end, the quiver was gone from her voice. She lowered the book. "I like that."

Eve grimaced. Bible thumping.

Jake gave Crystal's shoulders a squeeze. "I have it memorized. That way it's always there for me. How about if Aunt Betty helps you memorize it while Eve and I are gone?" He held out the book.

Betty took it, then leaned toward Crystal and whispered in her ear. The girl's face brightened. "Okay, Jake." She could barely contain her grin. Obviously they were planning something.

Eve scowled, her back and shoulders rigid as she and Jake left for the volcano.

* * *

All the way up the stream to where the jungle enclosed them, Eve clamped her teeth against the words hammering at her throat. She'd promised herself no matter how much Jake irritated her, she'd be nice. Ahead of her—katana scabbard strapped to his back, sword in hand—Jake sliced away plants as he walked alongside the stream. Left, right, left, right, slash, slash. The rhythm pounded on her brain—yet one more irritation to contend with. And for what? The path he was cutting was a waste of time. They'd find out at the top of the volcano which way to sail, and they'd leave the island in a matter of days.

She pressed her lips tighter against her teeth. Okay, what was bothering her was not the path. Not the rhythmic slashing. It was Jake's high-handedness with Crystal.

The words erupted through her lips like churning water from a broken dam. "Crystal has a fine mind. How dare you pollute it with your superstitious and obsolete dogma!"

Jake's head jerked. He turned to face her, his brow furrowed. "You mean the Bible?"

"Yes."

"That's quite a description." He resumed walking. "I take it you have an issue with it."

170

With the dam burst, the words no longer strangling her, she took up her good intention again to be nice. "Okay, let's be sensible. Give me one good reason why you put any stock in the Bible."

He chopped methodically at the vegetation, not breaking stride. "I can give you many good reasons. But if you want the central one, it's because God chooses to reveal Himself to us through the Bible."

"Come on, Jake! Every religion claims that in one way or another."

"Okay, you tell me, then. How else would He do it?"

"Through goodness in the world … and justice. And I see precious little of either."

"So, you see people treating each other badly and, for the most part, getting away with it?"

"I do."

He stopped again and turned, his eyes penetrating, his mouth tugged down in compassion. "Because that's what happened to you?"

"Of course." Indignation flared hot at his taking the argument to a personal level. "As it has to you. Didn't you lose Ginny under just those circumstances?"

The blood drained from his face. For a second, his body sagged. His hand holding the katana sword dropped to his side.

Her stomach wrenched. "Jake, I'm sorry! That was cruel of me."

Color returned to his face. He straightened and whacked the sword at a green sapling. Its crown of leaves toppled into the stream bed. "You made your point."

"My point was that God didn't stop Captain Emilio from killing Ginny—and all the other passengers."

"Captain Emilio killed them, Eve, not God." He turned on his heel and strode ahead, hacking with wider swathes at the foliage.

Hot lava rose to her throat. "And God couldn't stop him? Wouldn't stop him? Creates but doesn't control?" She rose on her toes and screamed at his back. "How does God reveal Himself on that score, Jake?"

He whirled around. "Don't sell Him short with your paltry knowledge, Eve. He executes justice. He holds every person accountable. Whether it's immediate or takes awhile, there is a day of reckoning."

"And while we're waiting, we suffer the consequences? What good is there in that?"

He took a deep breath. "We have the love of Christ to get us through it."

"A man who died two thousand years ago?" She belted out a laugh. "Get real, Jake. That's not what Crystal needs."

His lips tightened. It was the same dour expression he'd used when she had refused to talk anymore about Ginny's death. And now what had she done? She'd mocked his beliefs—beliefs that didn't even matter to her. She blew out her breath in exasperation. Was it that hard to be nice to him? They'd be here only a few more days, and then none of this would matter.

Jake said nothing until they reached the waterfall. Surprisingly, his voice was calm, devoid of even a smidgeon of anger. "If Jesus were just a flesh-and-blood man, Eve, you'd be right. There'd be no comfort because there'd be no hope—just victims making more victims."

"I didn't say there was no hope."

"Where is it, then?"

"I'm looking, Jake. I'm looking, but I know I won't find it in dry bones."

"Jesus is in Heaven, Eve. No bones were left behind."

She rolled her eyes and waded into the pool. *Sure, Jake.* She lowered herself into the water, closed her eyes, and relaxed. As she sank below the surface, sadness rolled onto her like a huge rock. *Be real yourself, Eve.* Was hope in justice from a courtroom any less ridiculous? Was hope in any flesh-and-blood man?

She sat up, sputtering water. Yes, there was hope. Not in one big hereafter Heaven, but incrementally, one moment at a time.

And right now, that moment was waiting at the top of the volcano.

Chapter 28

Jake caught broad glimpses of the island as he and Eve climbed the towering cone of the volcano, but the full panorama awaited his final step onto the stony rim. Here at last, spread below him and across the ocean to the horizon in every direction, was the answer he had expected. If Eve hadn't been beside him, he would have crowed at being right. Already she had the binoculars with its one preserved lens pressed to her eyes. Once she discovered the answer for herself, would she be willing to go along with his plans?

Her focus was on the horizon, first in a fast, wide sweep, then slowly. If he was right, the distant edge of the ocean, no matter how many times she circled around, would yield nothing. No ridge of an island or two or three darkling the sky. Nothing—because there were no islands. A platoon of dead Japanese soldiers had as good as whispered that information to him.

While he waited for a turn at the binoculars, he studied the island. Clearly, the volcano was extinct, or at least inactive. Its cradle was a bed of crumbled and jagged chunks of lava emitting the acrid smell of sun-broiled rock. The southern half of the cone had given way to a major lava flow that formed the elongated body of the island. A dense rain forest covered the land, with beaches here and there dotting the perimeter. From some hidden point lower in the cone, a stream flowed down the length of the island, ending in the swamp at the southern tip. A branch of the stream flowed east and cascaded down to the pool he and Crystal had discovered three days ago. Also to the east was a smaller lava flow that ended in the field guarded by the Lone Soldier. Nowhere was there any sign of civilization.

"I don't see any islands." Eve's voice was heavy with disappointment. She lowered the binoculars. "How far are these good for?"

"Twenty or thirty miles."

She thrust the binoculars at him. "Here, you take a look."

He examined the full circle of the horizon around the island, then the length and breadth of the island itself. "Nothing out there." He offered the binoculars back to her. "Want another look?"

"No." Her chin twitched her lower lip downward.

She wasn't going to cry, was she? "Some of the outer islands are hundreds of miles apart. I hoped that wouldn't be our case, but once I found the burial cave, I suspected it was."

"Why? What difference would the cave make?"

"Because the whole platoon died on the island. You'd think they would have tried at some point to contact their country or other troops to get off. Either they knew their location was remote enough that island-hopping was out of the question, or they sent someone off who didn't make it."

She flicked her hand in a dismissive gesture. "Or maybe the whole platoon died at once. Maybe leaving the island was never an option."

Jake raised his eyebrows. "Digging that burial cave took a lot of time and a lot of hands."

"What I mean is that it might have been their residential cave until they all died at once." She folded her arms across her chest and glared at him. "It makes sense. The Lone Soldier could have put them in there and slept somewhere else."

Could she ever talk to him without getting mad? "No question about it—he certainly didn't elect to stay in that death chamber. That's why we need to hunt for a second cave. We need to get all the facts we can to make a good decision."

"Decision? What decision?" The wind flung Eve's hair into her eyes. Behind her, dark clouds appeared on the horizon and sped toward the volcano as if it were a bull's eye in target practice.

He pointed at the clouds. "Rain's coming."

She glanced over her shoulder and back at him. "What decision? What is there besides getting off this island? I've got things to do, Jake—an important deadline coming up. So, what do we need to do to get off? What's the battle plan, General?"

"Colonel," he answered automatically. A deadline? Eve had avoided telling them what she did for a living, just as she'd dodged telling him what she meant by linking Ginny's death to herself and Captain Emilio. Irritation scuttled like a scorpion over his nerves. The woman had more secrets than the island.

"What about the boat?" The wind whipped her words now, as well as her hair. She shielded her eyes and peered at him. "With the boat, we don't care how far away the next island is."

"I need to look at it more closely, see what damages it sustained. Mine split in two before I got to the island. We can't risk that."

"We should go back today and start the repairs. Betty said you found a safe path."

"Safe in daylight. It will be dark by the time we stop to get fruit. And we sure don't want to camp out in the jungle. A campfire is no guarantee against snakes, you know." She flinched, and satisfaction swelled his chest. "Besides, I want to find that second cave first."

"Another nook and cranny search?" She heaved a loud sigh. "What's with you having to play Soldier Boy all the time?"

A sour taste rose on his tongue. "Those dead soldiers you're putting down might very well save our lives. Finding that burial cave put a sharp sword by my side and bayonets near yours and Betty's."

Eve opened her mouth, but he stepped closer and twisted up the volume knob on his voice. "And what about Betty? Have you thought about her? She's not doing so well, is she? She's not up on her feet and walking." He pointed at the dark clouds. "Are you going to leave her out in the rain with the monsoon season upon us? Or Crystal? Do you think a cave might gain us some comfort, even if it's for only a few days while we repair the boat?"

Her eyes narrowed as his voice rose. She thrust out her chin and opened her mouth again. He turned the volume knob to full blast. "And, yeah, I am a Soldier Boy, and because of that I know what I'm doing—can you latch onto that? I got us food and water. I got us weapons. And I'm going to get us shelter. And you know what? That's not the end of my Soldier Boy list. We need to set up a signal fire, and we need to start a ship watch. There are four of us here, not just you, Eve. There's more to do than just charge blindly ahead on a fool's mission."

Eve's eyes widened. Her mouth clipped shut. She stepped back, neck, shoulders, and arms stiff. His words—his rage—had shut her up. About time! He was tired of having to deal with her sharp tongue and mulishness.

The downpour crossing the ocean hit the mountaintop and pelted them with tiny missiles. Eve stirred, eyes blinking against the assault, and without a glance at Jake, turned and climbed down the steep cone.

He followed. The ferocity of the rain drove them slipping and sliding down the slope of the mountain. At the waterfall, they stopped to collect fruit. Neither said a word.

The sourness in his mouth was gone. In its place was the sweet taste of having said what he wanted, how he wanted. If Eve wanted a confrontation, from now on he'd give her one, nothing spared. No more Mr. Nice Guy trying to win her to his viewpoint. No more sympathy for burgeoning tears. Her head and her heart were as hard as lava. Wielding a hammer was the only way to deal with this stony woman.

* * *

The downpour was unrelenting. At first the sheet of water was only a visual impediment that caused Eve's feet to slip, her fingers to lose their hold. Then the numbness gripping her body wore off. Cold penetrated to her bones and pinched the scratches on her skin. But what hurt was not the sting outside, but the sting inside. Over and over, Jake's words lashed her heart. *A fool's mission. A fool's mission.* On the steep precipice of the volcano, his words had stopped her cold. He was right. Horribly right. And she didn't know what to do about it.

The whip of rain on her skin felt justified. What was wrong with her that she had turned a blind eye to Betty's and Crystal's needs? Hadn't she vowed on the lighter to look out for them until they got back to civilization? And here she was, oblivious to Betty's injury, willing to have her endure the discomfort of cold and rain, all so that Eve could hurry back to nail Danny Romero.

And Jake—why did she get so irritated with him? She couldn't make it through one day without chastising him for something. Ungrateful wretch, she was alive because he had saved her life—twice. What was wrong with her that she couldn't concede to his plans? Would a day or two delay be that hard to live with? Didn't being alive top winning a trial?

At the waterfall, she couldn't bear to look at him. *Soldier Boy*, she'd called him. Why put him down? Why mock the skills that had protected their lives and sustained them with food and water?

She trekked after him downstream, grateful for the rain that hid her tears and drowned the sobs jerking her chest. Jake was right. She'd tied herself so tightly to her mission that she'd lost sight of everyone else. Lost sight of the bigger picture beyond her own little world, her own little concerns, her own little agenda. Her mind swirled. How could she balance the enormity of Danny Romero's crimes against the worth of three people whose lives she impacted right now?

She didn't know. It beat against her head like a judge's gavel. She didn't know, she didn't know, she didn't know.

Ahead of her, Jake stepped out of the stream. They must be near camp. She inhaled deeply to pull herself together. Poor Betty and Crystal—were they huddled under the canvas sail to ward off the rain? A cave would be nice. How she would love the warmth of a campfire to dry her skin and stop her shivers.

"We're over here," Crystal shouted.

Eve peered around Jake. In front of them, glowing through the dense rain, was the flicker of a campfire. She sheltered her eyes and stepped forward. "Crystal?"

"Right here." A figure rose next to the firelight. "We made a tent."

"A tent?" Eve stooped and entered the shelter. Jake stepped in beside her, water dripping from the end of his nose as he leaned forward.

"I was worried about you," he said. "And look at you two, all toasty and dry."

On the other side of the fire, Betty spoke up, her voice cheery for the first time since her foot injury. "I come from a family of campers, so I figured out how to rig this to the three trees. Crystal did an awful lot of work helping me out." She put an arm around the beaming child snuggled next to her.

The sailcloth was draped as a lean-to, the point of the triangle secured to one tree, high enough to sit under. The other two points were tied to the bottoms of the other two trees and clamped to the ground with an assortment of large stones, shells, and sticks. A small pit in the center protected the fire from the wind, which fluttered the tips of the flames in a fairy dance.

"Well, then, how about a tour of this magnificent mansion?" Jake sat and scooted as far under the shelter as the top allowed. He extended his arms and legs toward the fire. Eve followed suit opposite him.

Crystal crawled closer. "We started before the rain came, so all our kindling and firewood are dry." She pointed to a pile of leaves, grass, and twigs half-buried in sand at the back of the tent. "I put the big sticks and some stones on top so nothing would blow away." A gust of wind blew across the floor in timely illustration.

"Good thinking." Jake moved his limbs to expose more skin to the fire. Eve shifted her legs to accommodate his.

"Aunt Betty tied down the bottom corners of the tent, and I tied the third one up there because she couldn't stand up."

Eve peered at the elevated corner jerking a short loop of rope in the wind. Would it hold?

"Then Aunt Betty dug the pit in the center so everyone could sleep close to it, and I brought in the fire. We couldn't start one inside, you know, away from the sun."

"Looks like you thought of everything. Good job, both of you." Jake exhaled a long sigh. "Last thing I expected to find was a fire."

Eve nodded, her chattering teeth a cover for the fact that she couldn't speak. Not without crying.

"What did you find out from your trip?" Betty asked.

That somebody is a self-centered fool. Eve pinched her lips together to keep the edges from tucking down.

Jake cleared his throat. "We could see the entire island. It's completely covered in jungle except for a few beaches. No signs of civilization anywhere. No islands on the horizon, either."

"So, now what do we do?" The cheeriness in Betty's voice deflated.

"Repair the boat."

Eve inhaled a shuddering breath of gratefulness. Had he said that for her benefit?

"But first we need to find permanent shelter," he went on. "I'm afraid a typhoon would make short work of this wonderful little tent of yours. Tomorrow morning, I'm going to look for a second cave. A cave I suspect the Lone Soldier might have used."

Eve glanced at Crystal. The child's chin was quivering. Could Jake really ensure no snakes would enter? And what if caves were exactly where snakes went during a typhoon?

He must have seen Crystal's expression too. "How about if you and Aunt Betty take charge of a signal fire and ship watch for me, Crystal? Just because no islands are nearby doesn't mean there aren't any ship lanes."

Eve caught her breath. Ship lanes? If they could spot one, they could sail out to it. That's what they should do first—find a ship lane.

"What do you want to do, Eve?" Jake's question startled her. Shame welled up that she'd been thinking of only herself again.

Suddenly the answer to her dilemma popped into her mind. Danny Romero's drug trade enslaved untold numbers of addicts and prostitutes. Her purpose to bring him to justice was no fool's mission. But it didn't require her to sacrifice the welfare of others. She could hold the two in balance. Jake would never know about Danny Romero, but he'd never have cause to call her a fool again.

"Find the cave." Her words came out strong and clear. "I don't want Betty and Crystal to sit through another torrent like this." Warmth surged from her resolve and spread throughout her body.

Across the fire, Jake's expression was stern. It said that until she proved herself, her words were hollow. But he'd see. She'd be right by his side tomorrow, searching for that cave. And she'd look out for everyone from now on, not just herself.

"Crystal, let's show Jake and Eve how you did with Psalm Twenty-three."

Eve grimaced as Betty nudged Crystal forward. Okay, she'd have to work on the religion thing—bite her lips to keep her mouth shut. It galled her in particular that adults would impose their beliefs on vulnerable children.

Crystal crawled around Eve and Jake to stand under the highest point of the tent. Behind her, the rain had settled into a steady patter, reflecting the firelight in its drops. The child smiled, obviously self-conscious, just as obviously pleased with their attention. She opened her mouth and sang.

The melody rose clear and sweet from the depths of Eve's memory. Tears blurred her vision. The words were familiar. She knew them, every one of them. Her lips trembled, aching to sing them.

She was five years old, sitting on her mother's lap. Her mom's arms were wrapped around her, loosely, so that together they could sing the Twenty-third Psalm. She sang the melody while her mother sang the descant. Every night at bedtime they practiced until she knew every word. Then a car accident took her mother away. All by herself, Eve sang the psalm, huddled under the covers at night, wanting her mommy. Then came the day she understood her mommy would never come back. She never sang it again.

The sharp crack of clapping hands echoed against the raindrops. Eve joined the applause, her teary eyes matched by Betty's and Jake's. She held back the sobs wrenching her chest, stuffed away the memory into the deep crevices of her heart.

What she couldn't do anything about mustn't be allowed to create cracks in her armor.

Chapter 29

Eve's scream woke Jake. He sat up, confused by the shriek, the shadow hovering over his head, the dark lumps stirring close by. Of course … he was in the tent. Eve squealed again, identifying herself as the lump two arm-lengths away. Farther back, next to the kindling, lay Betty and Crystal. His heart jumped at the level of fear in Eve's next yell. He scrambled to his knees. A bad dream? Or snake?

He scurried to her side, eyed one of the bayonets that stuck upright in the sand a foot away. He grabbed it and crouched next to her, ready to jump back if he found the coils of a giant python looped over her. She broke into a pant, the contortions of her face highlighted in the glow of the fire's coals.

No snake. No critter of any kind that he could see. She whipped her arm up and thrashed at the air. A dream. She was having a nightmare. He grabbed her hand to bring her terror to a halt. "Eve, wake up! You're—"

Her foot crashed into his face. Pain stabbed lightning hot under his eyes. He let go of her hand and fell backwards, dropping the bayonet to grab his nose with both hands.

"Wolves!"

The hair on the back of his neck pricked. "Eve, you're dreaming. Wake up!"

She scrabbled to her knees, her eyes so wide the whites around her irises gleamed in the firelight. He sat up, still cupping his nose. The iron taste of blood seeped into his mouth. Dark spots dropped to the ground from between his fingers.

"Wolves—I thought they ..." Eve gazed at his fingers. "Oh, Jake, I'm sorry! I kicked you, didn't I?"

"Jake?" Betty rose onto one elbow. "What's going on?"

"Eve had a nightmare and kicked me in the face." He got to his feet and stepped outside the tent, pinching the bridge of his nose to stop the bleeding. When, oh when, would he learn to stop rescuing this fool of a woman?

A full moon had replaced the storm clouds, illuminating the campsite in stark grays and whites. His feet were bare, but he had no problem picking his way over the rocky soil to the stream. He lay down at the edge and buried his face in the water.

"Jake." Eve touched his back. "Jake, let me see."

Her voice was unsteady. She hadn't recovered from her nightmare, yet she had chased after him to make sure he was all right. The hardness in his heart softened at her concern. He pushed back from the stream and sat up.

She squatted next to him. "It doesn't look broken, but I can't tell for sure."

"I'll be okay. Won't be the first time if it's broken. Is it still bleeding?"

"No." She sank into a sitting position, criss-crossing her legs. "Jake, I'm sorry. I ..." She stared down at her hands. They were trembling.

"Sounded like a bad nightmare. Wolves, you say?"

"They're chasing me." She inhaled a shaky breath. "I'm running through a forest, shouting for help, but my father ... he's not there." Tears brimmed in her eyes and spilled onto her cheeks. "They always catch me. Always. I try to fight them off, but their teeth rip into me—"

Terror, sharp and piercing, sliced across Jake's chest. The memory slashed at his throat so that he couldn't breathe. He gasped.

"Jake?"

"The dog." He shot his hand to the scars on his right cheek.

"The pit bull?"

"It just kept tearing me up. That's all I remember. Ripping me up …" He stopped.

"I'm sorry. It must have been awful. My nightmare is nothing. I feel stupid."

"No, please. I don't even know where that came from." He shook his head to dispel the specter. His heartbeat leveled. "Does your dream happen a lot?"

"I don't know what triggers it. I go months, then I have it."

Guilt stung him. Had he caused her nightmare by chewing her out at the volcano?

"What about you?" she asked.

He shrugged, feeling stupid himself now. "Like I said, I don't know where that came from. I never dream about the attack. I was two years old and foolishly walked up to a chained dog with pups. We'd always had dogs, so I wasn't scared of its bark. My dad got me away before the dog did any real damage."

"Those scars looked pretty serious to me."

"They only became a problem when I got older and the kids teased me. So I coped by beating them up." He touched his nose, recalling the first punch he had taken. "That's when my father started me in a wrestling program. Instead of hitting my critics, I tossed them to the ground and pinned them till they squealed 'uncle.'"

"Maybe I need to learn how to pin wolves."

"What about your father? You said he wasn't there."

She stiffened and looked away. "It's only a dream, Jake." She tossed a pebble into the stream and rose to her feet. "Thanks for rescuing me once again. I hope it didn't cost you your nose."

"It'll be fine." Other than hurting like crazy.

They walked back to the tent in silence. He wanted to ask more questions about her dream, but she'd slammed that door shut. Dream? That was like calling a five-alarm fire a weenie roast.

One thing for sure—he'd misjudged Eve. She wasn't simply a hardheaded woman. Something had happened to make her tough. He rubbed the scars on his cheek. And she hadn't had a dad there to help her like he'd had.

They reached the tent and returned to their sleeping spots. The campfire had snuffed out, but the moonlight was as bright as a streetlamp. At the back of the tent, soft snores puffed from the Betty-lump.

"Eve?" he whispered.

"Yes?"

"You know there's a heavenly Father."

"That doesn't help, Jake. Good-night."

He could take her hostility now. Tonight, Eve's dream had unlocked a secret. No man was trustworthy, and no man was going to boss her around. No doubt there would be more revelations trickling down from this one. He cushioned the back of his head against his arms and suppressed a groan. *Please, may my nose be the only casualty.*

* * *

Jojo slapped the wad of pesos onto the table. The uneven legs rocked under his hand, rattling the chairs shoved against the table legs. The noise got him the attention he wanted.

"Go away, we're closed." From the back of the restaurant, his mother's voice echoed against the hard surfaces of pots and pans hanging on hooks above metal appliances. She stuck her head out the doorway. A sharp inhale followed by the snapping on of lights told him she'd spied his hulk at the table. "What do you want? I told you not to come here."

She plodded into the room as if she weighed two hundred pounds instead of eighty. A broom with a handle longer than she was tall trailed her like a tail. He smirked as her eyes sought out the pile on the table before turning to him. "What do you want?" she repeated, emphasizing the *want* with sullen petulance, as if he were the beggar.

"Are you behind on the rent?"

"I owe a little. I'll catch up."

"You get kicked out of that rat's hole, you won't find another."

"I've got friends."

"Your boyfriends?" He sneered. "All they give you is disease."

"One gave me worse." She glared at him as she did every time she threw the word at him. "A monster."

He grinned. The one good thing his American father had given him was his size.

"And a murderer. You killed that sailor that disappeared off the ship, didn't you? Everyone is talking about it. Said you loosed some crated zoo animal to make it look like they fought and fell overboard."

He sniggered at his cleverness. Thanks to the leopard, no one had been able to fix the blame on him.

"They'll drag you off to prison, and this time you'll stay."

"And then what will you do for money? Make your home with the street children and become their mother?"

"Monster! Because of you, I have no babies!"

He grinned a second time. Best thing his size had ever done was shred his mother's womb at birth. He put his hand on the pile of money. "Maybe you don't want this, then."

The flare of her nostrils was barely perceptible before she lifted her chin and stalked toward the kitchen. He laughed so that his voice bounced off every hard surface in the room as he left. When he peeked back in a minute later, the pile on the table was gone.

* * *

Jake set the bunch of green bananas on the tent floor. These would have to do for this morning. His nose throbbed as if Eve had plunged a bayonet into his face instead of her foot. The only motivation he felt to move a single muscle today was to find that second cave.

A tarantula crawled out of the fruit, a big, hairy brute. The opening scene from *Raiders of the Lost Ark* leaped to mind. His spine tingled at the thought of tarantulas parked on his back from hauling the bananas. He brushed the spider into the fire pit before it could crawl away. It burst into flames and popped. He'd read they were good to eat roasted, but he suspected he'd already pushed the women's threshold with the snake meat.

"Whoa, that's what Eve did to your face last night?" Betty rolled herself into a sitting position.

Crystal opened her eyes and blinked. "Wow, you look like a raccoon."

"Good morning to you too. Watch out for tarantulas in the bananas. I already killed one." He was disappointed when they barely responded to his poke at them. No eeks or scuttling away. They were adapting to life on a wild island better than he had expected.

"Sorry, Jake." Eve sat up and yawned. She didn't have black eyes like he did, but last night's stress tinted the areas under her eyes a faint gray.

"Are you up to exploring today? You could stay here and rest." Good grief, he was back to feeling sorry for her. Her nightmare had tossed the hammer right out of his hand.

"I wouldn't miss it. All I need are a couple of bananas and I'm ready."

And a dip in the stream, a drink of water, and a trip to the designated toilet area. He huffed at the delays.

When she was finally ready, he snatched up Crystal's torch and the lens to light it. They walked down the stream to the cove so he could observe the location of the trench from a distance. The stream emptied into the left side of the cove; to the right, rocky ground rose to the cliff he and Eve had fallen over. Between the two areas lay the cove's beach, the minefield in back of it that hid the trench, and above it the abrupt rise of rock stretching far away to the volcano. A second cave had to be somewhere in that rock.

They returned to the spot where the log had pushed them over the edge of the cliff. Their first task was to look for more booby traps. When they found none, they tramped the length of the trench and back, then the rocky section between the trench and the cliff.

"Logically, the cave should be here, near the cliff's edge," Jake grumbled, "but I don't see any more openings. Nothing but rock. I wonder if I can see anything by looking down on this area from above."

He climbed to the height of a two-story house above the trench. The area proved to be a mini-plateau, about thirty feet in diameter. Closest to the side above where Eve stood, tall grasses and shrubs grew, while the rest of the plateau was bare rock. Peculiar that one section had life, while the rest was barren.

Using a stick, he parted the foliage and found several bamboo pongee sticks stuck in the ground. His mouth went dry. He was familiar with them from Nam. The hidden, razor-sharp spikes had injured a number of his buddies. The tips of these were dull, battered by decades of sun and rain, but the memory of the deadly spikes still sent a shiver up his spine.

The trap's presence was further evidence that he was close to something. His heart beat faster. Was something buried among the pongee sticks? Another swipe, deeper this time, disclosed what the foliage had been meant to hide: a rusted pulley. Running over the top of it and back down into the rock was a cable. Excitement pulsated through his nerves. The Japanese soldiers had rigged a counterweight.

Shoving aside the decayed pongee sticks, he reached down and grabbed hold of the pulley. Clockwise, it wouldn't budge. He pushed hard in the opposite direction. This time it turned.

"Eve!"

"What?"

"I found a pulley. See if it makes any of the rocks move." Straining against the resistance of rust, he rotated the mechanism a full circle.

"Yes, a stone moved," she hollered.

He climbed down to her side, his heart hammering. This was beyond anything he'd imagined. He and Eve put their hands flat against the rock she designated and pushed up. Grating in protest, showering a powder of gray cinder, the rock slid to the height of their kneecaps and stopped.

He got on his hands and knees and peered into the darkness. "We found it."

Chapter 30

The entryway wasn't as dark as Jake expected. Must be because of light entering around the pulley. His stomach tightened with anticipation. Imagine, a cave with a pulley door! What other features would the cave have? If the soldiers had been on the island any length of time, they may have kept improving this home away from home.

Eve crouched next to him.

"Let me check for booby traps before we go in. The Lone Soldier might have left us with his last hurrah." He probed the passageway with a stick. When nothing happened, he took a deep breath and crawled in.

He stuck his head back out and beckoned Eve. "You've got to see this!"

"Shouldn't I light the torch first?"

"You don't need it. The cave has its own light source."

"Really?" She scrambled inside.

He laughed at the surprise on her face as she rose to her feet. They were standing in a large chamber with more than ample headroom. To their right, on the north wall, three small openings admitted light.

"Clever." He ambled over to them. "You can't see these windows from the beach because they're on the seaside of the cliff. From the ocean, they look like nesting birds dug them."

"Hooey—so that's what I smell. Birds."

The odor was overpowering, even at the windows with an ocean of fresh air outside. He shoved the empty nests overboard. "Best do this before Crystal wants to make pets of them."

In front of the windows lay a stone hearth, open on all sides so that one could walk around it. "No need for torches. Between the windows and the hole for the pulley, there's enough light to see during the day, and they'd have the hearth fire at night."

"Look, furniture." Eve strode to the other side of the chamber, where a long table of bamboo slats was surrounded by ten handcrafted chairs. A large tripod stood against the wall, a cauldron placed upside down on the floor next to it. "I bet they used that for cooking on the hearth."

"And look here." Jake set a basket on the table. "A whetstone, cooking utensils, chopsticks, hooks and lines for fishing."

Eve reached in. "Needles and thread!"

They investigated the room and brought more treasures to the table. A broom and two buckets, a small cast-iron pot, an axe and shovel, a dismantled radio.

Jake tried out the radio to no effect. "Batteries are dead."

"What's this?" Eve thumped a large book onto the table and opened it. The yellowed pages were filled with tidy columns of Japanese characters.

"Probably journal entries logging war data." He unfolded a map inside the cover and spread it on the table. "It's in Japanese, but it's clearly the Philippines." An arrow pointed to a miniscule dot positioned at the extreme eastern edge of the Philippines. It lay on the southeast border of a sea-lane that threaded west through the larger islands and then north to the capital.

"This is where we are." He placed his finger on the island. "I suspect the soldiers' mission was to report on traffic in this sea-lane leading to and from Manila. If so, that means we should be able to spot ships too. It also explains why the windows are on the north wall. This room was an observation post."

Eve carried the map to the windows and peered out. "Would the sea-lane be the same today as back then?"

"No question about it." As his eyes adjusted to the dim light, he spotted a darkened corridor in the wall farthest from the windows. The narrow hallway contained five ledges carved into each side. "I found the sleeping quarters," he called over his shoulder. The beds were empty except for disheveled sleeping mats. No skeletons. With the exception of the Lone Soldier, the platoon lay at rest in the burial cave. No snakes, either—he double-checked the ledges to make sure.

He reentered the chamber. Everything they needed to survive was here. His heart raced with excitement at the unexpected provision.

"Look at this place." Eve swiped her hand at the room. "It's covered with bird poop. Everything—floor, table, chairs. No wonder it stinks."

He surveyed the room with new eyes. Indeed, what must be decades of bird droppings plastered everything forming a horizontal surface, with splatters on the walls, to boot. He cleared his throat. "It's nothing a good scrubbing can't handle. I mean, look around you—this room is fantastic! It's like a miniature banquet hall in a medieval castle."

Eve's mouth dropped. "You can't mean you still want to—" She stopped, pressed her lips together, and glanced around the room. "You're talking about taking a day to clean this, aren't you?"

"Yes." He clenched his teeth. Here we go again.

Her nostrils flared as she sucked in a long breath through her nose and slowly released it. When she spoke, her voice, though tight, was an obvious attempt to be amiable. "How about if I work on the signal fire to speed things along while the three of you work in here?"

She wasn't going to argue with him? Tension ebbed from his shoulders. "Sure. Good idea."

"Where?" She slipped the map back into the book. "Up where you found the pulley?"

He crawled outside after her and gazed up the steep incline to the plateau. "It's a bit of a climb, but, yes. It's handy to the cave, and the fire would be visible to the north."

"I'm on it." She took off at a trot across the trench.

He returned to the cave to grab the two buckets. Outside again, he paused and rubbed his head. Now, how was it he'd ended up with the job of scrubbing while she did the hauling?

* * *

191

Betty groaned as Jake lifted her into his arms. Honestly, she'd have been better off if the land mine had blown her foot clear off. Then she'd have only a stump to heal instead of the shredded flesh aching on the bottom of her foot. At the look of concern on his face, she bit into her lower lip. "It's okay, Jake. I'm dying to see this cave, and I'm glad to have something helpful to do for a change."

"You're awful light. We need to fatten you up somehow."

She snorted. "We're all skeletons." She looked back at Crystal. "You coming, child? Are those buckets too heavy?"

Crystal grunted a response that must have meant she could handle it. The two buckets were half full. The water sloshed against the sides like miniature tsunamis as she held them out from her body in an awkward balance act.

"We'll take the shortcut," Jake whispered in Betty's ear. "The going is rougher, but this way I think we'll get more water to its destination."

The shortcut meant climbing the rocky incline east of the stream, all but sliding down its other side into the trench, and then wading through waist-high grass to the rocky bank at the other end. Betty clutched Jake's neck. How in the world would Crystal manage this?

"Don't look back," he warned. "Our Gymnast of the Ocean Cliff will figure it out."

Across the trench—good grief, almost two stories high—stood Eve. "We have to climb that?"

"No. The cave opens into the trench. Eve is setting up our signal fire. You may want to join her after you see the task we face."

"Nonsense. We'll have the place clean before sundown."

They waited at the entry for Crystal to catch up with them. Her mouth was set in a tight downward curve that dammed welling tears from spilling onto her cheeks. She kept her gaze on Jake, her stare reproachful but desperate with trust as she put one foot in front of the other. When Crystal's steps faltered, Betty spied the Lone Soldier half-hidden nearby in the grassy bank. Oh my, he was a heart-stopper.

Jake captured the buckets before Crystal dropped them. "Good job. Doesn't look like you spilled a drop. Do you two want to say hello to the Lone Soldier before we go in?"

Betty was surprised when Crystal didn't slink to her side. Instead, the child stood her ground and turned her head toward the tattered sentry. "Hello."

Poor child. Betty extended her hand to Crystal. "Another time, Jake. I'm ready to see this cave."

They crawled inside, Jake first, then her, then Crystal. This time, Crystal sidled up to her while their eyes adjusted to the semidarkness. The odor of bird poop overwhelmed her nasal cavity. "Whoo-ee!" Cuddled against her, Crystal giggled. That was good. The stench was not. Had she said they'd have this place clean by sundown?

"Rather than have you crawl over these bird deposits, let me carry you to show you around. Do you mind?"

She stifled a groan as Jake lifted her. She'd never get well in a place smelling like this.

With obvious pride, as if he'd carved out the place himself, he introduced Crystal and her to the cave's features. He was right; after the cramped tent, it was like walking into a luxury hotel. Except for the mess left by the birds.

"They chopped the whole room out of this rock?" Awe echoed in Crystal's voice. "It must have taken forever."

"Not that long." Jake edged a chair out from the table. "The rock is magma, part of the lava flow. It's easy to dig out, although there are a lot of sharp little rocks in it that are like pieces of glass."

He set Betty on the chair, pulled out a second, and lifted her injured foot to rest on it. Did the man not see the white plaster of bird droppings he'd set her on?

He hauled in the two buckets of water and plunked one onto the table. "You start with the tabletop while I work on the chairs. Then I'll bring the cauldron over and you can work on it. It was turned upside down, so it shouldn't be much trouble. I'll bring you more when you're ready."

The man's work ethic certainly wasn't hurting. "What do I scrub with?"

"Here you go." He dug deep into his pockets and retrieved four clumps of tightly twisted grass. "Two for you and two for me. Crystal, you'll bring more water as we need it, and in the meantime, keep us supplied with grass." He reached into a basket on the floor. "Here's a knife—cut the grass so it's long enough to twist into scrubbers."

Knife? Betty gulped. She would never give Crystal a sharp knife like that. But to defy Jake in his buzz-saw work mode was too daunting to consider.

"Cut away from you like this"—Jake slashed the knife into the air— "not toward you like this, so you don't cut yourself. Got it?" He handed the knife to Crystal. "We'll go through the scrubbers quickly, so keep at it until I need you to fetch water."

Crystal glanced at Betty and scurried out the entryway. Jake tipped the bucket onto the table, sloshed water over it, and attacked the surface with a scrubber in each hand. "I'll catch the far corners for you before I start on the chairs."

A stench rose from the wet table, clogging her throat, wrenching her stomach. She leaned over and vomited onto the floor.

Jake halted. "You okay?"

"The smell …"

"It won't be so bad once we get the area near you cleaned up. I'll move the chairs outside and postpone cleaning them so I can work on the windows. That's where it's the worst, from their nesting. Fortunately, the gulls are big enough not many of them got inside." He tackled the table with even more vigor. "Just let me finish up here first."

She sat back, her head woozy. He splashed more water over the tabletop, wiped the gooey moisture onto the floor, and emptied the last of the water onto her vomit. "There." He threw his shredded scrubbers onto her diluted stomach contents and grabbed a broom leaning against the wall. "I'll sweep this outside and be right back."

She'd barely taken a breath before he returned to drag away the chairs.

"I gave Crystal the bucket to fetch water from the beach. We'll pour this other bucket over the table so you can get it done and out of the way." Before lifting the pail, he held up his hands to display two new scrubbers. "She's doing a good job with the grass. You can be proud of what a hard worker she is."

Betty quirked her mouth at the praise. Would he think her a shirker if she asked to switch jobs with Crystal? Water spattered her face and neck as he poured it onto the unscrubbed portion of the table in front of her. He dumped what was left onto the windows and set the bucket near the entryway.

"If you can finish up before she comes back, we'll rinse off the table with her bucketful and send her off for two more."

Well, she couldn't just sit there while he worked on the windows and Crystal toted water. Gripping a scrubber in each hand, she rubbed at the pool of goo in front of her. She gagged, but nothing rose from her stomach. All right then, if she was going to have to eat off this table, it was going to get a good scouring. She held her breath and dug in.

Two buckets of water and four grass scrubbers later, she sat back, satisfied the table was as sanitary as it was going to get. She moved on to the cauldron and utensils, stretching to lay them side by side across the table.

"You're standing!" Jake's surprise broke her concentration.

Goodness, she was! Somewhere along the line she had lowered her injured foot, pushed back her chair, and leaned against the table to rest on her good foot. "So I am!" Warmth at the achievement flooded her body. She dared to touch the toes of her injured foot to the floor. "Maybe it's time for a moccasin and cane." Jake appeared ready to jump to it. "Tomorrow," she admonished. "I want nothing more today than to get this place clean."

"Anyone ready for lunch?" Eve crawled inside, wiping at her knees as she stood. "Is that what I think it is at the entryway?"

"The, uh, puddle? I was going to get rid of it when we finished." Jake gestured at the room. "So, what do you think? Does it smell any better?"

"I don't know how you can stand it." Eve covered her mouth and nose. "All this water has done is magnify the odor."

Betty cringed. Had she gotten used to breathing the foul stuff? "I'm ready to eat if you can help me get outside, Jake." Although he carried her to the cave door, she still had to crawl out, right through the ratty scrubbers and bird muck he'd swept through the entryway. Outdoors, his hands, legs, and clothing revealed he'd crawled through it several times.

Her own hands, like his, were white with a thin layer of the goo they'd been scrubbing. She shuddered. "Take me to the cove, Jake. You and I aren't touching anything more until we clean up."

After lunch, she made him bring the chairs for her to wash off directly in the cove. The salt-laden air cleared her head and lungs. Across the field with its hidden land mines and fence and trench, Jake and Eve and Crystal labored like determined ants.

Every time Crystal fetched water, Betty received updates.

"Jake carved hash marks on the wall to show we've been on the island seven days."

"Eve took our tent down and brought it over."

"Jake swept the muck over the cliff. Phew-ee!"

"Eve wanted to build a fire to dry out the cave, but she said the hearth still smelled, so she's scrubbing it all over again while Jake and I cut grass for the beds."

And with a fit of giggles, "A gull flew in and made new messes!"

The sun was casting a kaleidoscope of reds and oranges over the ocean by the time Jake retrieved her. "The cave is ready, but how about if we take a look at what Eve's done with the firewood?"

Well goodness, he didn't tell her it meant having to latch onto his back like a turtle shell. To scale the steep slope, he had to use both hands while she clung with all four limbs wrapped around him. He slipped twice, and once had to reposition the stranglehold she had on his neck. How had he and Eve ever made it up the cliffside they'd fallen over?

Crystal, reigning Gymnast of the Ocean Cliff, scampered easily to the top to join Eve. "Wow, look what Eve's done!"

Oh my, it was impressive. Not only had Eve carried every twig, stick, and leaf to the new site, but she had also built a platform of large stones to stack the wood on. With the rope from the lighter, she had battened down the sailcloth over it to prevent the wood from getting wet.

Obviously pleased with everyone's praise, Eve untucked a pointed end of the sail and propped it up with a sturdy stick. "And look, we can also put the sail at a forty-five-degree angle, like this, to protect us from sunburn when we're watching for ships."

The job looked just about right for a lame, old lady who couldn't do much else, but Betty wasn't sure turtle-backing it up there on Jake was something she wanted to do every day.

With far less hassle going down than up, they descended to the cave. The muck was gone from the entryway, and a fire crackled inside on the hearth. While the moisture hadn't entirely dissipated, the improvement in reducing the odor of the former feathered tenants was gratifying. Crystal's seashell platters lay on the table, stacked with a variety of fresh fruit. A five-star hotel couldn't have received a higher rating than these accommodations the four of them had worked so hard on.

Jake carried her to the pristine table, which surely deserved as much praise as Eve's pile of sticks and stones. No one said anything, but she beamed when Jake brought her a cane and a well-padded moccasin for her injured foot. The man was a marvel. Really, if anyone deserved praise, he did.

"So, Jake, tomorrow we light the signal fire and start work on repairing the boat." Eve all but said *at last!*

"Not quite." He set his coconut on the table. "Now that I can safely leave you three in the cave, I'm going to walk the perimeter of the island. I don't feel comfortable working on the boat when there might be things on the island we don't know about yet."

"Like what?" Eve's response was quick.

"Well, for one, we have no idea what's on the other side of the island."

Betty's spine tingled. Surely anything threatening would have showed up by now. And if there was something bad, what if it got Jake?

Chapter 31

"I'm going with you." Eve blocked Jake's exit from the cave. "And don't tell me no."

"No." He emptied the morning's fruit onto the tabletop and readjusted the katana scabbard on his back.

She huffed. "You shouldn't go alone."

"Should we leave Betty and Crystal here alone?"

Her mouth twitched down at his logic. There was no way she would abandon Betty and Crystal, if that's what accompanying him meant.

"I'll be back tomorrow by sundown." He stuffed some of the fruit into his pockets, stepped around her, and crawled outside.

Then she'd just do her own exploring. The rocky slope above the signal fire would be perfect.

She grabbed the kitchen knife and hacked furiously at the fruit. Nine weeks left before the Danny Romero trial. Each day she stayed on the island was a prison cell that bound her and freed Romero. She had to get off. One more day—she would give Jake one more day. Tomorrow, if he didn't start work on the boat, she would. It had survived an explosion—repairing it couldn't be that hard.

After breakfast, she helped Betty assemble the moccasin for her injured foot, then lugged the tripod to the hearth and hung the cauldron while Crystal fetched two buckets of water from the stream. Mussel soup to surprise Jake was the target of Betty and Crystal's day. Fine, because the last thing she wanted was anyone's company.

She picked up one of the bayonets. "I'm going to check out the slope above the signal fire. I'll bring fruit when I return."

The two chefs barely acknowledged her departure.

On the plateau, she stopped to inspect the firewood. In spite of last night's wind and rain, the sail was tight and everything under it dry. Satisfaction with the job she'd done raised her spirits. She was tempted to start a signal fire, but Jake had creeped her out with his concern about what might be on the island. No sense attracting unwanted attention while he was gone.

The slope proved an easy climb, with occasional shallow craters and large boulders breaking the monotony of bare rock stretching toward the distant volcano. Although she didn't know what to look for, she kept an eye out for booby traps.

Her heart jumped when she spotted what she was sure was a trail—a man-made one. The path wound around several boulders, crossed a small stream, and ended at an opening between two vertical rock formations. She squeezed between them and halted, her heart pounding at what she found on the other side.

Before her lay a garden. Its loveliness spoke of human hands crafting every square inch. Not only had a pocket been dug into the lava to cradle the garden, but the walls had been chiseled into artful geometric designs. Across from her, a miniature waterfall splashed in a cascade of descending ledges to several small pools linked across the garden. It wouldn't have surprised her to find goldfish with graceful, flowing fins gaping at her from the water.

The reedy grass of the Lone Soldier's field had taken root in the garden, but the invasion was sparse. On impulse, she began pulling the trespassers, stacking them in a mound behind her. A passion to restore the beauty of the garden overtook her and she worked feverishly.

Flowers, watered by the pools and sheltered from the sun by the lattice of weeds, released sweet fragrances as she uncovered them. Unfamiliar with all of them, she reveled in the glory of their colors, their forms, their scents. She imagined the soldiers finding them in the jungle and transporting them to the garden. At the exposure of a cluster of petite, white flowers, her breath rushed from her lungs.

Sampaguitas.

This flower she knew. Its name meant *I promise*. She knew because eight months ago she had made a promise to a sixteen-year-old prostitute—

* * *

The phone rang as Eve entered the District Attorney's office. The receptionist's desk was unattended. She punched the speakerphone button and peeled off her scarf and gloves, spattering the floor with specks of snow.

"Federal prosecutor's office, Evedene Eriksson speaking."

"Eve!" Debra Baker, her bud at the state attorney's office, shrieked at her. "We've got a trafficking witness! Hurry! Cook County Hospital ER."

"On my way!" She grabbed her purse, hustled outside, and hailed a cab.

The driver flew across Chicago at the promise of a doubled fare. Debra grabbed her by the arm in the emergency room and pulled her to a small room. A nurse nodded at Debra and left, closing the door.

A hospital bed, straddled by two chairs, took up most of the space. Its occupant, a slender teenage girl, was covered by a white sheet up to her chest. Arms, bare shoulders, and face bore a spectrum of black and blue bruises. Her left eye was swollen shut. Blood caked her lips, both ears, and a swathe of cuts across her cheeks. Although the girl's hair was colored red, the slanted corners of her eyes identified her as Asian, and the honey color of the skin on her hands, as part Caucasian.

Eve's chair crackled as she sank onto the plastic cushion.

"Alicia, this is Evedene Eriksson. She's—"

"I know. I've seen her before. I want to testify."

"Testify against whom?" Eve searched her memory, but the girl's face was too messed up to recall.

"Romero."

Eve's heartbeat skyrocketed. "Danny Romero?"

"You told us at the jail you'd help us if we testified against him. I didn't care then, but now he's tried to kill me."

"Danny Romero tried to kill you?"

"His men."

Eve leaned forward. "I need hard facts, Alicia. Proof that will hold up in court."

"I got them."

"All right." Eve fetched her notebook and pen from her purse. "Let's begin with your name and birth date. The real ones, not what's on your ID."

"Marikit Santos Torres, August 23, 1965."

Sixteen years old. Definitely underaged. Eve's hand trembled at the thought of finally nailing Romero. "Where were you born?"'

"I don't know. Here? I've always lived in Chicago."

Eve slapped her pen onto the notebook and turned to Debra. "Why did you call me? If she hasn't crossed state lines, federal has no jurisdiction."

"Hear her out. Go on, Alicia ... Mari. Start at the beginning."

Eve waited two breaths before the girl finally opened her mouth.

"My mother's pimp started me when I was twelve. A year ago he sold me to a club. We got rounded up one night by the cops, and that's when I heard you at the jail. I didn't know who Danny Romero was, but I asked around and found out stuff."

With her good eye, Mari studied Eve. "You were pretty and smart and powerful, and for a while I wanted to be like you. I never went to school after sixth grade, but I read a lot."

"I can help you—"

"No, you can't. Nobody'd ever give me a job. Anyways, I liked the club. I had a bed and food and TV and pretty clothes. Then they promoted me, said I'd be part of a special group, the Sampaguitas."

How could the girl think there was anything special about prostitution? But this was just a kid, a sixteen-year-old kid, held in bondage for four years, and who knew how many before that? "Is this group connected to Danny Romero?"

"Yes. The Sampaguitas are his. I moved to a different club. His club."

The idea of "special" galled Eve, but the question had to be asked. "What's special about the Sampaguitas?"

"All of us are Asian. No one can do"—she looked down at her body— "this to us."

"Are all of you children?"

"I'm the oldest."

Eve wanted to scream, but instead she asked, "Why the name Sampaguitas?"

"It's the national flower of the Philippines. We're supposed to be from there, but some of us are Japanese, Chinese, Vietnamese. Anyway, Americans can't tell the difference." She shrugged. "It's a small, delicate flower. The name means 'I promise.'"

"Promise what?"

Mari's chin trembled, and she hung her head.

"Never mind. Tell me about the proof you have."

"When we were put together at the club, some of the little girls cried, but after a while they stopped. Not Tala, though. Even with the drugs, she still cried. Maybe because she's the youngest."

"How young?"

"Eight."

Eve closed her eyes. So what if Mari saw her pain. The girl needed to see it, needed to feel it, needed to be kicked harder than those bruises with it. She opened her eyes and met Mari's.

"I wanted to help her." Mari's voice quaked. "I didn't want her to be stuck like me for the rest of her life. She had a home and a family, and she told me their address—"

"What state?" Eve swallowed. This would be the deciding factor. It had to be across the state line for her to get involved. For her to get Danny Romero for trafficking. Child trafficking.

"Indiana."

Eve slumped back in her chair. She scribbled down the address, her heart thumping. "What happened? Did you help her?"

"I didn't know how to get her home. I couldn't take her there, and I couldn't send her all by herself." Tears trickled from Mari's good eye. "I should've called you."

Dread squeezed Eve's gut. "Should've" meant something had gone wrong. Impulsively, she slipped her hand over Mari's. The slender fingers were cold. "What happened, Mari?"

Mari took in a shuddering breath. "I sneaked out with Tala and took a taxi to Child Services. I knew they'd ask me questions and maybe even hold me if I went inside with her, so I told her what to say."

"What was that?"

"To just keep saying her parents' names and address—that's what mattered, to get her back home to them, and then they'd look out for her. She didn't know stuff like Romero's name or the club address, and I didn't tell her."

"Go on."

"Once she got inside the building okay, I went back to the club. Nobody saw me. There was a big stink when they discovered she was gone, but no one suspected me. I was happy, figuring she was home safe and all with her mum and dad."

Her voice fell. "A week later they brought her back. She didn't talk to me or no one. And she didn't cry any more, either."

For several heartbeats, none of them spoke.

Eve glanced at Debra's blanched face and knew she was thinking the same thing. How could someone who should have helped little Tala betray her instead? She steeled herself to ask more questions. "Did you find out how she got taken back to the club?"

"No. Everyone was scared to talk to her. Scared even more 'cause she'd stopped crying all the time. I kept thinking what they must of done to her, scared of what they'd do to me if they found out."

"It looks like they did."

"I ran—that's how they found out. I couldn't stand hanging around waiting for them to get me. I sneaked out just like before, but this time they were watching. They made me tell everything and then beat me up. That's when I knew they were going to kill me, because no one was allowed to hit us." Sobs shook her chest in quick gasps.

The nurse poked her head into the room. Eve signaled "one minute" and turned to Mari. "How did you escape the men?"

"I don't know. I woke up in the hospital."

For the first time since Eve started the interview, Debra spoke. "They dumped her into the Chicago, but a patrolman saw them and fished her out. It was touch and go. You're a lucky girl, Marikit."

"I want to testify against Danny Romero!"

Eve released the girl's hand and stood. "Thank you, Mari. We'll take you to a safe place until you can. With your help, we'll put Danny Romero behind bars. I promise you."

"And send Tala home?"

"Yes. And send Tala home."

A week later, Eve and Debra were the sole attendants at Marikit's funeral. An anonymous benefactor paid for it. A bouquet of Sampaguitas sat on the coffin, mocking the two mourners. Mocking their failure to find Tala. The club. A group of Asian girls called the Sampaguitas.

"I made a promise to you, Marikit." Eve dumped the flowers into the trash and stomped them flat. "I'm going to put Danny Romero behind bars."

* * *

Rain pelted the Japanese garden. Eve hunched her shoulders and gazed around her. Her heart pounded. She'd made a promise, and no matter how long it took, she'd keep it.

She sheltered her eyes and peered up. The sky glowered with dark clouds that roiled from horizon to horizon. This storm was going to last awhile. Jake had chosen a bad day to walk around the island.

Across the garden, she spotted a second entrance. Betting it would lead to the stream that flowed from the waterfall pool, she cut a path through the vegetation until she stumbled onto the stream. Already the water was overflowing its banks and hurtling toward the ocean. At the waterfall, she picked the fruit easiest to reach and waded downstream to the cave. No sense battling the rain attacking the bare mountainside she had climbed that morning.

She entered the cave, soaked to her bones, teeth chattering. Betty and Crystal scooted a chair close to the hearth and handed her a coconut shell of their seafood concoction. "Sit and sip," Betty commanded. "We don't have towels to dry you off, but between the fire and the soup, we're going to stop those shivers."

The soup tasted like diluted ocean water with lumps of chewy sea creatures she presumed were mussels. But the broth was hot and she was cold and she drank every bit of it. When her body stopped shaking and she could put two words together, she told them about the Japanese garden.

"Those soldiers took a long time carving out this cave and planting that garden." Betty's voice was somber. "They made this island their home, didn't they?"

"Well, we're not." The words blazed from Eve's heart. She had a promise to keep. "Tomorrow, Jake will be back and he'll start repairing the boat. In a few days we'll sail for the sea-lane."

She paced the floor, restless for Jake to return, restless to end the day and start a new one. The cloud cover and rain shut out the sun, so they had to guess when evening came.

"I'll wait up for Jake in case he comes back tonight." Betty shooed them to the sleeping ledges. "Get your sleep. You're going to have a busy day tomorrow."

But when Eve arose the next morning, he hadn't returned. They waited all day through a whipping rain, and he still didn't show up.

Chapter 32

Sunlight was poking through the cave windows when Eve got up. Her heart jumped. No more rain. No more sitting in the dark inhaling the acrid stench of soggy ashes, with only cold chowder to eat. Today they would get something done so they could finally get off the island.

She glanced around the cave. If Jake had returned last night, there was no sign of him. His bed was empty, the firewood in the cave hadn't been replenished, and there was no good-morning fruit dumped on the table. Today made three days.

Her stomach tightened into double knots. Why hadn't she insisted on going with him—or would she, too, have vanished, leaving Betty and Crystal to fend for themselves?

She fought the sparking across her nerves. She had to get ahold of herself before Betty and Crystal woke up. Have a plan ready for the three of them. Crystal could take over the chores of gathering fruit and firewood since Eve would be off working on the boat. It would only be for a few days.

She stopped. Maybe that's where Jake was, repairing the boat. It would be just like him to make the repair, rainstorm or not, and sail pleased as could be into the cove today, not a thought given to their worry about where he'd been.

She shook Betty and Crystal awake. "The rain has stopped, and Jake's not back. I'd like to take Crystal with me to get fruit and firewood—"

"Nonsense." Betty sat up. Wisps of dried grass from the bed tangled in her hair. "You should look for Jake, not fool around with what we've already got. Crystal can fetch firewood from under the canvas, and we can make more soup."

"I could be gone for several days, and you'd have no—"

"Look for Jake. We don't need fruit. If we run out of wood, Crystal can go upstream for it."

Eve sighed. She'd just have to say it straight out. "What if I disappear too?"

Betty took Eve's hand. "Look for Jake. He saved our lives, and we're not abandoning him."

Guilt stabbed her. Once again, without even thinking about it, she'd chosen Romero's trial over Jake. "All right." She helped Betty hobble to the table. "I'm going to the boat first. Maybe he's there, repairing it. But, please, be careful while I'm gone. Don't take any chances." She picked up one of the bayonets and left.

A sharp wind rustled the stalks of grass in the Lone Soldier's field and whipped her hair into her eyes. Gray clouds hovered around the sun, boxing it in, promising rain. Ignoring the hunger pinching her stomach, she trotted across the trench, stopped at the top of the incline to check the broad expanse on the other side for Jake, and hurried to the stream for a drink. She hadn't climbed the rocky cliff beyond the stream since they had arrived at the cove a week ago. Scaling the precipice was easy with her moccasins, but farther on, at the ocean cliff, with its sheer rock face and seething water far below, her heart pounded. Had they really climbed up the side of this?

She should have listened better to Jake's description of the path he'd made through the jungle to circumvent the cliff. She'd made a mistake by assuming he'd be there to show it to her. A mistake to think he'd be there to protect and lead her and Betty and Crystal. She should have known better. It was best, always best, to make sure you had control over what was happening in your life.

Rain spattered cold drops that in minutes soaked her clothes. The jungle path was clearly her only option. In spite of the time it would take to follow the path, fighting vegetation beat a fatal misstep on the cliff's wet side. This way, too, she'd be prepared for getting Betty and Crystal back down to the boat. Besides, she was hungry. She'd find something to eat along the path and get out of the rain.

The jungle's edge offered several entries. One bore fresh cuts on its trees that had to have been sliced by Jake's katana sword. The farther she went, however, the more obscure the trail became. The cuts and obvious broken branches that guided her at first became difficult to find. She doubled back and corrected her path three times before she gave up and hacked her own trail with the bayonet.

She found mangosteens and ate, swatting away tiny, winged competitors at every bite. They crawled into her hair and under her clothing and inside her moccasins, leaving itching gravesites when she smashed them. As soon as she got out of this jungle, she was going to strip down in the rain and scrub every inch of her body.

Would she ever get out, though? For all she knew, she was looping circles, or worse, heading straight into the interior of the island. At some point, the path needed to veer back toward the ocean. She should be moving downhill, too, from the top of the ocean cliff to the plateau where they'd rested.

The logic calmed her. She bore left in what she hoped was a turn seaward and oriented herself to journey in a descent instead of climbing. At the sight of chopped tree branches that all but glowed like neon signs, she let out a whoop. She had found Jake's path! Soon the scraggly trees of the ocean coastline crowded into the jungle against a backdrop of gray sky and drizzling rain. The crash of ocean waves against rock boomed louder as she trudged through the thinning trees.

Unwilling to overlook anyplace she might find Jake, she climbed the stony path to the plateau where they had rested at the bottom of the cliff. Nothing. Nothing on the rocks far below where white foam frothed like spittle. Ridiculous to peer over, flattened on her belly, whimpering as the wind lashed her shirt and hair, but she had to look.

No stripping down to wash the bug bites, either. Water ran from the top of her head down every inch of her body and pooled inside her moccasins. By the time she descended to the next level of jungle, she was shivering uncontrollably. The warm air was no deterrent to wet skin chilled by the wind off the ocean.

She passed the clearing where Jake had cut the moccasins for her, climbed down to the beach where Betty had challenged her that Jake was a good man, and at last stepped onto the long stretch of sand she had stumbled across holding onto Jake's and Betty's shoulders. Their journey to the cove ten days ago seemed like ages now, so much had happened.

The tree line at the back of the beach afforded little protection against the rain. The wind swirled the drops in a heavy mist between the trunks of the towering palms and tossed it far back into the slapping leaves of green vegetation. Rubbing her arms, teeth chattering, she plodded one squishy step after another, squinting for a glimpse of the boat among the trees.

"Eve!"

She halted. "Jake?"

He stepped onto the beach. She ran to him, laughing, crying, furious. Should she hug him for being alive, or smack him for making them worry?

He grabbed her arm and pulled her out of the pummeling rain to the boat. "What are you doing here?"

"Looking for you, what do you think?" Anger flashed heat to her skin but subsided in a snap when she saw him shivering, fists jammed into his armpits to warm his hands. "Why didn't you come back to the cave? Did you find something on the other side of the island?"

"Nothing but sand and trees—except for these." He pointed to a pile of thick bamboo poles propped upright against the boat. Their tips were poked between the branches of a nearby tree to keep the wind from blowing them down. "Took me two days to drag them here. Look at those babies, they're perfect for building outriggers for the boat."

She forgot all about chiding him. "How long will it take?"

"A day, two at the most, once the sap leaches out."

"Sap? We have to wait on that?" She touched the wood. It was slick beneath her fingertips, supple, far from hard like the bamboo table and chairs in the cave.

"If we want the boat to float, we do."

"How long will that take?"

He shrugged. "I'll have to keep checking. Days. A week. Two weeks."

She held her breath to keep from screaming. "Can't we use some other kind of wood?"

"Why would we do that when bamboo is exactly what we want?"

Her huff punched a hole in the mist. "I told you. I've got an important deadline coming up. I've got to be there."

"What kind of deadline? Be where?"

"A court date." There, she'd told him! She folded her arms across her chest, defying him to ask more questions.

But he did anyway. "When?"

"August 24, nine weeks from now."

He smiled, no doubt pleased he'd pulled the information out of her. "Not a problem. A few sunny days to build the outriggers, and we'll be off this island long before then. I promise."

Promise? She huffed another hole into the mist. How good was he for that?

Chapter 33

"What's with the torches?" Jake tumbled an armload of dripping fruits onto the table and sloshed wet footprints to the hearth. Fingers too numb to bend, he fumbled out of his drenched shirt and moccasins to stand shivering before the fire.

"Crystal and I want to see the burial chamber." Eve shoved the torches away from the wet fruits and began cutting them. "Will you take us?"

The force of her whops on the starfruit left no doubt what his answer had to be. Ten days and the sap still wasn't finished exiting the bamboo. Every other day, either he or Eve or both had checked on the progress. The Japanese garden had proven a pleasant diversion during the wait, but the moments of sunshine had been rare. The burial chamber would serve as a good distraction. Besides, the cave still held secrets. Barring the presence of giant pythons, he wouldn't mind exploring that escape tunnel.

"All right, let's go after we eat." No sense waiting to dry his clothes. The rain would soak him all over again, but that didn't mean he'd forego toasting his skin now and seeing if his toes were still alive.

They formulated a plan while they ate. They'd leave Crystal at the entry until he and Eve ascertained that it was safe for her to join them. He didn't mention searching for the escape tunnel. It only made sense that Eve would return with Crystal to Betty while he scoped out where the second tunnel led.

Sheltering coals crammed into the small cast-iron pot, they tucked the four new torches under their clothes and dashed to the burial cave's entryway. Inside, the sound of their pants echoed in the blackness, as if the ghouls had crept up and hovered nearby. Add the prospect of a snake or two, and the spookiness pricked Jake's arms with mountain-sized goose bumps.

He held the first torch against the coals. It hissed to life and filled the close space with the stink of burning synthetic rubber. Everyone coughed until the odor expanded into the tunnel and dissipated. When he raised the torch from the pot, a dim halo of light softened the darkness.

He rose to a crouch. "Watch your head, Eve. You can't stand up all the way. You okay here, Crystal?"

Her answer was a squeaky mew. Eve reached a hand to the ceiling and got to her feet in a stoop.

He slid the katana sword out of its scabbard and held it at his side between him and the wall, ready for action. "Grab my belt in back so you don't stumble into me, and we'll head out."

"Got it—ready, Colonel, sir."

He grinned. As far as he was concerned, she could call him that all day. "Twenty steps forward, then we'll hit a sharp right turn." He refrained from adding, *Forward, march.*

At the corner, he peered back for a glimpse of Crystal. A faint glow from the rim of the pot gave the only evidence she was there. "We're going to disappear around a corner, Crystal. Hang tight until Eve comes back for you, okay?"

"I will." The courage in her voice puffed his chest with pride. It was going to be hard to leave this little gal when they got off the island.

He straightened as they entered the burial chamber, waited for Eve to do the same, and shifted to position the torch between them. "Can you see them?"

"I sure can smell them. Phew-ee! And I thought the birds were bad."

"If there's trouble, I want you to run back to Crystal and get out."

"You didn't leave me in the ocean. I'm not leaving you in the cave."

A lump formed in his throat. Sometimes the woman deserved kudos, in spite of her cussed orneriness.

He sidled around the chamber, holding the torch low to the floor to spot snakes, the katana sword ready in his right hand for an attack. When they arrived at the niches occupied by the corpses, he ignored the skeletons and checked, first quickly, then more thoroughly, for animal life in each bed. When he was sure they were in no danger, he exhaled what felt like an M1 Abrams tank. "Okay, let's light the second torch and send you for Crystal."

While Eve was gone, he gathered up bayonets and looped them in their scabbards over his neck and shoulders. A Marine could never have too many weapons.

"It's horrid," Eve warned Crystal as they joined him. The two inched toward the skeletons, Crystal hugging Eve's arm, her free hand pressed over her nose and mouth.

"It's like a haunted house at Halloween, except for the smell." Crystal glued herself to Eve's side as they examined the soldiers.

"The torches will burn out any minute now. Time to head back." He would use the last two torches to explore the escape tunnel once Crystal and Eve left.

"Wait, Jake. Over here." Eve stooped. "Another passageway. I bet it's the escape tunnel you told us about."

Great. "Probably. It's where the snakes went, anyway. I'm going to check it out as soon as you and Crystal leave."

"Not by yourself, you aren't."

He sighed. "We don't know what's in there. It might be a whole den of snakes."

"Uh-uh. This tunnel was carved to go somewhere."

"Then take Crystal back to Betty first."

"I want to go with you guys. I'm not scared."

"Oh, c'mon, Jake. Let's light the third torch and go for it. You lead the way, and we'll be fine. If something happens, I'll make sure Crystal's not hurt."

"Pleeeeeeease, Jake!"

He growled at their stubbornness, at the sputtering torch expiring in his hand, at his own reckless impatience to push ahead. "All right, give me that torch—but put plenty of space between you and me in case you need to get out of here."

He lit the third torch, handed Eve's back to her, and entered the passageway. Like the entry tunnel, this one forced him to walk at a stoop. He held the katana sword ready, every nerve end zinging on Code Alert. The monster head that had lifted from the pile of coils two weeks ago was fresh in his memory. Would his torch distinguish the snake's camouflaged skin from the gray hues of the cave walls? His mouth was dry at the prospect that it wouldn't.

"Coming in," Eve shouted behind him. Her voice reverberated off the walls. "Crystal is holding onto my waistband. My torch is about to go out, but I can see yours."

The tunnel sloped steadily upward. Pain shot up his back as he was forced to stoop lower and lower. His head scraped the ceiling and a gritty powder dropped onto his brow and eyelashes. "It's getting narrow up here. We're going to have to crawl." He lowered himself to his hands and knees. Carrying the torch in one hand and the sword in the other was awkward. Sharp cinders in the cave floor stung his knees. "Stay a safe distance back. This is going to be slow going."

The katana thudded a flat clank each time he moved forward. He had to be careful not to jerk the torch so the head wouldn't fall off, but he didn't want to go so slow it would burn out before he saw the end of the tunnel. Or ran into a snake.

"Our torch is out," Eve called, "but we can still see yours. We're on our hands and knees now."

He couldn't afford to pause and glance back. "My torch is still good."

"You okay, Crystal?" Eve asked.

"I can't see you, but I can touch your moccasin ahead of me." Crystal's voice sounded farther away than he liked. As soon as he saw the end of the escape tunnel, he'd tell them to catch up with him.

The walls began to squeeze in on him. The top of his head. Then his shoulders. "I'm on my belly now," he shouted. Why had the soldiers narrowed the tunnel? It would slow down their escape.

He scooted forward on his stomach, squinting to see what the halo of light revealed ahead of him.

The tip of his sword rammed into stone. His heart stopped. Had he been fooled into entering a faux tunnel? Was that why it narrowed—because he'd arrived at a dead end?

His torch hissed with a sudden spike of light. No! It shouldn't be dying already!

Then it clicked. Air! Somewhere, fresh air was entering the tunnel. He let go of the sword, switched the torch to his left hand, and ran his right hand over the wall. There! Partway up the wall, the tunnel turned a corner. He held the torch up to the opening. The head hissed with another spark.

His shoulders pressed too tightly against the wall for him to turn. He was like a huge human plug. "Eve, can you hear me? The tunnel turns a corner to the right up here. We're almost at the end."

"I can't see the torch anymore." Her voice was faint.

"My body is blocking it. I'll wait for you and Crystal."

"No, go ahead before the torch goes out. We're fine, aren't we, Crystal?"

He didn't hear an answer, but evidently Eve did. "She's right behind me. Go on."

The torch was burning faster with the new supply of oxygen. He should at least check out the turn in the tunnel before he had to use the torch tucked in his belt. If he could see daylight, he wouldn't need to use their last torch. "I'll go ahead a ways and make sure we're at the end."

He poked the lit torch into the hole and squirmed in after it, trying not to scrape the blade of the sword against the wall. Dust from volcanic ash sifted into his eyes, nose, and mouth as he wriggled through the tight quarters. He'd be covered with it from head to toe by the time he got out.

And there up ahead, at the top of a steep flight of stairs, was the exit. He grinned. Not far away at all. He rushed as fast as his legs could climb. With his body plugging the light, Eve wouldn't be able to see where to go.

At the top, he crawled under a short overhang of rock and stood up. A haze of sunshine lit the surroundings. The scent of flowers permeated the air. He should have known.

"I'm out!" he hollered down the hole. "I'm in the Japanese garden!"

* * *

Crystal squirmed sideways to run her palm over the bumpy cave floor. If she didn't find her sandal, she'd have to leave it behind and walk around outside with one shoe off, one shoe on. The escape tunnel was supposed to be short, not long and creepy like this one. She wiped at her eyes. She hated having to pretend to be brave, when all she wanted to do was cry.

"Still okay, Crystal?" Ahead of her, the noise of Eve's shuffling crawl stopped. "We're going to have to scoot on our stomachs from here on." A grunt followed. "Whoo, the floor is cold!"

"Wait a minute, I lost my sandal." Crystal swallowed a sob and backed up until her knee struck the hard leather sole. "Okay, I've got it now." It wouldn't slip onto her foot. If only she could sit up instead of trying to wriggle her toes into it.

The *schlip-schlip* of Eve's moccasins dragging against the floor made a different kind of echo. Like what a big snake would make. Chills ran down Crystal's spine. She pushed the sandal forward with her knee and slid her right hand into the leather straps. There, she didn't need the stupid thing on her foot anyway.

She crawled after Eve but had to flop onto her belly before her fingertips found Eve's moccasins. *Schlip, schlip.* Nothing to worry about. She gulped back the whimper scratching at her throat.

"I'm at the corner. Are you okay, Crystal?"

A corner? Crystal's heart beat faster. She bit her bottom lip to keep from yelling *Wait for meeee!* like a big scaredy-cat. She'd told them she wasn't afraid, so she'd better act like it or they'd never take her anywhere again. "I'm okay."

She wriggled forward, holding her breath as the floor pinched her bare arms and legs. "Ouch, ouch, ouch, ouch." Saying it out loud helped it not hurt so bad.

At Eve's call, she hushed. All she could hear was "see light." Eve sounded far away, but she couldn't be. Maybe it was because the corner stopped the echo from being so loud.

She scooted forward, rubbing her left palm against the wall until it slipped off into emptiness. She'd found the corner! Tears jumped to her eyes. Using both hands to define the turn, she wormed her way into it. "I'm right behind you!" She inhaled a stuttering breath of relief. Any minute now she'd see the light too.

But where, oh where was it? The tunnel tightened around her. Dust prickled into her nose, and her eyeballs stung like she was in a sandstorm. She squeezed her eyes shut and covered her nose and mouth with her free hand. It slowed her down, but that was okay. She'd get to the end, no matter how slow or fast she went.

Strange roots poked at her, so close they rubbed against her head and down her body. Good thing she had the sandal covering her hand to push them aside. If there were roots, then there was a tree somewhere above her. She must be close to the end of the tunnel. She opened her eyes. Nope, no light.

Her free hand touched one of the roots. She squealed. The root was pointed and sharp. Pinpricks zipped down her neck to her tailbone. She stuck her finger into her mouth and gagged at the taste of gritty ash soaked with blood.

A howl crashed out of her lungs, bursting from the dam where she'd stuffed the ghouls and the darkness and getting left behind. "Help!" She yelled it over and over.

"Crystal!" Jake's voice grabbed hold of her like a big hug. "I'm coming. Tell me what's wrong."

"I'm stuck."

"Can you back up?"

"No. I'm in a trap with sharp sticks."

"Don't move! Stay absolutely still until I get there."

Her chest heaved with snuffly sobs she couldn't stop. She was tired of being brave. Tired of proving herself. She was a crybaby, and she didn't care any more. From now on, she'd stay with Aunt Betty.

"I see you, Pumpkin. I'm right behind you."

She broke into fresh sobs.

His hand grasped her bare foot. "I'm sticking the torch up here so I can see. Looks like a trap, all right, but we're going to get you out just fine. Where's your other sandal?"

"In my h-hand."

"Good. I'm going to take off this one and push it up to your shoulder. See if you can reach it."

Heat from the torch warmed the back of her leg as he removed her sandal and guided it up her backbone to her neck, then sideways to her shoulder. She reached back. "I got it."

"Atta girl. Now put your hands into your sandals so you can push against the sticks and scoot ahead. Once you're away from them, I suspect you'll see the end of the tunnel and can get out."

"Nooooooo. They'll cut me. They cut my finger when I touched them." More pinpricks galloped down her spine, just thinking about the razor slice on her fingertip.

"I looked at the sticks up close, Crystal. They're bamboo, and they're cut on the side away from your body. The soldiers imbedded them in the wall at a slant so that they bend away from you when you crawl out of the tunnel. You won't get hurt, but anyone crawling into the tunnel from the outside will get stopped by the sharp points. It's only a one-way trap. The way we're going is an escape tunnel."

"I ca-a-an't." Hopelessness tumbled out of her in a cascade of tired sobs.

"Sure you can. You're already halfway through. You didn't get hurt until you touched the ends, did you? Your sandals will protect your hands now."

"No-o-o-o."

"I'll be right behind you."

Her cut fingertip tingled against the hard leather of her sandal. "I ca-a-an't, it hurts."

"Pumpkin, you can trust me. You know I'd never let anything harm you. That's why I'm here, to help you. When we get off the island, I want us to stay friends—to talk on the phone and go see each other. That's how important you are to me."

Warmth flowed into her. She could feel her heart beating, the air moving into her lungs and out again. Her bones felt strong, like maybe she could move after all. She took a big breath. "Okay, Jake."

She wedged her hands farther into the sandals and scooted forward. The bamboo brushed against her but didn't cut, just like Jake had said. The last sticks snapped the air as she left them behind. The cold floor pinched her arms and legs again, and dirt sifted into her eyes and nose—but that's what you had to expect if you went crawling through tunnels.

Ahead of her, a bubble of light shimmered. "I see the end of the tunnel, Jake."

The sticks rustled behind her as he pushed through them, grunting.

"You okay, Jake?" She giggled that now she got to ask the question that *he'd* kept asking *her*.

The exit dropped her onto a big fern. The gurgle of running water told her the stream was nearby. She sat up and shifted her sandals to her feet before standing. A moment later, Jake squirmed out of the tunnel, his shoulders squished by the narrowness of the hole. She giggled at how funny he looked, all black from head to toe.

Then she ran to his arms and cried and cried. Not because she was scared.

But because Jake had made her a promise, and she knew he'd keep it.

Chapter 34

At last, four weeks on the island and they were ready to leave! Jake tugged the lighter out of the slapping waves and up toward the tree line. His heels sank deeper into the wet sand as he braced himself against the boat's resistance. The bamboo outriggers on either side wobbled with each yank. They had worked better than he'd hoped. Once he added the sail, the boat would skim right through the choppy water. All that was left was a last trip to the volcano top, and then he and his fellow castaways would be on their way to the sea-lane.

Rain started up as he reached the tree line. With the outriggers attached, the boat was too wide to be pulled into the trees. It would fill with rainwater, and he'd have to bring a bucket to bail it out before they sailed. During the monsoon in Nam, the dampness of constant rain and mist day after day had made life miserable. Here, it was even worse, as if the island were the center of the heavens' target practice range.

He set out at a dogtrot for the cave. If the sun came out, he'd grab the binoculars and see if he could beat the next downpour to the volcano's cone. He hoped Eve wouldn't insist on joining him, or even Crystal. When he traveled alone, he could be with Ginny.

A miasma of sadness enveloped him. It absorbed him until he no longer felt the rain pounding him but became part of it. Cold. Fragmented. Spilling aimlessly. A loneliness, vaster than the universe, gripped his insides. Soon they'd be headed home. But not him. He had no home. Only an empty house.

Brett and Dana rose to mind and shook him hard. *Dad!* He blinked. He loved them, too, didn't he? Their lives were important to him. What were they doing now at the academy? How had Brett done with the rifle skills? And Dana—were the guys giving her a hard time or falling head over heels in love with her?

A sweet tenderness seeped into the hollow inside him. He'd go to the Point first thing when he got back. Maybe he'd relocate near them. They'd never get over Ginny's death, but they could comfort each other, move on with God's grace to find meaning in their lives.

The rain stopped as he approached the stream near the cave. The landscape was greening up except where the volcanic rock formed an impervious armor over the ground. In the Lone Soldier's field, the grass all but sang in the breeze. The ghoulish sentry was totally hidden from sight. If they hadn't arrived in the burn of summer, they never would have discovered him.

He entered the cave long enough to grab the binoculars. Betty was alone inside. He paused. "Sun's out. How about if I set a chair outside for you?"

She followed him, her cane tapping energetically across the floor and preceding her out the cave door like the antennae of a beetle. "Where are you off to? Eve and Crystal are making a day of gathering coconuts for the trip."

"The volcano. I'm going to check out the sea-lane—get a better idea of how far away it is and how frequently it's being used."

She let him help her into the chair, then waved him off, turning her face to the sun and closing her eyes. He appreciated that she didn't try to detain him. In the three weeks since they'd moved into the cave, she had become more and more cheerful as her mobility increased, thanks to the cane he'd carved for her. Without books to read, he found the rainy days hard to put up with, but she seemed content, whatever the weather.

Eve, though, was always uptight. She disappeared often, returning chilled, teeth rattling, to stand before the hearth fire. He knew she was counting off the days until her court date. He was too. It was now his deadline as well as hers. He'd promised he'd get her off the island in time for it.

At the volcano, he focused his attention on the horizon to the north. His heart beat wildly when he spotted a ship—a tiny dot that crawled steadily along the horizon. The vessel was barely discernable with the binoculars, but the steady, straightforward path distinguished it from a whale or other meandering object. As the day wore on, he spied two more ships. The pattern of travel was the same. It was clear they were on an ocean highway, following the shortest path through the islands to their destinations.

So he'd been right about the island being an outpost. The soldiers could readily observe and report on enemy vessels, with the advantage that the island was just far enough off the path that no one would notice it. The bad news was that at that distance, no signal fire would be noticed. A boat would need a reason to come to the island. The uninhabited beaches and cove said that so far, no one had found a cause. Even the motherland of the Lone Soldier had dismissed coming.

Rain swept in, hiding first the sea-lane, then the panorama of the island below him, and finally, everything within arm's reach. He descended the cone by touch more than sight, plastering his chest and hips against the stone, securing his foothold before releasing the grip of his fingers to search for a new hold. When the ground leveled to where he could walk, he stumbled off-course into the stream. He fell face first. The tumult of water submerged his head as if an iron hand forced him under. He came up fighting mad.

The stream would make an easy ride back if it weren't for the waterfall at the end. He fought the current and crawled onto the bank. If this was what the deluge was like on land, what would it be like in the middle of the ocean? If they left the island now, would they be safe? The question called for a hard decision.

* * *

"I saw three ships on the sea-lane." He let his excited companions chew on that part of the news. As chilled as he was, he needed the comforts of fire, chowder, and fruit before facing the second part of the news with them. The cave was filled with the damp, woody scent of the coconuts and firewood Eve and Crystal had dumped inside. Their exuberant chatter in anticipation of the trip ricocheted off the cave walls like ping-pong balls.

"I thought you were going to bring the boat to the cove." Eve pulled up a chair next to his and sat, extending her bare feet toward the coals.

"I took it out for a test run. It's ready, but I want to sail on a sunny day. Or at least start off on one so I'm pointed in the right direction."

"Today would have been perfect." She picked up a stick and jabbed it at the coals. "We shouldn't have stocked up on coconuts. We wasted the day."

"Not really. I needed to confirm the location and distance of the sea-lane. It's far. Farther than I expected."

"What difference does it make? We just head north."

Betty limped over, cane in one hand, a coconut shell of fish-fragrant chowder in the other. She handed the shell to Jake. "What's your guess at the distance?"

"Assuming the range of the binoculars is a max of thirty miles, I'd say thirty. The ships were barely discernible."

Eve shrugged. "So?"

"So, if everything went perfectly, at five knots per hour it would take six hours to reach the sea-lane. We haven't had six hours of straight sunshine since before we moved in here."

Eve quirked another shrug. "As you said, we start out in the right direction and keep going, rain or shine."

"That was my thought until the downpour on my way back from the volcano. Trouble is, we're as good as blind in the rain. There are no markers on the ocean. We could go round and round in circles. We could head the wrong direction. We could even be in the sea-lane and miss a ship passing right by us. Or worse, it could plow us under." He squared his shoulders for the reaction that was sure to come. "Trouble is, the rain has raised our risk to an unacceptable level."

"Unacceptable?" Eve jumped to her feet as if a coal had landed on her toes. "Are you saying we shouldn't go?"

Betty gaped at him. Crystal stepped next to her, her blue eyes as wide as he'd ever seen them.

"No. Well, yes. I'm saying you should stay here." He set the coconut shell down. "I'm saying I will go by myself."

"What? Why?" Eve's voice rang with bewilderment.

"Because it's too dangerous for all of us to go. In this weather, on a storm-tossed ocean, we'd each need to wear a life vest. We have two left, not four."

"Then you and I can go." Eve flung up her hands. "We'll send someone back for Betty and Crystal."

"No." His breath froze at the thought of Betty and Crystal forever stranded on the island. "If we didn't make it, chances are Betty and Crystal would never be found. That's a chance I won't take."

Betty rapped her cane on the floor. "We should all stay. What's the hurry? We have everything we need to wait out the monsoon."

"I have a deadline to meet," Jake said. He glanced at Eve. He'd made her a promise, and he would keep it.

"Foolishness!" Betty rapped her cane again. "Your life is worth more than any deadline. You'd miss it, anyway, if you died getting there."

"Jake, no." Eve shook her head. Shook it over and over, in fast little jerks. "Betty's right. It's not worth dying for."

He tossed off a laugh. "I'm not going to die. If tomorrow is sunny, I'll head out. And the day after that"—he smiled at them as if there were no question about the outcome—"we'll all be headed home."

Chapter 35

Jake awoke restless, nerves on edge like when his battalion was preparing for a sweep in Nam. The soft puffs of Betty's snores punctuated the silence of the sleeping corridor. He slipped out of bed and padded across the cold floor to the hearth for his moccasins. A faint glow painted the sky outside the three windows. His heart pounded. Unless the light was peeking from under heavy rain clouds, he'd be setting sail today.

A sharp squawk from the direction of the table startled him. He whipped around. Gulls. Three of them. The beak of the largest opened into a wide V and emitted a hiss. He sat so he faced them and hurriedly assembled his moccasins. Eve or Crystal could take care of the birds. If the weather proved fair, he wanted every available second to be aimed at the journey, not gull-chasing.

He circled to the cave door and raised it. The gulls repositioned to follow his path but didn't leave the table. He crawled outside, tipping his face upward to determine his destiny.

He got to his feet and gawked at the sky. No gray overcast. No dark clouds. Only a scattering of feathery, white ones against a brassy sky. Yet he could feel the drop in atmospheric pressure—a sure sign a storm was on its way.

He climbed to the plateau above the cave to see what an ocean view might tell him. A gust of wind tossed dried leaves and twigs at his head as he accessed the top. Kindling and some of the larger sticks lay scattered over the ground. He blinked. Eve's tidy stack of wood was in disarray.

Worse, there was no sailcloth covering it.

He spun around to scan the trench and minefield for where the wind might have dropped the sail. Nothing. He raced to the other side of the plateau. No sign of the sail on the ocean either.

He was sure he had secured the sail last night, tightly enough that the wind shouldn't have dislodged it. The wind was strong, but certainly nothing unusual for the monsoon. How could this have happened?

The answer walloped him in the stomach. *Eve!*

He dashed back down to the cave. The gulls squawked and flapped their wings but stayed on the table. He checked the sleeping ledges. His was closest to the chamber, then Eve's and Betty's and Crystal's. Only Betty and Crystal were in their beds. He checked the other six ledges. All of them were empty.

And a life vest was missing.

Betty rose to her elbow. "Gulls again? I was trying to ignore them."

"Eve's gone. And so is the sail."

"Oh, Lord, no!" She sat up. "What's the weather like?"

"Clear skies and a strong wind. She'll think that's a good sign, but I can tell a storm is coming. There's a low pressure front. And the sky's a funny color."

"Surely she'd turn back when she saw the rain clouds."

"There aren't any. Just little white ones."

Betty's hand flew to her throat. "Take me outside, Jake. I don't like the sound of this!"

"Can't. I've got to go after her."

"No, wait! If this is what I think it is from my travels, she's in big trouble. You need to know."

He huffed at the delay but picked her up and carried her past the complaining gulls to the cave door. They crawled outside.

"Do you want me to take you to the plateau?"

"No need to, Jake. That sky says typhoon. That's why those gulls are inside. They're looking for shelter."

He took off running.

* * *

Stepping from the jungle onto the beach where Betty and Crystal had landed, Jake drew in a startled breath. Dark clouds camped the sky like a bivouacked army. Beneath it, the ocean was heavy and rolling, restless with suppressed energy. The wind whipped inland, rattling the leaves on the trees. Surely Eve had caught the warning and sailed back to the island. Or maybe he was right behind her and could stop her before she left.

The noise of the coastline had changed. No gulls rode the air currents. The surf's steady lap was now a rough swash foaming at the beach's edge. Palm fronds clattered in combat. The heaviness of imminent danger permeated the air like an invisible fog. It pressed against his skin and clogged his lungs.

He ran along the edge of the beach, straining to see any movement on the ocean's surface. If Eve had made it out there, she must be attempting to return. The wind by itself would sweep her in. Or had the current caught her and was dragging her out to sea?

Halfway down the beach, the strength of the wind forced him to retreat to the tree line. He moved from tree to tree, mooring himself against the gusts. It would get worse as the center of the typhoon got closer. The wind was strong now, but not yet vicious. Typhoons advanced slowly, at a rate of seven to ten miles per hour. If he could find Eve, they could still get back to the cave before the worst of the storm hit.

Rain broke from the clouds and sliced bullets into the sand. His heart sank when he arrived at the four sticks marking the murdered sailor's grave. Sure enough, the boat was gone. A path of disturbed sand showed where Eve had tugged the lighter to the ocean.

There wasn't much he could do now. Except keep looking. He couldn't give up until it was clear she hadn't survived. If the current had caught her, she wouldn't be too far out. She could still make it back to shore.

The beach ended, and he entered the jungle. He'd traveled the boggy terrain five times now, two of them to haul bamboo for the outrigger. One time he'd ended up in the quagmire of the swamp. His hair stood on end at the memory of the crocs he'd run into. No doubt they were instinctively quiescent in the threat of a typhoon, but the ones he had seen were big guys. He didn't want to put their appetites to the test.

At the next beach, he fought the wind and rain to inspect the shoreline for the boat. The gale was pushing harder now, probably forty miles an hour. He staggered forward a step at a time. He couldn't see worth spit, but he was sure he was on the beach at the southernmost tip of the island. It was where he had dragged Eve ashore when he rescued her from the ocean. God had saved them from being swept out to sea then. *Please, God, save her again.*

He all but stumbled over the lighter. It was on its side, half submerged by the waves pounding the beach. The left outrigger was gone, and the one on the right was broken. The sail was still attached, but the mast was broken in two. Both oars were missing.

He searched around the vessel for Eve, then extended his hunt up and down the beach. Had she made it to shore with the boat, or … ? He swallowed back the thought.

"Eve!" He hollered until his throat hurt. His voice was no challenge to the gale whipping about him, but he kept at it. He plodded up and down the shoreline, tunneling through the wind, examining the churning waves pummeling the beach. His stomach was leaden when he returned to the boat and inverted it. His heart sank further when he saw the crack down the lighter's middle. He ran his fingertips over it. Numb as they were, he could still feel the split was beyond repair. The boat would probably break in two just hauling it up to the tree line.

He wrestled the waterlogged sail off and tugged it backwards over the sand toward the thrashing palm trees. Anger and grief wrestled in his gut. Anger with God for not protecting Eve; grief for the loss of her life. Anger with Eve for taking things into her own hands; grief for his failure to realize that of course she'd do that.

He entered the tree line and hunted for a place to stow the sail. Wet and heavy as it was, there was no way he could lug it back to the cave. The challenge of making it back there himself was increasing with every passing minute.

Shaking with cold, he returned to the beach to orient himself. The storm-tossed ocean frothed like a rabid dog, leaping and snarling at the black clouds overhead. The wind beat at the trees with a thousand fists and shrieked at their resistance. His legs and knees trembled. Never had he seen power like this.

"Jake!"

He spun around. "Eve?"

Was the wind fooling him? But, no, there she was, a short distance off, sitting with her back against a tree. She was slumped to one side, arms and legs sprawled, wet hair plastered against her head and face. Her hands, knees, and the lower half of her legs were caked with sand from crawling to the tree.

He ran to her and stood, heart pounding, gazing in disbelief. With all his might he wanted to grab her and shake her. Hard. "What were you were doing, taking off like that? I told you I'd—"

"It wasn't your call, Jake." Her face reddened, and her shout flamed as hot as his. "It was mine."

"Yours? I don't recall that decision."

"Do you recall I said no? That was my decision. You always assume yours overrides mine."

Acid scalded the back of his throat. "Do you realize there's a typhoon coming? Thanks to your uninformed decision, the boat is damaged beyond repair. We now have no way off this island you were so eager to leave."

The tightness in Eve's face deflated. She turned her head to the side and vomited what looked like a stomach full of salt water. For the first time, he saw the walnut-sized bump on her forehead.

"You're hurt." He knelt beside her and examined the lump. "Do you have any other injuries?"

She shook her head. "Not that I know of. I was thrown out of the boat. My head struck the edge."

He looked her over for other signs of damage. The life vest had afforded at least some protection to her vital organs. "Everything okay in there?" He tapped the vest.

"I'm fine."

"Can you walk?"

"A little ways." She let him help her to her feet.

"How about a long ways? We want to get back before the full force of the typhoon hits."

"I can't. Let's just go inland and wait it out."

"Inland is croc land."

She shook her head in obvious exasperation. "Okay, Colonel. You go your way, I'll go mine."

Flames bit the back of his throat again. "I didn't come here to leave you in the middle of a typhoon."

"Did I ask you to come? You can stop being a hero, Jake. Stop trying to save me." She leaned against the tree and slid back to a sitting position. "I'm staying here."

Before he knew what he was doing, he grabbed her by the shoulders and pulled her to her feet. "If you thought your nightmare about wolves was bad, listen to the howling of that wind! That's what you need to be afraid of! That's what's chasing us, and, like it or not, you are going with me!"

Her head rolled, and she vomited again. He stepped aside to avoid the spew but didn't let go of her. She straightened to a wobbly stand, clutching his arms. Her fingers were ice against his skin.

"Wolves?" She laughed weakly. "Okay, Jake. I'll go. At least you came, didn't you?"

His anger fizzled at the reminder of the other part of her dream. Her father had failed her. Of course she wouldn't trust easily. Life had taught her to look out for herself because no one else would.

"I'm here"—he softened his voice —"and we're going to help each other, okay? Lean against my back and reach around to clasp your hands at my waist." He rotated and felt her body slump against his spine. He reached back, grabbed her hands, and brought them together at his belt buckle. "Atta girl. Now match your steps to mine. It will take both of us to fight that wind. Both of us, you hear?"

Her answer was slurred. "Both of ush? That makes ush both colonels, you know."

Oh boy. That hit to the head really rang her bell. He dared a step forward and felt her chest heave. A spread of warmth pooled onto his back. The pungent odor of stomach contents whisked forward with the wind.

He folded her hands under his and took the next step. "No way, lady. I just now got promoted to General."

* * *

They staggered through flailing vegetation to avoid the worst of the wind while still keeping the beach in sight. More than he feared the storm, he feared the crocs. He hadn't thought to bring one weapon with him. And now he had to haul Eve's almost deadweight straight through the edge of the beasts' territory.

The beach ended, and he had no choice but to cross the patch of jungle leading to the next beach. Croc land. Nervous sweat dripped from his armpits, replacing the pelting rain.

The path he'd hewn on his previous trips lay submerged in water. After several ankle-deep steps, he stopped. Eve was slipping down his back. If he had to run, her dragging feet wouldn't just slow him; they'd be a handle for croc teeth.

"Eve, I need you to put your arms over my shoulders." He crouched, scooting her higher onto his back as she flopped one arm and then the other onto either side of his neck. He grasped her forearms at his shoulders and stood. Her feet fluttered helplessly against the backs of his calves.

"Can't walk," she protested.

"You can walk when we get to the next beach. Right now I want you to keep an eye out for crocs."

"Like that one?" She slapped her left elbow against his shoulder.

He swiveled in a half-turn. A blur of gray parted the reeds at a distance in a dead aim for them.

Adrenalin jump-started him into a run that would have won the gold medal in the one hundred meters. The hurdles too. He pumped muscle, leaped fallen branches, and ran like he'd never run before.

Only you can't outrun a croc in its own territory.

The thought sank in as his chest squeezed out the last molecule of oxygen in his lungs. He inhaled desperately, mouth wide, throat burning. He toppled to his knees and let go of Eve to break his fall.

Eve's shriek matched the wind's. Her nails scratched through his shirt as she slid down his back. *God, no!* The croc had her!

He scrambled to his feet and whirled, still gasping, to face the beast. Eve lay on the path, struggling to get to her knees, swiping mud off her face. There was no croc.

He didn't wait to see why. "Run!" He swept her up, heaved her over his shoulder, and staggered forward. Ten steps and the wind hurled them off his feet. Sand, coconuts, and palm fronds assaulted them as he fell. They had reached the beach.

"You okay?"

Eve answered him with a groan and dry heaves.

He barely had enough energy to drag her out of missile range. He set her down and slumped against a palm, facing inland toward the bog while he caught his breath. A pile of coconuts next to him was ammunition in case of a croc invasion, though he doubted the reptiles would venture out this far. Not with a typhoon working up its own appetite.

"We've got to go. We still have time." The rest of the journey would be a piece of cake compared to this.

The fury of the storm hit as they approached the ocean cliff. The path he'd created around it proved no protection. They went inland into unfamiliar territory, where the canopy battled the storm for them. Except for the howl of the wind and the tremor of the trees, there was no sign of life. The monkeys and other canopy-dwellers had fled. Exhausted, Jake fell asleep, cushioning Eve's head on his thigh.

The quiet woke him. He roused Eve. "The eye is here. We've got to get down to the cove before the typhoon hits again."

The nap had done Eve as much good as it had him. Although still woozy, she insisted on stumbling after him, leaving him free to hunt the trail he had marked. They emerged at the top of the ocean cliff and gazed with astonishment at the clear sky forming a crystal blue dome over beaches strewn with debris and fallen trees. The ocean, however, strained in huge waves that said the storm wasn't over.

"The eye won't last long." He forced himself to keep a pace Eve could match. "We'd better get to the cove before the wind starts up again. We don't want it to catch us on that open field."

The descent proved too much for Eve's shaky legs. He helped her climb step by step down the rocky path to the stream. They paused for a drink, but it didn't stay in Eve's stomach. She hung her head and gasped shallow breaths.

"We're almost there," he soothed her. "Just a few more steps."

At the trench, she collapsed. He carried her the rest of the way to Betty and Crystal's welcoming arms. She was out cold, and his stomach buzzed with worry that she had internal injuries.

Chapter 36

Eve shrank from the coconut shell of sea chowder Betty thrust in her face. "No thanks." Her stomach lurched at the reminder of ocean water scouring salt up her esophagus the whole trip back from the boat yesterday. She'd slept all day, but tonight, as soon as everyone joined her at the hearth, she wanted to apologize for wrecking the boat—and their best chance to leave the island. Her failure sat heavily on her stomach, as bitter as the salt the ocean had forced down her throat.

"You haven't eaten anything all day." The shell teetered as Betty set it at Eve's feet.

"Can't." How could she, when Romero's trial would proceed without her now? Everyone thought she was dead.

Crystal approached and with a loud clatter dumped an armload of wood onto the floor. She sighed heavily and sat to feed the branches one at a time into the fire. "I'm bored. Jake, can you finish telling us the story about you and Ginny?"

"Don't pester him, child." Betty lowered herself into the chair next to Crystal and yawned.

The yawn meant Betty would be heading to bed in minutes. If Eve were going to apologize, she'd better do it now.

But she couldn't roll the two-ton rock off her chest. She gazed glumly at the coals sparking red in the intermittent gusts from the windows. None of the others had a stake in the boat like she did. What did they care, really? Only she had a reason to get back home. Frustration pinched her stomach.

"I don't mind, Betty. I like talking about Ginny." Jake took a seat on the other side of Eve and put his bare feet on the hearth's edge. The four of them sat side-by-side so the caldron afforded some protection from the wind and rain whistling through the windows.

Jake stretched his arms toward the coals and wiggled his fingers. "I told you about our time at the fair. Ginny never would date me, but we became good friends. I found every excuse I could to be with her. I sat next to her in school, walked down the hall with her between classes, asked to study with her for exams. I even drove all the way out to where she lived to help with odd jobs around the place. Her father was an inventor and was often away on business. There was always something I could do. I had a schoolboy's crush and was madly in love with her. I was sure that somehow I would find a way to win her."

He withdrew his arms to his sides. "Then tragedy struck. At the beginning of Ginny's senior year, both her parents died in an accident. Her only surviving relative was her grandmother, who was in a nursing home."

"Poor thing," Betty murmured.

"Did Ginny have to move away?" Crystal stopped poking the fire to wait for Jake's answer.

"No. Permission was given for her to live with a family that belonged to her church so she could complete her senior year." Jake fell silent.

"Let me guess." Betty leaned forward in her chair to peer at him. "It changed things between you and Ginny."

"Yes. The Millers—the family she lived with—were stricter than her parents had been and didn't want us getting together outside of school. When it was time to leave for college, Ginny told me it was best not to see each other or even correspond."

"That stinks!" Crystal jabbed a branch at the coals.

"I told her I loved her and wanted to marry her. But she said our relationship could go nowhere and now was a good time to end it. I was crushed, but what could I do? I went on to college and concentrated on my studies and athletic scholarship. I did my best to forget her. Then, in my sophomore year, I roomed in a dorm suite with three guys on my wrestling team, and guess what?"

Crystal giggled. "I know. They were all Christians."

"You're right. God used them to wrestle me to the mat and pin me. I asked Jesus to be my Savior and turned my life over to Him."

Eve suppressed a groan.

"So you called Ginny and finally got together?" Betty grinned at her guess.

"Nope. I figured God had firmly closed the door on any romance between us. But as it turned out, Ginny was meant to be part of my life after all. My father died of cancer while I was in college. Ginny came to his funeral and I told her I'd become a Christian."

Jake's voice broke. "My dad was the best. He'd have been happy to know he brought Ginny and me together."

Eve squirmed at the grief in his voice. The ache pinching her stomach catapulted into her heart. Except now the pain wasn't about missing the trial. It was about something worse. Something far worse. She quelled a sob that rose to her throat.

"I'm turning in." Jake rose abruptly to his feet. His chair rocked backwards. He righted it and left without another word.

Crystal and Betty gazed in silence at the fire. Seconds later, they followed him, bidding Eve good-night.

She eased the bumpy route of her pain with a deep sigh. Well, so much for apologizing about the boat. Didn't matter. There'd be lots more nights they'd sit around with nothing to do, thanks to her. The apology wouldn't mean much to them, anyway. Once the typhoon hit, Jake and Betty had resigned themselves to waiting out the monsoon season. If anything, they would try to console her, maybe ask questions about why she'd been so determined to attend this mysterious court date.

Should she just tell them everything, come clean now that they'd be stuck together for who knew how many months?

The pain scuttled back to her stomach. And have Jake hate her day after day all those months? How many times had he rescued her? Each one would be a knife in his heart that he hadn't saved his wife but had saved the person behind his wife's death. Eve slumped forward and wrapped her arms around her chest.

No, if he was this emotional about his father's death from more than twenty years ago, he certainly wasn't going to be understanding about the circumstances of Ginny's death. The only reasonable course of action was to bide her time until they got off the island.

The ache snaked back to her heart, jolting the emotion aroused by Jake's unfinished story. Something … She swallowed as the ache crept up and squeezed her throat. Something about Jake and his father. The respect, the tenderness that had choked Jake's voice … She clapped her hands over her face. Her father. It was about her father.

She hated him.

The pain twisted inside her like a buried dagger, scarred over but never removed. She had pushed it away and pushed it away, put it out of her mind, interred it in a tomb of forgetfulness. But it was still there.

She sat up, ramrod straight. All right, then, it was time to deal with the issue. Get over it. Move on.

She clenched her teeth. At the boat yesterday, Jake had brought up her dream. That was her clue. The ache thudded heartbeats in her ears as she forced herself to think through the nightmare. Wolves. Wolves caught her. Were they her father, something he had done? No. The answer was solid, sure. The tightness in her throat loosened.

What, then? Again, with equal clarity, the answer asserted itself: not what he'd done, but what he hadn't done. Some way he hadn't been there for her. Some way he had abandoned her. Rejected her for something else.

Bile curdled at the back of her throat. What? she yelled at herself. She placed herself on the witness stand—young, a child, maybe Crystal's age. *What?* she yelled at her. The child cowed. She was only scaring her with the yelling. *What?* she pleaded. The child stared back with blank eyes. She wasn't going to tell. Couldn't tell. The child couldn't see what the "what" was.

Eve stood up. Sweat coated her skin. Her body shook. *It's okay*, she soothed the child. *It's okay that you don't know. It will come.* She felt that with certainty. The answer would come.

The island would give it to her.

* * *

Jojo walked down to the harbor in Manila and sat on a piling. Sea gulls circled the dock, squawking. Pools of captured ocean water and dead seaweed dotted the beachfront. The smell of the ocean was strong, freshly released from the turmoil that had battered the harbor and the city beyond it.

Exhilaration pounded his nerves. The first typhoon of the season had come and gone. The power, the relentless violence, was his power too. Four more months it would build. And build. Build until the monsoon ended, and he took his first step. With spring would come the big, fancy yachts to fill the empty slips in the marina. This year he would examine each slick vessel until the right one came along. This year, for sure, he'd find it and make it his. This year he was ready.

The harbor had become his at age six. He'd sat on the wharf and kicked his legs and waited. Waited for his father. His mother had described him. Tall, with wavy blond hair, handsome like Clint Eastwood. And rich. His stomach squeezed with excitement. A rich *americano* with a big, fancy, white yacht.

She told the story over and over, how she had waited on the handsome man in the bar of the restaurant he and his friends frequented. She was young and slim then, with large, brown eyes that gazed yearningly after him. She'd had all her teeth then, too, and they were white like oyster pearls. Whenever the *americano* looked at her, she smiled. At last, he invited her to come aboard his big boat to tend bar at a bash he gave for his friends.

When the party was over, he came to her drunk and paid her for her services. It hadn't been hard to end up in his bed. She didn't stay until morning because she didn't want the crew to find her, but when she went back after work, the beautiful boat was gone. Nine months later, Jojo was born. Stupid woman, she didn't even know the name of his father. But he'd come back. And he'd recognize his son. His mother said they looked just like each other in the face.

But not any more. Jojo ran his beefy hand over the stubble on his cheeks and chin. His mother said he was ugly with his face cut up and scarred. Six of his teeth were knocked out in prison brawls.

So what. His father wasn't coming for him.

And that didn't matter either. Jojo flicked his tongue over his lips. He couldn't have a father, but he could have a yacht.

He had two of the crew picked out to run the boat. And he had the island picked out to hide on—right at the outermost edge of the Philippines, complete with a cove to hide in.

This year he was ready.

PART 2

January–June
1982

Chapter 37

The island bustled with spring like a young bride unpacking her honeymoon trousseau. Every breath Jake took was fresh with the scent of flowers and warm sunshine nursing tender green shoots. Wildlife teemed everywhere he went. Three days of exploring the awakening island brought him back to the cave with news he could hardly wait to share.

The evening sky, released from four months of monsoon cloud cover, sparkled in pinpricks of starlight. The cave door stood open and warmth flooded his chest that three people dear to him awaited his arrival. The red glow of coals highlighted their figures as they rushed to greet him. His heart caught at how their clothes hung on them like handouts two sizes too big from a refugee bin.

Crystal hugged him. Betty fetched him a cup of her seafood chowder. Eve scooted a chair out from under the table for him. He sat, inhaling the tangy aroma of the soup, the smell of charcoaled wood embedded in the cave walls, the odor of sweaty bodies subdued by the coolness of the cave. For the first time in three days, he felt at peace.

With a start, he realized the cave was home now. He'd been eager to escape its imprisonment, its monotony of month after month of monsoon dampness and incessant chatter from his roommates. The three days of freedom, however, proved the real prison. His ache for Ginny when he'd been alone day after day hollowed out his insides. Raw despair drove him back to the cave, thankful for his three companions. With them, he could forget the sharp blade of grief piercing his heart. He could go on living.

With them, he had a purpose for his life. Save them. Protect them. Bring them back unharmed to civilization.

He sipped his soup while they reported on cultivating the Japanese garden during his absence. Ginny had been like that, needing to unburden herself of her news before she could listen to his.

Three bowls of soup later, his turn arrived. They gathered around him with faces expressing eagerness for his news now that theirs was depleted. "First thing I did," he said, "was check out the stand of bamboo I used to build the outriggers. Unfortunately, the typhoons had destroyed it. I found three others with culms that might be the perfect size for a raft, but they're still growing. It may be months before they're the right height."

Eve's shoulders slumped. "So we sit around some more."

She hadn't complained once during the long wait for the monsoon to end—Jake had to give her credit for that. Still, restless tension had been evident every day in her voice, the way she chopped fruit, her solitary walks on the beach in spite of the driving rain. Whatever was supposed to have happened on the missed court date in August, clearly she hadn't given up on it.

"No sitting around at all. I found mahogany stumps in the swamp—"

Eve's head jerked up, and he hurried to finish before she could interrupt him. "The trees might have been cut by the Japanese soldiers, but there are enough stumps it could also mean loggers have been to the island. We need to start our shipwatch at the volcano top again and get the signal fire going."

"Do the cuts look recent?" Eve frowned, but her voice had no edge to it. "Could loggers have come and gone without our knowing it?"

"No." He emphasized the word. It would be just like her to insist they move to set up camp at the swamp. "Enough time has gone by that the bog almost covers the stumps. No one would have waded in there who didn't want to be croc meat. But younger mahoganies are nearby. They might be worth a logging ship's return."

"I'll start the shipwatch tomorrow." Eve paused. "Unless you want to."

Ah, now for the news he was truly excited about. "No, go ahead. I'm going to try my hand at catching a deer." He grinned as their mouths fell open.

"Deer? Jake, you're full of surprises." Betty's thin chest rose and fell with a half laugh. "You saw deer?"

"Not deer, but their scat at the pool. I suspect spring is pushing the wildlife into new territory and we'll see animals we never guessed existed here."

"Fresh venison." Eve's sigh bordered on a gleeful moan. "How will you catch it?"

"Since we don't have suitable weapons for hunting, I'm doing it caveman style. I'm digging a pit."

Crystal's gasp swallowed half the air in the cave. "What if a tiger or something falls in instead?"

Betty huffed. "Crystal, you know tigers don't live in the Philippines."

Crystal snapped back. "I told you I've heard something when I gather fruit. Not a roar, but a yowl, sorta high and screechy like a cat."

"Yes, and Eve told you she's heard it too, that it's some kind of monkey." Betty scowled. "There are no big cats in the Philippines—no lions or tigers or leopards or cheetahs or anything like that."

Crystal's lower lip shoved out. Jake took one of her hands in his. He wasn't the only one feeling the effects of being cooped up for four months. "I'll keep an ear out for your critter while I dig tomorrow. No telling what new animals we'll encounter now that spring is here."

Crystal's glare stabbed all three of them. "It wasn't a monkey."

Jake squeezed her hand. One thing he'd learned in Nam was to never discount another person's fear, no matter how illogical it seemed. He'd do well to apply it to this island too.

* * *

The game trail sloped from a densely timbered hillside to a shallow ravine dominated by a lone buttress tree. Jake stood under the tree where the path curved toward the waterfall pool. Perfect. The thick undergrowth molded the trail into a chute that would force his prey to walk straight into his trap. Trouble was, he needed to get it dug by the end of the day. Any longer, and his presence at nightfall would scare the deer into finding another way to the pool.

He marked out a rectangle roughly four by six feet, then used the pick to loosen the dirt, a shovel to heave it, and the axe to hack away roots. The topsoil was easy, barely an inch deep. Beneath it, the island's volcanic rock was soft and porous, but difficult to work with because of the sharp cinders that scratched his skin. The damp material dried quickly in the heat and turned into dust that irritated his eyes and congested his lungs. Before long, his skin, hair, and clothes were black from the mixture of sweat and dirt. At least there were benefits—the dirt formed a second skin that thwarted the cloud of pesky insects hovering around him.

He paused only to hydrate and eat the fruit and fish he'd brought. When the pit was deep enough that his fingertips barely reached the top edge, he carved footholds on either side of the far corner to climb out. Rays from the sun, parked directly over the buttress tree, declared the day half gone. His arms and back ached, but there was no time to rest.

A mountain of excavated dirt blocked the path. He covered his nose and mouth with his shirt against the cloud of dust he'd raise, and flung shovelful after shovelful into the undergrowth. When the path was clear, he dragged branches to the pit and wove a framework across the hole. It had to be strong enough to hold a camouflage layer of dirt and leaves, but frail enough to collapse under an animal. The scat and hoof prints at the pool indicated the deer were small, perhaps no larger than a Great Dane, but lighter in weight. The victim would have to fall immediately, before it could gather its wits and leap across.

Dead leaves from the buttress tree covered the game trail, making his last task of disguising the pit easy. He stood at the top of the timbered incline and squinted down the path at his finished handiwork, half admiring it, half worried he'd miscalculated the correct dimensions. Would a deer fall in, only to escape with a simple bound? Or would the lingering scent of a human deter any deer from coming in the first place?

* * *

He awoke before sunrise, aglow with anticipation. He tied on his moccasins, remembering how as a young boy he'd rise at daybreak during duck hunting season to check the rural ponds. The thrill of imminent discovery had heightened every nerve ending as he crept up and over a pond's dam, wary not to be spotted by his prey. He never knew what he'd encounter, a flock or empty water.

Was this morning too soon? Would he discover the trap empty, dismantled by a civet or other animal heavy enough to fall in but nimble enough to climb out? Questions lined up like dominoes that needed only to be tipped against each other to fall in a clatter.

He strapped the katana sword onto his back and, as an extra precaution, a bayonet onto each thigh. At the last second, he grabbed the axe. There was no leftover fruit on the table to eat, but his stomach was too jumpy to want it anyway. He left, paused long enough to drink at the stream, then sloshed uphill against the tumbling current.

Entering the rain forest was like crossing an invisible line after the wide, open space of beach and field and ocean. The rain forest was a cocoon of warm, humid air framed in by a wall of perpetual shadows. The only illumination was a haze of sunlight that slipped unbidden between the layers of leaves and down and around the columns of tree trunks. A cacophony of noise echoed from the high reaches of the canopy. This was a world alive, but in hiding. Jake's nerves tingled on high alert.

He intersected the game trail and stepped with the light tread of a cat over the tamped earth. Halfway up the timbered incline that dipped on the other side to his pit, a bellow like a calf's rose on the air. His heartbeat doubled. He'd caught his deer!

At the top of the hill, he halted. The hoots and clamor from the canopy were absent. The deer's plaintive call echoed in a dome of silent treetops. Nothing moved. The dried leaves on the game trail, the green brush on either side of it, the huge buttress tree—none of them fluttered or waved or rustled. Everything was as still as a painted canvas. The back of his neck prickled.

Silly to be spooked. He wasn't in Nam. No sniper held him in his sights.

He resisted the urge to slip out the katana sword and strode to the pit to stand at its edge. The framework had imploded. Branches and broken sticks and dry leaves lay scattered across the black soil of the hole. Below him, huddled against the wall, a small, dark brown deer with antlers knelt on one front leg, the other leg extended at an awkward angle. Foam dripped from its mouth, and its chest shuddered in gasps between its wails.

Jake leaned closer. Those cries weren't from pain. They were from fear.

An angry, high-pitched yowl pierced the air. Jake's nerves flashed lightning hot. Every hair on his body stood on end. Before he could straighten, something heavy thudded onto his back. Needles dug into his shoulders and buttocks.

He ducked his head as the weight of his attacker impelled him headfirst into the pit.

Chapter 38

Years of wrestling clicked an automatic response. Jake tucked his head into a wrestler's forward kip and somersaulted to land with a whop on his back on top of his attacker. A stunned yowl from beneath him morphed into a shriek. Jake shot feet and hands in a spread-eagle to the pit walls and pressed his weight down hard onto the writhing lump. Whatever kind of animal it was, there would be no win for Jake if it gained its feet.

The needle-sharp claws embedded in Jake's shoulder blades and buttocks dug deeper as he bore down. He clenched his jaws against the white-hot pain sparking behind his eyelids and pushed harder. The animal's breath was hot on the back of his neck, but its teeth made no contact. The sword handle must have caught the animal's open mouth and was pinning its jaws open. The harder Jake pressed down on the animal, the closer he would bring his neck to its teeth. He'd have to ease up.

The bellowing deer, its injured leg caught under Jake's shoulder, lunged at Jake's head. He jerked his face to the other side and felt an antler shear skin from the back of his neck. Before the deer could pull away, Jake whipped his head back around and imprisoned the prong against the katana handle. Now there was the double impediment of sword handle and antler protecting his neck. The animal pinned beneath him shrieked and struggled harder.

Jake gasped in a lungful of air to exert more pressure on top of the animal. His arms and legs trembled with the effort. The deer's frantic lunges to free its antler were loosening the pressure of Jake's head against its prong. And the animal beneath him was squirming closer to escape.

Help me! I can't leave the women to die!

The animal gave a sudden shove against Jake's back. He felt its hips wriggle free. The end of a long, ropy tail lashed the wall from side to side.

The air whooshed from Jake's lungs. A cat—he was fighting some kind of big cat!

He gasped a lungful of air, stoked by the identity of his attacker. This was no mere scrap with an animal he could chase away. Only one of them would get out of this alive.

The hard lump of the cat's head had slid down to Jake's shoulders. His neck was no longer a target. With relief, he released the deer's prong.

The cat wriggled lower. Its breathing was rapid, grasping for air. But still its body inched downward. It would be out from under Jake long before he could suffocate it.

He would have to take a risk. His legs were shaking so badly they'd soon be useless.

In one swift movement, he let go of the wall, grabbed a bayonet from each thigh, and aimed their steel tips on either side of him into the cat's ribs.

The animal screamed. Its claws dug deeper into Jake's flesh, driving a shriek from his own lungs. He squeezed his eyes shut against the searing flames and locked his mind onto a single goal. Find the vital organs.

Over and over he plunged the thin blades into the cat, tilting first to one side, then to the other, to expose its ribs to the bayonets. Blood soaked his hands. The raging cat wriggled lower and lower. Any minute its imprisoned jaws would reach the end of the katana sheath and be free to sink into the small of Jake's back.

He jammed the blades higher into the cat's rib cage. Why wasn't he hitting its heart? Its lungs?

The cat's hind claws embedded in Jake's buttocks slipped free and raked down the backs of his thighs. Fire streaked from his rump to his knees. He screamed, for a moment loosening his hold on the bayonets.

This was it. With a last surge of strength, he thrust the two bayonet blades deeper into the cat. In his mind, he inched their tips together. Inched them through heart and lung. Inched them to touch in a kiss of death.

The cat coughed a raspy gag. Its fangs pinched Jake's spine as they slid clear of the katana sheath. Jake stiffened, waiting for the teeth to crunch down. His fingers gripped the bayonets, buried them deeper into the cat's heaving sides. If he died, the cat died with him.

The cat's hind legs slackened. Dropped. Its body shuddered.

Jake held his breath. Waited to make sure. His feet slid numbly down the wall. His legs collapsed against coarse fur. The cat didn't move. Still, Jake couldn't let go of the bayonets.

Above him, the rectangle of sky and buttress tree branches flickered with light and shadow. Bird calls and monkey hoots echoed from the canopy. The scent of blossoms and green leaves drifted down from the underbrush. The jungle had resumed its life.

He inhaled a slow, shuddering breath and turned his face toward the deer. Its head lolled near Jake's. A whisper of air wheezed from its throat. It no longer stood on its hind haunches but had slumped flat to the floor.

He unlocked his grip on the bayonet handles finger by finger. His hands dropped to the cinder floor like dead geese onto a duck pond. He grunted, raised his left arm, and rolled off the cat, away from the deer.

The cat rolled with him.

Jake's heart slammed into his ribs. He grabbed the katana sword from its sheath, only to knock his fist into the wall crowding his head. The sword clattered to the floor. To fetch it, he had no choice but to keep rolling, putting the cat on top of him.

The thought of fangs sinking into his neck sent his adrenaline pumping. He whipped onto his side far enough to snatch up the sword and spun back. But instead of facing the cat, he rolled onto its body. Pain spiked to a new peak as the cat's claws once again jabbed into his shoulder blades.

His head swam. The cat was dead, but its claws still held him captive. He inhaled diaphragm-crunching breaths and rolled to his side. Gritting his teeth, flinching with each prod of the sword, he pried the claws free.

Pain rode over him like an armored tank. He lay flat on his stomach and breathed heavy swallows of air until his head stopped reeling. Blood trickled down his sides from the wounds in his shoulder blades. The furrows raked down his thighs by the cat's hind claws throbbed. The palms of his hands stung with scratches from pressing them against the wall's sharp cinders. The gouge in his neck from the deer's prong burned like someone held a smoldering rod to it.

But he was alive.

Thank You. He closed his eyes and let his trembling body, alive against all odds, be his prayer. Slowly, his breath steadied. His head cleared. Strength seeped into his bones and sinews.

He rose to his hands and knees and opened his eyes to gaze at his assailant. It was a cat, all right—a leopard. Its coat was patterned in darkly outlined ovals, the largest running along the spine and graduating into smaller ovals as they descended toward the belly. Stunned, he recognized the animal from pictures in his travel catalogues. It was a clouded leopard, native to Southeast Asia, but certainly not to the Philippines. How had it gotten to this island?

Flies swooped in on the carcass like bombers on an air raid. No way—this prize was his! He removed the bayonets and lifted the cat to the edge of the pit and shoved it out. He wasn't leaving the deer behind either. He put it out of its misery with the axe. Boosting it out proved another matter. Its weight had to be three times that of the cat. The strain of heaving it out sent fresh blood flowing from his shoulder wounds. He sat with his back against the wall to shield his injuries from the flies, and put his head down. When the dizziness left, he retrieved his weapons and climbed out of the pit.

Around him, the jungle sang. The island hailed him. Victorious conqueror, give glory to your God! He swatted flies and laughed. It was good to be alive. Good to feel joy in his heart. Good to be God's beloved.

He reassembled his weapons, draped the cat around his neck, and grabbed the deer's antlers to drag it behind him. He staggered forward, an entourage of flies attending him.

Now to see if the victory included making it all the way back to the cave.

Chapter 39

At the slope descending into the trench, the weight of the deer took charge. It tumbled into Jake and sent him and the cat somersaulting. The flies lifted in an angry buzz and resettled. There was no getting away from them. Fresh blood gushed from the wounds on his shoulders. He stood, but fell to his knees and vomited. Hail the conquering hero.

He dropped the animals outside the cave door. Blood soaked his shirt, plastering it to his back. Someone needed to sew him up before the flies became the victors.

Mercifully, the cave door was open. He didn't have to work the pulley, just crawl through once he got his gear off. "Hello?" His voice was barely a whisper. With painstaking effort he peeled off the sword and bayonets. Somewhere along the path, he had dropped the axe.

"Betty?" he croaked. "Eve? Crystal?"

No answer. He crawled inside and found the cave empty. Dimly, he recalled their plan to go to the Japanese garden this morning.

He staggered to his feet and leaned against the wall to thwart the flies that had followed him inside. The fight with the leopard had taken him to his limit. Getting back to the cave had pushed the limit further. No way was he going to make it to the garden for help.

Sleep. He lurched toward the sleeping hall but crumpled to the floor before he got as far as the table. The coolness was a shock to his skin. He rolled onto his back to let it soothe the fire in his shoulder blades and legs.

A shriek cut the air. Crystal scurried into the cave. "There's a—"

"'S okay," he interrupted. "They're dead." He pushed himself up to a sitting position. Crystal's shape blurred in the light of the doorway. He blinked, but she stayed fuzzy.

"'M hurt—need help. Get"—Jake wracked his brain—"Eve." Or was it Betty who mended their ragged shirts and shorts? The room spun. "Hurry."

Crystal sprinted out the door. She shrieked again as she passed the animals. It hurt too much or he would have laughed. He sure loved that little girl.

So tired. He closed his eyes, felt himself topple. Didn't matter. What he needed was sleep.

Stupid flies. He slapped at the air.

* * *

"Jake?" Eve scanned the interior of the cave, impatient for her eyes to adjust to the dark. Her chest heaved from the mad dash down the mountainside. Would she even hear him over her thundering heartbeat? Crystal had said he was on the floor. On the floor! That alone said her help was urgent.

The murmur of blowflies led her to him. Nasty things! She grabbed the broom and swatted at them until they rose in counterattack. Spying Jake folded sideways on the floor, she cried out and beat furiously at them. They circled and came back to the fray, but her intensity finally won out.

"Jake!" She dropped beside him and probed for a pulse in his neck. The blood on the leopard's carcass outside told her the cat wasn't the only victim.

He was alive, but his heartbeat was faint. "Jake, help me." She slung his left arm across her shoulders and pulled his chest off the floor. His head wobbled. "Help me, Jake. We need to get you up."

He stirred, raised his head. "'N my back. Need t'sew my back."

Her stomach jumped in protest. She was no surgeon. "Let's get you to the table and see what you're talking about."

She fell on top of him at the first attempt to raise him. His yelp told her his injuries were more than scratches. Her arms and chest came away sticky with blood. She didn't dare wait for Betty and Crystal to arrive to help her.

On the second try, Jake staggered to his feet but toppled her. She rose quickly and supported him in a slow shuffle to the table. As gently as she could, she lowered him onto the table on his stomach and helped him crawl all the way onto the bamboo slats.

The firelight flickered on shirt and shorts soaked with blood. She'd have to cut away the back of his shirt to reveal his injuries. His shorts were already torn open at the legs. Her hands trembled as blood pooled onto the table between the slats. She had to hurry.

She poured the last of their drinking water into a pot, set it on the coals to boil, and made a quick mental list: disinfect needles and fishline in case she needed to sew him up. Also boil something to clean his wounds. His shirt. She would use that since there was no other cloth available.

No need to disinfect a knife. She shuddered. At least she wouldn't be cutting into him. Sewing him up had to be better, if that was what was required. She cut a length of fishline, dropped it into the pot of water along with several needles, and steeled herself to slice away his bloody shirt.

He'd said his injuries were on his back, but where on his back? The shirt was matted to his skin. None of it looked bloodier than any other part. She settled on cutting the side and shoulder seams to remove the shirt, first from his chest, then from his back. That would give her two pieces of cloth to work with.

When she tugged the front part of his shirt free, his body was deadweight, his breathing steady. Good. If he was unconscious, he wouldn't feel her peel off the back part stuck to his injuries.

Tears streamed from her eyes as she nudged the material away from his spine and shoulders, only to send new blood prickling through the old. "Oh, Jake! Look at you! First the dog, now a cat!"

She fetched the needles and fishline from the steaming water and dropped in the two pieces of Jake's shirt. The water burst into brilliant crimson. How long before they were disinfected? After a restless minute, she fished out one piece, let it cool briefly, and gingerly bathed Jake's back and rump. She alternated the cloths, washing and rinsing, washing and rinsing until at last she uncovered the four wounds.

The scratches on his buttocks had stopped bleeding, but not the wounds on his shoulder blades. She threaded a needle, took a deep breath, and—as fast as she could—sewed the slashes closed. She willed Jake not to wake up. *How can you believe in a God who let this happen to you?* Her whole body shook by the time she sopped up the blood on the table and spread the two rinsed cloths over his sutures to keep the flies off.

"We're here." Crystal poked her head into the cave.

She'd forgotten about Betty and Crystal. Her world had narrowed to Jake's mauled back and the bloody needle and thread pinched between her thumb and forefinger. Had it been minutes or hours? "I'm at the table." Her voice trembled in sync with her body.

"Eve?" Betty crawled in after Crystal and got to her feet. "Are you okay?"

"No." She choked back tears. "I had to sew him up. The leopard got him bad. Really bad, really deep." She looked down at her hands. Jake's blood had stained them pink. "I've never sewn up a person before." In spite of herself, she broke into sobs.

"Run and get water, Crystal. You don't need to cry too." Betty handed the bucket to the child and hobbled over to Eve. "You were brave to do that, very brave. I don't think I could have done it."

Eve blubbered as Betty put both arms around her. Betty's frail body was warm and smelled of flowers and earth and sweaty underarms. Eve clasped her tightly to her chest and sobbed.

When Crystal returned with the bucket, Eve dribbled clean water over her hands and splashed the tears from her face while Betty and Crystal checked on Jake.

Betty lifted the cloths one at a time and peered under them. "Looks like you did a good job. From what I can see, the bleeding has stopped and he's sleeping just fine. When he wakes up, we can move him to his bed. Doesn't look like he'll want to sit on that backside for a while."

In spite of herself, Eve laughed.

"Let's get at those animals now and reward this poor man for his wounds." Betty patted Eve's arm. "Are you up to it, dearie, or do you want to rest?"

"Anything to get rid of these flies."

They went outside and examined the animals. The leopard's paws and claws were red with Jake's blood, but there was none on its mouth. She shivered at the size of its fangs. Jake wouldn't be here if the leopard had sunk those ivories into him. "It jumped onto his back but didn't bite him."

Betty held up the katana sword. "Look at the hilt, all chewed up. Jake must have stopped those teeth with it somehow." She dropped it and swatted away flies to pick up the two bayonets. "Completely covered in blood. That's how he killed it, with these." She thumped the leopard's side with a bayonet. The flies heaved upward like a cape caught in the wind, giving a momentary glimpse of the carcass before they resettled. "There, in its sides."

"So what do we do with them?" Eve stepped away from the incessant buzz, from the two mounds of insect-crawling-over-insect. "I don't know a thing about how to skin a cat or butcher a deer." But she did know how to pitch the whole mess over the cliff.

"We'll do our best, just like you did with sewing up Jake. Crystal, fetch something to keep the flies off us while Eve and I haul Jake's prizes down to the beach." Betty set her jaws in a tight clench against the swarm of flies, snagged the cat's tail in one hand, her cane in the other, and set off at a careful limp down the rocky path to the cove.

The deer's antlers stuck out of the packed flies like the mast of a ship in a storm-tossed ocean. Eve sighed. There was nothing to do but grab ahold of the prongs, swat a windshield-wiper space in front of her eyes, and trudge after the determined old woman.

"You and Jake can make moccasins from the deer hide, and that shirt of yours has faced its last mending. I expect Jake will need new clothes now too." Betty sounded as gleeful as if they were heading off on a shopping spree.

Crystal loped onto the beach, dragging a palm frond almost twice her size. She stuck the woody stem into the sand, stood the branch upright, and waved the frond sideways, back and forth over a wide swathe of sand. Clever. Both animals fit under the child's gyrating fan.

With the flies effectively distracted, Eve and Betty skinned the pelt from the leopard and the hide from the deer. Betty and Crystal then scraped the flesh off the skins and stretched them out to dry while Eve took on the task of cutting up the deer and spearing the meat onto branches for roasting. She and Crystal disposed of the carcasses while Betty set the meat to cook. They'd never eat it all before it spoiled, but Eve was glad for the challenge.

She checked on Jake every chance she got. He never moved, never shifted his position on the table. His stillness jammed her heart into her throat every time until her shaking fingers found his pulse and she could breathe and swallow again. When they woke him to transfer him to his bed, she examined his sutures. Every place she had poked the needle was swollen and red.

What if she hadn't sufficiently sterilized the needle and fishline? What if, instead, she had infected him?

They had no antibiotics. Nothing. Nothing whatsoever to help him.

Chapter 40

Crystal trailed Betty down the dark, sleeping corridor. She helped her aunt crawl into bed and then climbed into her own. There had been no sound from Jake as she passed his ledge. Her lower lip trembled. For three days she'd been allowed only glimpses of him as he lay asleep, and she sorely missed him. What if he died, and she never got to say good-bye, never got to tell him she loved him? Eve, in particular, had been watchful as an owl. There'd been no chance to sneak in even a little love pat on the way to bed.

What she needed was a plan.

She began at breakfast. "Mmmm, this fruit is juicy—you always find the ripest, Eve. And your venison stew last night was scrumptious, Aunt Betty." That ought to win her some favor.

Next, do something special to help them out. "Want me to clean these?" At the stream, she washed out the two cloths from Jake's shirt that Eve and Aunt Betty used to cool his fever. No matter how hard she scrubbed, she couldn't get rid of the bloodstains. Just touching the stains squashed her stomach into a hard lump.

But so far, so good. Now for the hardest part of her plan—getting around Eve the Owl to be alone with Jake for a few seconds.

She waited until they went to the beach for their morning mussel hunt. "Oh, I forgot to fill the water bucket when I took the cloths to the stream. Can I do it now?" Aunt Betty always put more water into the cauldron when she added the morning's catch of mussels. She'd be grumpy about a delay.

Sure enough, her aunt huffed. "For goodness' sake, child, go ahead. Don't dillydally like you usually do."

"I won't." She wanted to dash to the cave and get the bucket before Eve could protest, but it might look suspicious. She turned to Eve, who was ankle-deep in the cove, hands buried in the water.

Eve straightened. Crystal's heart pounded while the Owl hesitated. "Don't bother Jake," she finally said.

"I won't. I promise." Crystal forced herself to trudge at her normal pace across the beach and up the rocky incline to the cave. A sideways glance showed Eve still standing straight and tall, hands dripping water, staring after her. Crystal's backbone prickled under the hot gaze. Maybe she shouldn't carry out her plan after all.

She crawled into the cave and was out in seconds with the empty bucket. Should she wave to say, "See how fast I was?" or should she act like it was no big deal and just walk across the trench? A peek revealed that, sure enough, Eve hadn't moved. Well, let her stand there and watch all she wanted, nothing was going to happen.

At the stream she filled the bucket half full. Better two or three trips a day than trying to lug a full bucket. Even with half a bucket, she always spilled water while climbing down the steep hill to the trench. Back home, her grandma and grandpa would have squawked about the spill, but here everyone was grateful just to have water.

She was halfway across the trench before she bothered to look down at the beach. Both Aunt Betty and Eve had their backs to the cave. Crystal held her breath and walked faster. If they didn't look up, they wouldn't know she was in the cave, much less how long she was in it.

At the entrance, she crawled in, turned back around, and tugged the bucket into the cave, oh-so-careful to not let it scrape against the rock. No telling how good Eve the Owl's ears were. The thought made her stomach jitter. She'd better hurry, just in case.

No need to wait for her eyes to adjust to the dark. Just feel her way along the wall to the sleeping hall, and Jake's ledge was first.

His breathing was soft, like he was blowing feathers. She restrained a giggle. Her fingers found his head—good, his face was toward her. She could make out his form now, stretched on his stomach along the ledge. "I love you, Jake," she whispered. She leaned forward to kiss him. To steady herself, she placed her hand on his back.

Jake woke with a shriek. "Leopard!"

Crystal's heart leaped to her throat. She jumped back as Jake tumbled off the ledge. *Thud.* The air left his lungs in a great whoosh. A million seconds went by. Then she heard him gasp the air back in.

What had she done? The jitters she'd calmed moments ago exploded like the mine Aunt Betty had stepped on. Crystal fled. Her shin hit the water bucket hard enough to tip it clanking to the floor.

She didn't know she was crying until she flung herself into her aunt's arms.

"Sweetie, what's the matter?"

Eve splashed in from the cove, her steps churning the shallow water into miniature geysers. "What happened? Is Jake okay?"

Crystal cringed. The broken promise, the lie she'd told on purpose—she had done the unspeakable, and Eve's eyes were searching out her very soul. She couldn't let her find out. "I don't want Jake to die!" she wailed. "I love him!"

Eve's glower softened. "He won't die. We won't let him. He'll be okay, you'll see."

Crystal buried her face into Aunt Betty's shoulder and sobbed. What had she done? Oh, what had she done to her beloved Jake? He was lying on the floor, and she had just left him there. She should tell them about it, but she couldn't, she just couldn't.

* * *

Jake got to his feet and groped his way to the table. No sitting down, the way the slashes in his thighs burned. The fall had slammed him onto his back. Had any of the sutures ripped open? He felt like someone had poured gasoline over him and set it on fire. Flames on the inside of him too. His mouth and tongue were an ash heap. He needed water.

He shuffled to the spot where they kept the water bucket. It lay empty on its side. He rubbed his face. Hot. Hot all over. Where was everybody? Outside? One of them would get him a drink.

Stooping to crawl through the door sent his head spinning. He flattened himself against the floor and absorbed the coolness of the stone into his bare chest and cheek. When the dizziness passed, he grasped the bucket handle and squirmed outside on his belly.

Fire licked his shoulder blades and buttocks as he clambered to his feet. He gasped bursts of air in and out of his lungs. Nausea rose in a clog from his stomach to choke his throat and the inside of his nose. He threw up on himself, unwilling to test his balance by bending over.

A chill swept over him. He leaned against the cliff, soaked the morning's soft heat into his palms and forearms, the side of his face, his heaving ribs. Finally his breathing calmed. It struck him that although his wounds burned, the torment from the last few days of feeling skinned alive had left. He remembered buddies in Nam screaming from stitches received with no pain relievers. Now he understood.

The shivers subsided, but a headache landed like a swarm of bees taking up residence inside his skull. He recognized the symptom. A dehydration headache. He had to have that water.

A glance over his shoulder located Betty, Eve, and Crystal. They were walking with their backs to him far down the beach, where the corner jutted into the ocean. They wouldn't hear if he yelled.

He'd have to get the water himself.

Bracing with one hand against the cliffside, he crouched and picked up the water bucket. A wave of nausea swooped over him, but disappeared when he straightened.

He inhaled a deep breath. Atta boy, he could do this.

* * *

At the end of the beach, the women stopped to give Betty a rest. Crystal plopped down where the waves teased the shoreline. She squiggled her toes deeper and deeper into the wet sand. They'd get completely buried, and then a wave would come and dig them out and she had to start all over again. It was a contest. Her toes against the waves—sorta like her and Eve.

She just knew Eve was going to dig out what happened with Jake. Dig out the lie. Dig out the promise Crystal had made knowing she wasn't going to keep it. And now she was going to get caught. She was the toes. Eve was the waves.

It was obvious what Eve was doing to catch her. First Eve asked Aunt Betty questions about places she'd traveled to and which places she liked best. Busy talk. Talk to give Crystal time to calm down. Time for Eve to set the trap. Crystal knew it as sure as if she'd watched Eve put the cheese on the mousetrap and pull the spring back.

Then, sure enough, Eve asked Crystal the same questions. Where had she been and what had she liked and why? The questions were little crumbs for the mouse to nibble to get it over to the trap. And just like the mouse, Crystal went after the crumbs, knowing what was happening, wanting with all her mousy heart to resist, but oh-so-wishing to please Eve that she couldn't stop.

Eve stood and looked at Aunt Betty. "How about if Crystal comes with me to pick fruit for lunch?"

Crystal shivered. Eve had got her to the mousetrap and was pulling back the spring.

"That's fine, as long as you help me to the cave so I can check on Jake." And Aunt Betty was playing right along.

Would he still be on the floor where she'd left him?

They got to the cave. Between thinking about how she'd made Jake fall and how Eve was going to make her tell everything, Crystal scrambled as fast as she could up to the little plateau, and then on up toward the Japanese garden. Maybe she could think of a way to distract Eve's attention. Fall, maybe, and act like she was hurt. But no, that would be another lie. She was through with lies. She just wanted to get away with this one so Eve wouldn't despise her and never trust her again.

Crystal walked faster, but Eve stayed right beside her, talking and talking, all friendly-like. Crystal's ears were so stuffed with the tears she held back that she could hardly hear the words. But this was the big cheese talk, all right—all this kindness to lead her straight into the trap. Then, *snap!* the spring would pop and she'd have to confess. She began to sniffle, just thinking about it.

Aunt Betty shouted their names, and she halted. Eve did, too, and they ran back to the cave. They stopped on top of the little plateau and peered down. Aunt Betty stood outside the cave entrance, yelling their names until she and Eve showed up. "Jake's gone! He's bleeding!" She pointed at the trench and began hobbling along it with her cane. "There's a trail, see?"

"Stay there, Betty. Crystal and I will find him and bring him back." Eve climbed down the plateau to the trench, but Crystal stayed where she was. She scoured the trench ahead of her aunt until she saw Jake at the very end.

"There he is!" He was lying like a big crooked *X* in the long grass. "Jake! Jake!" She plunged down the plateau and ran toward him, screaming his name.

Eve ran ahead of her, but suddenly froze in a dead halt. Fear closed Crystal's throat. She caught up with Eve and stopped too. She couldn't move. All she could do was stare.

Jake lay on his stomach. One arm was crooked over his face; the other was stretched out beside him, fingers clasping the bucket handle. Swarming over him was a mass of huge, blue-green, metallic-colored blowflies. They were packed in heavy clumps over the stitches on his back. Crystal gasped when she saw flies crawling in and out of Jake's nose and mouth.

One tiny, little lie, and this is where it led.

Chapter 41

For sure, Jake was dead.

Horror crawled over Crystal's insides like the blowflies crawling over Jake's outside. She should help him, but her feet wouldn't move. At a gasp behind her, she turned numbly to observe Aunt Betty hobbling up to them. Her aunt's eyes bugged out, and her mouth and nostrils flared wide as the air swooped into her lungs.

"Get those flies off him!" Aunt Betty shoved her and Eve aside and rushed toward the still figure. She flailed her cane in heavy arcs over him until the flies rose like a swirling tornado to envelop her.

Crystal and Eve broke out of their stupor and ran to her rescue. They pulled her back until the angry horde returned to its feast.

Aunt Betty refused defeat. "Check his pulse!" she yelled to Eve. "Crystal, fast as you can, bring a bucket of water!"

Crystal grabbed the bucket and ran for the stream. She looked back once and saw Eve crouched beside Jake's head. Her aunt was attacking the horde again. This time the flies looked like they were losing.

Filling the bucket was her daily job and she had learned how to do it efficiently. Still, the stream was shallow, and filling the big bucket even halfway took time. She splashed water into it to hurry the process. She had to get back. Maybe Jake really wasn't dead.

She began to pray for him, then stopped. God wasn't going to listen to her! This whole thing was her fault. Jake would still be asleep on his ledge if it weren't for her. She had woken him up, and if Jake were dead, then clearly it was because of her.

The knowledge squeezed the life out of her budding soul. She understood she hadn't done anything to deserve her father's abandonment and her mother's death. But Jake, that was different. If he died, if she was guilty of his death, then she deserved to lose God.

She steeled herself against the reality awaiting her in the trench. Everything inside her became quiet. The breath in her lungs ceased. Her heart didn't beat. Though she moved on the outside, on the inside she either lived with Jake or she died with Jake. Her guilt could bear nothing less.

* * *

Eve scooted back from checking Jake's pulse as Betty splashed water from the bucket again and again over his back. The flies rose in a dark mass and attacked Betty, but she merely squinted her eyes against their assault and kept pouring. Jake didn't flinch under the impact of the water on his raw sores, but when she splashed water onto his face, he groaned. Next to her, Crystal drew in a sharp breath.

With a pang, Eve realized Crystal, too, had feared him dead. A fear that had sunk sharp teeth into Eve's heart and brought up all kinds of unsuspected feelings for Jake. Feelings that said he meant far more to her than she had imagined. Her head still whirled in confusion. She shoved the emotions aside and reached for Crystal's hand. It was cold and limp. "He's going to be okay, sweetie."

Crystal said nothing.

"C'mon, let's get him out of here." She got Crystal to help her take Jake's arms and pull his chest onto Eve's back, then hoist him higher so she could bend forward and carry him turtle-back. The flies now struck at her. They batted against her eyes and every inch of exposed skin, buzzing in her ears with the high shrill of a dentist's drill.

"Lead the way," she shouted at Crystal. Clutching Jake's arms to her chest, she staggered forward, eyes slitted against the dive-bombers. At the cave entrance, while Betty and Crystal warded off the flies, she dragged poor Jake inside on his stomach. It took all three of them to heave him from the floor onto the table.

"Quick, more water." Betty sent Crystal skedaddling with the bucket.

Swatting away the flies that rode Jake in, Eve examined his injuries. "Hard to tell with all this dirt, but his stitches look okay."

"You can bet those flies laid eggs in them," Betty growled. "However many buckets it takes, we're going to clean them out."

It took three buckets before Betty was satisfied. Jake was shivering by the time they tucked him away on his ledge. Eve piled coals into the small pot and placed it as close to him as she dared to warm him up.

The coolness of the cave fought her efforts. She rubbed his arms and legs to stimulate his circulation. A lump lodged in her throat. *Come on, Jake, don't scare me again.* Fear rocked her a second time, harder than it had in the trench. *Please, Jake.* She couldn't bear the thought of losing him. Of living without him.

When at last his skin warmed and his teeth stopped chattering, she left him to Betty's care and hustled to get fruit before dusk arrived. The venison soup they would have eaten for supper was peppered with blowflies. Nobody commented about insects in their food anymore. They simply spooned them out. But this was too over-the-top to stomach.

She made the trip a quick pick—whatever looked ripe, whatever was within easy reach. Her nerves still crawled from the sight of Jake covered with flies, lying in the trench like an abandoned corpse.

Jake dead—the possibility shredded her. Left her insides dull and jumbled, like the island in the gray morning after a typhoon. All the toughness she'd hammered into her brain over a lifetime was now mush. The carefully guarded soft spots in her heart were in disaray. She was no longer clear as to how she felt toward whom and what.

Jake. Her breath dammed her lungs so she couldn't breathe. Believing him dead had blasted the ramparts protecting her heart. Had flung hidden feelings sky-high. Feelings freed, revealing themselves warm and tender toward this man.

They frightened her.

What was happening? The air locked up in her lungs shuddered out. All she knew for sure was that she wanted to hurry back. Not to Chicago. Not to a new Romero trial. But to the cave.

To Jake.

* * *

When she returned, Betty sank into a chair next to her at the table, clutching a damp wad of Jake's shirt. "He's got a high fever. We should take turns watching him tonight." Her voice trembled. "He was delirious while you were gone."

Eve gave her a quick hug, as much for her own fear as Betty's. "Let's eat and I'll take the first watch. You get some rest." There was no way she'd sleep if Jake needed tending.

Crystal hardly touched her food.

"You all right?" Eve placed her hand on Crystal's. There was no response. No turning of the wrist to clasp Eve's palm, no entwining of slender, little fingers with Eve's.

The child shook her head.

"He'll be okay."

"You keep saying that."

"I keep meaning it. You want to keep watch with me awhile?"

She was surprised when Crystal declined. "I just want to go to bed."

"Me too." Betty leaned heavily on the table and stood. She pointed to the small pot of water. "I'm using his shirt to mop off his brow and keep him cool. You can check him for fever anytime."

Eve followed their shuffling footsteps into the dark sleeping corridor. Betty grunted as she did every night when Crystal helped her onto her ledge. A soft rustle identified Crystal's climb into her own bed. "Goodnight, darling," Betty called. Crystal's response was faint.

Jake was lying on his side. Was he awake? She leaned over him, her heartbeat quickening. His breath warmed her cheek, and she jumped back, startled by how close she'd come to him. The second piece of shirt lay in a tidy bundle over his brow. She scooped it off and replaced it with the cooler cloth from the pot.

At her touch, he opened his eyes. "Water." His voice rasped like parched reeds in a sea breeze. Alarm seized her breath and held it. He'd been in pain the last three days from the stitches, but not weak like this. Crystal's fear seeped into her bones. What if he did die? What if she were wrong that he'd be okay?

With trembling hands, she fetched a coconut shell of water and slid her hand under his head to help him take small sips. It reminded her of her first conscious moments on the island, when Jake had fed her drops of coconut juice after rescuing her from the sea. He'd done everything he'd promised, hadn't he? Found them water, food, shelter. Made her moccasins, saved her how many times? She owed him everything, and all she'd ever done was give him a hard time, gone her own way.

Betty was right that first day of their trip up the island, when the two of them had argued about Jake. Eve inhaled a slow breath, ready now to accept the truth of Betty's words. Ready to admit what she'd so vehemently denied back then.

She lowered her face to Jake's ear. "You're a good man, Jake." She jerked in a second breath. May as well own up to all of it. "We—all of us— love you."

* * *

In the middle of the night, Jake's cries startled Eve out of a doze. She pulled herself to a wobbly stand from the chair she'd placed next to his ledge.

"Ginny! I can't find you!"

Pain daggered her heart. He wanted Ginny. Of course he would …

Her fingers confirmed what the darkness obscured. Sweat soaked his hair and beard and pooled beneath his chin onto the bed. She ran to change the cloth slipping off his forehead. "Shh now, you're okay." His face and arms and chest steamed with heat. She brought the pot over and used both cloths to cool him. The bony corrugation of his ribs beneath the damp cloth brought tears to her eyes. He had paid a heavy price to care for her and Betty and Crystal. An unaccustomed tenderness swept through her.

"Ginny!" He grabbed away a cloth and pressed her empty hand to his mouth. His lips were chapped in ragged furrows that scraped the soft inner circle of her palm. For a second, she yielded to the heady tingle of intimacy that coursed up her arm and pushed the breath from her throat. His grip tightened.

No!

She jerked her hand away. What was she doing? Shame at her response to his touch—a touch meant for Ginny—clamped her throat and rocketed heat up her neck to her cheeks. This was wrong, totally wrong.

It was her fault that Jake was here. Her fault that Ginny wasn't.

Cold fingers seized her arm, and she jumped. Betty stood next to her. "Eve, are you all right?"

It took a moment to realize what Betty was referring to. She was crying. Shoulders shaking. Chest heaving. Muffled sobs pushing through her nostrils. She opened her mouth and sucked in little chokes of air. "I—" She didn't know what to say. "He's calling for Ginny."

Betty slipped an arm around Eve's waist. "He did this afternoon too. Poor guy, he loved her so much. It will take a long time for him to move on."

The tears wouldn't stop. "You were right all those months ago, Betty. He is a good man. I never met ... never thought ..." She struggled to untangle her thoughts, to speak words that made sense. "Jake has been nothing but good to me, and I've been so ... so—"

"Blind?" Betty offered. "Belligerent? Ungrateful? Stupid?"

Despair suffused her at the ease with which Betty summoned the gruff words. She collapsed into the chair and covered her face with her hands. She should be the one dying.

Betty put her arm around Eve's shoulder and pulled her into a bony hug. "Those are harsh words, dearie, but you know, I thank God for you. You jumped right off that lighter and swam out to Crystal and me and dragged us to safety. We wouldn't be here if it weren't for you. And look how you sewed Jake up and saved him from bleeding to death. Every day you go out of your way to help make Crystal and me comfortable and happy."

"But not Jake."

"You've been hard on him, no question about it. But now that you see the good in him, all that will change. Every day can be a new day in which you bless him just like you have Crystal and me."

Bless? She recoiled at the religious word. All right, bless, then—she'd do her best to make him happy. A sigh heaved from her chest. At least the word gave her a handle on how to swoop up and manage all those wild emotions that had leaped out when she thought Jake was dead.

"Ginny!" Jake's cry brought her to her feet.

Betty shot her palm to his forehead. "We've got to bring this fever down or ..."

Eve gulped, finishing the sentence. *Or they'd lose him.* She dunked both cloths into the water and thrust one at Betty. They mopped his head, his chest, his limbs. Her hands and arms shook.

How could it be that she'd finally found a good man—maybe the only one to ever walk into her life—and now she might lose him forever?

Chapter 42

Once Betty and Eve were sound asleep, Crystal crept off her ledge and sneaked by the three exhausted adults. All night she had stifled her sobs so no one would hear her. The sun was poking orange rays through the cave windows. At least she could get fruit for them now that it was morning. She hurried so Aunt Betty wouldn't worry about where she'd disappeared to, but nobody was awake when she returned. Okay then, she'd do more. Anything to please them, to relieve the weight of guilt on her heart.

At the stream, she filled the water bucket and rinsed out the two cloths and lay them in the sun to dry. With one eye on the cave in case anyone woke up, she hunted mussels, cleaned them, and added them to the cauldron. All that work, and still everyone slept.

Her own eyelids wanted to drop into slumber, too, but she couldn't bear to walk by Jake's bunk to get to hers. The horrid *thud* of his fall yesterday kept echoing in her head. Even worse, what if she slipped past him and there was *no* sound because he'd stopped breathing? The thought pinched spasms in her stomach and squeezed her lungs so tight she couldn't breathe.

She gasped in air and forced her imagination to picture Jake up and at 'em, smiling so big all his front teeth showed, beckoning her with a pat on the ground to sit beside him on the beach and read the Bible together.

He'd like it, wouldn't he, if she kept the hearth fire going too? She fetched firewood from the plateau until her legs ached from the climb and in itched from the dirt and sweat. A speedy dip in the stream brought o the last task she could think of, cutting up the fruit.

The sharp knife set her insides jittering. Slicing the mangos and star ples wasn't a problem, but peeling the weird red fruit covered with green hair was something Eve always handled. Well, she had learned how to open coconuts, hadn't she? A little practice and she could peel the creepy red and green fruit too.

She yelped as the knife split open the soft flesh of her thumb. The knife clattered to the floor and skittered toward the sleeping hall. Before Crystal could retrieve it, Eve rushed into the room.

No, not the Owl! Crystal's insides shriveled into the darkest corner of her heart.

Eve stopped, glanced at her, then the food, then the knife. "Oh, thanks for getting the fruit—that's exactly the lift I need. You want help?" She picked up the knife.

"I cut myself."

"Let me see." Eve took Crystal's hand and examined her thumb. "Want me to sew it up? I'm getting pretty good at the job."

Was she kidding or not? Crystal jerked her hand away. "That's okay. I'm fine."

A *tap-tap-tap* against the rock floor announced Aunt Betty's arrival. "What'd you do, cut yourself? I told you to leave that knife alone." She leaned on her cane and seized Crystal's thumb. "Now look what you've done, on top of all our other troubles!"

A grunt from the sleeping corridor jerked their attention to its doorway. Jake stumbled into view. He leaned against the wall, his chest and palms flat against the stone for support. "Help me." His voice was raspy.

"Jake! What are you doing up?" In two steps, Eve was at his side.

"Need you ... look at my back."

"What's wrong? It's not bleeding. Let's get you back to bed."

"Help me ... to table." His words, whispered with effort, were nevertheless insistent. "Need light to see."

Fear punched the air in Crystal's lungs. *See what?*

Eve's voice softened. "Okay, lean against my back, then, like I did against yours during the typhoon." She slipped Jake's arms over her shoulders and trundled him with small steps to the table. Crystal swiped away the fruit and helped Eve lay Jake on the bamboo slats. Eve brushed away wisps of Jake's hair plastered in sweat to his face. "Okay, what do you want me to do?"

His answer scraped out between heaving breaths from the journey across the room. "Get close … Look."

Crystal's stomach knotted at how feeble his voice sounded. How he lay with the bumpy bamboo slats poking his face. How his arms lay limp by his side, like jellyfish washed ashore by the tide. She blinked back tears and forced herself to join Eve and Betty at the table.

At best, the light in the cave was dim. She leaned over and squinted at his back. The pattern of the cat's claws marked four short furrows down each shoulder. The blood had dried into black lines puckered with miniature, pink volcanoes connected by fishline where Eve had sewn Jake up. Tiny, white dots the size of rice embedded the pink bumps.

No! Surely those dots had not moved. She bent closer. Every one of them wriggled and fidgeted.

She jumped back with a scream. "Maggots!"

As if choreographed, Eve and Betty leaped back with her. Their faces mirrored her horror.

Jake released a heavy sigh. "Thought so." He raised his hand and opened his palm flat. "Let me see."

Eve inched forward to peek at his back. "Trust me, they're there. Some are already under your skin."

"Show me one." When no one moved, he murmured, "Crystal?"

"Gross!" But how could she refuse? Wasn't she the cause of this invasion in the first place? If Jake had to bear it, so did she. Suppressing a whimper, she brushed a stubby, white larva into her hand and held it out for Jake's inspection. It wriggled toward the crease line below her fingers. She squealed and dumped it onto his palm.

He shoved his hand level with his eyes. "Good. A maggot."

Aunt Betty squeezed Crystal's arm. "Get me that bucket of water. We're getting rid of them right now."

"No!" Jake's voice raised the hair on Crystal's arms. He lifted his head and shook it with surprising vigor. "Don't."

"He's delirious." Aunt Betty pushed Crystal toward the bucket. "Get the water."

"Stop!" Jake boosted himself to his elbows and twisted around to frown at Betty. "They eat dead flesh. They'll help my wounds."

"I won't allow it, Jake." Tears brimmed in Betty's eyes. "I won't have you eaten alive by worms."

"Wait." Eve grasped Crystal's arm. "I've heard about this, Betty. In some parts of the world, maggots are used medically to remove decay and prevent gangrene. It may—" She halted and pressed her lips together. When they stopped quivering, she continued. "It may be Jake's only chance."

Silence smothered the cave. Air vanished from Crystal's lungs. Pulse and heartbeat quit. The words swallowed her soul. *Jake's only chance—to live.*

The creak of the table shattered the quiet. Crystal jumped, her heart ramming her ribs. Across from her, Jake slid his legs off the bamboo slats to a shaky stand, his arms, braced against the table, equally shaky. His head drooped as if his neck had turned to rubber. "Take me back."

Eve helped him to his bed. She returned to sit next to Betty and put an arm across Betty's slumped shoulders. Crystal couldn't distinguish the words Eve mumbled into Betty's ear, but it wasn't a hard guess. "He'll be okay." How many times had Eve said that? And look at Jake now.

Crystal's insides ached. She wanted Eve's arm around her. Wanted Eve's hand smoothing her hair away from her face. Wanted, yes, even the empty words of comfort. But she understood she was unworthy. The words "eaten alive" cut deeply into her heart. Jake might die, maybe was dying right now, alone in bed. Slowly eaten by worms.

She sniffled bumpy, little sobs of air into her lungs. At last, here was someone who loved her for no good reason in the whole, wide world—and she had as good as killed him.

When she crawled onto her bunk that night, she hardly closed her eyes before Jake's cries awoke her.

"Ginny!"

The soft patter of Eve's feet, the tap of Aunt Betty's cane, the slosh of two cloths dunked in water—they all said the same thing. The worms were eating Jake.

There were no more tears left to cry. Only a deep chill, and the certainty that tomorrow Jake would be dead.

Chapter 43

Eve entered the jungle at the place where she had hacked a path to her favorite tree. The opening cut in the thick growth bordering the stream formed a narrow arch that allowed her to slip through without being scraped, poked, or slapped by branches and leaves. More importantly, the bare earth of the trail removed chances of stepping on a snake. The fewer the challenges she had to face, the better she could focus on keeping Jake alive.

The twitter and hoots from the canopy overhead spoke of the continuity of life. The contrast of Jake's deliriums last night, for the second night in a row, squeezed her heart. Which was worse, his fever and ravings while she and Betty frantically sponged him off and tried to comfort him, or the periods of utter stillness when she held her breath to see some small sign that he was still alive?

She batted away pesky insects hungry for her eyes. If only Crystal had risen early to gather fruit again for their breakfast, she could have grabbed a morning nap. But the child had remained on her bunk, curled in a fetal position rather than stretched out, half hanging off her ledge, as usual. Poor thing, no doubt she had slept as little as the adults and was filled with the same mind-numbing dread.

It was just as well. With Jake finally sleeping, she wanted to get out anyway. The cave that had been such a welcoming refuge was now a tomb sucking away her every breath. For a second, the image of the Japanese soldiers in the burial cave flashed into her mind. A shiver jabbed down her backbone.

She broke into a trot. They wouldn't end up like those soldiers. No one was going to die. Not Jake. Not Betty. Not Crystal. Not her. They'd all make it off this cursed island. From now on, she'd refuse to think otherwise.

At her approach to her destination, a flock of brightly colored broadbills swooped away in noisy protest from the towering tree. Leaning into its upper branches was the crown of a second tree that had toppled over. Its mossy trunk created a steep but convenient bridge to the first tree. From there it was an easy climb to the canopy. With practiced skill, she crossed the bridge and scaled the tree. The hole made by the fallen tree allowed her a view of the sky and, in the distance, the gray top of the volcano baking in the morning sun.

So, where was the closest troop of monkeys today? Although she couldn't see them through the layers of green leaves, she had no problem hearing them. All she had to do was follow the noise, and whatever the monkeys were feeding on became the next meal for their human cousins. Since monkeys simply filled their stomachs and moved on, there was always something left for her to pick.

This time it was mangos. She carried her haul to the waterfall pool and deposited the mangos inside a shallow corral Jake had constructed. After harvesting two other fruits nearby, she bathed, then plodded downstream with the fruit pouched in her dripping shirt.

The coolness of the water rushing over her ankles soothed her. Really, there was no reason to worry about Jake. In spite of two nights of fever, he was at least eating and drinking during the day. With the chill of the cave to counter his fever, and the maggots to consume his dead flesh, he should recover. It was foolish to entertain any other possibility.

Foolish to think her feelings toward Jake had changed in any way too. Fear of his death had simply colored her admiration of him with hyped-up drama. The courtroom demanded data in black and white—facts had to be facts. And that was her venue, the courtroom, not the stage. The black-and-white fact was that her ambition to win *United States vs. Romero* had resulted in nineteen deaths. That had to be the basis for any emotions connected to Jake.

Sobered by her reality check, she arrived at the cave and spotted Crystal, bucket in hand, wading in the cove's shallow water. Betty must have sent her out to gather mussels to distract her. They certainly didn't need more meat with all the venison still on hand. Especially with nobody eating much of anything the past five days since Jake's injury.

Betty greeted her with a dour face. "He had more deliriums while you were gone." She eyed the fruit with glazed disinterest as Eve dumped it onto the table. "It's those maggots crawling inside him that are making him sick."

"You've been picking off the ones on the outside, haven't you?" Eve paired the accusation with a sharp look and raised eyebrow.

"Every chance I get," Betty shot back. "I don't understand how those eggs hatched so soon, anyway. It takes at least two to three days, not one."

Eve took over what was usually Betty's job and sliced the fruit onto a seashell platter. "The eggs must have been laid at the pit. I swear every fly on the island followed him to the cave."

Sudden horror drove stomach acid to the back of her throat. "Oh, Betty, I boiled the cloths before I washed him off, but I must have sewn some eggs in with the stitches!" She laid the knife aside and drew in a breath.

"I tell you, Eve, we need to cut them out."

The thought of slicing into the tender, pink flesh on Jake's backside brought more acid to Eve's throat. "No. Absolutely not. Cutting him and digging around for maggots will only make things worse. Promise me you'll drop the idea."

Betty grumbled, but Eve made her give her word. Should she hide the three knives to make sure?

She called Crystal in to eat, but none of them consumed more than a few bites. Betty's new batch of mussel-venison soup fared no better.

At midday, Eve took soup to Jake to encourage him to at least sip the broth. His body was hot, drenched with sweat. Before she could fetch the cloths and water to cool him, he called out for Ginny. Betty crawled off her bunk from a nap and hobbled without her cane to his side. "The time between his deliriums is getting shorter. He's getting worse."

Anxiety the size of a boulder rolled into Eve's stomach. She sped to get the cloths and water. When at last Jake lay in a restless slumber, she climbed onto her own bunk and tossed and turned in a vain effort to sleep.

At dusk, his fever returned, rising and rising, his shouts for Ginny growing more and more frantic, until what seemed like hours passed before his fever broke. This time he slept without moving, his breathing so shallow that Eve and Betty checked his pulse again and again. Neither of them could swallow a morsel of food, and they didn't protest when Crystal refused to eat.

When the sky was a grim black against evening stars, Jake's fever broke for the fourth time that day. "We've got to keep him hydrated," Betty said. While one of them mopped his body with one cloth, the other dribbled water into his mouth from the second cloth.

The cycles continued into the next day, and the day after that. Jake refused any nourishment but water. The cries of sorrow and grief during his deliriums drained Eve's sensibility. His fevers robbed her strength. Each time she slept, she rose to the possibility that today might be the day Jake died.

He became the hub of the wheel around which she and Betty and Crystal revolved. She and Betty took turns caring for him, one sleeping as best she could while the other tended him. Crystal stepped up to the plate and nursed the nurses. She prepared the food and insisted they eat. She cleaned the dishes, fetched the water, woke one when the other was spent. She monitored the days for them. Today was the sixth day, the seventh, the eighth.

It was the one consistent request Jake made, asking, "What number day is it?" Or, as he grew more feeble, merely, "Day?"

On day nine, Crystal told her Jake gave her a thumbs-up, though he could barely lift his hand. "What's that mean?"

Eve was at a loss. "Must be to encourage us." But why? Each day he got only weaker and weaker. Disgustingly, each day the larvae got bigger and bigger.

On day ten, he spread his lips into what had to be a smile and lifted a trembling finger to point to Heaven. Stunned, they interpreted it to mean that today he would die.

The maggots were now almost half an inch long, forming horrid little humps under Jake's skin. But on day ten, they became still. Jake's cycles of delirium and fever stopped. His skin was pale, his arms meatless. He lay quiescent, his breathing barely discernable.

Eve spent the night in a chair next to his ledge, her heartbeat fluttering thunder at every shallow breath he wheezed in. His forehead was cold. Too cold.

Trembling, she awoke Betty and Crystal. "We need to say our good-byes."

Chapter 44

Crystal crawled onto the ledge with Jake. The dried grass beneath him stank of urine and body odor and, up near his head, a little bit of vomit. She stretched out next to him and stared at his face until she could see his mouth half-hidden in his beard, and above it his nose and eyelids. Would he hear her? Probably not, but she had to tell him. For her sake. Tell him everything.

His left arm pillowed his head. His other lay between them. She copied him, an arm under her head, the other resting next to his. Her fingers brushed against the curly hair on his forearm, and she slowly lifted her palm until her hand lay like a fragile egg on a soft nest.

She chewed her lower lip. No crying. No Crybaby Crystal. She inhaled through her nostrils until her lungs were tight with air. She'd be brave and begin with the worst. The sneaky plan, her lie, everything. It was more than she could carry in her heart anymore. She released her breath and snuffled in more air through her nose. She'd tell him how sorry she was, and beg him to forgive her.

Then she'd tell him how happy he had made her—the happiest in her whole life. She'd thank him for taking her to see the rain forest, for teaching her how to start a fire, and how to mark a jungle path with broken branches. For telling her about him and Ginny, for spending his mornings teaching her Scripture and about God. For the Twenty-third Psalm—she mustn't forget that.

She had a long, long list. The only thing she wouldn't tell him was that he mustn't wait for her in Heaven. She wouldn't be coming. She didn't deserve to be there.

She opened her mouth, but the words snagged in her throat. Her hand left its nest and flew to his beard and clutched hold. "I love you, Jake! I don't want you to die!"

And then little sobs came hicupping out, making her forget everything she wanted to say. She'd thought about it for so long, needed so much to tell him. But all she could do was cry.

Jake stirred. He opened his eyes and inched a finger to her lips. "Hush," he whispered. "I'm going to live."

* * *

Jake could count his ribs protruding like row after row of sand dunes in the fleshless skin of his chest. How many days had he gone without eating? He groaned when he heard that Betty had thrown out the venison stew, claiming it was too old to eat. He'd hardly gotten a bite of it. That afternoon, he insisted Eve help him to the table for their next meal. Enough of lying in bed—it was time to celebrate his resurrection from the dead!

The pressure on his buttock wounds as he settled his weight into the chair called for jaw-clamping grit. If he didn't move, he might make it through the meal. The women sat around him with smiles so huge he swore their happiness lit up the cave. All three of them were gaunt in the face, deep hollows under their eyes. For the first time, it hit him how much they had suffered alongside him the last two weeks. His gut tightened all the way up to his throat, making it hard to swallow. The island had tied the four of them together in a way that superseded even the close camaraderie with his battle buddies in Nam. Only his family topped the growing affection he felt for his three fellow survivors.

"Clear up a mystery for us, Jake." Betty rubbed and patted his left hand as if she were the mother of the Prodigal Son returned home. "What were the thumbs-up about? Especially when you smiled and pointed up?"

"Ah, that!" Jake speared a bite of pineapple and held it up to his mouth. "More field-emergency knowledge from Nam. I knew that on the tenth day, my body would peak in producing its own antibodies. I figured if I could last until then, I might live." He waggled his eyebrows at Crystal. "And, praise God, it looks as if I will."

She didn't laugh at his merriment. A shadow flitted across her brow at the mention of God. Then, as if to please him with an appropriate response, she tipped up the corners of her mouth.

His gaiety ratcheted down a notch. If anyone would be traumatized by his death, it would be Crystal. She had made him, not merely a hero to idolize, but her father to treasure and love. Those were big shoes to fill. He winked and gave her his best grin. With all his heart he wanted to keep in contact with her after they got off the island, but would telephone calls and visits be enough?

If Ginny were alive, he'd be tempted to see if he could adopt Crystal. But Ginny wasn't alive. He gulped back the bitter taste of sorrow. Well, thank God that—at least for Crystal's sake—he hadn't died.

"Mind if I check your stitches?" Without waiting for an answer, Eve stood and leaned over his chair. The warmth of her breath tickled his skin. "They look good." A fingertip poked one of the puncture wounds on his right shoulder. "That's a scar. Does it hurt?"

"No."

"How about here?" The fingertip slipped to the tender flesh bordering the scar.

"Ouch! Yes."

"And here?" The finger lifted and pressed down a tad farther away.

"No." Must be his uninjured flesh, although every inch of his body had hurt like the dickens the first several days after she'd sewn him up.

"Jake!" Her voice was tense. "The maggots—I can't find them!" Her fingertips flitted over his stitches like sharks in a feeding frenzy.

"Stop!" He twisted away from her instruments of torture. The movement pinched his buttock wounds against the bamboo slats of the seat. He leaped from his chair and spun away to shield his back from the maniacal fingers. "Get away! The maggots are gone."

Eve stepped back, her eyes wide. "Oh, Jake, not deeper into your—"

"No! No, they left my body." Her concern was gratifying, and she'd been a trooper with all the help during his illness, but doggone the woman, she had a way of literally getting under his skin! He drew in a deep breath to calm down. "They crawled out to pupate."

"You felt them leave?" Betty's mouth turned down in disgust.

He laughed. She groused when they entered his wounds, groused when they left. "They wiggled their way out a couple days ago. I suspect you can find their cocoons around my bed."

Betty snorted. "I've got better ways to spend my time, thank you."

Eve faced him with folded arms. "Those stitches should be taken out. It won't be fun. All we have are knives, no scissors."

Weariness descended like a cement block on his brain. He eased back into his chair. Perhaps he wasn't quite up to being resurrected after all. "Let's think about that for tomorrow. One last bite of fruit, and I'm ready for bed."

"Wait." Crystal rose from her chair to stand before him, eyes fixed on the floor, mouth tight above a trembling chin. "I have something to tell you."

* * *

Crystal couldn't bear to look at Jake. Her insides shook at what she was about to do. She clasped her hands tightly in front of her.

She had bound her fate to Jake's. If he lived, God was not lost to her. But if he didn't live, she would have to bear her guilt forever. Not even Aunt Betty and Eve's forgiveness would be sufficient. Only Jake's would do. He was the one who had suffered because of her.

She forced out two words. Forced them from the rat-infested dungeon in her heart. Forced them to her tongue. Opened her mouth, pushed them out. "I lied."

Shame stripped her into scorching nakedness. Her knees quaked so that she could hardly stand. "I lied to Aunt Betty and Eve. I did it on purpose."

Silence echoed against the cave walls. The acrid smell of wood ashes, the sweet scent of pineapple, the sour odor of Jake's unwashed body crowded her nostrils. Relief and dread prickled the back of her throat so that she had to swallow hard. Her insides tingled.

Jake reached over and took her hands into his. They were warm against the ice of her skin. She dared to sneak a glance at him. His face was grave, but his eyes were kind. They encouraged her to tell him more. "I told them I'd fetch the water and not go near you. But all along, that was my plan."

"You lied because you wanted to see me?"

She hung her head, nudged her chin up and down once.

"And you haven't apologized to them?"

Her chest knotted. He didn't get it. Her betrayal was against him, not them. The air in her lungs was barely enough to squeak out the terrible truth. "My lie almost killed you."

His eyebrows shot up. "How's that?"

"You left the cave to fetch water because of me."

"Going outside to get water was my choice, Pumpkin. You're not to blame for my decision. Do you understand that?"

"No." Reluctantly, she put the last piece into the puzzle so he could see the whole, ugly picture. "I touched your back and you fell off your bed. After that you chose to get the water."

"I see." His thumbs rubbed the backs of her hands in gentle circles. "Let me ask you a question. I took Ginny on the *Gateway* cruise. Does that mean I killed her?"

Crystal gasped in horror. "No! Captain Emilio killed her."

Jake nodded. "And it was a clouded leopard, not you, that almost killed me. "

The logic filtered slowly into her brain. Captain Emilio set off the blasts—if he hadn't, Ginny and all the others would still be alive. The leopard attacked Jake—if it hadn't, Jake would have no injuries to die from. Air leaped into her lungs in an explosion of joy.

"Then I haven't lost God either!"

Jake's eyebrows jumped again. "Why would you think you had?"

"Because … I wouldn't deserve Him. Not if I'd killed you."

"Crystal, all of us have reasons why we don't deserve God. Bad things we might do one time, bad things we do over and over again."

Crystal frowned. Her brain felt like Jake had taken an eggbeater to it. "So none of us can have God?"

"Yes, we can. We become God's beloved when we believe in Jesus. I gave Ginny a pearl necklace I bought especially for her on our wedding day, and it was always hers after that. In the same way, Jesus gives His forgiveness—that He paid for on the cross—to His beloved, and it's always theirs after that. That's how we can have God."

"Even when we're bad?"

His mouth pulled down at the corners, and his eyes looked so sad it made her breath jerk. "I hated being bad to Ginny because I loved her and wanted to please her. I always apologized and tried never to do it again. It's the same with God. We hate being bad to Him."

She got it. The love needed to go both ways—and why wouldn't she love God if He loved her that much? Something light, something full and fizzy and crazy with happiness, filled her insides. She squeezed Jake's hands so tight her bones crunched. "Lying is bad. I don't ever want to do it again."

"Tell Him that, Pumpkin."

She took a big breath, withdrew her hands from Jake's to weave her fingers together, and closed her eyes. "Dear Jesus, I believe in You, and I want to be forgiven forever. I'm really, really sorry I lied, and I don't want to ever do it again. I want to love You as much as You love me." She paused. "And thank You that Jake didn't die. Amen."

She opened her eyes and grinned shyly at Jake. Light from the cave windows reflected on tears brimming in his eyes. He drew her to him in a tight hug, and she hugged him back, certain the dizzying happiness inside her was oozing into his insides too. She had God and she had Jake. Both!

"Don't forget Aunt Betty and Eve," he whispered.

The guilt, although nowhere near as heavy as what she'd taken to God, pinched out stomach acid. She turned to face her aunt first. "I'm sorry I lied. Can you forgive me too?"

Aunt Betty's mouth curved downward. "I'm disappointed, child, but I forgive you. Come give me a hug too."

She went hesitantly into Aunt Betty's arms, sorry deep down now that she saw how hurt her aunt was. Lying was a hateful thing to do to people, as well as to God. "I'm sorry," she said against her aunt's shoulder. "I won't ever do it again."

Aunt Betty patted Crystal's back and released her. "I'll be looking for that."

New sorrow bit her throat. In other words, she'd have to prove herself. She had lost something precious, something that would not be recovered easily. She swallowed back tears, feeling more and more the enormity of what her lie had done.

It was going to be even worse with Eve, the real target of her lie. Eve—her Losers Club buddy, her friend who didn't look on her as just a dumb kid, her heroine who'd saved her and Aunty instead of looking out for herself, who'd been brave enough to sew up Jake and save him too. Over and over, Eve had shown love to her, and what had she done in return?

A sob lurched from her lungs. Please, God, she couldn't lose Eve! She ached to throw herself into Eve's arms and cry and cry and beg forgiveness. "Eve?" Her voice cracked. She turned a full circle, probing the cave's darkness. "Where's Eve?"

"She hasn't come back?" Aunt Betty twisted in her chair to glance over each shoulder, as if already needing proof that Crystal spoke the truth. "She sped out of here back when you said Captain Emilio killed Ginny."

Heart thumping, Crystal scrambled outside. High overhead, the sun beat down on an empty beach and swashing whitecaps beyond the cove. The grass in the trench sagged, releasing the sharp scent of baked vegetation. No one but her and the Lone Soldier were there. "Eve," she shouted. "Please don't be mad at me. I'm sorry. I'm really, really sorry!"

* * *

Halfway up the slope to the Japanese garden, Eve hesitated at Crystal's plea. Poor child. It was obvious she was upset, that she needed the assurance of Eve's love and the comfort of her forgiveness. But not yet. Not when she had her own emotional bomb to recover from.

At the garden, she paused to admire the progress they'd made in reclaiming its beauty. Miniature shrubs and bushes, dainty constructs of rocks formed into stepping-stones and bridges, and pools of water flowing from diminutive waterfalls were restored to view. With the grass gone, the garden's only enemy now was the noonday sun, unobstructed by the boulders on the east and west that hindered its morning and evening rays.

The heat of the stone pathway soaked into her moccasins as she followed its meandering trail through patches of flowers. A dizzying aroma of perfume clung to the air. At the spot where she had discovered the Sampaguitas, she sat down and inhaled a breath that sucked every molecule of oxygen off the island and spun her into giddiness.

Giddiness because she had been absolved of murder.

Of any part of murder.

Jake and Crystal had placed the guilt squarely on Captain Emilio's shoulders. All those passengers on the *Gateway*, dear Ginny—Captain Emilio was the murderer, not she, not even indirectly. Not even for boarding the *Gateway*.

All this time she had believed she was the linchpin, but she wasn't. It was Captain Emilio who was the key player. He had chosen to target not just her, but all the passengers. She didn't understand his choice, but clearly the blame was on him and his decision. He, and he alone, bore the guilt.

She released the air from her lungs with a loud laugh. Shouted it out. Her rump was flat on the ground, but, oh, was her soul ever soaring! Spinning and dancing and whirling like a gull riding an eddy high above the earth.

She was free! Free from her self-imposed, misplaced guilt for Ginny's death! For the deaths of all the *Gateway* passengers.

Her euphoria segued into a long sigh. Free now, too, to look at those tumultuous emotions battering her heart for attention. Emotions about Jake she didn't want to look at.

Because once she freed those feelings, once she granted them their own life, she would have to kill them.

The feelings weren't hard to figure out. With her misplaced guilt relocated to Captain Emilio, they stood on the ramparts of her heart and jumped and waved and hollered. Insisted on recognition. Demanded action.

She closed her eyes and clamped her jaw against the emotions, but there was no denying them.

She, who had never loved a man, who had scoffed at the idea of romantic love bearing any authenticity—*she* was in love.

In love with Jake Chalmers.

Who was in love with his wife.

Her stomach tightened in a spasm. She wrapped her arms across her chest in a tight squeeze. It was the only hug she was going to get. The only comfort. No one would ever know about these feelings. What was never meant to be would be buried on this island. Buried with a platoon of Japanese soldiers. She mustn't be like Lone Soldier, watching and waiting for what would never come.

She rose to her feet and gazed at the Sampaguita flowerbed. Waited for her heartbeat to level out. Her breathing to calm. The sun was hot on her head. Sweat beaded her skin. She lifted her chin and drew in air through her nostrils. "I haven't forgotten you, Mari. It's two Romeros now. Danny for you, Captain Emilio for me."

Old dreams still awaited her. She closed the coffin lid on what could only be an empty hope and slipped it into the soil with the Sampaguitas.

To stop her lips from quivering, she pinched them between her teeth and went to find Crystal.

Chapter 45

Jake poured the last of the water over his head. Oh, what he wouldn't give to be able to trek up to the waterfall pool and bathe like a man. None of this ridiculous sponging off with rags out of a pail of water in the trench. He pulled on the briefs and shorts Eve had washed and mended and laid out to dry before she and Crystal left on their morning fruit hunt. Today for sure he'd have to step up to the plate and begin a recovery routine.

"You decent out there?" From inside the cave, the tap of Betty's cane grew louder.

"Not if I don't get my belt. I seem to have lost a little weight these past two weeks." He pulled the waistline of his shorts away from his stomach. He could fit two of him in there.

Betty crawled outside with her cane in one hand, his belt in the other, and handed it to him. Instead of standing, she scooted to the side to rest her back and head against the cliff and stretch her legs in front of her. "My favorite time of the day. Sun high enough to warm, but not to burn." She patted the trampled grass next to her. "Come sit. I want to tell you something."

He glanced down the trench. So much for starting an exercise routine. He'd never make it down and back, anyway. How could a mere spit bath be so exhausting?

He stepped past her to sink into a cautious sitting position against the cliff. His incisions were still sore from Eve removing the stitches.

Betty turned her head to face him. "I've been wanting for several days now to thank you for how you handled Crystal and her lie. You're a wise man, Jake. You've been good for Crystal. She's blossomed on this island in a way I'd hoped only in my dreams to see."

Wise? Maybe three days ago when he'd been on a high about escaping death. He hunched forward, not wanting to meet her eyes. "Can I ask you a question?"

"Of course."

"What was it like for you when Frank died?"

She paused, inhaling deeply, as if steeling herself to open a cobwebbed vault. "Devastating. Frank cheated on me several times in our marriage. I thought I would be glad when he died, that at last I would be free of the shame and hurt."

Her voice quivered. "But the shame and hurt didn't go away. Instead, I discovered I'd stuck with Frank because I believed his affairs were my punishment—punishment for deserting God so I could marry Frank, knowing he wasn't a believer. Then, when he died, I had no one. Not him, not God. Only worse pain, worse loneliness. Each day was a black hole I had to get through by myself."

Jake squirmed. He shouldn't have asked her the question, shouldn't have provoked this painful confession. He sat back and slipped his hand over hers. "I'm sorry."

"No, it's all right. I've come full circle now. When I arrived on this island, I thought it was further punishment. But when you explained God's forgiveness to Crystal, I realized that even though I'd deserted God, I'd never ceased being His beloved. I never stopped believing in Him—I just wallowed in my guilt instead of having the sense to come back home." She laid her other hand on his, sandwiching his big hand between her two small ones. "Jake, you not only helped Crystal, but me too. I'm back in the sheepfold where I belong, and I'm singing halleluiah!"

He eked out a smile, but her joy was hers to exult in, not his. He wasn't a lost sheep. He'd never strayed from the sheepfold. So why had the green pastures and still waters been taken away?

"What about you, Jake? How are you doing?"

His gaze shifted to the Lone Soldier. He pulled his hand away and pointed at the skeleton. "That's how I'm doing."

"I don't understand."

His chest tightened, radiating tension up his neck to his jaws. "I miss Ginny terribly." He cast a wry smile Betty's way. "You heard my ranting. Later I wondered, is Ginny what I want, more than I want God? Is that why I find no comfort in Him?" He shook his head. "No. There's no doubt in my mind. No doubt in my heart. I want God more than I want anything or anyone."

He turned his head to the skeleton and spat out the words, "Just like the Lone Soldier wanted his motherland."

Betty sat in silence, her brow furrowed. When she spoke, her voice was soft. "Sounds to me as if you're saying you've been loyal to God, but He hasn't been loyal to you. Jake, you know God doesn't abandon His loved ones."

He scowled.

"He hasn't abandoned you, Jake."

"No?" He twisted to confront her, eyeball to eyeball. "Then what has He done to my life?"

* * *

Above them, Eve stood at the edge of the small plateau, her fingers gripping her shirt tighter with every word until her knuckles paled. Jake's answer to Betty, mounting like the red-hot lava of an erupting volcano, stunned her.

Not about wanting God—she didn't care about that. But about being abandoned. *Abandoned.* Her heart pounded so hard her whole body shook. That was the horrifying truth undergirding her nightmare about the wolves.

Her own volcano erupted with frightening intensity. Whatever terror the wolves were, her father hadn't rescued her from them—that part she understood. What was new was that he hadn't cared. Hadn't cared! He had abandoned her to them. Had made that deliberate choice.

The shock registered a 7.0 on the Richter scale of her heart. It knocked flat every thought, every memory, every emotion. Except one. The one that revealed her sprawled by the roadside, dumped like trash from a fleeing vehicle.

She turned numbly as Crystal, panting, her shirt as stuffed with fruit as Eve's, skittered off the mountain path and onto the plateau. "Thanks for waiting. I dropped the mangosteens and had to chase them."

Eve blinked. Below them, Jake and Betty craned their necks to spot them.

"We're ba-ack," Crystal sang out. She sat on her bottom and scooted down the plateau to the trench. "We are fruit-rich!" She giggled and lowered the front of her shirt to reveal her cache. "C'mon, Eve, no fair jumping!"

Eve backed away from the edge and obediently slid down the plateau. She clasped the fruit to her chest as if it were something precious. Something she must not let go of. Inside the cave, she gently deposited the fruit onto the table.

A mental fog, so thick she could hardly push through it, stilled her hands, her feet, her brain. She stood, vaguely aware of Jake bumbling off to the sleeping corridor, of Betty and Crystal pawing over the fruit spread across the bamboo slats of the table.

"Did you hear me?" Betty whispered fiercely. "Jake needs your help!"

That caught her attention. She elbowed out of the fog. God-abandoned hero needs help of father-abandoned wolf victim. "Sorry," she mumbled. "Tell me again."

"Exercise," Betty hissed. "Help him recover. Keep him busy with goals. Get him over this grump hump he's facing."

"He knows how to exercise, Betty. He doesn't need me nagging him. We'd both hate it."

"You said you'd be a blessing to him from now on. Well, here's your chance."

Blessing? Keeping her distance would be the blessing, not ramping up time spent with him. A feeling of light-headedness weaseled into her heart at the thought of an excuse to be with him. Could she handle it without giving herself away?

She shook her head. "Sorry, it won't work."

"You can help him get his mind off his problems," Betty persisted. "Give him something to be successful at. You owe it to him."

"I don't—" *Owe him anything?* She gritted her teeth. Only her life. Her heart, too, although she couldn't reveal that. "Okay, Betty, I don't think he'll go for it, but I'll offer."

And hope, for her heart's sake, that he rejected it.

* * *

Sighing, Eve set two stones weighing some five pounds apiece onto the flattened grass halfway down the trench. Her heartbeat quickened as Jake stuck his head out the cave door and inched his way like an ancient, emaciated tortoise into the morning sunshine. She ached to help him to his feet, to feel his arm clasping her shoulders while they plodded side by side down the trench for his morning walk. But that was not what Jake wanted. His plan was recovery, not intimacy. Fine. That's what she'd help him with then.

She stood with her hands loosely at her sides. No folding her arms—that looked authoritative. Jake was the one in charge here; he'd made that clear. She was still surprised he'd agreed to let her assist him with an exercise plan. The patter of her heartbeat slowed at remembering the expression on his face when she'd offered. Definitely not a look of appreciation. More like she was cod liver oil, distasteful but good for the health.

"I found two rocks for you." She retrieved them from the grass and held them up. Oh, good grief—she was acting like a ten year old trying to win the approval of a dumb boy too young to be aware of girls yet.

"Good. Thanks." Jake didn't even glance at her. His attention was focused on where he placed his steps on the uneven terrain of the trench.

Ah, that was probably why he'd said yes. For him to trip now, or to fall short in any of his exercise goals, meant humiliation. Betty or Crystal would give him sympathy and be easy on him, but certainly not Eve. No, he'd think of her as being as hard-nosed as a boot-camp drill sergeant. She crunched her bottom lip between her front teeth. So, was that a compliment or a finger pointing to yet another of her faults?

His smile when he reached her set her heart thumping even faster. So what if the grin was because he'd gone the distance without stumbling— that big flash of teeth said he was sharing the success with her. She couldn't help but return the smile. But she didn't compliment him. Not when her role was to be the tough guy.

"Ready?" As soon as he stopped next to her, she held out the two stones.

He settled his puffing with a big intake of breath, took hold of the rocks, and shifted his feet into a wider stance. "Curls first, then presses."

She counted for him, her stomach clenching toward the end at seeing him strain to barely lift the rocks. Her sigh at the finish was as heavy with relief as his. "Good job, Jake." An understatement, really. She relieved him of the stones and set them where no one would trip over them.

The last part of his plan was to walk back to the cave. How was he going to do that when, simply standing there, his whole body trembled from his exertion with the stones?

Sometimes you just had to overrule good intentions. Stepping past him, she took his hand and fastened it onto her shoulder with her own grip. She pivoted to face the cave. "Jailbird's march," she commanded. Her step forward forced him to step with her. His weight jolted through his arm to her shoulder, so that she had to brace herself to keep from sprawling on the grass. But he didn't protest the change of plans. Step, brace, step, brace. Slower than an ancient tortoise, they made it back to the cave door without falling.

Jake sank to his knees at the entrance and sat back against the cliff with a deep huff. Crawling inside didn't look like a viable option.

"I'll get us some water." She brought them each a coconut shell filled from the bucket inside the cave.

"Didn't realize I was this bad off." Jake held the shell with both hands to drink.

"You did well. I was impressed." She let the compliment sink in. Then, with a wicked snicker, "Ready to do it again tonight?" That was the plan. His plan. And she was the tough guy helping him out.

His cheek twitched in a half-hearted smile.

A week later, the trench was an easy walk. They moved the routine down to the cove, where Jake could also bathe. Heavier rocks and longer distances were added, until, at the end of a month, he announced he was fit and ready to resume his responsibilities. His body was no longer a mirror image of the skeletal Lone Soldier, but was filled out with regained weight and muscle.

In fact, he looked quite good. With shaggy, dark auburn hair curling onto his neck, his beard a startling orange, and the katana sword strapped across his bare chest and back, he rated the title of Island Warrior. He laughed at that.

He laughed a lot now, smiled a lot. Betty beamed at the change. "Nice work, Eve. Nothing builds up a man like achieving his goals."

If only the laughter and joy were in reaction to her. Oh, she knew how to attract a man's attention, to let him know he was an item of interest. But that wasn't what she wanted with Jake. She'd had enough of shallow relationships.

Clearly he thought of her as a comfortable companion, nothing more. And that was how they'd remain.

She'd have no problem keeping her love a secret.

Chapter 46

Jake poked his head out of the sleeping corridor. "Eve, now that we've found the axe, do you want to check on the bamboo with me tomorrow?" The thought of tramping all alone over the island squeezed the juice out of his brain. Last time he'd been gone that long, he spent the whole time thinking of Ginny, missing her until it drove him crazy. The memories were sweet, but only in small doses. Three solid days would take him over the edge.

Eve hesitated before turning from the hearth fire, but Crystal whipped right around. "I want to go!"

Why hadn't he thought of that? "Works for me, Pumpkin. We'll be gone two nights, if that's all right with your aunt."

"Please, Aunty?"

Betty rose from her chair at the hearth to face Jake. "I wouldn't sleep a wink." Already she was wringing her hands.

"But I'll be with Jake. There's nothing to worry about."

"You'd be going through that croc land and around the swamp," Betty croaked. "Right, Jake?"

"Right." No way Betty would relent after his and Eve's croc story from the typhoon. "Tell you what, Pumpkin, next time I go to the volcano top, I'll take you with me. Since we're all out of marshmallows, we'll roast a snake or two up there to gnaw on."

Snakes—the little ones—had become Crystal's favorite treat. From the glower on her face, though, not enough of a treat to replace a three day trip with him. Truth to tell, he was disappointed too.

"Take Eve with you if she'll go," Betty said. "Crystal and I will be fine."

He looked back at Eve. "You up for it?" Funny how they'd all changed. Eight months ago he'd never have thought city-girl Eve capable of roughing it. Now she was all smiles at the prospect.

Her voice percolated enthusiasm. "I've been wanting to check out the bamboo."

"Good, then I'll get you up early with me." He ducked back into the sleeping corridor. Guess he had changed too. Eight months ago he'd have died rather than ask Eve along. But once her drive to attend that court date got out of her system, she'd proven herself a real trooper. Much more cooperative. Likeable, even.

His eagerness to leave woke him several times before enough light peeked through the portals to warrant rising. He roused Eve, and they slipped out quietly to avoid waking Crystal. He wouldn't put it past the child to sneak after them.

Eve chuckled at the idea. "And risk Betty's wrath? I don't think so."

Good point. Winning her aunt's trust was proving a tough challenge for the poor kid.

He strapped the katana sword onto his back, and Eve fastened a bayonet onto her side. Last night, she had finished everyone's moccasins made from the deer hide. They weren't bad, considering she hadn't known how to cure the hide, but the the two shirts made from the leopard skin were as stiff as armored vests. She wore hers over her ragged T-shirt, but he was waiting until his stitches healed. And no matter how much she protested, he was going to wear his inside out with the soft fur next to his skin.

He took off at a trot, Eve easily keeping pace with him. She was only inches shorter than he, compared to Ginny, who was a foot shorter and needed him to slow down for them to walk together. Walking or running, Eve's long legs were a match for his. She'd demonstrated that well enough during their exercise sessions. Only after he'd won their last few foot races was he ready to declare himself fully recovered.

In no time at all, even with stopping to pick fruit, they arrived at the beach where Betty and Crystal had landed. Where he'd swum out to rescue Eve. He paused to gaze at the tossing ocean. Now that he knew how far away the tip of the island was, he marveled that the current hadn't swept the two of them out to sea.

God's intervention? Or just the way things had worked out? If he hadn't rescued Eve, she wouldn't have been there to sew up his wounds from the leopard. He'd have bled to death. Crystal and Betty would have been left alone and defenseless on the island. Gratitude at how the events had lined up swelled his heart.

But if God were going to intervene, why not do it before Captain Emilio killed all the passengers? He clenched his teeth. None of this needed to have happened. He should have been back home with Ginny, spending their last days together.

Beside him, Eve raised her voice above the caws of gulls soaring overhead. "This is where you swam out to rescue me, right?" She squeezed her right hand in her left and looked down. "I was stupid to be angry at you for pulling me ashore by my hair instead of appreciating the fact that you'd saved my life." She quirked a weak smile out of one side of her mouth. "I guess sometimes the trivial right in front of our eyes blocks the significance of the big picture behind it."

"You were pretty traumatized after a day in the ocean."

Her face grew sober. "I was. I've never been so scared in my life." A shiver imbedded her next breath. "The ocean was endless. Nothing in sight above the water, everything to dread below the water. It was like a glimpse of eternity. A glimpse of—" She stopped.

"Of God?"

"Yes." She shook her head, her eyes casting back and forth across the sand. "He's so completely unfathomable. He's just ... out there. You don't know what in life is going to strike you. You don't know where there's safety. You're always at risk."

His head spun. Wasn't that what he'd been feeling? Struck by God, no rhyme or reason? He filtered through his stock answers for her, but came up empty.

"Anyway"—Eve huffed a snort of self-conscious laughter—"my hair survived quite well." She touched his arm, a swift gesture that flitted away without settling. "Silly to bring it up, but, well, thank you for holding on and not letting go. I'm glad it served as a towrope."

He glanced at her hair. The sun had bleached its deep honey color into a kaleidoscope of blonde highlights. Ginny's hair had done that, too, brightening under the summer sun to a shiny copper orange. Her hair was curly in fine wisps that framed her face. Eve's was a thick curtain that hung behind her ears and partway down her back.

He blinked away the comparison. "You're welcome." What do you say to someone whose life you saved? *Make it count now that you know how precious life is?*

That wasn't what he heard God saying to him. More like Jake Chalmers' life hadn't counted in the first place.

* * *

Could the trip have started out any better? It was all Eve could do not to shout her joy. Finally, that ridiculous incident about her hair had been dealt with! Would apologies for her other offenses bring the same relief? Jake would have to hold her hand just to keep her from floating away. Maybe on this little excursion she could reverse all her past wrongs with him. Three days—oh what a sweet journey lay ahead!

"Croc land," Jake announced as they crossed from beach to bog. As if she wouldn't remember the spot.

They trudged single file, their moccasins making soft sucking sounds with each lift of a foot. Although they were at the far edge of the swamp, only a stone's throw from the ocean, the trees effectively cocooned them in damp heat and a stench of rotting vegetation. A welcome committee of mosquitoes escorted them the entire way. She swatted them at every step. "I hope these guys aren't carrying malaria. I've got more bites than I've got hairs on my head."

Jake peered over his shoulder and grinned. "It's the gals who bite."

She rolled her eyes. Correction was not conducive to the good time she planned with Jake. "I don't care about the gender; I care about the disease."

"They'd have to bite an infected person to be carriers. I think we're safe."

"Then how about if we go into the swamp to see the tree stumps you found?"

"You mean the mahogany? You like being eaten alive?"

They emerged from the jungle into blazing light reflected off white sand—a warning that their feet, even with moccasins on, would pay the price of a noonday sun that ate shadows for lunch. Within minutes, their clothes were soaked with a second coat of sweat.

Jake stooped and brushed aside the sand at his feet until he reached the cooler layer underneath. "Mosquito repellent." He smeared handfuls over every inch of his sweaty, exposed skin. Eve followed suit.

At a rise of land that disappeared into the swamp, Jake dropped the axe to retrieve on their return and scanned the landscape. "There's a lot of new vegetation here since I found the stumps. Ten to one it's covered them up, but they're not far." He pointed at the tree line. "You can see the young mahoganies from here."

She stepped up onto the grassy strip to follow him into the bog. Ahead of her, dozens of slender trees ten to twenty feet high rose from the muddy water at the swamp's edge. Beyond them, larger trees, ferns, and moss-covered logs layered the swamp like a moldy onion seen from the inside out. The odor of rotten eggs clogged her nostrils.

"Hang in there," Jake called back. "A few more minutes and the smell will be so overwhelming your brain will shut it off."

Eve snorted. Only a man would find that comforting.

The rise of land ended where a thick, gnarled tree with knobby roots clasped the bank. The tree leaned out over brown water so glass-smooth, it reflected the tree in perfect detail. Without hesitation, Jake climbed into the branches. "Okay, I can see the stumps."

Eve hoisted herself onto the lowest branch opposite his. On either side of the tree, the young mahoganies increased in size until they stopped abruptly at a series of stumps. Their tops were flat, obviously cut. Some were rotten, some bore shoots of flourishing offspring. Both indicated years had passed since they'd been harvested.

"Look!" Jake lowered his voice. "A deer, over there. We're downwind, so it doesn't smell us."

Eve spotted the creature on the other side of the bog. She crouched lower on the branch. "It's a doe," she whispered. "She's lovely! I wonder if she has a fawn nearby."

The doe approached the bank cautiously. She studied the water, took a step, stopped. Studied, took another step, stopped. Finally she reached the water's edge. Her front hoof sank into the mud, and she shrank back onto her haunches.

Eve held her breath.

The deer's ears twitched. She looked around, straightened, took another step forward. The hoof sank alongside the first one. She gazed out over the brown water. At last she lowered her head and drank.

The water opened with a sudden upsurge. A huge crocodile lunged forward and grabbed the doe's head in its jaws. In a blink, the croc and deer were gone. The water swirled once, twice, then smoothed into its former glaze.

"Oh!" Eve leaped up in horror. Her foot slipped, and she fell. Her ribs thudded against the branch and bounced off. She grabbed the limb and held on for dear life. In her mind's eye, she saw the croc leave the drowned deer and head for her legs dangling inches above the water.

She jerked her knees to her chest and looked down. The mirror-smooth reflection showed her eyes wide, her chest heaving. The water was only feet away. She couldn't stop looking. Her folded legs trembled. The joints of her fingers pinched.

Below her, the surface of the water broke. Flowed smoothly off a bumpy, gray wedge. It rose and lengthened into a snout. Two knobs at the wider end opened into filmy slits. The eyes gazed up at her.

The wedge swam away, made a U-turn, and submerged. She screamed as a trail of ripples headed straight toward her.

Chapter 47

Jake launched himself through the tree and snatched up Eve's right hand. With a mighty tug, he jerked her onto the branch with him. At the same time, the water split open and a gray missile propelled itself upward. Gaping jaws snapped at Eve's feet. Water spattered them as the croc's head slapped back into the swamp.

The tree lurched under the impact of their weight on the lower branch. Inch by inch, then faster, it tipped lower over the water. Half its roots slipped loose from the muddy bank and rose with equal speed skyward. "Jump!" Jake shouted. He gripped Eve's hand tighter and hauled her after him in a flying leap. They landed flat on their faces halfway up the bank.

"Run!" he screamed. Eve needed no urging. Grabbing hold of reeds and tree roots, they scrabbled up the bank. From the corner of his eye, he caught a flash of gray scales punch out of the water onto the bank below them. "Croc!" he bellowed.

At the top of the embankment they scrambled to their feet and bolted for the beach. The question was not if the croc would chase them, but how far before it caught up with them.

"Split up," he yelled at the beach. Whichever person the croc followed, the other could swing back, grab the axe, and strike. He had his sword, and Eve, a bayonet, but they couldn't risk stopping to face the croc and end up thrown off their feet before they got their weapons out. A foot or leg severed by powerful jaws was not a price he wanted to pay.

Eve veered to the right, so he swung left. He turned his head as he ran to catch a glimpse of the beast. It wasn't following him.

He halted in a swift about-face and yanked the sword from his back. The croc wasn't pursuing Eve either.

Chuffing air from his heaving chest, sword held at the ready, he crept back to the rise of land. He spotted the animal, immobile, halfway down the strip. The beast was huge. If there'd been elephants on the island, the croc could have eaten them for breakfast and still been hungry for dinner.

Jake backed away. No attacking this baby. It was hard to swallow his spit, just looking at the monster.

When the croc finally returned to the swamp, Jake retrieved the axe and trotted to where Eve sat waiting for him at a safe distance. The track of tears on her face cautioned him against exclaiming over the reptile's size. She didn't need to know. "You okay?"

She stood and rubbed her arms, hunching her shoulders into a slow shrug. "All I can think of is how glad I am you didn't bring Crystal."

A wave of nausea swept over him. Crystal would never have outrun the beast. His knees almost collapsed, and he took a step to steady himself. "Yes, thank You, God." He couldn't have saved her. And he'd never have forgiven himself. Never.

Eve walked over to him and wrapped shaking arms around him. His surprise lasted a second, then he closed his eyes and put his arms around her. He needed the comfort as much as she did.

* * *

What was she doing? Startled by her boldness, Eve stepped away from the solace of Jake's arms. Good grief, she had hugged Jake. She blinked. And he had hugged her back! A shiver of excitement radiated up her chest to her throat. So what if the catalyst was mutual terror! It took all the restraint she could summon to not slip her hand into his as they commenced walking.

Near the end of the beach, they passed the spot where Jake had towed her in from the sea, and where, farther back at the tree line, they had camped in exhaustion their first day on the island. Jake neither stopped nor commented. His pace was short of a jog, his expression one of determination. Clearly they were on this journey to inspect bamboo, and she needed to keep her mind on that. She quelled a huff.

The snap of croc teeth inches below her toes and the scrape of its scales crushing vegetation as the beast hurtled after her faded with the challenge of entering unfamiliar territory. Although Jake had explored this side of the island twice, it was new to her. Fewer beaches skirted its perimeter, and the jungle encroached to the edge of the rocky precipices. They spent more time climbing in and out of crevices than they did pushing through jungle brush. But how could she complain when the ache in her calf and thigh muscles was more than compensated for by Jake's strong fingers giving her a hand up?

By the time they reached the first bamboo plants, the sun was chasing clouds in the west. Jake peered at the tops of cane twice his height. "This is the smallest stand. They've shot up nicely, but their culms have no size yet. Probably won't for years."

She resisted the temptation to sink to the ground, remove her mocassins, and wiggle her weary toes. "How did you find bamboo way out here? Seems like a blindfolded man would have had as good a chance."

"Actually, this was a shortcut." Jake grinned. "Bamboo spreads by sending up new shoots from its roots. Once I found the first stand, it was merely a matter of scouting out others nearby. I suspect typhoons knock out the older cane each year. The stands I used for the outrigger sure got flattened anyway."

The outrigger—ouch. Something else to apologize for. She mustered a deep breath. Asking forgiveness wasn't as easy as she'd thought. "About that, I—" What? Was she wrong to take the outrigger? To spare the others by endangering only herself? Her apologies needed full integrity to be genuine. No confessing wrong-doing for something she wasn't actually guilty of.

Jake raised his eyebrows, a prod to finish her sentence.

The leaves of the bamboo rustled in a breeze. Almost as if the gust swept through her, the answer whooshed from her heart: truth was, her only interest had been to fulfill her wishes. What anyone else wanted hadn't mattered.

The answer hit her hard, like a cane to the back of her knees. She dropped with a thump to the ground. No matter how she coated her motive with good intentions, it still came down to looking out for what she—and only she—wanted.

Jake stooped at her side, his hand on her shoulder. "Are you okay? I'm afraid I exhausted you getting here."

"Jake." She choked out the words. "I'm sorry about taking the boat." But it was more than that, wasn't it? She had as good as stolen it. "I, I was selfish ... it belonged to all of us." She gulped in a breath, squeezing back moisture in her eyes. "All your hard work ... I messed it up."

For a moment that seemed to expand into eternity, he crouched unmoving at her side. His hand cupped her shoulder. The heavy odor of his sweat mingled with hers, overpowering the woody scent of the bamboo stand. Between her ears, the echo of her heartbeat pounded. In a flash, it struck home that her confession must have moved him deeply. *Jake, please. I want so badly to make a new start.* She closed her eyes. The wait was unbearable.

Finally, the weight of his hand withdrew from her shoulder. She opened her eyes to find him sitting squarely opposite her. His eyes fastened onto hers with such intensity her insides quaked at how he might answer her.

"The outrigger?" He pressed his lips together and shrugged. "We'll just have to build a replacement. But I appreciate your apology." His eyes bore deeper into hers. Clearly he wished to say more.

Did she want him to? She swallowed and lifted her chin in a tiny nod.

At her assent, the corners of his mouth tugged down and his voice deepened into raw emotion. "To tell the truth, it hurt that you didn't trust me. Hurt that I couldn't trust you."

The depth of his pain slammed a second blow. The fact that he dared to share it, that this very private, totally self-controlled man had revealed his heart to her, stretched her anguish to its breaking point. She longed to reach out, to open her arms to him, to make things right between them.

But how? How, when she didn't understand?

Her mind spun in bewilderment. Trust? What did trust have to do with her selfishness? She understood selfishness had repercussions—the courtroom handled their disastrous consequences all the time—but how was there any connection with trust? She stared numbly at Jake.

The fierceness of his gaze softened. "Tell you what." He got to his feet. "We're both tired. We'll camp here tonight and get a good start tomorrow. You rest while I check out some banana plants nearby."

She nodded. He was giving her alone time. A spasm pinched her stomach, leaped to her lungs, and rose to her throat. As soon as Jake's footsteps faded, hot tears sloshed onto her cheeks. She dashed them away with her fingertips. What was it with this island? It kept showing her up as a different person than she knew herself to be. She'd always been so sure of herself, so confident her decisions were for the good of mankind.

"My way or the highway." She remembered a colleague using the phrase to describe her. It fit. She'd rarely lost a court case in thirteen years as a federal prosecutor. Judge, jury, and sentence almost always confirmed her on what was right and wrong. So why place trust in anyone else?

At the crunch of fallen bamboo underfoot, she swiped the backs of her hands across her face to remove any trace of tears. Jake wended his way toward her, a cluster of bananas on his right shoulder. Her heart beat faster as he drew near.

Trust.

If it was that important to Jake, maybe a step forward would be to tell him she was a federal prosecutor. Tell him about the Romero case. About her being the target of the explosions.

An avalanche of fear rumbled from her brain to her heart to her toes. She gripped the banana Jake handed her. He had placed the responsibility for Ginny's death on Captain Emilio's shoulders. Surely she could trust him not to fault her too.

* * *

Jojo spat into the gutter. Aboard the transport ship, Eduardon hadn't seemed much shorter than his shipmates, but now the crowded streets of Manila showed him up to be the runt he really was. Keeping him in sight required a tighter leash than Jojo liked. All it would take Eduardon was a casual glance over his shoulder, a quick turn at a street corner, and he couldn't miss Jojo towering above the foot traffic. If the twerp got suspicious, Jojo would have to find someone else. But his gut told him Eduardon was the man, and if there was anything Jojo trusted, it was his gut.

Eduardon disappeared into an open doorway. Jojo lurked outside to the count of ten before thrusting his face next to the storefront's dirty window. Inside, Eduardon sat on a barstool, his back to the street, his legs dangling far above the litter on the floor. The dark room held only a few customers, and the bartender was quick to sweep Eduardon's coins off the counter and serve him. Jojo waited for the first drink to hit Eduardon's gullet, then sauntered in.

He took a stool one away from Eduardon's perch and ordered a whiskey. Eduardon glanced sideways at him but made no attempt at conversation. Of course not. They were both seamen, but Eduardon was an officer, Jojo a mere deckhand. Precisely why Jojo wanted him.

Three weeks together on the transport ship had quickly exposed Eduardon as Jojo's man. The crew laid out the sour-faced officer as a second-rate navigator, ambitious without success, angry at the hand life had dealt him. His wife had run out on him years earlier, and his money slipped away as easily. The only jobs he got anymore were on antiquated ships with crude captains and low-life crews. Eduardon's sneers made it clear he considered himself above them, though, in truth, Jojo saw, they intimidated him. A pilot and a proud coward—what could be more perfect?

Jojo waited until the man downed two more drinks and was squirming off the barstool to drop to the floor. "Hey, you looking to score some cash?"

Eduardon's face swiveled toward him, eyes narrowed above a barely checked sneer. "Like what?"

"You like cockfights?" Jojo knew it was Eduardon's passion.

Eduardon shrugged but followed Jojo out the door. Two hours and two bottles of whiskey later, after all the yelling and wild emotion of the cockfights had stirred some life into Eduardon, Jojo put the proposition to him. "You ever dream of sailing your own ship?"

"Pah. You think I earn that kind of money?"

"Forget the money."

"Forget … ? What're you talking about?"

"We start with a yacht. Take some rich foreigner's that nobody's gonna miss for a while. No measly barnacle bait, but a beauty—that's what we want!"

Eduardon's eyes shone in an alcoholic haze at the vision.

"Then we unload it, and we each start on our own boat."

"Nah." Eduardon pawed the illusion away. He hicupped. "Never get away with stealing it. Catch ya as soon as you hit the open sea."

"Not if we hide on an island."

"Islands're full of snitches. Turn ya in, or highjack it for their own pocket money."

Jojo clapped him on the back, careful not to jolt the pipsqueak off his feet. "Got the island already picked out. About as remote as you can get. No one on it, a small hidden cove on the north side. You can sail us straight there before anyone knows the boat's gone."

Eduardon twitched Jojo's beefy hand off his shoulder. "So you need a navigator, that it? Who else?"

"A deckhand and a cook. Got them ready to go soon as I say. All we need is the boat."

Eduardon's answer was long in coming, but Jojo didn't push him. Eduardon stared out at the ocean, dark beyond the harbor lights but filling the night with the incessant swash of its waves and the damp tang of seaweed and salt. "Okay. I got a cargo ship sailing out tomorrow. Be gone four weeks. You find that yacht, we've got a deal."

He turned and strode away. No staggering, no pausing to question which way, no bumping into the herd on the street. Jojo grunted. For a little twerp, Eduardon could hold his liquor. Good. That meant he'd remember they had a deal. Jojo would hold him to it.

Four weeks. Did the runt think he was going to be in charge because he was an officer? Jojo released a long belch. When Jojo's gut said they'd found the right yacht, that's when they'd make their move.

And that's when Eduardon would get his first lesson in kissing Jojo's toes.

Chapter 48

Eve was no ascetic when it came to fillng her belly, but when her fifth banana peel hit the ground, Jake reckoned it was her mouth she was stuffing, not her stomach. Okay, so she didn't want to finish their discussion about how she'd broken his trust. Disappointment rolled a five ton lorry over his hopes. To spare her a sixth banana, he called it a night. "We'll check out the other bamboo stands tomorrow. I think we'll find culms we can harvest in at least one of them."

He scooped out a shallow pit and used the binocular lens on the evening's fading rays to build a fire from dried leaves and bamboo scraps. The gentle breeze that seemed to have taken up residence among the tall cane drifted the smoke just enough to send the mosquitoes packing. Eve dropped right off to sleep, but his disgruntlement clamped shut his jaws and locked open his eyelids.

The scars on his back throbbed in the midst of tense shoulder muscles. He blew out a breath and inhaled slowly, consciously relaxing his muscles before shifting to face the fire. On the other side, Eve slept with her back to him. Her hair, tucked behind her ears as usual, hung like a shimmering curtain, reflecting the embers' glow. Her ribs rose and fell in the rhythm of a steady sleep.

His mind sped back to the croc and the hug that followed. The tightness in his jaws relaxed. That hug had opened a door for him and Eve. Had taken them beyond the camaraderie developed in their month of exercise together to a new level of companionship.

His pulse quickened, thrumming hushed, cotton-cushioned taps against his eardrums. He closed his eyes—remembering, savoring. Eve in his arms, seeking him out. Her remorse for taking the outrigger. The plea in her eyes to be reconciled with him. Something had happened with that embrace. Something that bared their souls. Freed her to apologize. Freed him to reveal the pain of her betrayal with the outrigger.

Eve's nightmare about her father and the wolves leaped to mind. His eyelids shot open. Of course. Why had he thought Eve could respond to what he'd said? She didn't know what trust was. Trust was a void, a chasm she couldn't cross.

But that didn't mean he couldn't cross to her. Bridge the void with a friendship that rose above her father's failure. That bridged his own void too. He swallowed back his aching loneliness for Ginny.

Piece by piece he'd build that bridge. Carefully. He didn't want to damage the fragile friendship they'd just achieved.

* * *

Eve sat up and brushed the grit of cane debris from her arms and legs. The bitter odor of last night's fire trailed an acrid scum down her throat to her stomach. Across from her, Jake sat with bulging cheeks, chomping the only item on their breakfast menu. When he reached across with a banana, she scrunched her nose. "If I have to eat one more banana, I'll vomit."

An unsuccessfully suppresed grin flicked the corners of his mouth. "We'll keep an eye out for something else on our way."

Could she eat anything anyway? Probably not until she admitted who she was to Jake. She stood and brushed off her shirt and shorts. What a coward she'd been last night. The timing would have been perfect. All she'd had to say was "Jake, I'm a federal prosecutor," and he would have taken it from there. Now she'd have to figure out how and when to bring it up.

Tonight. She curled her fingers into tight fists and shackled herself to the promise. In the meantime, she'd shove it off her plate so she could get through the day.

With no crevices to climb in and out of, their travel time to the closest bamboo stand was short. At its center, dozens of towering plants displayed thick culms. Eve encircled one with her forefingers and thumbs to form a fat *O*. "This size looks perfect."

"Too old." Jake pointed to patches of fungus on one woody stem after another. "I had to throw away a raft's worth of these last summer before I caught on. They won't hold up."

At the next stand, the diameter of several culms was two-thirds the size of the last ones, but with no fungus. Jake ran his hands over their sleek surfaces. "These will do, but there aren't enough."

The third stand contained more culms the same size. "All right, let's harvest these and stack them to dry, then go back for the others." He frowned. "The raft will be narrower than I want, but the trade-off might be it's easier to manipulate."

Cutting the bamboo proved no easy task. Between the whacks from the axe and the pressure of her and Jake's weight pushing against the stalks, the bamboo yielded its lumber reluctantly. Equally trying was positioning the leggy culms in a stack to leach their sugar and harden the wood. Her skin itched nonstop. Oh, what she wouldn't give for the cool massage of the stream next to their cave. At least when she and Jake returned in two weeks for the culms, all they'd have to do was drag them to the beach.

By noon, she was shaky from not eating. They'd found no alternatives to the bananas. On the north side of the island around the cove, they knew where dozens of fruit grew. But on this side, the unexplored jungle hid its cupboard from them. She gladly ate the bananas Jake had stuffed into his pockets, and more later that night at their campsite.

She ate two for supper before her stomach tightened around them like a noose. Okay, so she was a little nervous, but she was ready. Ready to tell Jake she was a federal prosecutor. She'd just wait until after he finished building his fire to decamp the mosquitos …

The bamboo stand hushed as he held the binocular lens steady. Didn't stir when the dry leaves wisped up smoke. Held its breath when they flattened to gray ash. A spark bit noiselessly into the shards of cane. Slowly, ticking off seconds, Jake leaned over the tinder and pursed his lips. A sharp puff broke the silence, and golden flames danced.

Her breath caught in her throat. *Now.* She needed to tell him *now.*

Four simple words: I'm a federal prosecutor.

"Jake—" His name came out strangled. Her brain set off an alarm, and her heartbeat accelerated. Acid pinched the walls of her stomach. She felt the blood drain from her face. Felt her cheeks and forehead and the skin on her arms and hands go clammy. The pulse in her throat lifted in frantic flight.

The bamboo swirled around her in a dizzying spiral. The dancing flames of the fire clicked off into darkness. Clicked on again at Jake's voice. "Eve!"

She blinked, found herself in his arms, his face inches from hers. Worry furrowed the skin around his eyes and across his brow. He lowered her to the ground and gently released her. "Are you okay? You passed out."

Her brain clicked into full power, and sorrow seeped in. The words "I'm a federal prosecutor" lay crushed and flattened on her docket. She couldn't say them. Couldn't take them to the man she loved for him to judge and pass sentence on.

The only words legible on her docket were *United States vs. Danny Romero.*

That was her destiny.

Not Jake.

Words came out of her mouth, but not the ones she wanted to say. "I, I'm okay now."

She swallowed back the wail that beat on her chest. Drowned it, like the croc had drowned the doe.

Chapter 49

Jake picked his way over debris and loose stones to the log that had shoved him and Eve over the cliff almost a year ago. His heart beat faster with each step. What had once almost killed them might now prove the very means of saving them. Huge boulders held the two halves of the log high above the sandbar and the hungry waves salivating at its edge. Above him, Crystal peered over the top of the cliff with its whiskery tree roots spiking its side. The faint odor of Betty's sea chowder emanated from the cave door, undaunted by the briny competition of the vast ocean.

The log was mahogany, no doubt carefully selected by the Japanese soldiers for its resistance to rot. Crumbling wood made for a lousy booby trap. If he could carve the longest half of the broken log into a dugout, it would accommodate at least one passenger. Connecting it to the raft would increase their chance of making it safely to the sea-lane.

He tromped around the battered log, studying it from every angle. After stripping away the bark, he'd have to create the boat upside down. Start at the top of the log to level out a flat underside, hack out arches for the bow and stern, then roll the log over to hollow it. Quite a task with an axe as his only tool. Maybe he could speed things up for the passenger's seat by using coals.

Ah, so much more fun than making a simple raft. He pulled a strip of bark from the log. Unfortunately, the lone axe allowed for only one workman on the dugout, whereas the raft benefitted from two sets of hands. His and Eve's. His grin broadened into a smile. In two weeks they'd go back for the cured bamboo. Spend days together assembling the raft. Sail it to the finished dugout, or vice versa, and attach the two. He gazed out at the tossing ocean. For sure they'd test the vessel's seaworthiness with the four of them aboard before sailing to the sea-lane. Then off they'd go, loaded with provisions in case they had to wait for a ship to rescue them.

Eve rounded the corner of the sandbar, and the sweetness of honeycomb rose up in him. "Hey, come take a look." He helped her up the largest boulder and took her arm to maneuver her around the worst of the debris. He'd need to make a safe path for her and Crystal to visit him.

"Do you see a boat in there like you'd hoped?" Eve studied the log.

"Call me Pygmalion, if you will." Jake waggled his eyebrows. "Keep me company when you can, and you shall see a beautiful maiden emerge."

Eve snorted, but her eyes danced. "Besides me?"

He liked it when she joked with him. "A better swimmer, anyway."

"What, my towrope wasn't enough for you?" She made a face at him. "Tell me what you have planned while we get fruit."

When she scooted off the boulders without his help, he found himself disappointed.

* * *

Did nobody but her notice the change? Crystal huffed as Jake and Eve disappeared around the bend of the sandbar. Could no one but her see that Jake and Eve enjoyed each other's company now? Preferred each other, even? They hardly went anywhere without the other. Okay, at first it made sense—gathering fruit and fishing and stuff together while Jake got over his injury—but, still, was sitting next to each other, arms touching, normal for them? Or helping each other, hand to hand, when they climbed trees ... or rocks? And what about the smiles and laughter and silly jokes?

Ha! She knew puppy love when she saw it. The kids at school were always leaping in and out of love like frogs on a hot skillet.

She withdrew her head from the cliff's edge and huffed louder, the noise lending at least some comfort to her sore heart. Should she point out the budding romance to Aunt Betty? She knew what Aunt Betty would do:

scold Jake and tell him not to make the same mistake she had made in marrying Uncle Frank. It was no secret Eve didn't cotton to God.

She hunched her shoulders and scrunched her nose. No, a big huh-uh. That idea made her heart even sorer. But what if Eve changed her mind about God? And what if she and Jake got married? Maybe, just maybe, they'd adopt her. She slipped her hands to her shoulders and gave herself an exuberant hug. Yes, that was what she wanted!

A sea gull cawed overhead and flew out to sea. Crystal squinted at the horizon of blue upon blue. It was empty, but what if they got rescued before Eve changed her mind? Jake had said any day now the loggers might return to the island for more mahogany. Rescue could be right around the corner. Or he might get the raft and canoe done, and they'd rescue themselves.

She chewed her lower lip. There must be something she could do to help move things along.

* * *

Tightening her grip on the branch above her, Crystal peered down, down, down through the layers of leaves to the jungle floor. Would Aunt Betty ever have a fit if she knew Eve let her climb this high! How many times had she watched *The Jungle Book* and wished she could swing through the trees and talk to the animals like Mowgli did? Well, forget it. Getting fruit with Eve was all the excitement she needed.

"Here you go." Eve climbed down a branch and dropped several mangos into the pouch Crystal made by holding out the front of her shirt. It was getting pretty full. She'd better hurry if she was going to carry out her plan. A simple question—how hard could that be?

"Eve?" She swallowed as her throat went dry. "Why won't you become a Christian?"

Eve halted in the middle of reaching for a mango. Crystal's heart stopped too.

"Really?" A corner of Eve's mouth jerked in a tic. She picked several mangos and brought them to Crystal. The look on her face said, *Are you old enough for this discussion?*

Crystal's heart went blippety-blip. She held her breath and stared back into Eve's eyes so she'd get the answer: Yes!

"Okay, young lady. To begin with, if there's a God, why doesn't He do something about evil?"

"Oh, I know the answer to that!" Crystal's insides lit up like a lighthouse from Heaven.

"Tuh!" Eve turned her back and climbed to a higher branch.

Crystal lifted her chin. Hey, how many times had she heard Eve talk about *Where's The Justice?* Enough to make Crystal think about it, that's how many! After all, she didn't have a daddy, and her mom had died from an overdose. Where was the justice in all that?

Sadness melted the anger tightening her chest. Like it or not, Eve was going to have to listen. "Grandma and Grandpa have a beautiful house." Eve glanced down at her, and Crystal's insides lit up again. "Everything in it is gorgeous and expensive. When I was little, Grandma wanted to keep everything safe, so she didn't let me into most of the rooms. She kept an eye on me any place I was allowed to go. I never messed anything up.

"Then one day Grandma had to be gone, so she left Grandpa in charge. He let me go wherever I wanted. He even let me feed myself, which I didn't know how to do very well because Grandma always fed me. I spilled on my clothes and on the carpet. Then I got down from my chair and wandered around and made little messes of things and broke some things. I didn't mean to, but Grandma wasn't there to stop me."

"I wouldn't have wanted to be in Grandpa's shoes when Grandma got home!"

Crystal giggled. "But that's how it's always been for me—Grandma, and after that, Grandpa, always making sure I didn't do anything wrong. Would you like God to do that to you?"

Eve's eyebrows flitted up. "You mean, be in my face all the time? No! But how about making us incapable of doing anything wrong in the first place?"

Crystal shrugged. "I don't think I'd like being just an animal." She looked across the canopy foliage at a troop of monkeys, and Eve followed her gaze. "I guess that'd be okay ..." Animals didn't abandon their babies, did they?

"Well, Christians haven't done a very good job of showing love to others. How about the Crusades ... and the Inquisition ... and the Salem witch trials ..."

"Huh?"

"When Christians killed people in the name of God, just because those other people weren't Christians."

"Oh." She didn't know about all that. "Maybe those people just thought they were Christians, or maybe they thought they were pleasing God." Her shoulders slumped. Why had she thought she could persuade someone as smart as Eve? They hadn't even gotten to the important stuff like Jesus dying for your sins, or Heaven where there was no sin. What a dummy she was. "Sorry." She could hardly look at Eve. "I was stupid to try to answer you."

Eve screamed so loud, Crystal almost jumped off the branch. The whites around Eve's irises flashed wide. She pointed at the top of the tree.

Crystal looked up. Slithering through the branches, headed straight toward her and Eve, was a huge snake. If it weren't for its movement, it would have blended perfectly with the foliage.

"Go!" Eve yelled. "Drop the fruit and go!"

Crystal's heart jackknifed to her throat. She grabbed the tree limb with both hands. The mangos in her shirt bounced off her feet and clattered through the branches. She skittered down the trunk so fast she almost beat the fruit. The long drop from the lowest branch was scary, but not as scary as the snake chasing her.

Before she could get to her feet, Eve landed with a *whop* on top of her. Crystal's breath shot out like a cannonball.

Eve rolled off her. "Branch broke on me." Her voice cracked with pain. Blood ran in a bright red ribbon down her right leg. Above them, the snake wound downward through the branches.

Crystal heaved air into her lungs, scrambled to her feet, and tugged Eve to hers. Arms locked on each other's shoulders, they ran side by side for the stream.

She stole a glance behind them. The snake was exiting the tree. Its head reached the ground while its tail was still unraveling from the tree limb. A python, thicker than Jake's arm. Her breath punched out of her lungs and back in again.

Eve's moccasin was soaked with blood. Every step left a trail for the snake to follow.

"Hurry!" She pulled Eve into a faster run. Eve groaned. Her weight grew heavier on Crystal's shoulders. Her stride changed to a limp. Crystal didn't dare stop for fear Eve would collapse.

Her mouth went dry. Eve was in no shape to defend them. That meant it was up to her. "Where's the bayonet?" She shook Eve's shoulder, hard. "Eve! Where's the bayonet?"

"Dunno." Eve's eyes were half-closed. "Lost." She stumbled, and they almost fell.

Crystal choked back a cry. Where were they? She'd forgotten to look for the broken twigs and branches that guided them to the stream. *Please, please, please, God! Help me!*

A rustling noise, soft at first, then getting louder and louder, rose to her ears. The snake—it must be closing in on them. Would it bite them to yank them down before it squished the life out of them?

Her breath rasped through her throat in painful bursts. Her legs wobbled. Eve's hand loosened its hold on Crystal's shoulder. Crystal tried to tighten her own grip on Eve, but her fingers were numb.

The rustling noise increased until it blocked out all other sounds. Her mind went blank, crowding out the reality of what would happen next. Her legs were her brain: *Run!* they commanded. Hold onto Eve and run.

Thick vegetation rose like a wall. They crashed through it. Two steps, three, then Eve's weight toppled forward. Crystal couldn't hold her upright. Couldn't let go of her. She extended her free arm to break her fall.

Her face registered the shock of cool water on her skin. She sputtered and pushed herself to her hands and knees. The stream—the rustling sound had been the stream! Beside her, Eve pushed her chest and head out of the water, choking, blinking. She whisked her hand back to her injured leg. Pink water swirled around her submerged arm and washed downstream.

Before Crystal could say anything, Eve inhaled a sharp breath. Eyes, cheeks, mouth, brow shaped a silent scream. Eve inhaled again and focused on Crystal. "Snakes can swim. Pull me downstream. Hurry."

Crystal sprang up, grabbed Eve's hands, and took off. She hauled Eve as if she were a galloping horse and poor Eve a sled. Fear cracked a wicked whip to speed her steps.

Chapter 50

"J-a-a-a-k-e!"

The shrillness of Betty's voice pierced Jake's concentration on the dugout. He looked up to find her head poked over the cliff's edge, her hands cupped to her mouth. Without a second thought, he dropped the axe and dashed as fast as his legs would run to her side. His heart thundered in his chest. He'd never heard Betty yell like that.

"Do you hear it?" Betty didn't wait for him to catch his breath. She pointed to the hill on the other side of the trench. "It's Crystal screaming."

He didn't stop to listen. He darted across the trench and up the hill. Cresting it, he halted only to whip the sword out of its scabbard and scan the terrain.

"Help!" Crystal's voice drew his eyes to where the stream emerged from the jungle. The bank was steeper there, and she was pulling on something half out of the water.

Eve.

He took off at an all-out sprint.

Crystal broke into sobs as soon as she saw him. He fell to his knees beside Eve. She was on her stomach, her head lolling from Crystal's efforts to tug her ashore by her arms. She was either unconscious or ...

Dropping his sword, he slid one hand under Eve's head, the other hand under her abdomen. "I've got her." Crystal let go, and he lowered Eve to the ground. Her skin was cold against his fingertips as he searched her neck for a pulse.

He found it, but it was faint. Her breathing was shallow. He swept her into his arms to carry her to the top of the embankment. "We've got to warm her up." Only when he lifted her clear of the water did he see the blood dribbling down the back of her right leg.

"What happened?" he barked.

Crystal had stopped crying and was facing the stream, legs apart, his sword held high in both hands, as if her next task was to chop off Goliath's head. Her jaw was clenched. When she turned to him, her eyes were as razor-sharp as the sword she held. Her nostrils flared. "Python."

Python? He did a double take at the half-pint Amazon in dripping shorts and tank top, standing guard between him and the stream. His jaw dropped in admiration.

"It was as big"—out of the corner of her eye, Crystal peeked at his biceps—"bigger around than your arm. It came after us through the tree. Eve fell out and could barely walk. It chased us … maybe down the stream too." Her chin quivered.

No wonder she'd bawled when she saw him. He checked the stream for the snake. "Come here, sweetheart. Bring the sword, and we'll warm Eve up with a big toaster hug."

He climbed the embankment and laid Eve on her side. After checking the stream again for the python, he crouched and pulled up the cuff on the back right side of Eve's shorts. A jagged cut three inches long stretched across the bottom of her buttock. The stream had washed it as clean as it was going to get. Already, the bleeding was subsiding.

He stood and took the sword from Crystal. "You were very brave. I can't tell you how proud I am of you!" She threw her arms around him, but she didn't cry. He smoothed back her wet hair, cradling her head. "When you're ready, I want to hear all about it."

She nodded and stepped back, her face sober.

"Here, let's warm Eve up, you in front, me in back. I'll keep an eye on the stream." Pythons typically lay in wait for their prey. Although this one might have been hungry, chances were it hadn't given chase.

Eve was shivering violently now. He set the sword nearby and hurried to lie down with his chest and hips and legs pressed to her backside. Crystal did the same with her back to Eve's front. When Crystal was settled, he reached over Eve and secured Crystal's arm. Goose bumps pockmarked it like icy land mines. He encircled the slender limb in the warmth of his palm and fingers and rubbed the length of her arm until the bumps disappeared.

With a happy sigh, Crystal launched into the details of her adventure with Eve. Details that lasted all the way to the cave while he carried Eve, and ended only after he placed Eve on her bunk. Then he got to hear the story a second time in bits and pieces, with even more details, when she shared it with Betty and Eve and him over the next several days.

* * *

"Jake, what are you doing!" Betty's voice rose in challenge.

He halted beside her at the cave door. "Why, bringing you ladies lovely flowers."

"Don't tell me those orchids are for us—they're for Eve."

"They're for all of you." But even as he insisted, he felt his face redden. "They're blooming all over the jungle now."

"I notice her favorite fruits are too."

"She's in pain, Betty. A little special attention helps, that's all."

"Special attention is what you'd give Crystal. Jake, you're as good as courting Eve."

He huffed, anger rising in his belly. "You're exaggerating things, Betty. I love Ginny. I miss her, and Eve's friendship helps me not to feel so lonely." He caught his gaffe. "Just like you and Crystal do."

Betty's voice softened. "Ginny is dead, Jake. You'll always love her, but that doesn't mean you can't fall in love with another woman. You should someday. But not Eve." She put her hand on his arm. "You know I treasure both of you. But, please, don't repeat my mistake of marrying a non-Christian. God's command has a sound basis."

It was all he could do to not throw the orchids at her. "I'm not in love with Eve. I'm not going to marry her. And I'm not disobeying God." He shoved the flowers into her hands. "I'll be at the dugout."

Silence followed him like a dark cloud stuck to the back of his head. Past the grass bowing in the minefield, past the waves unfolding against the cove's shore, past the ocean tossing froth at the island.

At the bend to the sandbar, Betty's voice pierced the quiet. "Don't fool yourself, Jake."

By the evening meal, his curdling guts had settled. He was no crabby old woman who nursed a grudge. Betty's concern was understandable. Decades of a miserable marriage, and now a renewed love for the Lord, motivated her to champion godly marriages, that was all.

"Don't be unequally yoked with unbelievers"—he was familiar with the Scripture verse. Not his problem. It didn't apply to him and Eve. They were just friends. Starting off as they had by butting heads from their first day on the island simply made their current affection all the more rewarding.

To make sure he wasn't fooling himself, he examined his feelings for Eve while he chipped away at the underside of the dugout. Everything was totally honorable, nothing in the least bit romantic. Nor did he detect anything different in Eve's behavior toward him.

There'd been that hug after the croc chase, but that had been purely for comfort. And the toaster hug a few days ago to warm Eve up? He swiped his mouth with the back of his hand. Okay, he was a little guilty of enjoying the embrace. But it wasn't sexual, wasn't romantic, just … comforting.

When Crystal called him to eat, he discovered the orchids artfully arranged in a seashell on the table. His gaze slid first to Eve, then guiltily to Betty. She quirked an *aha!* eyebrow. When he automatically sat next to Eve, as he had for the past several months, the same eyebrow rose again. After that, he refused to look at Betty.

That night, he awoke to the thumps of Eve tossing and turning on her ledge. The Dream. Before he could get out of bed, she woke with a gasp.

Her feet padded in a soft limp past his ledge. Her breathing was still rough. Seconds later, the cave door grated upward, stone scratching against stone. Had she gone outside? He hopped out of bed. The slitted windows showed it was still dark. What if in the confusion of her dream she walked the wrong way and stepped off the cliff, or walked the other way into the minefield? He followed her.

"Eve?"

Her silhouette stood out against the diamond-studded night sky. She was headed for the beach. She was in no danger. It was stupid of him to fear anything would happen.

Still, he quickened his pace to catch up. When he put his hand on her shoulder, she whisked around with a loud gasp.

"Sorry, I didn't mean to startle you. Are you okay?" A breeze tossed a strand of hair across her face. It just seemed right to reach out and brush it back behind her ear.

She caught his hand and pressed it to her cheek. "I had the Dream ..."

"I know. I'm sorry." Her skin was satin against his palm.

She began to cry, softly at first, then convulsively. He took her into his arms. She was shaking from head to toe. "You're going to be okay." Tenderness welled up from his chest into a mist that clouded his eyes. "You're going to be okay."

When her sobs quieted, he became aware of the softness of her body pressed against his. He stepped away and took her hands into his. "Let me pray for you."

She didn't protest. When he finished, a sigh wisped from her lungs. "Thank you, Jake. I'm going to sit out here awhile."

He didn't join her. Couldn't. Not when his heart was whooping and hollering at a party that, until now, he hadn't known was going on.

Maybe Betty was right.

He'd almost kissed Eve instead of praying for her.

Chapter 51

Eve handed Jake a vine and watched as he lashed it around two culms of bamboo lying at a perpendicular angle on the sand. Her arm muscles smarted from wrestling the last of the leggy canes through the jungle and around the swamp to the beach. Jake had insisted she didn't need to help—he'd already hauled a big load while she was laid up with her injury—but this was her first chance to get him alone. Her first chance to test him.

"There, we've got the frame done." He stepped back, hands on his hips. "The two longer culms will help us slide the raft to the water. I'm going to make the floor several layers high, so it's going to be a heavy bugger to push."

"Won't that make it more likely to sink?" It was hard to believe they'd be sailing away from the island in a matter of days. According to the hash marks on the cave wall, it would be June, only a few weeks short of a year from when they'd arrived.

She didn't have much time if she was to realize her hopes.

Jake tapped the frame with his foot. "Shouldn't. The culms are cured. A multi-level floor will give you gals a better chance to stay dry."

He instructed her how to lay out the bamboo into pontoons at each end of the rectangle while he worked on the floor between them.

She lashed bamboo until the roller coaster her heart was riding leveled out. One deep breath to assure a casual tone of voice, and she launched her question. "What was Ginny like?"

She scrutinized his face for reactions. Yep, there they were—a jump of the eyebrows, a quick, questioning glance at her, then wariness corralling his thoughts. She anticipated his answer would be slow in coming, his words carefully phrased. An awful lot of preparation on his part to a very simple question on her part. All unnecessary unless she was right: Jake was falling in love with her—and he didn't want her to know.

"Well …" Jake placed two bamboo culms into the lineup of the floor, cleared his throat, and finally looked her squarely in the eyes. In typical male fashion, he ticked off a list to answer her question. "Ginny was warm and giving and knew how to make people feel comfortable. She was very feminine and let me open doors for her, was always pleased with the little gifts I got her. She gave insightful counsel and helped me every way she could. She loved our kids and was involved in everything they did." He scratched his beard. "Why?"

The portrayal wasn't quite what she expected. She was used to people being described in terms of their accomplishments, not their character. The picture left her feeling strangely inadequate.

"I was wondering what you'd value in your next wife."

"Oh." Jake's shoulders slumped. "I'm not ready for that."

"What, for a wife, or for that kind of wife?"

"For a wife."

Her insides felt hollow. "What will you look for when you are ready?"

"God's will."

She grimaced. Why did he always have to bring up God in the conversation? "Would you consider someone like me?" The words jumped out of her mouth before she could stop them.

Jake's eyebrows shot up.

"It's hypothetical," she blurted. *Stupid!* She could ask a question like that, but couldn't tell him she was a federal prosecutor? Her cheeks heated as he studied her face.

"There are many things I admire about you, Eva Gray."

She flinched at the name, but he didn't appear to notice. His eyes rested with tenderness on hers. His lips softened into a smile. Her heart melted into a warm, oozy puddle.

"Of all the passengers on the lighter, you alone came to Betty and Crystal's aid. That took courage and a self-sacrificing attitude. There's no question but that your bravery saved their lives.

"And here on the island, you've never complained about the conditions, primitive and harsh as they are. You didn't expect me to find all the food for us, but you pitched in and helped. You saw things that needed to be done and did them without being asked. All those are wonderful qualities that cause me to have the highest respect for you.

"And then"—his voice lowered—"I owe you my life. I would have bled to death if you hadn't sewn me up after the leopard attack."

Not exactly the most romantic words she'd ever heard—more like she was was receiving a Medal of Honor—but the fact that he admired her gave her hope.

He shifted his stance and looked down before fastening his eyes on her again. Her heart skipped a beat. The tenderness was still there, but … saddened somehow.

"You're an amazing woman, Eve. But to answer your question, no, I couldn't consider you. The Bible makes it clear that God's will is for Christians to marry only other Christians."

"What? That's ridiculous!" She'd never heard such idiocy. She glared at him. Was Betty's marriage behind all this folderol? "I know of several successful interfaith marriages."

He shrugged. Obviously, their examples bore no authority with him.

Her mind leaped to another tactic. "What if I became a Christian?"

For the third time, Jake's eyebrows flashed up. They landed with the corners of his eyes crinkling above a huge grin. "Then you'd have to tell me everything about you."

She quirked a miffed half-smile at him. "I told you it was a hypothetical question."

The man laughed at her. She resisted whopping him with one of his precious cured culms.

Now what? Vacillating between anger and despair, she worked on the pontoons. Even if she told Jake everything and he responded well, what good was it if he didn't prefer her over his God? Once they finished the raft and paddles, they'd attach the sail and canoe, load up provisions, and off they'd go.

Good-bye island.

Good-bye Jake.

* * *

Within days of switching his stalking grounds to the exclusive Manila Yacht Club, Jojo found his prize. *Cameron's Castle*, a lovely pearl of a yacht, sailed into the marina and his gut snarled in triumph. Not only were the occupants *americanos*, but the owner was the very picture of his father. Tall like Jojo. Broad-shouldered like Jojo. Handsome like Jojo, except blond— exactly how his mother had described his *americano* daddy. No question that this was the yacht he must steal.

Everything fell into place. The crew, their wallets fat from payday, left the next morning for a weekend of pleasure. Only the first mate stayed behind to oversee the loading of supplies and to guard the yacht. When the owners returned from a stroll down the baywalk to sleep on board, Jojo sent word to Eduardon and the two crewmen, Philippe and Miguel. "Tonight we sail." The *americano* and his beautiful wife would provide the perfect entertainment for the trip.

He waited until the late-night traffic on Roxas Boulevard behind the club was down to a few stray cars. Waited until the club's tucked-away basin showed no motion on any of the yachts. Waited until the only threat to detection was the splash of oars as the four of them rowed to the yacht's mooring buoy.

Philippe stood on Jojo's shoulders to secure a rope ladder to the yacht's stern so he could climb aboard. Jojo followed him only high enough to peer onto the deck. At a noise above them, Philippe dropped to a crouch. Jojo didn't move.

A small head and narrow shoulders darkened the railing of the deck overhead. Before Jojo could draw a breath, the form withdrew. A hand replaced it, moonlight glinting on metal. "Who's there?"

Philippe stood. "Just me, boss."

The first mate stepped to the railing. "Who—?"

Philippe flung out his arm. The mate coughed and grabbed at his neck. His pistol clattered to the floor.

Jojo jumped aboard and raced to where the watchman had slumped over. Blood spattered the white railing and darkened the mate's neck and bare chest. Jojo grunted. What he wouldn't give to have seen the man's face when Philippe's knife landed.

Philippe reclaimed his weapon while Jojo retrieved the dead man's pistol and the key to the yacht's engine.

"You told me no killing!" Eduardon stood stifflegged on the deck, hands fisted at his side.

"This one couldn't be helped." Jojo thrust the key at Eduardon. "Quick, before someone sees your face in daylight."

Eduardon's mouth twitched downward. He didn't move. Didn't take the key.

Jojo nodded at Philippe. "Cast off and stand watch. Miguel and I are going below." He stepped past Eduardon, jabbing the key into the pip-squeak's chest so that he had to grab it. "*Now*, 'Duardon."

Without a backward glance, Jojo swept down the stairs. Rage burned through his arteries. "Check on him," he snapped at Miguel.

In a matter of seconds, Miguel returned. "He went to the bridge, boss."

The fire in Jojo's blood cooled. He smiled at Miguel. "Then we have guests to introduce ourselves to."

From loading supplies earlier in the day, he knew where the Camerons' stateroom was. He banged their door open and laughed when they bolted upright in bed. Cameron, naked as a peeled banana, jumped out of bed but stopped when Jojo aimed the pistol at him. His wife, clothed in a sheer, black nightie, grabbed the sheet and clasped it to her neck.

"What do you want?" Anger, not fear, blew hot in Cameron's words.

Jojo's belly tingled. So, the *americano* was brave, was he? Pleasure surged through his gut. He'd see how long that lasted.

He strode to the bed and put the pistol to the trembling female's head. "We want your yacht. Do you want your wife?"

Cameron's jaws tightened. "Leave her alone. I'll pay whatever you want."

Jojo jerked his head at Miguel. "Tie him up, but hobble his legs. He's coming with us." He didn't trust Miguel to watch them if Cameron offered a bribe. "Tie her to the bed."

The hum of the engine whispered outside the room. The floor and walls of the stateroom vibrated.

Jojo shoved Cameron out of the room, the pistol barrel jammed hard against the man's head. Before he shut the door, Jojo looked back at the woman. Her chest was heaving with muffled sobs.

His stomach prickled in anticipation. Cameron would be his appetizer; the female, his feast.

And for dessert, he'd deal with Eduardon.

Chapter 52

Eduardon sailed the yacht south onto the open sea, just out of sight of land. Blood pulsated in his temples, and his hands shook. Jojo had duped him! They had agreed no one would be hurt, that the watchman and Camerons would be abandoned on some deserted island. Yet, clearly, Philippe had been instructed to throw his knife to kill. As an expert knife thrower himself, Eduardon recognized the precision with which the knife had landed in the watchman's throat.

Now if they got caught, he was a conspirator. No one would believe his innocence. He never should have joined up with the big ape. He'd expected Jojo to try to cheat him of money, but murder—

He gripped the wheel until his knuckles turned white, forcing the trembling inside him to harden into a dead calm. He must outsmart the Ape. Gain the upper hand before they reached the island hideout tomorrow.

"Boss wants you." Philippe padded barefoot and shirtless to the wheel.

Eduardon's nostrils flared. Jojo was *not* his boss. But the two low-life crewmen thought so. Right there was Eduardon's first task: befriend Philippe and Miguel, win them to his side.

He released the wheel. "Perfect throw this morning."

Philippe grinned, revealing crooked, yellow teeth. "We have contest?" He nodded at Eduardon's slender knife, sheathed in leather on the left side of the navigator's belt.

Eduardon forced his mouth to smile. "Tonight?" To get things off to a good start, he'd let Philippe win.

He found Jojo and Miguel on the main deck. Miguel was tying weights onto the watchman's corpse. Eduardon swallowed at the rust-colored smears trailing from the watchman's body back up the stairs Eduardon had just descended.

More weights lay nearby. Next to them sat the yacht's owner, completely naked, his hands tied behind his back. Blood dripped from fresh cuts on his brow and the sides of his face. His teeth were clenched, but the tremors shaking his body screamed his pain.

Jojo stood over the man, head bent, eyes narrowed in an unblinking stare. He held a knife in his right hand. The blade was clean except for the tip. With a start, Eduardon realized Jojo had carved the man's face with the same cuts that scarred Jojo's.

The bones in Eduardon's legs turned to jelly. He stumbled, barely catching himself from dropping to his knees. Jojo's eyes snapped onto him, but Eduardon knew better than to look at him. He must not, must not show his fear.

"Ah, Eduardon." Jojo smiled. "Remember when you took that last job, against my wishes?"

Eduardon's mouth went dry.

"Mr. Cameron here is going to help me demonstrate what happens to people who cross me." Jojo's smile stretched wider. Keeping his gaze on Eduardon, he leaned over and slowly pulled Cameron's head back until recognition of what was about to happen registered on Eduardon's face. Then, swiftly, he slit Cameron's throat.

Eduardon recoiled. His back rammed into the railing. He grabbed onto it to keep from falling. Jojo's laughter, and then Miguel's, pierced his back like knives as he fled to the bridge.

* * *

Jake pulled the raft up next to the bobbing canoe below their cave and moored it to the same boulder. Building the raft had proved easier than sailing it up the coast today against the current. Eve collapsed the raft's sail and passed the two bamboo oars to him. He laid them in the canoe. "How about if you get tonight's fruit while I attach the canoe to the raft? It's late enough, we'll do the trial run with Betty and Crystal tomorrow."

To his surprise, Eve held out her hand. "Help me off, will you?"

Her slender fingers curled around his palm, and warmth shot up his arm to his chest. She stepped ashore but didn't let go.

"Jake …"

Holding her hand zapped an ache to his throat. He had to swallow to answer. "Yes."

She cast her eyes down, then raised them resolute to his. "You know I love you."

He blinked. She took his other hand, and the air in his lungs dragged out in a ragged breath. It took every bit of strength he could summon to not say he loved her too. He shook his head. "Eve, I—"

"If I became a Christian, I wouldn't know if I did it because I really meant it, or if I did it just to please you."

His arms trembled, wanting to pull her to him. "Eve—" He shook his head harder.

"Please, I want you to love me for who I am. Then we can deal with God. I'm ready to tell you everything you want to know."

The words whirled in his head. It was all there, wasn't it? Her promise to open up, her readiness to include God. Everything required to free him to love her.

He clasped her to him. Fire, fierce and sweet, swept through him. They would work through this. One step at a time. He slipped his hands to her face and allowed himself a kiss on the side of her mouth. His heartbeat accelerated. Two kisses. One on each side.

She closed her eyes and parted her lips. A moan, soft and shivery, rose from her throat. Her body melted into his.

No. He should stop. Let go of her. Talk.

Instead, he closed his mouth over hers. Tenderly at first, then, as she responded, with the hunger of having resisted so long. So many months.

The air in his lungs shuddered and expanded hotly in his chest. He pulled her tighter against him,

"Jake." She pulled away, her hands shaking on his shoulders. "I want to be with you. Always."

Always. The word dropped like a hand and drew a line between them in the sand.

There was a cost. A price for stepping over the line. The heat in his chest flickered. He let go of her.

Her fingers dug into his shoulders. "I know you love me. Please, give me a chance. You might not want me after you hear me out anyway."

Dread clogged his throat so that he couldn't speak. He didn't want to lose her. Didn't want a reason not to love her.

But she was going to tell him about Ginny, wasn't she?

He closed his eyes and nodded. He had to know.

Her hands slipped to her side, leaving his shoulders cold and abandoned. "I'll get the fruit and meet you in the garden at dusk."

He longed to reach out. To stop her. Everything in him shouted to go with her. Grab her hand and say it didn't matter. They'd gather the fruit together. Face the future together. Face the past together.

But he couldn't move. Couldn't step over the line.

He watched her disappear around the corner of the sandbar.

* * *

What sounded like the scream of a leopard pierced the jungle. Or was it a bird? A shiver prickled down Eve's spine and down her legs to the ends of her toes. She shouldn't have come without Jake. They were fools to treat the island like it was some kind of safe haven. Leopards, crocs, land mines, booby traps—the island was full of dangers that could have taken all four of their lives. It wasn't good to be alone.

She hastened to gather fruit from a spot high above the waterfall pool, keeping tuned into the monkeys. As long as they were screaming at her, she had some measure of assurance that no danger lurked nearby.

Her heartbeat settled, and she filled the pouch in her shirt with fruit. She loved that the canopy around the waterfall turned up its nose at the summer heat and filled the trees with never-ending bouquets of flowers. At the last minute, she selected a deep-purple orchid for her rendezvous with Jake.

Dusk tinted the slice of sky above the pool. She set the fruit and flower in the shallow corral Jake had made, and stripped and washed the sweat and grime from her clothes, her hair, her body.

She could hardly believe she'd declared herself to Jake. She'd always kept her emotions safely caged, stuffed away where no one could touch them. Their sudden freedom made her head reel.

Fear and exhilaration jockeyed in her stomach. Fear that Jake would reject her; exhilaration that he'd kissed her. Exhilaration that passion, for the moment at least, had won out. Fear that loyalty to God would in the end overrule.

Tomorrow they would leave the island. They would make a trial run of the raft and attached canoe with all four of them aboard, then move the provisions from the cave to the raft. One last hash mark scratched onto the cave wall, and they'd lower the door, kiss Lone Soldier good-bye, and sail away.

Tomorrow Jake would hold one of them uppermost in his heart. Her … or God.

Tonight she would find out which.

Chapter 53

The yacht carried more wine than hard liquor, but Eduardon managed to find a bottle of whiskey. He bolted half of it down to blot out the image of the knife slicing a red line across Cameron's throat. And before that, of Jojo's trance as he swayed above his victim, glutting on Cameron's pain. The man was as close to pure evil as Eduardon had ever come. Should the Ape ever discover Eduardon's jellied knees, he would feed upon Eduardon's terror and end his life in the same kind of bloody climax.

Winning the two crewmen to his side wasn't enough. He needed to get rid of Jojo.

At dusk, when Jojo disappeared below deck to the Camerons' stateroom, Eduardon left Miguel to man the bridge and met Philippe on the main deck for their contest. No longer could he allow Phillipe to win. It was imperative that Eduardon demonstrate his superiority and the right to command the ship after they disposed of Jojo.

They selected a target and began. The bottle of whiskey warmed their bellies and stirred a semblance of camaraderie. Philippe's tongue loosened. He told Eduardon about his acquaintanceship with Jojo. How he'd worked with him a year ago aboard a transport ship. How a crewmember disappeared at sea after an argument with Jojo. How—long story, short— no one dared defy Jojo.

"But we can—we should—when the man is a murderer," Eduardon almost blurted. Then he remembered the knife sticking out of the watchman's neck. Philippe's knife. Is that what it would take—stooping to their level, becoming a murderer himself—to be rid of the Ape?

He found a second bottle of whiskey and obliterated everything but the game from his thoughts. The contest was close. It wasn't hard to lose himself in the competition, to find it not at all unlike his beloved cockfights. Two scrappy cocks—that's what he and Philippe were—facing each other off, fighting to a clear decision point. And Eduardon, without question, was pulling ahead to the win.

A woman's screams shattered the night air. Both he and Philippe jumped. Miguel leaned over the rail and laughed. "The boss, he likes his women … chopped meat."

The screams didn't stop for ten minutes. In the meantime, Philippe won.

* * *

Eve entered the Japanese garden and emptied the fruit from her shirt into a small pool. Jake wasn't there yet. Good. Her insides shook, and her stomach was in knots. She needed to sit down, close her eyes, relax. Think positive thoughts.

She wove the orchid into her hair and pictured the garden behind her closed eyelids. In spite of the June heat, the garden—nourished by the trickling stream and numerous pools—was flourishing. The Japanese soldiers had planted their selections with care, with knowledge of each flower's need for sun or shade. She inhaled their faint perfume, trailed her mind in the stream's whispered serenade. Her fingers stopped shaking.

She had a plan. One that that would make everyone happy. Jake. Crystal. Betty. Even God.

If Jake chose her first—for who she was, and not because of what she believed or didn't believe about God—then she, in turn, would choose God. She would give Him a try.

A try because Jake said God was sovereign. That people were like grasshoppers. Not in *her* book. Some things belonged in *her* hands. Had to. The rest, God could rule. Then they had a deal.

Something brushed against her foot and she opened her eyes. A diamond-shaped head with slit eyes stared straight at her. The head hovered an arm's length away, topping the end of a pile of brown-and-green patterned coils.

She screamed and jumped up. The snake attacked faster than she could scramble away. It lashed around her legs like gigantic whipcords. She fell backwards, landing on its coils. With lightning speed, the snake looped itself around her. She couldn't get up, couldn't get away. The snake was all over her.

A spiral of bone and muscle squeezed her rib cage. She panicked. She needed to breathe. She exhaled, ready to gulp the precious air into her lungs. As if waiting, the snake tightened its crush. She couldn't ... fill ... her ... lungs.

For an eternity of seconds, she lay paralyzed, embraced in the snake's death grip. Terror seeped into her soul. Her last thought was of God. *Please, no! I—*

And everything went black.

* * *

Jake sped into the garden at Eve's scream. The sight of the giant python doubled him over like a sledgehammer to the stomach.

"Eve!" He caught his breath and bared the katana sword. The snake seized Eve so quickly that his dash to intercept it seemed in slow motion. His heart thundered in jolts as Eve disappeared into the huge, camouflage-colored cords.

He raised the sword above his head with both hands and brought the blade down hard. A V-shaped furrow opened across the coils, revealing red meat. The snake loosened its hold and thrashed about madly. Eve's limp body fell to the ground.

Before Jake could get to Eve, the undulating mass turned on him. Coils looped around his feet, rendering him immobile. An ugly, triangular snout rose up and struck at his face. He ducked, but the snake's lunge knocked him to the ground. The katana sword flew out of his hand.

He struggled to pull his feet loose. His left foot slipped free just in time to kick out and block the snake's next lunge. He screamed as the serpent's sharp teeth sank into his heel and its mouth engulfed his entire foot. The writhing snake slammed him on the ground and shook him from side to side. His head and arms flailed about like a puppet with loose strings.

The bayonet. On his second attempt, he managed to grab it from its sheath on his other leg and hack a slice out of the snake. The cut did nothing. He tried aiming a puncture blow, but the battering prevented him. Twice, the deadly coils looped around him. Each time, he slashed at them with the bayonet and opened up more snake meat. Each time, the snake let go. He worried the coils might pin his arms. If he couldn't wield the bayonet, he wouldn't come out the victor.

He had to change his tactics. He pulled himself into a tight curl and anchored his left arm around his left knee and calf, just above the snake's head. Then, again and again, like a mad man, he bashed the butt of the bayonet against the snake's skull. Again and again and again, until his arm ached and his breath came in gasps. Until his fist and the bayonet handle and the slit eyes became one in a sludge of gore and blood.

The ground vibrated as the writhing body of the python went into convulsions. For a terrified moment, he wondered if the snake was dead after all. Finally, the coils lay still. With a cry of revulsion, he tore the snake from his foot. Its teeth left a bloodbath from his ankle below.

He ran, limping, to Eve. She was on her back, her hair matted over her face and neck. There was no rise and fall of her chest. Her face, when he brushed her hair away, was flaccid. No pulse fluttered in her neck.

"No, no, no!" He didn't dare try chest compressions in case her ribs were broken. He opened her mouth, pinched her nostrils shut, and applied mouth-to-mouth resuscitation. Pythons killed their prey by suffocating them. If her heart hadn't stopped, if he could get her lungs going, get oxygen into her blood, she might live.

How could God do this to him—a second time! Was it because he didn't want to lose Eve, so God was taking the choice away, *mandating* His will?

Anger choked his throat. He jerked his mouth away from Eve's.

"Jake."

Eve's whispered rasp jolted tears to his eyes. He cried out and grabbed her into his arms. She grunted at the tightness of his grip and her eyeballs rolled back in their sockets. Her head lolled onto his chest.

He'd forgotten about her ribs. He stood, held her steady against the beat of his heart, and carried her down the mountainside to the cave.

Away from the snake. From the garden.

Away, if only he could, from God's callous control.

Chapter 54

Eve awoke with a start. *Snake!* Her rib cage wouldn't expand, wouldn't let her breathe. Air squeaked in helpless hiccups against her windpipe so that her eyes bulged like balloons about to pop. Darkness enveloped her like a body bag. She struck out at it, and her fist slammed against something cold and hard.

Please! Her appeal clung to the last molecule of oxygen in her lungs. She knew who she was calling to, but the name hovered beyond her reach.

Please!

In one shattering inhale, the barrier broke. Air barreled into her gasping lungs. Her heart slammed against her ribs.

Her sore ribs …

Jake! She opened her eyes, remembering the bumpy ride down the mountainside and Jake asking if her ribs felt broken. Not broken, she'd groaned, just super sore.

She was in her bed. Betty's voice, then Crystal's, floated into the sleeping hall. She swung her legs over her bunk and slipped her feet into her deer moccasins. She held onto the wall. It hurt to breathe and walk at the same time. No way she'd tell anyone, though. Today was the day they were leaving, wasn't it?

Something else. Even more important. She leaned against the doorway into the chamber, catching her breath, grasping at the elusive memory.

"You're awake!" Betty almost knocked her chair over, getting up from the table. "How are you feeling?"

Blue sky bathed in sunshine colored the window across the room. How long had she slept? "Where's Jake? Why is everything still here instead of on the raft? We're leaving today, aren't we?"

"I guess that answers my question." Betty plopped back into her seat. "Jake's getting fruit, and Crystal left to get water. We're waiting a day so you can recover."

"No." Eve straightened. "I'm fine. We can go."

"One day won't make a difference."

"I don't need a day. I'll tell Jake." If he was getting fruit, it must be morning. They'd have time to make it to the sea-lane before dark. "I'm going to the garden. If he comes back another way, tell him we can go, to start loading up."

"The garden! That's the last place you need to go."

Eve shrugged and emitted a self-conscious laugh. "I don't know why, but I have to see it." Before Betty could disapprove further, Eve grabbed a bayonet and crawled out the door. Her ribs protested each movement of her limbs. The pain was worse climbing the mountainside, but she couldn't leave without visiting the garden. A memory dogged her like a shadow in bright sunlight. She had to understand what had happened in the garden.

She prepared herself for what she'd find. A python, huge, its carcass an ugly blemish against the beauty of the garden. She'd seen plenty of reticulated pythons on the island the last several months, but none that size. Was it one of the same snakes Jake had encountered a year ago in the burial cave? Her head spun at the thought of being imprisoned in that small space with two of the monsters.

She slipped between the boulders guarding the garden's entryway and cried out. The flowers and bushes planted with such care lay in an upheaval where the snake had writhed in its death agony. The bridges and terraces, though still intact, stood in disarray. Flies blackened the snake's carcass, their movement giving it a macabre life in death.

Her knees forsook her and she collapsed to the ground. The purple orchid she'd braided into her hair lay torn and battered nearby. She picked it up and pressed its satin petals against her cheek. She'd wanted so much to be beautiful for Jake. Wanted to woo him to her side. Wanted—she swallowed—to not be a grasshopper in a world she couldn't control.

But she was a grasshopper. As easily crushed as the orchid.

A small landslide lay next to the miniature waterfall. She rose and selected a rock she could heft in both hands to carry it to the snake's head. She held it above the mass of blowflies and released it. The flies rose and settled again like a flapping cloth. As though driven, she returned with a second rock, then another and another until the skull lay buried.

She stood beside the ragged pile and stared at it. Her heart swelled as the elusive memory flooded her soul. "That's my headstone, isn't it?" she whispered. "It says *Helpless. Doomed to Die.*"

Joy spouted like a geyser. It wasn't Jake she'd called out to. It wasn't Jake who had rescued her. She laid the tattered orchid on top of the stones. "And it's my memorial too. I see it now, Lord. It says *Beloved. Saved to Live.*"

It wasn't until she crossed the garden to the other entrance that she wondered what Jake's answer to her was. Had he chosen God or her? She would ask him.

Not that it mattered now.

* * *

Crystal set the bucket of water onto the cave floor, careful not to let it slop over. "Done. Can I go play now?"

"Shut the door behind you this time." Aunt Betty thumped her cane. No doubt a scowl accompanied it.

Crystal scooted out the door. "What a grump," she muttered to the Lone Soldier. She stood to lower the door, then froze. A white boat was sailing into the cove. Froth-laced waves trailed it. She dropped to a crouch and poked her head back into the cave. "A boat, Aunt Betty! In the cove!"

Her aunt ran as fast as Crystal had ever seen her. She crawled into the trench and peered over the edge with Crystal. "A yacht. Glory be!" She clutched Crystal's arm as the vessel slowed and laid anchor.

The glint of sunlight on glass flashed from the boat. "Watch out, they're using binoculars." Betty pushed Crystal's head down. "Quick, get in the cave and shut the door."

"Wait! We gotta find out what they're going to do. Jake said no one could see the Japanese soldiers, so they won't see us either. Besides, it's probably okay if they do."

"Blast it, child, no, it isn't! Jake said we're to stay hidden until he checks anyone out, so don't you dare show yourself."

"Okay, I won't, I promise." Crystal suppressed a giggle. Aunt Betty must be as curious as she was to agree to stay in the trench. And that meant she must figure they were safe too. But this was more fun, anyway, to stay hidden and spy on the yacht.

Behind her, the cave door rasped as her aunt lowered it. Could the people on the yacht hear it?

Aunt Betty came up and crouched beside her. She put an arm across Crystal's shoulders. The heavy musk of her aunt's underarm and the shaky breaths that vibrated from her chest down her arm sent the creeps down Crystal's spine. Maybe this was a bit scary after all.

Two men lowered a boat from the yacht and boarded it. The sputter of a motor sent the sea gulls screaming. The hairs on Crystal's arms and the back of her neck rose. The boat shot straight to the stream that emptied into the cove. When the boat landed, the two men jumped out and dashed up the stream toward the jungle.

"We need to tell Jake." Crystal dropped onto her hands and knees to crawl as fast as she could down the trench.

"Oh no you don't!" Betty grabbed Crystal's ankle. "We're waiting inside the cave like Jake said." She didn't let go until they both were inside and the door lowered. "And don't you go sneaking off on me, either, young lady."

Chapter 55

Eve left the garden to wait for Jake at the waterfall. There was no telling where he'd gone to gather fruit, but he usually came to the pool afterward for a morning swim. Her insides buzzed with all she wanted to tell him. Then again, why delay when she could probably find him downstream?

The earth was tamped into a well-traveled path alongside the stream, which was now narrow and shallow once again from the summer heat, as it had been when they arrived a year ago. How long before the overgrowth would obscure the trail and their history on the island become as well-hidden a secret as the Japanese soldiers'? A sense of melancholia stole over her. For months, all she'd wanted was to leave the island. Now she counted her year here the most important turnaround of her life. The Romero trial was long over, and she couldn't care less.

"Hello there."

She jumped at the voice. Standing in front of her was a slender, cocoa-skinned man with black hair and Asian features. Her first thought was that he was one of the left-behind Japanese soldiers, that he'd been on the island all along, probably somewhere deep in the interior. Then it hit her that he was wearing an expensive Pierre Cardin shirt. It was way too big for him and covered up most of a pair of dirty, tan shorts. He wasn't Japanese, either. He was Filipino.

"You alone?" he asked.

Every cell in her body went on high alert. "Where'd you come from?" She kept her voice friendly but placed her hand on the bayonet strapped to her left leg.

"You need rescue? You and friends?"

He clearly wanted information. So did she. "Do you have a boat? Fishing? Logging?" How good was his English?

"Yes." He kept smiling while his dark eyes studied her. "You tell me how many I take home."

"Where is your ship?" She pointed downstream toward the cove. "There?"

She moved to step around him, but stopped when he reached under his shirt and pulled out a pistol. "How many?" he demanded, pointing the weapon at her.

The pistol unnerved her, but surely he wouldn't use it. He just wanted to scare her into cooperating. She unsheathed her bayonet and held it up, as if she could swat down bullets. She glared at him. "Show me your boat!"

Suddenly someone grabbed her arms from behind. A blow slammed the back of her knees. Her legs buckled, and she was yanked to the ground, the bayonet snatched out of her hand. From the corner of her eye, she glimpsed a second Filipino dressed in a similar shirt. He pulled a bandana from around his neck and tied her hands behind her back.

She got out one scream. Then the first man grabbed her hair above her brow with his left hand and jammed the pistol into her mouth with his right hand.

"You scream, I shoot. Understand?"

Eve's heart stuffed into her throat. She nodded.

He removed the gun from her mouth but kept it pressed against her cheek. "You tell me how many friends?"

They wouldn't believe her if she said she was alone. "One man." There was no doubt in her mind that Jake could handle these thugs. And, hopefully, Betty and Crystal were hiding in the cave.

"Where this man?"

"I don't know. He's gathering fruit."

"Where you live?"

"Up there, near a pool."

She listened while the two conferred about what to do next. Look for the man or take her to the boss? The boss won out.

"Get up." Her captor kept a tight hold on her hair at the top of her head and forced her to walk bent over. She had to face the ground, but it allowed her to see in back of her. The second Filipino fell behind until he was out of sight. The tactic had given him the advantage of sneaking up on her and subduing her. Maybe she could use the separation to her advantage too.

She clenched her thudding heart between her teeth. There had to be something she could do to escape. Ignoring the pain, she strained to loosen the bandana on her wrists.

* * *

Jake halted at the scream.

Eve?

He dropped the fruit in his shirt and raced down the tree toward her cry. At the sound of two men's voices, he stopped, aghast. Someone had landed on the island. Had slipped by him! And now Eve was in danger.

He turned off the path and worked his way through the vegetation to where he could see Eve and her captors without being seen himself. His heart catapulted to his throat when he saw Eve on her knees, head pulled back, the barrel of a pistol ground into the side of her face. It was all he could do not to shout and charge them in a wild rage.

The man holding Eve captive forced her to her feet. She was a good six inches taller, but he compelled her to walk bent over. With her hands tied behind her back, the position put her completely under his control. The second man waited until they were out of sight before trailing them, pistol in hand. Good. That made things easier.

He stepped back onto the trail after the second man passed. At the next bend of the stream, he approached the man from behind, slipped his left hand over the man's mouth and his right hand to his collar. He jerked the collar across the man's throat and kicked the back of his knees. A yank backwards pulled his victim off his feet so that his weight hung from the pressure point on his neck. Jake held the squeeze to the count of fifteen, until the man fell limp.

He dragged the body off the path into the foliage and stuffed the pistol into his own belt. The man was wearing tennis shoes. Jake ripped out the shoelaces and tied the man's hands and feet together behind his back. He used his knife to cut off a portion of the man's shirt, tore it in two, and gagged him.

How much time had passed? A minute? Two? Jake rushed down the path, his ears sharpened for any sound from Eve and her captor.

* * *

Eve strained for a peek ahead at their location. Yes, the junction of the game trail to her favorite tree was coming up. If she could get away, her captor might find it difficult to get a straight shot at her on the undulating path.

She stumbled on purpose and dropped to her knees. The man cursed and let go of her hair. She fell onto her back and yelped as her sore ribs hit the ground. The deception was risky. The man might kick her if he was angry. But he wouldn't shoot her. Lying on the ground, she looked anything but a threat.

For a moment, the man stood over her, his eyes sweeping her body. "You good mousemeat for boss." He smirked.

An icy fear pierced her, and in spite of herself, she gasped.

He laughed at her response. "Hey, Miguel, how about we get mousemeat too?" He pointed the pistol at her and walked back up the path. "Hey, Miguel!"

Gun aimed at her or not, she wasn't going to be anyone's mousemeat. Her adrenaline exploded like a bomb. The bandana was loose enough now to slide her hands over her bottom and legs and up to her front. She jumped to her feet and ran.

Her captor shrieked an obscenity. The pound of his footsteps sounded behind her. She turned the corner onto the game trail. For a moment it was silent. Only her own breath shuddering in and out of her lungs. Then he was behind her again, his footsteps faster, closer. She needed to open the gap or the chase would be over.

She grabbed a leafy branch and bent it forward as she dashed by. She released it, and it snapped back. Her pursuer squawked, and for a moment his footsteps faltered. Then he was after her again. The trick gained her six steps.

She rounded another twist in the trail. Her destination, the large tree that had toppled into a taller tree's branches, loomed ahead of her. Her ribs ached, pinching every organ in her heaving chest. Her lungs rasped like rusty hinges.

With a final surge of zip, she hurled herself up the fallen tree trunk. The climb was familiar, the slippery moss not a problem. A glance over her shoulder showed her pursuer much more cautious. Her lead gained another six steps. She climbed as high as she dared in the second tree and clung to its trunk, panting.

Should she shout for help? The pistol tucked into her pursuer's belt dissuaded her. He would shoot her for sure if she yelled. Or her shout might bring the second Filipino instead of Jake.

Mousemeat. She shuddered at what the reality of the word would mean for her.

And, just as certain, she realized she'd rather die than get caught.

Chapter 56

Eve worked at removing the bandana still binding her hands. She made a show of fumbling at the task and making squealing gasps of frustration. Below her, her pursuer had slowed and kept looking down at the ground. The towering tree was understandably unnerving. But if she was to implement the second part of her plan, she needed him to keep up the chase. He certainly wasn't going to walk away and leave her.

As if reading her thoughts, he took his pistol out of his belt and peered up at her. She took a quick breath and hollered, "I'm scared! If I climb back down, you won't hurt me, will you?" The quiver in her voice was genuine.

"Come down. I not hurt you."

Right. "I'm ... I'm afraid I'll fall. Can you come get me?"

"You come here."

She feigned a step downward, then drew back her foot and clasped the tree trunk. "I can't," she wailed. "You come. You aren't afraid."

The man swore and shoved his pistol back into his belt. The stink of his sweat grew stronger with each step closer he took. Whimpering, unable to stop mewls from squeaking out of her throat, she matched his progress with steps farther and farther out on the tree limb. When he reached the same branch and saw she had backed away from him, he fumbled for his pistol. "Why you go there? Come here to me!"

She tightened her clutch on the large branch overhead that angled in from a nearby tree. "Not if you're holding that pistol," she whined. "You need both hands to help me."

He left his pistol in his belt, grumbled, and held out his hand. His shirt was soaked, and his arm glistened with sweat. His hand trembled.

She extended her own shaking hand toward his, careful to keep a gap between them. "I can't move."

Holding onto an overhead branch, he inched his way toward her.

He was now an arm's length away. She retreated another step. The limb dipped under her weight. He hesitated.

What if her plan didn't work? What if he grabbed her after all? "Go away!" she screamed. "Don't touch me!" She took another step backward.

He lunged at her. With a shriek, she stepped off the branch. It sprang up like a cracked whip.

She plunged downward, then hung, kicking her feet as the large branch she gripped bore her weight. The man, however, was caught by surprise. He lost hold of his branch and crashed to the one beneath it. And then to another beneath it. He gained momentum as he fell. He hit a large branch but couldn't hold on. Flailing, yelping, he crashed through the remaining branches until he landed with a loud *whump* on the ground. He didn't move.

She regained her foothold. Half of her sobbed, fearing she had caused his death. The other half hyperventilated, fearing he was still alive. She climbed down and crept toward him. His body was submerged partway in the humus of the forest floor. One of his femurs protruded out of his abdomen. Blood oozed from his mouth and nose and ears. A look of horror etched his face.

Shaking so badly she could hardly stand, she scraped leaves and branches over his body. Part of her wanted to cover up the grisly deed she had participated in. Part of her, still wily and desperately afraid, wanted to ensure he wouldn't be found by his partners.

She whipped around when her peripheral vision caught someone approaching. The intruder made no sound. Her adrenalin skyrocketed at the thought of being captured a second time. She remembered the man's pistol and began digging at the mound she had just made.

"Eve?"

Jake! With a sob she ran to him and flung herself into his arms.

He held her so tightly she could hardly breathe. "I was afraid I'd lost you."

"There's another man—"

"It's okay. I took care of him."

"But there are more ... and a ship. I—" She stepped back and looked at the mound, then at Jake. "I—"

"What happened?"

"He fell. I set a trap. He followed me up the tree and I ... I couldn't let him get me."

"It's okay." He took her hands. "You were defending yourself."

Her chin and lower lip trembled uncontrollably. "Where ... where's the other man?"

"Back up the trail a ways. I left him unconscious and tied up."

"There are more," she repeated herself. "They came on a ship, probably into the cove. What if—"

She stopped, unable to voice her horror. What if Crystal had been playing on the beach? What if she and Betty had been captured?

"Let's find out what we can from our friend up the trail." Jake's voice was grim, clearly sharing her anxiety.

He took her hand and led her to the second man. He was covered with ants. Jake groaned. It was obvious from the number crawling in and out of the man's open mouth that he was dead.

"Now what?" She stared dispassionately at the body. For all her championing of life and justice, she found herself glad both scumbags were dead and she and Jake were alive.

"We'll have to go through the garden to check out the cove. If we go downstream, they'll see us."

They sped upstream, and, at the other side of the garden, crouched behind the last bit of outcropping rock to gaze down at the cove. She blinked at finding not a fishing craft or a logging ship, but a sleek, white yacht anchored in the middle of the cove. To the right of the inlet, where the stream emptied, a small motorboat was pulled onto the beach. Except for two tiny figures moving on the yacht, there were no other signs of human life.

"Do you think there are more than those two?" she asked.

"More could be below deck."

Including Crystal and Betty. Were they with the Boss? Her stomach punched bile into her throat.

Jake pulled her to her feet. "Let's go. They're waiting for the men to return. They won't do anything until they realize they've got a problem on their hands."

"What about Betty and Crystal?"

"That's what we're going to find out."

"Oh." She knew what that meant. The tunnel through the burial cave. Where snakes sought refuge from the heat. Her stomach looped into a series of knots. he couldn't go in there.

They paused for a drink at the garden's tiny waterfall. The water was warm and tasted like she'd licked a boulder. On the other side of the garden, thousands of insects swarmed the python's carcass. Gulls fought the flies to get a share of the meat. At their approach, the birds flapped away with shrill caws.

"What's this?" Jake pointed at the rocks piled on the serpent's head.

A thrill washed over her. She'd been so consumed by her captors she'd forgotten about telling Jake her good news.

She took his hand. "It's my grave. The old me." She laughed at the surprise widening his eyes. "Before the python squeezed out my last breath, I called to God. I don't remember all that happened, except that I woke up different ... alive ... believing."

"Believing what?"

"Everything we talked about all these months. Jesus, faith, God's forgiveness ... all of it. I'm a new person." Her heart was crammed so full she couldn't separate the treasure into its pieces, didn't know how to explain the radiance inside her.

Why did he look so startled? She grinned. "What, you don't believe He could save a sinner like me?"

Jake frowned. "It's just ... you were so adamant. So dead set against His choices, how He runs things ..."

Grasshoppers ... or mousemeat? God ... or the Boss? A deep contentment spread to every cell in her body. "I want Him in control, Jake. Even ... even when it hurts."

A painful smile twitched Jake's lips. "I'm glad." The smile broadened, and he swept her into his arms. "Or as Betty would say, Halleluiah!"

She wanted to laugh with him, but couldn't. Not when Betty and Crystal might be in trouble.

Chapter 57

One glance down the steep hole connecting the Japanese garden to the burial cave tunnel undid Eve. Her lungs locked. Her knees buckled. "I can't go in there without a light, Jake. That's where the python must have come from. It wasn't in the garden when I arrived."

He took her face into his hands. "I can't bear to leave you here. If anything happened to you …" His voice choked.

She closed her eyes. Focused on the warmth of his palms against her cheeks, the strength of his fingers. Jake loved her; she loved him. She could go anywhere with him, do anything for him. The vise clamping her lungs loosened, and she took a deep breath. "All right, I'll go."

He kissed her soundly and released her. "You can pray, you know."

Huh. She gave a half laugh. Weird to think that was available to her now.

Holding the katana sword and the confiscated pistol in front of him, Jake crawled on his stomach into the hole. She followed, stretching her hands forward, one flat against the wall, the other grasping Jake's foot.

The blackness swallowed her. So completely, she could see nothing. Not even her elbows brushing against her hairline with each movement forward. The heavy odor of her armpits clogged her nostrils. She shivered and began praying. *Yea, though I walk through the valley of the shadow of death, I will fear no evil, for You are with me.*

She followed Jake around the sharp curve into the tunnel leading directly to the burial cave. Her heartbeat quickened. She tried not to think about what awaited them.

The passageway enlarged, and they shifted from their stomachs to their knees. The stagnant smell of death and decay grew heavier. Her stomach tightened. Why hadn't she thought to dig up her captor's pistol? Or look for her bayonet? What help was she to Jake without a weapon?

"Okay, we're at the chamber." Jake's voice echoed eerily in the open room. "I'm staying on my knees and going for the opposite wall rather than feel my way around the perimeter. Hang on."

"No worry." The words shook out of her throat. "My fingers are permanently attached to your foot."

Cinders dug into her knees. Every two crawls forward, Jake stopped to sweep the katana sword in front of him. Each time, he braced for the possibility of the blade encountering something. Each time, she ceased breathing. When he resumed crawling, her lungs were good for two more swallows of air.

Would they hear a snake? The scrape of leathery scales on rock? The python had made no noise in the garden. No warning until the monster grazed her foot.

The sword clanked against something solid, and she jumped. The reverberation shot down Jake's leg to her hand. He reached back and squeezed her fingers. "We made it. We're on the other side."

"Attaboy." She leaned forward and kissed his fingers. They were icy cold against her lips.

The air outside the burial cave proved burning hot, insufferably humid, and incredibly sweet. She inhaled it in hungry mouthfuls. The cacophony of gulls and crashing ocean waves topped every concert she'd ever attended. Was there a way to hug God? A simple thank you didn't seem adequate.

Jake waved her to his side against the wall of the trench. "Still just two guys showing on the boat."

"There wouldn't be anybody inside the cave, waiting for us, would there?"

"Their bad luck if they are." He crawled to the door and lay flat on his stomach, pistol at the ready. "Betty, Crystal, can you hear me? It's Jake. Are you in there?"

When there was no answer, his jaw tightened. "I'm going in."

"Me too." She crawled over to him.

"I'm opening the door slowly so it won't be noticeable from the yacht, even with binoculars. Just a crack, enough to get inside on my belly."

He inched the door up and she held it while he squirmed inside. A moment later, his hand appeared and he held the door for her.

They waited for their eyes to adjust to the muted light. The room was deathly quiet. The fire was out. The cooking kettle was gone.

Jake stood up but motioned her to stay where she was. She understood: if there was trouble, he wanted her near the door so she could flee. Her heart thumped against her chest.

He flattened himself against the left side of the sleeping hall. Then he jumped across the opening and flattened himself against the other side. Her heart jumped with him. He had just made himself a target to anyone in the hallway.

Silence greeted his effort. He crouched and slipped into the dark passageway.

Time stood still. She pictured him checking out each sleeping ledge. There were ten. Any one of them could hold a man with a weapon. She held herself rigid, focusing herself as an ear. Even her heart seemed to cooperate. Tension muzzled the cave with empty echoes.

Then the noise came. Cries. Female voices. She jumped to her feet and dashed into the hallway. Jake had found Betty and Crystal.

* * *

The four of them laughed and hugged and talked all at the same time, until finally Jake took control. "Okay, one at a time, tell us what happened."

"I saw them first." Crystal said. "Aunt Betty and I watched them sail into the cove. She said we had to stay hidden."

"Good." Jake squeezed Betty's shoulder. Ten to one Crystal would have run to greet the boat otherwise.

"When two of them landed on the beach, we moved the kettle to the back of the sleeping hall," Betty said. "I was afraid they'd smell the seafood cooking if they came close enough, and they'd know we were somewhere around."

"Good again."

"And when we heard someone come in, we were scared to death till we saw it was you," Crystal exclaimed.

"Next time, use the clevis pin to lock yourselves in."

"Next time? Aren't we leaving on the yacht?"

"Betty, those aren't good guys down there." Eve crossed her arms in a tight squeeze. "Those men from the motorboat found me and took me prisoner."

"What happened to them?"

Jake grunted. "I took care of one of them; Eve, the other. They're both dead."

"You killed them?" The question shivered out of Crystal's throat.

Jake and Eve looked at each other. "Not on purpose, but yes," Eve answered. "It was them or me."

"I'm glad it wasn't you." Crystal ran to Eve and hugged her. "They must be bad men."

"I suspect they're thieves. Modern-day pirates," Jake explained. Crystal's eyes widened. "They probably stole the yacht."

He left them inside while he went out to check for activity on the boat. Betty dished up soup for them. No one had eaten since last night.

Eve brought him a bowl. "Jake, not that it matters now, but what was your answer going to be last night in the garden?"

He grimaced. "I went to the garden to say no to you; I left saying no to God."

"I don't understand."

"When you were alive, I could tell you no because I had hope—hope that things would change." The blackness he'd stuffed back into his heart in the garden seeped out like boiling tar. "But when you almost died, my hope died. I couldn't lose you. Couldn't give you to God. I love you—I didn't want to be alone."

The stunned look on her face tore him. He had failed not only God, but her as well. He took her hand. "I'm sorry. I thought I was strong. I discovered I was weak."

Her face crumpled. "That's what I wanted, Jake, to win out. I'm sorry I did that to you."

"You only showed me what was already there. I'm responsible for my decisions, not you."

A splash from the cove silenced them. A swimmer, headed for the beach.

Jake pushed Eve toward the cave door. "I need you to stay with Betty and Crystal. This guy is either retrieving the motorboat or he's hunting for the other two men. If he heads into the jungle, I can go after him."

"Can't we wait them out in the cave?"

"We've left signs all over the place—trampled grass, packed earth. They'd follow a trail straight to our door. The opportunity to pick them off one by one is too good to pass up."

"Then I want to come with you. Be your backup."

"Thanks." He brushed his lips over hers. "But I'm afraid your guerilla warfare skills are a bit rusty." He eased the cave door open. "Eve's coming in. Use the clevis pin to lock the door until I return. And, no matter what, no one leave the cave!"

He shut the door on their protests.

Already the swimmer had reached the shore. He looked Filipino, but much shorter and slighter in build than the other two. The man pulled a pair of glasses from a shorts pocket and put them on, then pulled out another item and unwrapped it. A pistol, protected by waterproof wrapping.

Jake ducked and ran halfway down the trench. Two gunshots pierced the air. At him?

He popped his head up high enough to see over the trench. The man was wading upstream toward the rain forest. He fired again, twice, the gun pointed straight up at the sky.

A signal to the other two men to return to the beach, no doubt about it. Jake's adrenaline spiked. He plunged into the burial cave tunnel. If he could race through fast enough, he'd exit the tunnel that ended at the stream and intercept the man, out of sight of the yacht.

Chapter 58

Eve jumped as the echo of two gunshots bounced off the cave door. She, Betty, and Crystal stared wild-eyed at each other.

"They're shooting Jake!" Crystal's scream ricocheted like cannonballs on the cave walls.

"Stop that!" Betty clapped her hands over her ears. "Goodness, child, maybe he's shooting at them. You don't know what's happening."

A second pair of shots followed. Eve's lungs crumpled as if they had been hit. Crystal broke into tears. Betty, seated between them, put her arms around them and began praying. She whispered, as if afraid the pirates might overhear.

How could you pray for something when you had no information about it? Eve stood. "I'm going to see what's happened."

"No! Jake said to stay here."

"I am, Betty. I'm not leaving. I'm just going to take a peek."

She was out the door before Betty could stop her. Jake was nowhere in sight. At the sound of a motor, she peered over the edge of the trench. The swimmer was taking the boat back to the yacht. Jake was not with him.

She sat down hard. Four shots and the man was returning to the yacht. Alone. It wasn't hard to guess what had happened. He had shot Jake and left him.

Stifling sobs, she raised the door a crack and told Betty and Crystal.

"Jake's dead!" Crystal wailed.

The words smashed Eve flat. "We don't know that. I'm going to look for him."

"But Jake said—"

"Betty! What if he's bleeding and needs help? Are we going to let him lie there and die?"

Betty groaned.

"I'll be okay. Don't worry. All the men are on the yacht."

She lowered the door. Sobs hiccupped from her stomach to her throat. Jake couldn't be dead. Couldn't.

At the hump of land between the trench and the stream, she flattened to the ground and wriggled over the rise. There was no cover at the top, and it meant exposing herself if anyone was watching from the yacht. But it couldn't be helped. She needed to find Jake—and fast.

She scanned the bare terrain from jungle to beach. No sign of Jake. No body crumpled on the ground. She got to her feet and ran. Too bad if anyone saw her! She would be in the jungle in another minute, and that was where she would find Jake. If anyone came, she knew a dozen hiding places where the two of them could be safe.

She hadn't even reached the trees before the guttural sound of the motorboat started up.

"Jake!" she screamed. Once the men landed, she wouldn't be able to yell without disclosing her whereabouts. She had only minutes to find Jake before the men tried to find her.

* * *

Jake emerged from the tunnel at the stream and hid in the bushes. For one crazy moment, he thought he heard Eve scream his name. But it couldn't be. He had left her in the safety of the cave. Upstream, monkeys shrieked an intruder alert. That's what he'd heard. The man must be up there, invading the monkeys' space.

He raced upstream toward the noise, pistol in hand.

* * *

367

Eve entered the tangle of brush and trees marking the edge of the rain forest. Jake could be hiding anywhere, his body concealed by the dense overgrowth. It made more sense to hide in the vegetation than to stay on the path where he could be spotted.

"Jake! Jake, answer me!" He had to be injured, even though she'd seen no blood in her hurry. Maybe he'd gone to the Japanese garden. He could hide in the tunnel.

The growl of the motorboat halted. She fled. Heart pounding. Ribs pressing. Breath shortening. Until she had no choice but to veer off the path and hide.

* * *

Jake arrived at the scene of commotion. He'd had to leave the stream bed to enter the rain forest proper. Why would the man leave the path? As the underbrush left off and the ground became bare beneath the giant trees, he slowed to guard against being seen.

The howl of the monkeys boxed his ears. He looked up. Specks of daylight sifting through the canopy revealed the object of the monkeys' wrath. A python, wrapped around the petite, lifeless body of an infant monkey.

Jake turned and sped back to the stream.

* * *

Eve lowered herself flat against the ground beneath a thick patch of green brush. She could see up through the leaves, but she was sure no one could see her. Immediately, a host of tiny, multiple-legged creatures invaded her body and clothes. No matter. They were nothing compared to the two-legged creatures hunting her.

The man she had seen return the boat to the yacht came first. He wore glasses and was short and slender, darker-skinned than the other two Filipinos. She barely glimpsed his grim face as he dashed by, pistol swinging in his right hand.

The second man took her breath away. Her bones chilled to ice. He was taller than Jake, layered in muscles, dark-complected but not fully Filipino. Scars carved pale ridges across his face.

The Boss. Whimpers crawled up her throat.

The man ran at a slower pace than his companion ahead of him. The first man's task must have been to catch up with her. This monster's was to search the vegetation for her. The stench of her fear radiated into her nostrils.

The ground shook as he approached. His eyes raked through the layers of brush and leaves and branches. She closed her eyes. Nausea swept over her. Suddenly she was back in The Dream. Wolves were after her, closing in on her. Only it wasn't a dream. In a flash, she realized the wolves were men—both in her dream, and now, in reality.

"Eduardon!"

Eve blinked.

The black eyes of the monster found hers. Held them. She couldn't look away.

Feet pounded on the path. The little man arrived, panting.

"There, in the bushes."

The foliage crunched as Eduardon stepped toward her. The trance broke. She bolted.

Heavier feet trampled the vegetation behind her. A vise clamped onto her arm. She was jerked backwards. A hollow laugh boomed in her ears.

"Look what scampered out of the bushes."

Mousemeat.

She screamed at the top of her lungs.

Chapter 59

The scream stopped Jake short. His heart lurched as he recognized it was Eve. What was she doing out of the cave? Had the man found it and seized the women? Or had Eve ventured out alone and been caught?

The racket of a struggle downstream spurred him to action. He crashed heedlessly into the foliage, using the noise from the ruckus to cover his rapid advance. If only he'd headed this way in the first place, instead of chasing after the monkeys.

A tall, muscular man had ahold of Eve. His hand was clamped over her mouth, but he was having difficulty subduing her. She thrashed about wildly, her eyes bulging from their sockets. Her captor, on the other hand, seemed to be enjoying the scuffle. Jake flared red with rage.

He spotted a second man standing out of the way of Eve's flailing arms and legs. The little guy with glasses from the motorboat. The one he'd intended to ambush.

With Eve's resistance distracting the men, Jake sneaked up behind the smaller one and rammed the pistol into his back. "Drop your weapon, now."

"What the—?" The man glanced over his shoulder. His nostrils flared, and he dropped his pistol.

Eve stopped struggling. Her captor shifted so that he stood with Eve in front of him.

"Let her go," Jake growled.

"You have a pistol in Eduardon's back?"

"I do."

The man pulled out his own pistol and gouged it into Eve's temple. "I'm going to count to three. If I get that far and you're still there running off your mouth, I'm going to put a hole in your girlfriend's head. So think about your situation: if you kill Eduardon, you lose your shield and I shoot you." He grinned, showing broken teeth. "You see, the real problem here is that you care about this female, but I don't care about Eduardon—and that means I win."

Jake didn't dare take a chance. He dropped his pistol.

"Get down on your knees."

Jake complied. Eduardon removed the katana sword and bayonets from their scabbards and flung them into the jungle. Then he picked up Jake's discarded pistol and examined it. "It's Miguel's."

"Where are my other two men?"

"Dead."

"Both of them?"

"Yes."

The captor bore his gun barrel further into Eve's skull, and she gasped in pain. Jake's eyes snapped to her face.

"You want me to be nice to your girlfriend, you don't try anything funny. Now, you get up and you walk all the way down to the beach with Eduardon here. And you," he barked at Eduardon, "you keep both eyes and both pistols on him. Don't hesitate to shoot, any excuse you want."

At the beach, Eduardon retrieved rope from the motorboat and under the big man's instructions stood Jake face out against the scrubby tree Betty had sat under a year ago with her injured foot. He looped Jake's chest in three tight circles around the tree, bound his wrists in back of the trunk, and finished with a last loop pinning Jake's feet in place.

Eve's captor dumped her on the ground nearby and told Eduardon to guard her. She collapsed onto the sand and remained motionless, her eyes dazed.

"So you killed my two men." The big man thrust his face only inches away from Jake's. The man's breath stank of rotten teeth.

When Jake refused to answer, the man turned to the side, whipped back, and rammed his right elbow into Jake's solar plexus. The air hurtled out of Jake's lungs and his head lunged forward.

"Nothing to say about what you did to them?"

Jake couldn't move. When he finally could breathe, he glanced at Eve. She was sitting up straight, widened eyes glued to his, mouth agape. Her chest shook in stuttered gasps.

His tormentor looked from Jake to her and back. He stepped away, then slammed his right fist into Jake's lowest right rib. "Oh, was that a rib I heard crack?"

Eve whimpered, and he smiled at Jake.

He slammed his left fist into Jake's lowest left rib. "Let's make this even now. Two cracked ribs." He laughed uproariously, as if he and Jake were having fun. "In fact, let's just work our way up, rib by rib, you think?"

"Stop!" Eve rose to her feet.

The monster whipped around. "Did you tell me to stop?" He took a threatening step toward her.

Eve rocked back on her feet, as if the force of his words had nearly tumbled her over.

Quickly, Jake twisted his bound fists around the trunk and fumbled at extracting his knife from his belt. No one had thought to search him after discarding his sword and bayonets. Finding the knife, he palmed it, straightened, and began sawing the cords on his wrists. If Eve could hold the men's attention for only a few minutes, he would be free.

* * *

Eve stumbled backwards to catch her balance. Had she really told the monster to stop? Her heart thumped so hard, her ankles shook.

"You don't like my fun with your boyfriend?" The brute tromped over and latched beefy fists onto her shoulders. "Don't worry, my pretty, I have other plans for your ribs." He shoved her at Eduardon. "Put her in the boat."

She fell against the little man, head spinning, legs numb as he tugged her to the motorboat. He pushed her over the side and she landed, groaning, on her sore ribs. Betty's sea chowder spurted out of her mouth.

Outside the boat, Eduardon's face reflected her terror. Her heart jumped. Maybe he wasn't a wolf like the others. "Please." She sat up, choking on a second wave of bile. "Help me."

Fear tightened the skin around his eyes. "Shut up."

He backed away and shifted his gaze up the stream. A huff of surprise shot from his mouth. The boat tilted as she swung around to look.

Jake was free, locked in battle with the other man. The brute threw Jake to the ground and kicked out savagely. He missed as Jake rolled away and scrambled to his feet. A hard punch sent Jake sprawling again. This time the monster's foot made contact. Jake grabbed it and jerked the man off his feet. Jake pounced on him, but staggered backwards when sand was thrown into his face.

Eduardon watched with the glee of a spectator in a ringside seat.

Eve slipped cautiously to the stern of the boat, within an arm's reach of the motor. Her heart leaped. Yes, the key was in the starter. As unobtrusively as possible, she rocked the boat. Inch by inch, it eased away from the beach. If Eduardon looked at her, she would hang her head over the side and pretend the sway of the boat was caused by her vomiting.

But Eduardon remained caught up in the fight. She rocked harder, holding her breath. Grain by grain, the boat slid over the wet sand.

She was an easy target for Eduardon's pistols. Her breath stiff in her throat, she wormed her way to the motor. Would he shoot her when she tried to escape? Or wade in and chase her? She scooted an oar toward her for a weapon. And if he shot her? She shuddered. Anything was preferable to becoming the monster's prey aboard that yacht.

Eduardon stiffened, and for the second time, she glanced at the fight. Jake was dominating. He landed a blow to the thug's sternum, a right to his jaw, another left to his sternum, another right to his jaw. The big man seesawed back and forth with each blow. At the third repeat, he collapsed. Jake leaped for the rope and hog-tied him.

"Hey!" Eduardon charged up the beach to the stream.

Eve grabbed the rip cord and pulled. Three times. Silence.

Gas. She squeezed the primer bulb on the fuel line. Her heartbeat outpaced her desperate squeezes. Was the motor in neutral? Yes. She tried the rip cord again. Silence.

She didn't dare look upstream at the men. Beads of sweat ran into her eyes.

She tugged on a small, red knob—the choke? This time she stood and jerked the rip cord all the way out. Four times. On the fourth, the motor roared to life.

The hairs on the back of her neck prickled. They would know now. They'd come after her.

She mashed the motor into reverse. It vaulted off the sand into the water, throwing her to her knees. Her forehead smacked the closest seat. Blood trickled onto her eyelids.

Eduardon ran toward her from the stream, shooting wildly with each pistol. "Stop!"

She gained control of the motor and shifted it into forward, tipping the motor to veer left. This time she braced herself for its leap and gunned it full speed ahead. Her spine tingled, waiting for the impact of a bullet.

Only when she arrived at the mouth of the cove did she look back.

Eduardon stood watching her, ankle-deep in the water. His arms hung at his side, pistols dangling. Ha ha! She wanted to wave. Stick out her tongue. Laugh hysterically. She had gotten away scot-free!

What about Jake? She scanned the area between the beach and jungle. Surely he had escaped into the rain forest before Eduardon arrived with his guns. She would hide with the motorboat in one of the tiny inlets and come back later. Later—*after* the yacht sailed away. She shivered. *After* the chance of becoming mousemeat was gone. No matter how long the pirates took, she would wait. Never, ever, would she let them capture her again.

But Jake and the other man were still punching it out near the three trees. She blinked. Hadn't Jake tied the man up?

The scene sorted itself out, and her heart thudded to a stop. They weren't fighting. Instead, one man was pommeling the other. Battering him. Striking him with hammer blow after hammer blow while the victim hung tied by his hands to the tree.

Jake would never do that.

The monster would.

She melted into sobs. Jake must have yielded to Eduardon's guns to give her time to get away. How long had she taken? And all the while, Jake had kept his eye on her. Waited for her to figure out the motor. Let them tie him to a tree and beat him up.

While she ran.

The brute would kill him.

In a daze, she cut the motor. She inhaled a shivering breath. Exhaled a prayer for help. Her heartbeat calmed.

At the sudden silence, the man swiveled around to stare at her.

"I'll make you a deal," she shouted. Her stomach felt knifed in two, but her terror was clamped in tight reins. "An exchange. The motorboat and me ... for his life."

The brute twisted back and punched Jake full in the face. Jake's head lunged forward. His body slumped until its full weight hung on his wrists.

"Okay, start swimming!" She started the motor and headed for the open sea.

Chapter 60

After a minute—enough time to make her departure believable anyway—Eve glanced back. Both pirates stood on the beach, the shorter one waving for her attention. Funny he didn't shoot his pistols to gain her attention. Was he out of bullets ... or saving them for her head? Her stomach melted to hot lead. Her heartbeat tapped faster. She made a U-turn and returned, cutting the motor at a distance she hoped a bullet couldn't reach.

"Do we have a deal?"

"Yes, come get us," Eduardon yelled.

Under better circumstances, she would have laughed. "I'll meet you at the yacht."

"Don't you want to check out your friend?"

She stood with the rip cord ready to yank. "Yes. Prove he's alive, or I leave."

Even at a distance, the big man's murmur to Eduardon sent chills down her spine. She swallowed three times to keep her terror under control. Eduardon trotted up the stream to where Jake hung by his hands, still in a slump. He slapped Jake twice on the face.

Jake raised his head. It wasn't hard to imagine his groan as his chin slipped back to his chest.

But he was alive. And the sooner she got the yacht out of there, the sooner Betty and Crystal could free him.

The cost to her own life was worth it. A sweet relief filled her soul, and she knew it was from God.

As soon as the two men splashed into the cove, she restarted the motor and sped to the yacht. The pirates had submitted to her demand way too easily. No question but that they had something up their sleeve. She needed to outwit them before they reached the yacht.

She idled the motor when she arrived. Immediately, the swimmers altered their paths to intercept her.

Of course, that was what they wanted—the motorboat. Then they not only had her, but they could swiftly return to finish off Jake.

Well, they could have the boat. But first, they'd have to chase it.

She aimed the bow at the cove's entrance, set the motor to full throttle, and jumped off. She treaded water to see if it stayed true to its destination or curved away with no hand to steer it.

It sped straight ahead and out the cove as if drawn by a magnet.

Then, what had to be the beefy hand of the monster pushed her head under water.

* * *

"No, Eve, they'll kill you," Jake howled. But she jumped out of the motorboat instead of riding it to freedom. He struggled against the rope dangling him inches above the ground. Eve's captors mounted the yacht's ladder, lugging her after them by her right arm as if she were a string of fish. He needed to get loose, needed to rescue her.

He spun around to the tree trunk and walked himself up it. The rope cut deeply into his wrists, so that it took three tries to reach the limb. Though the branch had borne his weight under the brutal attack of his torturer, it broke as soon as Jake climbed onto it. He smacked against the packed earth and cried out. Every bone, every muscle, every organ in his torso clamored.

He gulped in a breath and hurried to slip the rope off the severed branch and free his hands. The yacht motor purred to life and the boat dashed out the cove before he broke loose.

"Noooooo!" Biting back an avalanche of pain, he staggered up the incline between the stream and cave. The pirates must be chasing the motorboat Eve had set loose.

"Jake!" Crystal peered up at him from the trench. Behind her, Betty hobbled toward them like a three-legged frog in a race. He slid down and hugged them. "We saw them take Eve," Crystal bawled. "What are we going to do?"

"They'll come back for me. I'll rescue her then." He ran the length of the trench and climbed to the small plateau over the cave. The yacht was a white speck on the immense blue of the ocean.

His heartbeat accelerated. They'd return any minute. He needed a plan. Some way to board the yacht. Gain their weapons. Free Eve.

But the white pinpoint disappeared over the horizon. He stared at it in disbelief.

Crystal scrambled up beside him. "Where's the yacht?"

The answer drowned in a boil of darkness rising within him. He pushed it back. Waited for the boat to reappear. The darkness churned higher. He stood. Sat. Watched. Waited. Nothing changed on the horizon.

Trembling, he descended to the trench. Crystal followed and shrank wide-eyed against Betty as he paced back and forth. The darkness pressed harder. His chest heaved with the weight of drawing his breath.

The darkness clawed for release. Why should he hold it in? Hadn't evil wiped out his future with Ginny? Then demolished any hope of one with Eve?

A shard tore away and rushed to the surface. Why hadn't God protected them? Weren't believers the beloved of God, committed to His care? What hope was there if God wouldn't look out for them?

The darkness surged upward and exploded to the surface. "Why didn't You do something, God? What's wrong with You!"

Shaking so violently he couldn't walk, he halted near the Lone Soldier. His hand hovered over the sun-bleached skull, then reached down and wrenched the skull free. With all his might, he hurled it at the sky. It arced up and up, penetrating the deep dome of the heavens—the same heavens that had sheltered two lighters before they shattered fragments of people over the sea. The same heavens that had curved over a white pearl of a yacht before it disappeared over the horizon.

Betty's gasp stabbed his ears. He stood, dumbfounded, as if the skull had rocketed itself upward under its own volition. It sped upwards, growing tinier and tinier, until suddenly, as if batted by an invisible hand, it turned and plunged back to earth.

He ran to the edge of the cliff. The skull hit the ocean and sank out of sight.

"Jake, what have you done!"

He spun around at Betty's voice to find her and Crystal clinging to each other. They shrank back as he approached them, as if he were the ghoul itself, risen enfleshed from its watery tomb.

He didn't know what to say. Behind Betty and Crystal, the headless soldier tilted awkwardly against the trench. He stumbled over to it and ran his fingers across the depression in the soil where the skull had rested. His own head spun, so that he had to blink away the dizziness. He sank to his knees and leaned into the grim figure. He could think of nothing but to stare at the shimmering water. Stare until at last he saw what the eyeless sockets of the Lone Soldier had seen. His chest began to heave, and his whole body shook with convulsions.

Betty and Crystal ran to him and then put their arms around him.

"Someday his country will return for him," he whispered. "This soldier was loyal to his country. We don't know how long he survived here. Maybe years, maybe decades. One by one his companions died off until only he was left. And when his time came, when he knew he was going to die, he put on his full uniform and came out here and manned his position. He died looking out to sea, still waiting, still expecting."

He swallowed the hoarseness in his throat. "All this time on the island, I thought I was the loyal one, that God was the disloyal one. First He took Ginny, then Eve."

He hung his head. "This soldier has shamed me. I'm the disloyal one. Instead of looking to God and waiting on Him, instead of expecting good from His purposes, I counted the hardships, and I counted them against Him."

Sobs rattled unhindered from his chest. "I thought He had abandoned me. But it was the other way around. I abandoned Him." He covered his face with his hands. "God, forgive me."

Crystal sniffled. "So we wait and trust Eve will come back?"

Jake raised his head. "No." He planted a kiss on her forehead and stood. Strength glowed inside him where once the darkness had vanquished him. "We're going to act in trust."

He placed a hand on Betty's shoulder. "Quick, grab what you want and head for the raft. I'll help you board. Crystal, bring all the coconuts you can. We can't overtake the yacht, but we can go to the sea-lane and radio for help."

Betty grasped his arm. "Go without us, Jake. The raft is too slow. Take the canoe and go."

"No." He shook his head vehemently. "I won't leave you behind."

"We'll be fine."

"All sorts of things could happen to you." The possibilities lined up like troops called to formation. "I can't bear the thought of losing you and Crystal on top of everything else."

"For Eve's sake, every minute counts. Go, Jake." Betty shoved him toward the beach. "Disconnect the canoe while we bring the food and coconuts."

He paused, then hugged her fiercely. "I'll get the life vest."

Chapter 61

Eve stood on the deck and watched the island disappear. Next to her, the monster gripped her arm. "You see there'll be no swimming back to your boyfriend."

She forced herself to breathe normally, in spite of her erratic heartbeat. Knowing she was going to die made things simple. Made it easier to focus on her plan.

"I need a bathroom so I can clean up."

"You will address me as Master."

In spite of her resolve, her heart quaked. She stiffened her chin. "Okay, Master, where's a bathroom?"

His fingers bit into her shoulders as he swung her to face him. "I can see you're a feisty woman, so you're lucky I'm a patient man." His voice was light and friendly. Playing with her. A spasm jolted down her spine. "I'll wait until the first time you don't do as I say, and then I will discipline you. If you live through the beating, you won't be feisty anymore." He smiled as if he'd just explained how to win his undying love and affection.

"Being the nice guy I am, I don't want to hurt you. If I'm forced to beat you, it's because you're showing me you want me to." He shrugged and raised his eyebrows. "So you see, anytime I have to hurt you, it will be your fault. It will be because you want me to discipline you."

She refused to bat an eye.

A flame of rage flickered over his face. "This is where you answer with, 'Yes, Master, I understand.'"

She needed to back down to get her way. "Yes, Master, I understand." She lowered her eyes and waited in total submission.

He yanked her down the stairs and shoved her into a stateroom. "Shower and put on something pretty. I'll be waiting."

"Yes, Master."

"The closet is full of gowns." He pointed to a set of sliding doors that were full-length mirrors. "The former occupant didn't cooperate, but you will."

"Yes, Master, I will."

He shut the door and locked it. Relief swept through her that he hadn't stayed.

The room was filthy. A musty smell permeated it. Some kind of brown muck was spattered on the walls, the beautiful sea-green carpet, even the bed sheets.

She caught her breath. It was dried blood.

Discipline!

As if he'd heard her, the brute called out, "Don't keep me waiting."

He must have been lingering outside the door for her to realize what had happened to the former occupant. "Yes, Master, I'll hurry." This time, the meekness was genuine.

"When you come out, you'd better look like a damn princess. Otherwise, I'll to have to hurt you because you didn't try hard enough."

She swallowed hard to keep a tremor out of her voice. "Yes, Master, I understand."

His laughter accompanied the thud of his feet up the stairs.

She had to hurry. One chance—that was all she had.

She ran into the bathroom. Thankfully, no blood spattered the walls or floors. She locked the door, for what minimal security it afforded.

Everything she needed was at hand. She grabbed an eyebrow pencil and tore off a small piece of the bottom of a tissue box. *Help!* she wrote. *Survivor of Gateway. 3 others marooned on outer island.*

The information was bare, but enough to get a detective started. When the yacht came into the hands of the authorities, they would search the vessel with a fine-tooth comb, looking for evidence of what had happened.

An arrangement of cosmetics was grouped on the sink countertop. She pulled the lid off a cylindrical box of dusting powder, buried the note in the powder, and shoved the lid back on. A cloud of fine, white dust puffed into the air. She grabbed tissue, wiped off the sink and floor where the powder had settled, and threw it into the toilet.

She was a ticking time bomb. She stripped and showered. Ran to the closet, grabbed a gown and shoes. Put them on. Sped back to the bathroom for makeup and hair.

Jewelry. She didn't want to give the monster an excuse to hurt her. A jewelry box lay on the dresser. She helped herself to a diamond necklace and earrings.

Done. She slid the closet door shut and surveyed her efforts in the mirror. The gown, a turquoise satin sheath, hung loosely on her frame. The neckline plunged too low, but she wasn't changing clothes now. The necklace and earrings sparkled against the tan of her skin. Her hairdo and make-up added a touch of sophistication.

She swallowed back a sob. Yes, she looked like a damn princess.

* * *

Without an outrigger to balance the canoe, Jake had to battle the ocean as soon as he paddled beyond the breakers. The swell of the ocean created roller coaster troughs that required either an exhausting climb or a dizzying descent. Both threatened to roll the canoe. At the top of each trough, he reoriented himself to the north by looking south back at the island and west up at the sun. The ocean seemed determined to tug him away from the sea-lane.

His chest and arm muscles protested each stroke of the oar. His mouth was dry. Sweat blanketed his chest underneath the life vest. It was only a matter of time before he'd get a dehydration headache. If only he could stop for nourishment. But the tiny canoe fought him, wobbling as if it had a flat tire. To keep it upright, he had to use both hands on the oar, rowing first on one side, then quickly on the other.

Arching over the heat and weariness and thirst was his biggest obstacle. Time.

Time to reach the sea-lane before nightfall hid him from passing ships.

Time to find Eve before the brute ended her life.

* * *

Eve blinked at her image in the mirror. She had met her goal and beat the clock. The surge of adrenaline evaporated, leaving her scraped out and empty. There was nothing left now except to die.

Her knees buckled, and she collapsed to the floor. She put out her hand to brace herself. Her fingers brushed against a spot of rust on the carpet. She backed away, hiccupping spasms of lung-tight air. Blood!

The room spun. Confusion trickled over her brain like a spring melt. Was the blood hers or someone else's? She needed help. Wasn't there someone to help her?

"Time to come out!" a voice yelled. Three powerful knocks boomed on the stateroom door.

She shrank back. "Go away! You can't come in!"

* * *

"Go away!" she yelled at her brother. "You can't come in!"

He pounded on the door again. "C'mon, Evedene! C'mon out!"

"No! You're drunk! You and Roger go away or I'm gonna tell Dad when he gets home!"

To her twelve-year-old mind, there wasn't a more powerful argument than telling Dad. She smirked. She had used the threat plenty of times on Dax, and it always worked.

She nestled against her pillow and picked up her book to continue reading. Should she tell on Dax? At first it had been fun when her father was gone in the evenings to attend meetings with his boss, and the boss's son had stayed with her and Dax. Dax was fourteen and Roger was fifteen, and she'd thought it great stuff to sit between the two on the rec room couch and snarf down popcorn, guzzle pop, and stay up way past bedtime watching TV.

They'd done other crazy things too, like climb out onto the roof and lie flat against the steep incline, the rough shingles like sandpaper against their skin, while they gazed up at the black sky and laughed and told jokes. Or the time they'd gone out at midnight and, starting at one end of the block, had climbed over dozens of fences to sneak through everyone's backyard until they reached the other end of the block. They did lots of silly things their dads didn't know about, and she always looked forward to those evenings of fun and adventure.

But then Roger found her dad's liquor stored at the back of a kitchen cabinet. She joined them the first time they stole into the Scotch, but she didn't like the taste, and as the evening went on and the boys got stinking drunk while she didn't, she decided she wouldn't do it again. Soon drinking became the norm for Roger's visits, the talk became raunchy, the jokes dirty, and she withdrew to her bedroom. The boys didn't like her retreat, but with the power of tattling held over their heads, they left her alone.

She heard the boys mumbling now outside her door, a drunken giggle, and then the sound of something scraping between her door and the doorjamb. Suddenly the door burst open and the two boys fell laughing into her room.

"Get out!" She was aware she was wearing her short, summer jammies, and that after all the dirty talk she'd heard, she didn't want the boys seeing her with practically nothing on.

"C'mon, sis! You're no fun no more."

"Yeah, we wanna play with you. C'mon 'n play cards with us."

"I'm not playing anything with a bunch of drunks! Get out or I'm telling!"

"Hey," hooted Roger, "how 'bout Strip Poker? Two hands and you're in trouble, kiddo!" He howled and slapped Dax on the back.

"Yeah, little sister, you're growin' up, alrighty!"

"Get out, now!"

Roger's eyes were greedy on her. "Let's make 'er play, huh, Dax, ol' bud? Let's make 'er, yeah?"

Eve threw her book at the boys as they stumbled toward her. "I'm telling Dad!"

"I'm tellin' Dad!" Dax mimicked her in a high-pitched voice. He was too drunk to be scared of Dad.

Eve eluded them and ran out of the room. They howled in delight and gave chase.

Now she was scared. This was no game. She ran down the stairs, around a corner, and was momentarily out of sight. The coat closet! She slipped in, shut the door, and pulled the hanging jackets in front of her. Her heart pounded so hard she could hardly hear. She gasped tiny snuffs of air through her nose and tried not to cry. Her chest shook from the effort.

The boys passed her by. They were having fun. Howling with laughter while she cowed.

Back and forth they ran, guffawing, yipping like a pack of wolves. Then it was quiet. She knew what they were up to—waiting for her to come out of her hiding place, that's what. Well, she wouldn't. She would stay in the closet until Dad came home.

She slid to the floor and crouched against one corner, a jacket covering her from sight. It was hard not to cry. She hated Dax. She was going to tell on him for sure!

The closet door opened. She huddled under the jacket and held her breath. She didn't move one little bit.

"Found 'er!" Roger cried.

Then the jacket was ripped away and she was dragged out of the closet by her legs.

"Let go! You're hurting me!" She kicked Roger hard on the nose. He released her and clasped his hands to his face. She jumped to her feet and would have gotten away, except that Dax came up behind her and grabbed her arms. He pinned them behind her.

"Stop it, Dax! Let go of me!" She squirmed helplessly as his grip tightened.

"Got 'er, Roger."

Then Roger was in front of her, cussing, his nose swollen, though it wasn't bleeding. "Hold on tight 'cause she's gonna pay now!"

She screamed when he touched her, screamed minutes later when unbelievable pain knifed through her. And all the time, her brother pinned her arms and cheered Roger on.

They left her groaning, curled into a tight ball on the floor. She reached down and touched the area of pain. Blood smeared her fingers.

She hobbled to a chair in her father's room. When he arrived, before she could speak, he told her Dax had confessed everything. "They were drunk," he said. He kept his eyes from meeting hers. Why wasn't he taking her into his arms and rocking her like he had when her mom died and they had cried together? He just stood there.

Finally he said, "If I press charges, I'll lose my job."

She understood his shame then. She got out of the chair and went to her own room.

* * *

The door to the stateroom banged open, and Eve jumped. The scrawny man with glasses stood in the doorway. He held a pistol pointed at her. "Jojo wants you. *Now.*"

Chapter 62

Jake's head throbbed. The glare of sunlight on water brought stabs of pain to the backs of his eyeballs. He risked a squint behind him. The island, while not a speck, was at least a blob on the horizon. Was this what the ships saw from the sea-lane, or did he have farther to go?

He stuck the second oar into the water so the two paddles straddled the canoe and stabilized it. The sea was calmer now, not as combative—maybe he could manage a piece of fruit with one hand while he held the two oar handles with the other hand.

The overripe star fruit was soggy and bland, but the juice was as good as heaven-sent. Two more lay on the canoe floor. Best to save them in case he needed to eat with one hand again. The coconuts and other fruit required two hands and a knife to open them.

Ahead of him and to the east, a dark spot appeared on the ocean. His heartbeat quickened. A ship? He raised his hand to shade his eyes, then stood to wave frantically. "Hey!"

The two oars plopped into the ocean. The canoe wobbled, tipped, and tossed him in after them. He rose to the surface, sputtering.

It was a ship, all right, but hardly nearby. He and the canoe would be no more noticeable than a pebble in a gravel pit.

He swam to the canoe and righted it. Water flecked with soot sloshed in the shallow cavity he had burned out for a seat. The coconuts and star fruit were gone. He attempted to crawl aboard, but the boat rolled every time. Finally, he mounted it as if it were still a log, wrapped his arms and legs around it and rotated it until he splashed flat on his stomach into the cavity. The boat sank as his body displaced the water but rose when he squirmed his chest onto the bow.

Forget sitting up. Using both arms as oars, he paddled smoothly forward.

In the distance, the ship sailed in a steady path westward. Jake oriented himself to the same destination. A destination with a sky rapidly turning pink.

* * *

Eve rose to her feet and stared at Eduardon. For a moment, past and present collided. Her heartbeat thudded against her ears, shook every bone down to her wobbling ankles. Then past and present separated into their two monsters—her father decades earlier; Jojo now.

"Go." Eduardon's pistol prodded her below her left shoulder blade. She mounted the stairs to the lower deck on shaking knees. The past tore holes in her stomach. Clawed talons at her heart. She gripped the railing to stay on her feet.

Jojo would torture her now—beat her, slash her, stomp out her breath. But his torture was only to her body. Not like what her father had done. He had thrown her soul out the window. Left it splattered on the roadside for the vultures to eat. She fought the tightness in her chest to draw in air.

Eduardon grasped her arm and pulled her to the bridge's ladder. "Go."

Go where? To her death peaceably? She clenched her teeth and inhaled a deep breath. Not unless God willed it.

"Eduardon." She clasped the ladder and put a foot onto the first rung. "Together we can stop him."

"Shut up."

"Better to kill him than to let him kill me."

"I said, shut up!" He shoved her so hard the ladder bruised her skin.

"Do you need help?" The scarred face of the monster appeared above her.

Her throat constricted. Had he heard her? She ignored the thick hand extended to her and climbed to the bridge.

Jojo's eyes flickered over her. "Ah, you are a princess! Come, my beauty, get your reward." He poured a brown liquid into a shot glass. The pungent smell of whiskey assaulted her nose. The bottle was half empty.

She thrust her chin forward. "I don't drink."

He pulled a knife with a wicked curve from his belt and waggled it at her. "What good are you if you won't join in my fun? We will have to return to your boyfriend so you can watch while I cut his guts out. Or he can watch while I cut out yours."

"All right." She took the glass and sipped it.

"Down it."

She squared her shoulders and swallowed it in one gulp. Her face burned as the whiskey hit her empty stomach.

"Another," he bellowed. "One for you, too, 'Duardon. Put your gun down and join the party. Our beautiful princess can dance for us, eh?" He poured three drinks and handed one to each.

Eve clutched her stomach. "I'm going to throw up. I need something to eat."

Jojo took her glass and set it on the map table. Then he opened his right hand, splayed his fingers, and slapped her face. She couldn't help grabbing her cheek in surprise.

"I warned you about this earlier." He put the glass back into her hand.

She downed the whiskey. The liquor entered her bloodstream and fire spread throughout her body.

"I think she'd be good at a strip tease, don't you, 'Duardon?"

Flames scalded her cheeks. "I don't dance."

This time he hit hard enough to knock her to the floor. The shot glass rolled across the wooden planks.

He jerked her to her feet by her hair. "Then Eduardon here will be nice enough to help you."

The scrawny man took a step backwards.

"Ah, 'Duardon, I can see you want her. Tell you what, we will share her. I will let you go first." He released Eve's hair and pinned her arms behind her.

"No!" She struggled, twisting her shoulders, kicking her heels at Jojo's shins. "Let me go!"

"Look, she dances for you, 'Duardon! She likes you. You must come and join her."

Eduardon's face darkened into a scowl. "Let her go, you degenerate ape." He whipped out his knife and pointed it at Jojo.

The monster loosed Eve's right arm and thrust forward a pistol. Eduardon's face paled.

He flung his knife at the same time Jojo fired. The brute stumbled backwards, releasing Eve's other arm. She jumped away.

Eduardon crumpled groaning to the floor, holding his stomach.

Jojo clapped his hand over blood spurting from his neck. His head jerked and he reeled and fell, discharging the pistol in a wild shot. The bullet pinged off the laminate map table and clanked in a ricochet off the stainless steel trim overhead.

Eve's head snapped backwards, and everything went dark.

* * *

Darkness covered the sea. The roller-coaster heaves of the ocean had resumed. Water black as ink slapped Jake's face and snatched at the canoe. His tongue and gums stung from spitting out salt water. He clung to the dugout with all four limbs, the weight of his torso in the burnt cavity barely preventing the craft from rolling.

Two more ships had sailed by without spotting him. He'd have to wait for daylight now. No telling where the roller coaster would take him. Farther away from the sea-lane? Back to the island? Or out to a wasteland of water?

The dugout careened down another dip of the ocean and Jake tightened his hold. His arm muscles ached from paddling. From hanging by his wrists. From being attached to two cracked ribs. He didn't dare relax, even when the waves were flat. If he fell asleep, he might never wake up. Not on this earth, anyway.

Without warning, a hulk cut into his path. Lights dotted it from bow to stern.

A ship.

A SHIP!

It sliced through the water, churning waves at its sides that fanned out like sparkling plumage in the ship's lights. The waves caught the dugout and dragged it under, spinning it out of Jake's grip. He tumbled helplessly, unable to tell which way was up. He forced himself to remain limp until at last he felt the life vest lifting him to the surface. With a surge of energy, his lungs ready to pop, he kicked to the surface.

He broke through the water, yelling as soon as he could breathe. The ship, a tanker, plowed past him. Ridiculous to think anyone atop that mountain of steel would hear him, but he screamed anyway. "Help! Man overboard!" He waved his arms, splashed a target of geysers with his hands and feet, yelled his larynx raw.

The tanker climbed the roller coaster's opposite slope and disappeared.

His body drooped, every last drop of adrenaline spent. The dugout was nowhere in sight. He treaded water minimally to keep heat in his limbs. Hollowed of all feelings, he let the swell of the ocean carry him up the slope.

The bright lights of the tanker glowed startlingly close. A faint "Hal-loh!" echoed across the water. Adrenaline shot a fresh dose into his muscles.

"Here, over here!" He splashed up geysers for his rescuers' binoculars, shouted loud halleluiahs for their ears.

And for God's.

* * *

"C-C-Coast Guard. I need to talk to the Coast Guard." Jake's teeth chattered so hard it was no wonder the crewmen stared blankly at him. He clutched the blanket they'd thrown around him when they hauled him from the pontoon boat to the tanker's main deck. Okay, he'd try a simpler word. "C-C-Captain." At his third attempt, they nodded.

"Captain's on his way." A crewman pointed at a paunchy man in uniform descending the ladder from the bridge. The captain, puffing on chubby legs that strained his trousers, peered at Jake suspiciously.

Jake quelled the urge to pounce on the man and scream demands. The captain would be responding to a black-and-blue bag of bones with long hair and beard straggling past his shoulders, clad only in thread-bare shorts. A middle-age hippie, no doubt, who had fallen from some boat.

A sailor handed Jake a drink of water. The captain folded his arms across his chest, as if addressing a naughty schoolboy. "What happened?"

The sips of water helped. The words still croaked out, but without the stuttering. "I'm a survivor of the *Gateway*." The captain gave no indication of recognizing the name. "Stranded on an island over a year, three others with me. Pirates kidnapped one of us this morning. Need to radio the Coast Guard, intercept the yacht."

Jake's knees gave way and two of the sailors caught him and held him up. His breath rattled between sentences. "Name's Jake Chalmers. U.S. Marine Corps colonel."

The captain unfolded his arms.

Encouraged, Jake pushed above the fog of paralysis creeping over his body. "Need to send your coordinates. Yacht is"—he swallowed, dredging the name from numb brain cells—"*Cameron's Castle*."

This time the captain's eyes rounded. He turned on his heels and waddled at a close run to the bridge.

"Sounds like the stolen yacht the Coast Guard's looking for," a sailor said. He nodded to the other sailor gripping Jake. "The Captain will take care of it, Colonel Chalmers. Let's get you some rest."

Jake straightened to his full height. "No. I need to go to the bridge. I need to talk to them."

A sailor clattered down the ladder and ran over to them. "Coast Guard is coming for him. There's a cutter nearby."

Jake's heart did a flip. There was still a chance. A chance Eve was alive. A chance they could get to her in time.

Chapter 63

The cutter reduced its speed to approach *Cameron's Castle* with caution. Jake held his breath for so long, his chest ached. Two Coast Guardsmen on the cutter's upper deck stood by with rifles trained on the yacht. Jake's fingers itched to join them.

The yacht was floating aimlessly on huge swells of the ocean. Not good. Jake's breath broke loose from its prison, draining his lungs, shaking his knees so hard he could hardly stand. *Eve*. Brain and heart clashed over what the drifting vessel indicated of her fate.

Next to him, the captain hefted a megaphone to his mouth. "Ahoy, *Cameron's Castle*," he bellowed, first in Filipino, then in English. "This is the Philippine Coast Guard. Please respond."

The cutter moved closer and the captain repeated his command. When there was no answer, he motioned the first mate to close in on the yacht. His voice sharpened. "Prepare to be boarded!"

The cutter lurched against the yacht and several Coast Guardsmen secured an attachment while two others jumped aboard the yacht. Side arms at the ready, they dashed to the bridge and disappeared inside. It was all Jake could do to not hurl himself after them.

Minutes later, one of the guardsmen reappeared. "Send a corpsman," he shouted. "Two dead, one injured." He climbed down into the lower deck.

The captain put a restraining hand on Jake's arm. "In case you're thinking about rushing over there, don't."

"Of course not." Jake's scarred cheek twitched. "I know better." Truth was, the captain had caught him just in time.

A medical corpsman darted from the cutter to the yacht and up to the bridge. Watching him, Jake assumed an at-ease stance, but inside he was ready to bolt. Two dead, one injured. God knew which way he was voting on that matter.

Within seconds, the corpsman emerged. He cupped his hands to his mouth. "Need a medevac, pronto!"

At the same time, the second guardsman returned from the lower deck. "No one below," he yelled.

Jake was out the door before the captain could stop him. Although he'd been sitting the entire time they'd traveled from the tanker to the yacht, not one cell in his beaten, broken, worn out body had rested. He ran toward the yacht, aware of his feet stumbling. Of groping for support on the wall. Of careening down the ladder and staggering across the deck. Of having to crawl like a baby from one ship to the other.

But all he felt was the pounding of his heart. Pounding from his stomach to his chest. Pounding from his throat to his head. Reverberating in his ears, against his eyeballs, against the vast, dark cavern in his skull.

He climbed to the yacht's bridge, disconnected now from awareness of his body, lifted as if by angels' wings from rung to rung. When he stepped inside the cabin, the pounding shaking his soul stopped.

Eve.

She lay with her head in a pool of blood. The side of her face was matted in dark red.

No.

His gaze leaped to the two bodies sprawled on either side of her. The big man, the brute, was on his side, his face drained of color. His hands and the left side of his neck and shirt were soaked in blood. A short distance away, the little man lay on his back, his hands bloodied over a crimson flower that spread outward from his belly.

A movement at Eve's side startled his heart into erratic thumps. The corpsman knelt by her, unraveling a long, narrow piece of gauze. Jake fell on his knees across from him and watched numbly as slender cocoa hands raised Eve's head and wrapped the gauze around and around her head above her eyes.

Jake swallowed. "She's … alive?" He couldn't bear to hope without confirmation.

The corpsman nodded. "Bullet put in a good dent. Fortunately for her, the blood clotted."

When the corpsman finished the bandage, Jake carefully took Eve into his arms. Her eyes fluttered open and she stared up at his face. A weak smile flitted across her lips. "Jake. You came."

Unable to speak, he touched his lips to hers.

Her forehead furrowed. "Wolves—"

"They're dead," he rasped. "They'll never bother you again."

"… saved me …" Her voice sank and she closed her eyes. Her breath wisped in a steady rhythm against his skin.

The water lapped against the boat, rocking them with the gentle hand of a mother tending her newborn. He looked out the window into the deep dome of the sky. *Thank You.*

He hugged Eve's body to his chest and wept.

* * *

"Jake?"

At Betty's voice, Jake rushed from the side of Eve's gurney to the Coast Guard cutter pulling up next to his. The two ships rocked as they bumped together and were secured. He looked over his shoulder to make certain the corpsman had a good hold on Eve.

"I wasn't sure they'd get you girls to come out of the cave." He laughed, lighthearted now that Betty and Crystal were here. Everyone was safe. They were off the island and headed home. Their families had been notified, and the authorities were on the alert for Captain Emilio. He lifted Betty over the side of the second cutter into his while the young Gymnast of the Ocean Cliff scrambled easily from one ship to the other. He hugged both of them for a long time. A long, long time.

"We weren't in the cave," Crystal said when he released them. "We spent all our time looking for you to return. When we saw the Coast Guard coming, Aunt Betty guessed you'd sent them."

Betty's face creased into worry lines. "They wanted to know where the dead men's bodies were, but we told them you'd have to show them. Are you and Eve in trouble?"

"No. It's standard procedure. They'll identify them and send them home for burial. Same with the Japanese soldiers." His heart warmed at the thought of the Lone Soldier's wait finally being over. Then he remembered that the island guardian's skull lay at the bottom of the ocean. He ducked his head in remorse.

"Is that Eve on the upper deck?" Betty gripped his arm. "All they would say was that she was safe."

"Yes." He took their hands and led them to her. "She has a head wound," he whispered, although Eve wouldn't have heard him. She had slid back into unconsciousness after their brief exchange on the yacht. "A medevac is coming to take her to Manila for surgery."

"Will we go with her?" Crystal picked up Eve's right hand and gently sandwiched it between her two hands. Jake recognized what she was doing. A toaster hug.

He took in a quick breath. "Yes. We'll all fly back on the helicopter."

"And then what? Home?" There was no eagerness in Betty's voice.

Home. His heart leaped at the thought of seeing his children again, of holding them in his arms, of catching up on their lives. But beyond that, home was back on the island, wasn't it? Not so much on the island as with Eve and Betty and Crystal. The year had melded them into a family under God's sovereign hand.

The sadness on Betty's and Crystal's faces mirrored a sudden despondency in his own heart. Home for Betty, he knew, was an empty house. For Crystal, it was with grandparents whose love for her was questionable. He and Eve would have each other, but was that enough?

He cleared his throat. "Three things happen now. First, we go to Manila and stay with Eve until she's okay. Second, we go home to our families and give them big hugs. And third, the four of us get back together again."

"Forever?" Crystal squealed.

Eve's eyes blinked open. Her lips moved slowly, and the three of them leaned in close.

"The perfect plan," she mumbled. She smiled and placed her other hand on Crystal's. One by one, the four of them sandwiched their hands together in a giant toaster hug.

The End

A MAP of the island can be found at
http://donandstephanieprichard.wordpress.com.

For updates on the SEQUEL to Stranded,
sign up for our NEWSLETTER at the same site.

Dear Reader,

It was a lot of fun for us writing this book, and we hope it was even more fun for you reading it! It would mean a lot to us if you would post a comment ("review") on Amazon at http://www.amzn.com/B00OQGJBUY about our book and your experience reading it.

CONTACT us at http://donandstephanieprichard.wordpress.com— we'd love to hear from you!

Want to keep up on the progress of our next novel? Sign up for our NEWSLETTER at http://donandstephanieprichard.wordpress.com and occasionally receive tidbits like how to build a raft and yummy recipes like Roasted Python or Mussel Stew.

Check out our *Stranded* boards on PINTEREST at www.pinterest.com/stephprichard. You can add your movie star candidates for our four castaways if you'd like. Is there a movie in the making? Ha! We wish!

Please join us on our FACEBOOK page at www.facebook.com/4u2read. Sometimes we hand out prizes, but mostly we run from crocs and compare our times.

ACKNOWLEDGEMENTS

Special thanks to the following for helping us with our book:

Dr. Betty Ray for medical advice and over-the-top enthusiasm

Brenda Anderson for best-ever critique partner
(www.brendaandersonbooks.com)

Carrie Lynn Lewis for techno enlightment
(www.carrielynnlewisauthor.wordpress.com)

Danielle Hanna for social media savvy (www.daniellehanna.com)

Natalie Hanemann for outstanding editing
(www.nataliehanemannediting.com)

Ken Raney for gorgeous cover design (www.kenraney.com)

32834873R10228

Made in the USA
Middletown, DE
19 June 2016